THE FORGOTTEN (

AMERICAN CIVIL WAR, 1860 TO 1865

DECEMBER 26, 1862, MANKATO , MINNESOTA
HERE WERE HANGED 38 SIOUX INDIANS
(OUT OF 303 CONVICTED)

PEACE AND PROGRESS

outskirts
press

Chapter 1
Sergeant-Major Cheever

April 19, 1865: The American Civil war was winding down. About April 2nd the Confederate Government evacuated Richmond and became a government on the run. In Virginia, on April 9th General R. E. Lee surrender the main Confederate army to General U.S. Grant.

On April 14, President Lincoln was shot in Washington D. C. and he died on the morning of the 15th. The Nation was stunned and went into deep mourning. His open casket was placed in the capitol rotunda for public display on the 18th. It was scheduled to be on display for three days. The remains were viewed by tremendous, solemn crowds that day.

While the war was winding down there was still a lot to do. Confederate President was still loose with most of his government's officials. The Confederacy's second largest army commanded by

General Johnston was still a fighting force to be reckoned with. His army was being hounded by General Sherman's troops in North Carolina. General Kirby-Smith's Confederates still held Texas and western Louisiana. The manhunt for Lincoln's assassin and his gang was being conducted by thousands of soldiers and lawmen in and around D. C. .

While some of the Union troops were still fighting the Rebs, others were preparing to go home and be discharged. One of the first guys lucky enough to be sent home early was standing with his hand on the batwing doors on the Palace Saloon in Atlanta, Georgia. He looked back over his shoulder and shouted, "Goodbye and good luck!"

The door swung open. A whiff of stale beer from the bar trailed the man in a Yankee uniform as he stepped out into the bright, noontime sunlight. The chevrons on his uniform proclaimed his rank to be Sergeant-Major. His uniform was faded and showed some wear and tear, but it was neat and clean. He appeared to be as fit as a fiddle. His muscular, six-foot plus frame gave him an appearance of confidence and competence.

His face looked more formidable than handsome. It was tanned to deep mahogany and sported a black bushy mustache across his upper lip with a goatee across his bottom lip and chin. The mustache and beard were his way of hiding his deformed jaw. His bottom jaw stuck out slightly beyond his top one. He became self-conscious about the jaw when he was ten years old and a girl, he tried to talk to ran away yelling, "Stay away you freak with the funny jaw."

On his head was a black, felt hat. There was a cord around the crown with its two tassels dangling over its front brim: identifying it as cavalry issue. It showed the hard use it had endured by its battered appearance and the band of sweat stain that circled it. His tunic had two badges sewn on its sleeve. They proclaimed him to be a scout and a sniper. His pants were standard cavalry issue with the yellow strip down the legs. On his feet he had a pair of scruffy, dusty riding boots.

He surveyed his surroundings in obedience to his well-honed awareness of the need to know if danger lurked there. Seeing no threats, he stepped down into the street. Little puffs of dust appeared where his toes touched down.

In his left hand he carried a long black bag. It wasn't hard to figure out that the bag carried his rifle. Around his waist were two holsters with button down flaps to hold the guns in place. The flaps of the holsters were stamped C. S. A. indicating they were "spoils of war". Each had the butt of a pistol protruding from it. The one on his left hip had its butt facing forward for a cross body draw while the right was situated for a natural right-hand draw. The handles appeared to be of a modern design suggesting they were Colt revolvers. Veterans would be willing to bet that those expensive revolvers were battlefield booty also. On the back of his gun belt hung a Bowie knife in its sheath.

Crossing his chest were two straps. One was attached to buckskin pouch while his canteen hung on the other. It was obvious to anyone in the know that the pouch held his ammunition. He also had a knapsack on his back that appeared to be stuffed with all the rest of his earthly possessions.

He had just left his troop of scouts for the last time. It was sad for him to think of the finality of this goodbye. He had counted on these men to have his back for over two years now. They had never let him down. But the war was over, and he had his orders. Those orders instructed him to deliver a package to General Sheridan in Jackson, Mississippi and then proceed home to be mustered out.

His transportation voucher put him on the 1:30 train to Jackson and then to Vicksburg, to seek transportation to his discharge destination, St. Paul, Minnesota. He was authorized to use any form of transportation available.

He walked down the dusty street between clap

board, false front buildings. Even though he was intent on reaching his destination, nothing escaped his scrutiny. After a three-block jaunt he entered the train station. He glanced at the clock over the ticket counter, time was 12:50 and he thought, '*Plenty of time.*' He took off his hat and used it to swat the dust off his jeans. He also took this opportunity to look around. He saw nothing that alarmed him. He ambled over to the ticket window and waited for the clerk to address him.

"What can I do for you Yank?"

Bill dug his travel voucher out of his shirt pocket and handed it to him.

" Do you have some identification to prove you are this Wilbur James Cheever?"

Bill took out his wallet and showed the clerk his service card.

The clerk looked at the card and grunted. "Going home are you Yank? Well, good riddance! We've had enough of your ilk down here." The clerk handed Bill his ticket accompanied with an emphatic nod. The look of disdain on the clerk's face backed his unfriendly comment.

"I'll miss you too Reb." replied Bill.

"Well at least that ape president of yours got what he deserved."

Bill's hand flashed across the counter, grab the

front of the clerk's shirt and jerked him off his feet. "I'd be careful who I said that to if I were you. It might just be a pissed off Yank like me. If I weren't in such a good mood about going home, I'd kick the living shit out of you. But since I'm in such a good mood I'm only going to make you blush over your disregard for human life." With that he slapped the guy across his right cheek hard enough to make his teeth rattle and then backhanded him across his left cheek equally hard. The clerk's cheeks were bright red as Bill dropped him and he fell to his knees.

Bill looked around but didn't detect any threat of retaliation. He did receive some looks of disapproval, but some were supportive also. There was still a 15-minute wait before the train would load. Bill found an empty spot on a nearby bench and surveyed his surroundings again.

The station was filling with people. Several businessmen types had their heads together in deep conversation. Each was contributing to the cloud of smoke that was engulfing them. The station was becoming permeated with the smell of cigar smoke. They ignored a shoeshine boy who tried to sell them a shine.

Giving up on the businessmen as prospective customers, the shine boy wandered off yelling, "Shoeshine! Get the best shine in Georgia, only 25¢!"

Bill waved the boy over and said, "See what you can do with these dirty, old boots of mine."

"Yes Sir." With that he sat down on his shine box and got to work.

Bill continued to watch the growing crowd. There was a family with four kids in tow. Mother must have scrubbed them until she got to the very bottom layer of skin. Bill could smell the homemade soap ten feet away. Bill thought, '*I remember when I was little, and Ma would wash me. She was a ferocious scrubber.*' Bill noticed the husband was wearing a gun.

A farm couple sat together on the bench opposite Bill. The wife had a new, pretty, red, gingham dress on and clutched a straw basket covered in the same cloth. The hair that escaped her red with white polka dot bandana was sun faded blond. Her eyes had spider webs at the corners and the skin on her face looked like finely tanned leather. Her face let her world know she spent a lot of time in the sun. She smelled like lilacs. Her boots didn't fit the rest of her outfit. They were scruffy, run down at the heel cowboy boots

The husband had ruff hewn features. He was dressed in new bib overalls and a new red/blue/brown plaid shirt. He looked a little uncomfortable in his new outfit. He did have a soft aroma about him that said "horse". On his head he had a new straw hat. His hands looked hard and calloused as a farmers' hands should. Bill thought, '*those two look like who they are supposed to be. Nothing to worry about from anybody I see here.*'

The time passed quickly, and the crowd grew accordingly. Finally, the conductor called, "All aboard."

Bill flip a 50-cent piece to the shine boy and said, "I didn't think those boots could ever look this good again."

"Thanks Mister."

The crowd was in a festive mood as it moved slowly toward the platform and climbed into the waiting cars. Bill moved along with them until he climbing the stairs into the coach attached to the baggage car.

He selected a seat near the back of the car and propped his rifle bag against the wall, slipping out of his knapsack and adjusting everything to make himself as comfortable as possible before he sat down. It would be a long trip to Jackson, and he intended to make the most of his down time.

He assumed a position which suggested he was asleep. However, under his lowered hat brim, his eyes surveyed all his fellow passengers; where they were seated and how they were acting.

In the first two front seats of the car on the side opposite Bill, sat four of the businessmen still deep in their conversation but, thank goodness, without their cigars.

In the third seat sat an elderly lady in all her finery. She must have bathed in some flower scent Bill couldn't place but he sure could smell. Sitting next to her was a drab waif. Bill wondered '*how can the girl sit next to all that perfume and not swoon. The girl must be the woman's servant and can't afford to complain.*'

In the fourth seat was the woman in her red, gingham and her husband. That dress was an attention getter.

In the seat behind the couple was a rosy cheeked young lady with a little too much meat on her bones. However, she would attract her share of beaus because of her womanly shape and endowments.

There was a good-looking young man in the seat behind her. Bill would bet a month's salary that this young man had all the attention from girls that he could handle. The rest of that side of the car was empty.

On his side of the car, the first seat was empty. The next three seats were occupied by the couple with their four children. The children, under the watchful eye of their parents were behaving like the poster children for a manner's advertisement.

Behind the family were two love birds struggling to keep their hands off each other. Their decorum was being shattered more and more with each second that went by. Finally, the mother of the children turned and said, "Well I never." This was accompanied with a withering look that had enough frost in it to put out any smoldering ember that might be about to burst into flame.

The seats between the love birds and Bill were empty. Behind Bill was a grizzly old timer of undetermined age and occupation. He had his hat tilted over his eyes, his chin down on his chest and emitting snort like snores as he slept. His clothes appeared to be as old and as beat up as he was.

Bill's attention shifted to a new entry. The man's appearance was not what bothered Bill, the rough, unkempt look was common in Georgia these days. It was the feeling that there was something familiar about this man. The newcomer was dressed like a typical cowpoke with a low-slung holster and gun on his hip, a Stetson on his head, a plaid western cut shirt and blue jeans. He was dusty and sweaty as if he had just gotten off the trail.

Before Bill had time to speculate where and when he might have run across the guy, a second man entered the car.

The second man looked as unkempt as the first one. He also was dressed like a cowboy and heeled with a gun and holster. He waited patiently while the first man took his own sweet time surveying the car. Finally, he sat down in the unoccupied front seat. With the aisle clear, the second guy proceeded to the back seat of the coach on the opposite side from Bill.

An alarm bell went off in Bill's brain. This was a classic set up used by train robbers; one in front and one in the back of the car. Slowly, Bill unbuttoned the flaps over his pistols and slipped them out onto the seat. They lay there hidden by his trousers. Next, he took off his hat and placed it on the seat. Then he rummaged in his knapsack until he found a small mirror which he propped up so he could see where the man behind him was located. He finished his act by scratching his head and smoothing his hair. After rearranging his knapsack stuff, replacing the mirror, securing its flap and returning it to it place in his gear; he then turned in his seat and leaned his back on the train wall. From this position he could see both the front and the back of the car out of the corners of his eyes. He replaced his hat, tilted it over his eyes and resumed his sleep sham.

There was a long shriek from a whistle and a squeal of iron on iron as the engineer released the locomotives breaks. The drive wheels jerked the train a couple of times before it started moving smoothly down the tracks.

The train moved through the Georgia pine

country all afternoon with the clack-clack of the wheels to provide a peaceful accompany meant to help the miles speed past . Bill thought, '*Georgia really is pretty if you're not dodging bullets.*' Several sawmills and furniture factories seemed to be working again. Bill thought, '*Work is the best tonic for erasing what's been ailing this country these last few years.*'

About 6 PM, Bill felt some hunger pangs. He rummaged in his knapsack until he found some jerky and hardtack for his evening meal. He had just started gnawing on a piece of salty jerky and soaking the hard tack in water from his canteen when there was a tap on his shoulder. The old timer seated behind him, who looked like a prospector asked," Hey youngster, would you have any of that grub you could spare?"

"Sure." was Bill's reply. Bill handed a chunk of jerky and a square of hardtack over his shoulder.

The food was taken, "Thank you!" came back.

About 9 o'clock the train started to slow down. Bill thought, 'if anything were going to happen this would be the time and the place'. He cocked his revolvers and became extra alert.

The first indication that his hunch was coming true came from the man in the front of the car. He turned his head and nodded toward the back of the car. Suddenly he jumped to his feet in the middle of the aisle while drawing his gun. He shouted, "Hands up, this is a hold up!"

Simultaneously, the man in the back stood up and started his draw only to receive Bill's first bullet in his chest. Bill didn't stop to watch the result that his bullet had but he did hear the satisfying clatter of the gun hitting the floor. He immediately raised his second gun and fired at the man in the front of the car. His aim was true, and the man crumpled where he stood. Bill was shocked when a bullet whiz by his ear shattering the window beside him. Immediately his instincts took over and he identified the shooter as the farmer who accompanied the red, gingham dress. Bill's third shot knocked the farmer down, spraying blood all over the lady in red.

Confusion, screams, sobbing and gun smoke filled the coach. The mother of the children was having trouble calming them down, her husband, gun in hand was trying to help her. The children's frightened sobbing filled the car with their fear.

The aristocratic lady had fainted and was being attended to by the waif. This was a lucky break because the lady's faint put both her and her young attendant completely out of Bill's line of fire toward the farmer.

The old timer behind Bill checked the guy in the back of the train and proclaimed, "This guy is dead!

He's going to stink; he shit his pants." He confiscated the robber's guns just in case he was wrong.

The good-looking guy and the businessmen had their guns out. One of the men in front checked that outlaw and proclaimed, "This guy is dead too! He is already becoming a stinker."

The good-looking guy checked the sham farmer and chimed in, "This guy is still alive but bleeding badly."

The male half of the two love birds, with his gun in his hand was standing over his partner being very protective of her.

Bill said, "Somebody grab the lady in red, she was in on this too!"

The robust, busty young woman grabbed the woman in red and pulled her out of the seat. Then she flopped her on the floor and lay on top of her.

"Everybody get down as close to the floor as you can. I expect there will be more of them showing up! Any of you fellows that know how to use a gun, man the windows on both sides of the coach. The next bunch will be riders."

There was a hubbub as people found a spot on the floor or drew their guns to defend the train. All was ready when five riders leading four horses rode along it shooting at the windows as they went. When they got to Bill's car, they were greeted with a volley of lead. Two saddles were emptied, the other three broke off the attack and rode away followed by the six empty saddles.

The car was full of the acrid smell of gun smoke. However, with all the broken windows, the smoke and smell dissipated quickly as the train came to a stop.

The woman in red's wounded partner was slumped over, filling their seat, so her captor dragged her to vacant seat across the aisle, lifted into her seat and trapped between her captor and the train's wall. Her head was on her chest and she was sobbing. Her dress was stained a deeper red on the back where she had landed in her partner's blood when she was flopped on the floor. Her basket was upside down in the aisle and the gingham cloth that had covered it was under the seat. There was nothing in the basket but under the seat with the cover cloth was a six gun. Since the fake farmer had not shown a gun on himself, Bill guessed the gun he used must have been the contents of the basket.

Bill holstered his guns and waited for his after battle shakes to quit as the adrenaline drained from his system. Shortly he got hold of his emotions. Feeling in control again, he got up and went up and down the aisle asking each person if they were ok and thanking them for their help. He stopped at buxom lasses' seat and praised her for the great job she had done.

Bill had just returned to his seat when a conductor entered the car. His shoes and the cuffs of his pants were covered with drying blood. He glanced down at the dead robber in his path and asked, "Who is this guy?"

One of the businessmen spoke up, "He acted like he was the leader of the gang. We have another dead robber in back and a wounded one in a seat halfway back. We also captured a woman who was part of the gang. The people on this car had an organized defense by the time the riders got to us. The two downed riders resulted from our volley. All the credit for foiling this robbery attempt should go to the soldier in the back of the car. His alertness and actions were decisive this evening."

Chapter 2

Accolades

The conductor said over his shoulder to his companions, "Get this guy out of here." He stepped back on the cars platform so the men could grab the dead man. After the body was gone, there was a large pool of blood on the floor where he had been laying.

Stepping back into the car and avoiding the blood as best he could, the conductor called out, "Is anyone else hurt in this car?"

The answer was a resounding "**Only the crooks!**"

The conductor started up the aisle to where Bill was seated. On his way he glanced at the wounded fake farmer noting the bloody mess caused by his wound.

On his way he took a notebook and pencil out of his pocket. When he reached Bill he said, "I and the Railroad thank you for your help tonight. What is your name and unit number? I am going to need it for my report to the authorities."

At this moment, the two train crewmen reentered the car and waited for their next orders. The boss pointed at the wounded man. As the two came to retrieve the wounded man everyone could see their overhauls, shirt sleeves and dirty gauntlets were covered with blood. "Take him to the aid station and then come back for that last stiff. Also, get a cleaning crew in here to clean up this mess." The crewmen left carrying the bleeding robber in his new bib overalls.

"Now, what's the name and unit?"

"I am Sergeant-Major Bill Cheever detached from the Sixth Minnesota, currently on an errand for General Standish, commander of the Atlanta occupation forces."

"Well Bill, I am delighted to meet you. May I shake your hand?"

Bill stood up and said, "Of course." The two men warmly shook hands.

The door of the coach opened at that moment and the two train men reappeared.

The conductor turned to Bill and said, "As you can imagine, I have things to do that need to be done. I hope the rest of your trip goes better than this." Then he exited the car.

The trainmen picked up the last dead outlaw

from the back of the coach leaving another pool of blood. As the trainmen passed Bill's seat he asked, "Were the two we knocked off their horse's dead or alive?"

"Dead. One of them had two slugs in him, the other guy gained the weight of four. All three of the dead robbers are stretched out in the baggage car. This guy is on his way to join them. The cleaning crew we be here to clean up this mess when we reach Tuscaloosa." with that, the men and their burden left.

Now that the action was over, the tension drained out of the people in the coach and they all started talking at once. The sobbing of the lady in red formed a counter point to the happy talk of the other passengers. "**Oh, shut up!**" her captor told her in a stern voice.

The after-action remorse that plagued him throughout the war set in. *'When will this need to kill end. I just want to get home and settle down in some peaceful place, have a family and live the good life.'*

It took 45 minutes more to reach the Tuscaloosa, Alabama station where the train was scheduled to take on water and fuel.

The Tuscaloosa Provost Marshall had been notified of the attempted hold up by the train's telegrapher. A squad from that unit with a wagon showed at the station about the same time as the train. They were there to collect the dead and arrest the prisoners. It turned out there was only one prisoner, the lady in red. Her companion had bled to death on the way to the city.

They also had a cleaning crew with them. After cleaning the blood pool at the door to the car, the cleaners asked all the passengers to exit while they finished their work.

The buxom lass continued tending to the lady in red as the passengers waited beside the tracks. Soon a Lieutenant leading the squad came along and took the lady crook into custody. The squad escorted the prisoner away as the Lieutenant called out "Is Mr. Cheever here?"

Bill stepped out of the group of passengers and replied, "Here sir."

The Lieutenant strode over to him and offered his hand to Bill. While shaking his hand warmly he said, "I talked to the conductor and heard his account of tonight's action. What a great job you did. I hear you are on your way home. Too bad for us. We still need good men down here. Where are you headed?"

"St. Paul, Minnesota."

"Good luck on your trip and your future." Offering his hand again. Bill shook the hand and the Lieutenant turned and disappeared after his men.

The cleaning crew had finished their job and

bade the waiting passengers to reenter the coach. They left the pungent odor of disinfectants as a reminder of their work. Also, while the passengers were out, all the broken windows had been replaced, they were good to go.

One good thing came out of the delay. While all the other activities were being played out, Tuscaloosa's Women's Christian Society who usually sold bag lunches to train passengers showed up but hesitated to approach. The attempted robbery made them reluctant to venture on to the train. The conductor finally convinced them it was safe to enter and sell their lunches. So, while all the other things were going on the ladies moved through the train hawking their wares.

Bill brought two of them and handed one to the old man in the seat behind him. The aroma that escaped the bags when they opened them made their mouths water. The only thing that exceeded the aroma was the taste of the meatloaf sandwich itself. Both Bill and the old man thought the meatloaf sandwich was delicious. They had only good things to say about the Pecan cookies and peaches also included in the lunch. It was a happy, well fed bunch that left Tuscaloosa for Jackson, Mississippi this night.

The train was about an hour and a half behind schedule at this point. There were no further incidents along the way.

Bill finally dropped off to sleep about midnight. It wasn't long after he fell asleep that he started thrashing in his seat; he was suffering through his reoccurring nightmare. This nightmare was the re-living of his one, man to man fight during the war. He and a Reb were skirmishing in a copse of woods during the battle at Chattanooga, Tennessee. They surprised each other and a knife battle erupted. Bill finally found an opening and skewered the man. He was looking into the Reb's eyes at his pain, his fear as he realized he was dying and the blank look when death came. He had found out the hard way that there was a big difference between shooting some-one from a distance and killing closeup and personal with a knife. He had maintained his fighting edge after that but after every fight where he killed an enemy he relived, in his dreams, the dying look in his victim's eyes.

The old codger in the back seat shook Bill awake and said, "Are you okay youngster? I've had those after-action dreams myself and I know they're tuff to live with."

"Thanks for waking me. I'll be alright now." It took a while for sleep to come again, but eventually he slept quietly through the rest of the night.

The train moved on through the night arriving in Jackson about 8 o'clock in the morning. As it came to a stop at the station, Bill appeared on the platform between the second and third cars. He stood there for a moment scrutinizing his surroundings. He had left his stuff on the train except his side arms.

No one was there to meet him, but he didn't look like he had expected anyone. He took a second look around noting the other people debarking from the train. Satisfied, he headed toward the station and disappeared around it.

The street leading from the depot to the Jackson City Square was full of people hurrying about their business. The sights, sounds, and smells of the city reminded him of nowhere in particular and everywhere in general. There were no telltale signs that this was a city occupied by hostile forces, but it was.

Jackson, being the capital of Mississippi, had the appearance of being fully restored from the ravages of 1863. After the siege of Vicksburg ended on July 4th with General Pemberton's surrender to General Grant, Grant decided he had had enough of General Johnston's army hanging around his flank and rear.

To relieve this pressure, Grant sent General Sherman to retake Jackson and push Johnston's army back far enough to negate his presence in the area. Sherman accomplished this by the end of the summer. This campaign started Bill's personal climb up the promotion ladder. He had become a Corporal by summer's end.

His reminiscing ended as Bill entered the door of General Sheridan's headquarters. There were several desks organized around a waiting area. The area smelled kind of musty, the furniture looked somewhat battered, the rug was thread worn, and the walls could certainly stand a coat of paint. Each desk had a sign over it identifying the function or the persons for whom the clerk was the gateway.

Bill saw the desk with General Sheridan's name over it, so he walked over and said to the corporal setting behind it, "I have a package from General Standish to General Sheridan. I have orders to personally deliver it to the General."

"Whom, shall I tell the General is calling?"

"Sergeant-Major Cheever just arrived from Atlanta."

The clerk told him to wait and then disappeared through a convenient doorway. In almost no time the clerk returned and told Bill the General would see him immediately. Turning, the clerk motioned Bill to follow and returned to the doorway from which he had just emerged.

The General was standing by his desk, waiting for them when they entered his office. He wasn't a very tall man, but he had eyes that burned through you and commanded your attention. "I commend you Sergeant Major for your performance on the train. Nice work. The provost Lieutenant said in his report that your fellow passengers, all of them, lauded your alertness and decisive action." He extended his hand and gave Bill's a hardy shake. "If the war were still on. I would be recommending you for a medal. Have you had anything to eat this morning?"

Bill's answer was to shake his head no.

"Good" said the General. "The best reward I could think of for you was breakfast prepared by my chef and attended by my staff. Please sit down."

Bill set down but immediately stood up again, saying, "I almost forgot the package I have for you, Sir." as he handed it to the General.

The General didn't seem curious about the contents of the box and simply laid it on his desk unopened. "Corporal get someone to man your desk. You take a message to the train's conductor instructing him to hold the train until Bill gets back."

Next, he rang for his orderly. "Check the officer's mess to be sure there is plenty of hot coffee. Then assembled my staff and tell them our guest is here for our congratulation meal. Have them there and ready in ten. Tell the chef he's on the clock."

"Yes sir!"

The General sat down at his desk opposite where

Bill was seated. "Smoke?" he asked as he reached for the humidor on his desk. He opened it and the smell of good Cuban cigars escaped into the room.

"No thank you sir."

"Mind if I do?"

"No, please do."

"Were you with General Sherman at Vicksburg?" as he selected a cigar and prepared it to smoke.

"Yes sir!"

"How about his campaign to retake Jackson and push General Johnston out of the state?

"Yes sir!"

"Did you go with him to Chattanooga?" The General took a match out of a box on his desk and scratch it on the side of the box. The match burst into flames accompanied by the smell of burning phosphorus and sulfur. He held the flame to the end of the cigar and puffed it to life. All other smells were replaced by the aroma from the cigar smoke. The General seemed to be enjoying the first puff as he let the smoke trickle out his nose and the corners of his mouth.

"Yes sir! I saw your magnificent charge up the cliff. That was thrilling."

"Thank you for remembering. My blood was up that day. How about all those battles during his Atlanta campaign? Were you in any of those?"

"Yes sir! All of them."

"Did you go with him from Atlanta to Charleston?"

"No, sir! I returned to Nashville to work for General Thomas. My squad was tasked with roaming the countryside as scouts and to keep the peace. However, I was in the Battle for Nashville when Thomas all but annihilated Hood's Rebels."

"Well, Bill, that is quite a service record you have. Your action on the train explains fully why you wear the stripes of a Sergeant-Major." The General snuffed out his cigar and laid it on the ashtray on his desk. "We better get to breakfast now. We don't want to keep my staff waiting too long. I've already upset their usual routine; oh well, it won't kill them."

When they arrived at the breakfast table the staff was seated around it. Bill was shown to the seat of honor at the head of the table. Each of the staff members had a plate in front of them with an egg something or other on it. Before the General sat down. He introduced Bill to his staff and introduced his staff to Bill. As the General sat down the chef slid one of those egg concoctions out of his pan onto a plate and served it to him.

"Are you familiar with French omelet's Bill?" asked the General.

Bill shook his head no.

"The chef makes the omelet, but you make it yours by selecting any or all of the ingredients the chef has displayed around him."

Bill chose cheese, bacon, and onion. The chef immediately whipped up Bill's choices into a huge omelet, slipped it on a plate, put the plate in front of Bill and disappeared.

"Gentlemen let's eat." ordered the General.

There wasn't much smell from the omelet, there was quite a bit of texture to its surface, but one bite and Bill didn't care about anything but its great taste.

As they ate, Bill was asked question after question about the train robbery attempt. The other topic of interest was the goings on around President Lincoln's assassination. A Lieutenant asked, "Isn't this the last day of viewing at the rotunda?"

One of the other officers answered, "Ya, the bodies of the President and his son will be on the train to Springfield tomorrow. The route they are taking is very around about with lots of stops so people can mourn his passing."

Sheridan said, " I hope they catch that Booth bastard soon."

Chapter 3

Memories and Reflections

T wo hours slipped by before Bill returned to the waiting train. He had a toothpick in his mouth and a job well done look about him.

Out of habit he gave a quick look around. Next, he reported his return to the conductor, releasing him from the General's restrictive order. As he walked to his coach, he felt relieved, his assignment was completed, and he was free to concentrate on getting transportation home. On reaching his car, he swung up to its platform and disappeared inside. The odor of the cleaning solutions that had been used still hung in the air. He found his gear where he had left it and after rearranging it for the afternoon's ride, he sat down. He opened the window in hopes of airing the car out.

As he looked around, he realized he had the car practically to himself. The old geezer had said,

"Thanks and goodbye." as they left the train together few minutes after they arrived in Jackson. The only passengers remaining in the car were two of the businessmen and the buxom lass. No new riders had entered the car.

Train gave out a long whistle. Shortly after the whistle sounded, the train's drive wheels started to churn adding their noise to the din of the activity going on around the station.

Despite the clickety-clack of the train's wheels, Bill's attention was riveted to the passing scenes. He remembered, '*how cold, wet and frustrated he and his buddies in the Sixth Minnesota were as part of General Sherman's Corps probing the area north of Vicksburg.*

They had seen their first action during the Corp's attempt to take the heights above the Grand Bayou. They couldn't see their enemy dug in on the top of the bluff during that engagement but the Rebs could see them. Five guys in our regiment were wounded and two were killed. I didn't even give it a thought when I dragged the wounded Sergeant out of the line of fire. I was just young, dumb, and lucky. That made war a lot more real for us than all that time we had spent occupying forts. All we wanted was to find a route around the city to dry land. However, all we found was a maze of bayous, swamps, dead-end rivers and rebs blocking our way.

'*He thought of how relieved we all were when*

General Grant finally ended that nightmare effort by floating some transports down the Mississippi River past the Reb's guns at Vicksburg.

Next, Grant marched the troops down the west bank of the Mississippi where they met up with the boats at a hamlet named Hardscrabble. Then he sent troops across the river to establish a beachhead. All that accomplish, he sent the entire army across. General Sherman's Corps was the last unit to cross because we had to march the farthest to get there.

General Pemberton took his troops out of their defensive works to chase Grant's army. Grant kept us on the move which thoroughly confused his enemies. During all that marching neither I nor my friends ever saw a live reb who wasn't a prisoner. That early spring campaign turned out to be a big, happy camp out for us.

There was one event I remember as if it were happening today. At an evening formation of the Corps my name was called out and I was ordered to proceed to 'front and center'. The Corp's Brass, including General Sherman and the Honor Guard were arrayed before me as I saluted. A Sergeant with a scroll stepped forward to face me. He unrolled the scroll and read, "This 'Citation for Valor' in the face of the enemy is here by awarded to Wilbur James Cheever for the act of pulling a wounded comrade to safety during the action at Grand Bayou. There were some more nice words about what I had done that I don't remember now but I do remember the great feeling when the Sergeant who read the citation introduced himself as the guy, I had pulled to safety that day. That scroll will be waiting for me when I get home.

Things changed in a hurry for us as the Army turned to attack the city. As the train approached the Big Black River Bridge, he remembered, *this was his first action since the assault on the hills at Grand Bayou. He had hope that this time he would be able to see the enemy so he could fight back. He vividly remembered that, as his squad rushed up to support the right flank of the attack on the bridge, he stopped and took aim at a Reb who was posed to shoot at the Yanks attacking across the bridge. A fountain of blood was visible as my bullet smacked into the side of the reb's head. My first thought was what a nice shot I had made. On second thought it became both satisfying and sickening. Horror came over me for a minute or two as the Reb disappeared behind his works. I was just 18 then. I vomited all over the place.*

I remembered, 'As a kid on the farm, hanging on my dad's pants leg, crying, and pleading for the life of the chicken whose neck was stretched across the chopping block about to have it cut off. I remember my Sergeant coming over to calm me and get me back to concentrating on the work at hand. He reminded me that my mates were depending on me holding up my end of the fight. A few Reb bullets whistling past my head did the rest. I killed several other rebs that day. It got easier and easier as the day went on. Soon I was thinking of them as targets and not as people. By the end of the day, it became kill and look for another target. I never loss my killer instinct after that but after every fight I struggled with my feelings about what I had done.'

More memories crowded into his mind as the train approached Vicksburg. He saw the still visible scars made during their siege of the city. These brought back old memories of the, *'sights and sounds of their attacks on the defenders works. The hurrahs of the Yanks intermixed with the high pitched, keening reb battle cry still rattled around in his head'*. He thought, *'will I ever be completely free of my memories of the horrors of war?'*

By the time the train pulled into the Vicksburg station, Bill was convinced that

'War is anything but a civilized activity.'

It was about 5 in the evening when they reached Vicksburg. Bill got off, knapsack on his back, pistols in his holsters, and bag with rifle in his left hand. As he walked into the city he thought, *'This place is still a shamble, I wonder how the rebel citizens are getting on'*. He didn't see much visible evidence that the inhabitants were working hard to restore their city. *'Oh well,'* he thought, *'they asked for it and they got what they asked for.'*

He moved down the street toward the center of the city. As he rounded a corner, he found himself in front of a noisy, little saloon with the familiar saloon odor coming out the door. There was a piano playing inside and lots of laughter drifting out of its open door. Bill thought, '*They might even have a free lunch.*' He pushed through the batwing doors and headed toward the bar. The bar was crowded but he managed to find a spot to snuggle into. "A tall, cold beer please barkeep." he said. While waiting for his beer, he looked around the room. Most of the guys wore Union Blue. The girl's dresses were obviously old, before the war styles and showing the ravages of time.

Bill was startled when a hearty voice shouted, "Bill, Bill Cheever you old son of a gun. How are you? Where have you been?"

Before Bill could answer, the piano player started in on "Clementine". This prompted every would-be vaudeville entertainer to join in with their own personal rendition of the words to the song. The din of the clash between the mismatched words and music filled the barroom with sound that would be thought wonderful by the singers, but the non-singers would find hard on their ears.

Bill looked in the direction of the shout and feasted his eyes on an old friend, another Minnesotan.

"Jake, it's so good to see you! What have you been doing with yourself the last two years?"

They approached each other with a handshake and typical man hug, one arm delivering a hearty slap on the back. Clementine came to an end and the piano player took mercy on the crowd by playing a little-known waltz.

"I've been right here in Vicksburg, on garrison duty." replied Jake Olson, "How about you?"

"I've been traipsing all over the South. Old Billy Sherman took us across the South chasing the Rebs under Joe Johnston. What a slick fox Johnston turned out to be. When we finally got him pinned with his back against Atlanta; Jeff Davis gave us a present. He turned the Confederate Army over to that brave, bold, impatient Texan, General Hood. General Hood, remaining true to his nature immediately came after us. Old Billy whipped those Rebs every time they showed themselves. Pretty soon Hood tucked his tail between his legs and the whole bunch of Rebs skedaddled. After we took Atlanta General Sherman split the Army, taking some 60,000 with him to the sea." Bill continued. "My group of scout/sharpshooters were sent back to General Thomas at Nashville. Our mission was to roam the countryside looking for possible trouble. I was there when Thomas destroyed Hood's army. After that, my group scouted around and when the war fizzled out, I was back in Atlanta. From there I came here. Now I'm looking for a way to get back to Minnesota. What about you Jake? How's garrison life?"

"Well, Bill, my brother is here too"

Bill broke in, "Just a minute Jake, my beers here. You want one Jake?"

Jake shook his head no, "I've got one over at my table; come on, let's go over there and sit down."

Bill stopped at the bar and picked up his beer and followed Jake across the room to a corner table. The table was covered with red and white check-ered oilcloth and had four, blue kitchen chairs for seats. "This is sort of my table in the evening." Jake said. "One of the perks of being a regular and able to come a little early to claim it." They both took a seat.

Jake and Bill clinked glasses and Bill said, "A toast to getting back to Minnesota soon." and they both took a chug of beer.

"As I said, Tom's been here the whole time. You know how he is. He'd organize a contest between ants if he were stranded in the middle of a desert. With him here, there's been all kinds of action. He got a ball and bat from up north and we have regular baseball games every Saturday. Races and boxing at least once a week. He started a chess club, a debate club, and a theater group. I'm not sure how we find the time to stand guard duty. When do you expect to get back to Minnesota?"

The music and singing had started again but it was far enough away so they could ignore it.

"I'm going as soon as I find transportation. You don't know of any possibilities, do you?"

"I know there is a big riverboat expected any day now. I heard it was going to take a load of liberated prisoners up north. I think it's called the Sultana. The liberated prisoners are scheduled to load tomorrow, and the Sultana will leave ether tomorrow or the next day. I don't know how much chance there is to hook a ride. I heard there's about 2000 liberated prisoners on her passenger list."

"Do you have any idea where I should go to find out if I can go with them?"

"Let's see, I know there is a camp for paroled prisoners out on the edge of town. That's where the liberated prisoners are being kept. That seems to be your best bet. A dodo, Major Williams is in charge. I don't care much for the man but I'm sure he's the one to see." Jake answered.

"I think I'll just mosey on out there. It won't hurt, and who knows, I might get lucky." Bill muttered to himself. "But, before I go, let's eat and chew the fat for a while."

Jake recommended the bar's specialty, Slum-Bullion Stew. When the bowls arrived, Bill saw it had peas, carrots, and small red potatoes in a reddish broth. The aroma escaping out of the bowl and its appearance signaled that the broth contained onions, tomatoes, and beef bouillon with special seasonings. Hidden in the broth were a generous portion of beef chunks.

As Bill wiped the last remnants of the sauce from his now empty bowl with his last crust of bread he said, "Thanks Jake. Momma would be proud to serve a stew that tastes like that at her table.

It was 7:00 that evening before Bill and Jake parted. They talked about old times in Minnesota, the Sioux uprising was a hot topic as they remembered friends that had survived and those who had perished. Of course, they talked about Lincoln's Funeral train that would start its way across the country tomorrow.

Bill felt a warm glow from the pleasant meeting with Jake. Before Bill left the saloon, he asked the bartender for directions to the camp where the former prisoners of war were being billeted. Armed with the bartender's information Bill made a beeline for the camp. He thought, *Sultana, I wonder what kind of a ship she is?* He had no trouble finding the camp.

Approaching a sentry, he said, "Excuse me, I'm

looking for a Major Williams. Could you tell me where I might find him?"

The sentry looked skeptically at Bill and asked, "Who are you?"

"I am Sergeant Major Wilbur James Cheever, service number 32-512-63, detached from the 6th Minnesota for scouting duty. Reporting in from the Atlanta area." Bill replied.

The sentry snapped off a sharp salute. Bill returned it, maybe a little more haphazardly than the sentry's. The sentry turned and called out, "Sergeant of the Guard." A wiry, little man with sergeant's stripes on his sleeve detached himself from a group of soldiers lounging on the ground nearby.

"What is it Kramer?" he shouted.

"This man wants to see the Major." replied the soldier named Kramer.

"Send him over here!" shouted the Sergeant. Turning, the Sergeant said, "Private Brass, take this man to the Major."

Another man detached himself from the group of soldiers, "Yes Sergeant." said the soldier called Brass as he snapped his salute to the Sergeant. The Sergeant saluted back. "This way soldier" not waiting for an answer, Brass led the way down the dusty road into the camp. Cheever followed behind.

Bill could see shelters and men scattered

everywhere and anywhere. They must've dropped where they were when told to fall out. Small cooking fires also dotted the landscape. The smell of burning wood and sizzling steaks gave the grove of trees the camp was pitched in a nice, homey aroma. Up ahead Cheever saw a large tent which he took to be headquarters for the camp. He became sure of his clever deduction when Brass headed right for it. Lounging around fire pit with a nice fire in front of the tent were three officers, a Lieutenant, a Captain and a Major. Bill made another clever deduction, he thought that must be Major Williams. Sure enough, Brass pulled up in front of the Major and saluted smartly; the Major returned the salute from his chair.

The Major's face had a sour, scornful look that shouted, how dare you disturb me while I am enjoying this fire. His black hair was short, gelled to make it stand up straight and cut to give him severe flat top. His blouse was buttoned fully even though he was setting by the fire and was obviously hot.

Bill thought, *'This is not a sympathetic soul. I doubt I'll get anywhere with him.'*

"Sir this is Sergeant Major Wilbur James Cheever. He just arrived in Vicksburg from Atlanta. He requested to be conducted to you sir."

"Thank you soldier, you're dismissed now. Return

to your guard position." The two exchanged salutes again.

The Major turned to Bill with the question, "What name do you answer to Mr. Cheever?"

"My friends call me Bill, sir."

Chapter 4
Fate in the Making

O n January 3, 1863, the steam powered piston, side wheeler riverboat Sultana was launched in Cincinnati, Ohio. The Sultana had a wooden hull 260 feet long and 42 feet wide. She had two upper decks and a hurricane bridge. She was powered by four steam boilers fired with coal and served by two large smokestacks that overshadowed her upper deck. Her crew numbered 85. She was built to accommodate 376 passengers. Her expected use was transporting contraband cotton from New Orleans to St. Louis.

Her hull was black like most river boats and her upper decks were white. After the Sultana was launched, she moved from Cincinnati to her home port of St. Louis. The Sultana usually steamed from St. Louis (Missouri) to Cairo (Illinois) to Memphis

(Tennessee) to Vicksburg (Mississippi) to Baton Rouge (Louisiana) to New Orleans (Louisiana) and stopping at the same ports of call on the return trip to St. Louis. On the way to New Orleans, her cargo was usually supplies and troops for the Union Army. On the way back to St. Louis she carried produce (cotton, sugar, etc.) and travelers.

The Sultana's Last Voyage

About midnight on April 13-14,1865 the Sultana, with her Captain J. Cass and crew left St. Louis for a typical trip to New Orleans. From the time the Sultana left the dock at St. Louis it was helped on its way by the strong, spring, flood current. They reached Cairo, Illinois in almost record time. The crew unloaded its Cairo bound cargo and loaded the cargo headed downstream.

Cairo was in a festive mood; news was that General Johnston was negotiating the terms for surrendering of his entire army to General Sherman. The Sultana's captain and crew were planning to stay over and join Cairo's celebration that was scheduled for that night and leave for Memphis the next afternoon.

The celebration was a blast. Kegs of free beer were situated at each intersection, several bands marched around serenading the crowds with patriotic songs and spontaneous marches by the citizens with lots of cheers for the Union. The captain and crew straggled back to the boat one or two at a time. It was well after 12 o'clock when the last one checked in.

However, the next morning found Cairo in turmoil and shock. News of Lincoln's assassination had arrived during the night. Captain Cass immediately saw an opportunity to make some more money. He thought '*Where we are going people would not have heard this news*. He knew the war had destroyed the South's telegraph system and that it had not been repaired yet. He scoffed up a big armload of Cairo newspapers. The people down south would pay premium prices for the news the papers contained. All he needed to do was to get there first. He immediately gathered his crew and they cast off for Memphis. April 15, 1865 was going to be a busy day.

The trip to Memphis, with waters of both the Ohio and Mississippi pushing them was faster than any of them had ever made the trip before. The Sultana reached Memphis early afternoon on April 15th. Cass sold his ten cent newspapers for ten dollars apiece. Business was brisk until the news started to spread by word-of-mouth. The Sultana's crew had taken care of unloading the Memphis bound cargo and loading the downriver stuff. Captain Cass immediately got the Sultana underway again, they reached Vicksburg the next morning.

On reaching Vicksburg, The Captain was back to pedaling more of his newspaper stock. The newspaper idea was beginning to be a very profitable enterprise for the Captain. Once again, the crew took care of Sultana's Vicksburg business.

For the last week, Lieutenant Colonel Rubin Hatch had been investigating every riverboat captain scheduled to docked here. He was searching for a captain who would be willing to join him in making lots of money from his insider position. Captain Cass, he had heard, had a reputation on the River of being easily influenced by money. His crew wasn't shy about extra money either. After seeing the Sultana at the wharf this morning, he came down to the harbor seeking Captain Cass to present his deal and find out if Cass was interested. Hatch spotted Cass hawking his papers on a busy corner of the fish market. The Captain obviously was not a fastidious person. While his hat with his badge of authority on it was spotless, his hair hanging down from the sweat band was shoulder length and look like it was a tangle of oily globs. The Captain had on his dress uniform, but it was less than impressive with all the stains and wrinkles prominently displayed on it. He didn't seem to be aware of his shabby clothes as he stood there trying to look like a proper Captain. He obviously wasn't impressing any of his customers.

Hatch approached the Captain and said in a low voice meant for only his ears, "Are you the Captain of that big riverboat tied to the wharf?"

Cass nod his head and whispered, "Yes."

"Are you interested in a deal that will make us both a lot of money?"

"Always willing to listen, Colonel."

A Man passing by stopped and said, "How much for a paper?"

"News hot off the press. Ten bucks US, not that confederate ass wipe."

The man grumbled under his breath, "Highway robbery." Still he dug in his pocket and came up with a five-dollar bill and five ones. Taking his paper, he went down the street still grumbling.

The Colonel introduced himself, "I'm Ruben Hatch, chief quartermaster at Vicksburg." He was interrupted again by a loud **"Whoopee!"** that came from the paper buyer a half a block away. This was followed by a gleeful **"That old bastard finally got what he deserved."**

Hatch looked after the elated Reb but almost immediately returned to the deal he was proposing to Cass. "I'll see that at least 1400 former Union prisoners of war are assigned to the Sultana for transportation back north." Hatch said. "The government will pay you $5 for each enlisted man and $10 for each officer transported." He said, "My fee for arranging this will be 25% of the take. Do you take it or leave it?"

Captain Cass was elated with the goldmine he was being offered. He thought 'the *bribes a little steep but the payoff should be tremendous.*' "It's a deal!" The two conspirators shook hands.

Hatch said, "It will take a few days to bring the last of the returning prisoners from the Confederate prison camps. Some are coming from the Selma; Alabama area and the rest are from the Sumter Camp located at Andersonville in Western Georgia. They will be brought here to Vicksburg."

Cass said, "This will fit my schedule perfectly. I still must reach New Orleans with my downriver cargo, pick up my upriver cargo and then return to Vicksburg. With arrangements made, the two men shook hands again and parted.

Cass shut down his newspaper enterprise posthaste. He was sure he could pedal the remaining newspapers in New Orleans. He also knew that if he weren't here to take the load of prisoners, some other ship and captain would jump at a chance to make this windfall. Thus, by late afternoon on the 16th the Sultana cast off from the dock and was on her way.

By early morning on the 17th they reached Baton Rouge. It didn't take long for the crew to complete the ship's business there. Captain Cass decided, given the strength of the current, he would cancel the scheduled upriver stop there and so informed the Port Authority.

Early on the morning of the 18th, the Sultana arrived in New Orleans. Lots of work awaited them in that morning. The captain would have to complete his newspaper enterprise. The crew would have to unload the New Orleans bound freight and passengers while upload the upriver cargo which included a small herd of livestock, 120 tons of sugar, 70 cabin passengers. They also had scads of people who would endure the trip on the deck. However, the crew knew their business, and by hard work everything was shipshape by nightfall on the 18th.

Immediately, the Sultana was on its way back to Vicksburg. There was no stopping this time, but progress was slow. The mighty Mississippi which had propelled them to a record-breaking trip downstream might cause this trip to break the record for the slowest upriver trip ever. The river was about as mighty as it could be at its high flood stage. These were the highest floodwaters in many years. The tops of the trees along the riverbank were all you could see of them and in some spots the river spread out so wide you could not see either shore. The Sultana's steam boilers had to work at higher than usual pressures to give her paddle wheels enough push to make headway against the current.

The Sultana was winning the struggle against the current until about an hour south of Vicksburg when one of her boilers sprung a leak. At reduced steam pressure, she was verily making headway against the current. She limped into Vicksburg at breakfast time on April 21st. This was about a day longer than it normally took to get from New Orleans to Vicksburg.

As soon as the Sultana was securely tied to the wharf, Captain Cass sent his chief engineer, Nathan Wintringer, to fetch a mechanic to repair the damaged engine. Captain Cass stood on the foredeck looking anxiously down the dock towards where Wintringer had disappeared. After what seemed like an eternity, Captain Cass saw the lanky form of his engineer hurrying back clutching a small guy's arm. The small guy's feet were hardly touching the boards of the dock as Wintringer pulled him along.

The little man had on some of the filthiest, oiliest bib overalls on ever seen on planet Earth. His engineers cap sat on top of his head with brown curls sticking out from under it. His beard was brown and curly like his hair. Captain Cass thought, *'this guy looks just like one of those Irish elves.'*

NEIL GILLIS

"**Captain**" called Wintringer, "**this is Mr. Brimley; he claims to be the best steam engine mechanic in Vicksburg**. Mr. Brimley this is the Sultana's Captain Cass."

"Good day to you Captain." said the smiling Brimley. "Please lead me to the ailing monster."

"Right this way Mr. Brimley." said the Captain. "We have a busted steam line." With that, he turned and started down the ladder to the engine room. Brimley and Wintringer followed close behind.

The boiler room was hardly big enough to hold the ships four boilers. The black crew sprawled on the deck by the coal bins. The bins were almost empty. The trip up the Mississippi fighting the currents seem to have depleted both the coal and the energy of the black crew.

Ignoring the black crew, the Captain said, "the problems in the steam feed pipe between boilers one and two Mr. Brimley."

"Ah! Let's take a look." replied Mr. Brimley.

With that, Brimley started examining the offending pipe. After examining the problem pipe, Brimley continued checking all the rest of the Sultana's pipes and boilers. At last he grunted, "It looks like the rest of the pipes and equipment are sound enough. Replacing the broken pipe should be all that's needed. Do you have any replacement pipe handy?" looking questioningly at the captain and his engineer.

"I don't think so." said the engineer. "Can't we get some in Vicksburg?"

"Ha-Ha!" chuckled Mr. Brimley. "We've had a war around here you know!"

"Well, what can we do then?" asked the Captain.

"I can scrounge up a piece of pipe and manufacture a sound splice with it." replied Brimley.

"How long will that take?" asked the captain.

Brimley stroked his goatee and seemed to enter a trance-like state. Suddenly he snapped out of his trance and said, "I believe it will take about four to five days if we're lucky enough to find that piece of pipe in that time."

Captain Cass looked like he'd swallowed a lemon. In an anguished voice he screeched out "That is impossible! I can't have this ship layover here that long. One day, even though that will be a strain; that's all the time I have for this repair."

A burst of sound from the deck stop their conversation. What a din of animal noises. Lots of moos, some oinks and a clatter of hooves cascaded down through the open hatch.

"That must be the crew unloading the livestock." said the ships engineer.

The three men looked at each other as if to say, "What can we do now?"

Brimley said, "Well, I did make a repair on a piece of pipe like this once. We were out to sea when a steam line broke. Search as we may, we couldn't find a replacement pipe. So, I hammered the bulge in the pipe until the two sides were together and match pretty well. Then I wrapped boilerplate around the weak spot to strengthen it. I completed the job by welding everything up."

"How long did that take"

Brimley stroked his goatee again, "I think I could get that done in a couple of hours for you."

"Great, can you do it right away?"

"I guess I could put off the other things I had planned to do today. It will cause some pain for my other customers but not so much I can't stand their bitching."

"How much will that cost?"

Brimley stroked his goatee, "I think I can get that done for, say $30 U. S."

"Why that's highway robbery."

"Well, I figure $10 of that pays for the work I won't get today because you're in such a hurry. Another $10 of that pays me for my time and any supplies I will need. The last $10 pays me back for the 10-cent newspaper I paid you $10 for the other day. Take it or leave it; which will it be?" said the smiling Brimley.

"I have no choice," said a pouting Captain. "it's a deal."

Mr. Brimley turned to Wintringer "Do you have an anvil available?"

"Yes, I'll have it set up down here right away. It will be waiting for you when you're ready to start the repair."

"Can you also remove the broken pipe so I can start closing the gap as soon as I get back?"

"Sure, we'll have everything ready for you by the time you get back."

Their plans made, Brimley excused himself to go round up the tools and materials he'd need to make the planned repairs. Captain Cass went off to make plans with the Army for the delivery of the freed prisoners that afternoon.

The rest of the morning of the 20th the crew scoured the deck to clean up the mess left by the livestock, filled the coal bunkers, and got the Sultana ready to load the horde of prisoners they knew would be boarding that afternoon.

The stage was set for fate to take a hand.

Chapter 5
A Way Home

Early evening on April 20, Bill stood before Major Williams waiting for what would come next. "Okay Bill, what are you looking for from me?" asked the Major.

"Sir, I was hoping I could catch a ride on the Sultana when she leaves." stammered Bill. "I'll do anything to earn my passage, sir."

"Do you have your orders and travel voucher with you?".

"Yes sir." He fished in his pocket for his papers and presented them to the Major.

The Major gave the papers the once over, nodded his head and thought, *This may solve the new problem I got dumped on me today. He is a Sergeant-Major so no one can accuse me of not doing my due diligence by selecting him on such a short acquaintance. I just can't look this gift horse in the mouth and reject him because I don't have references. His rank is all the reference I need. That's it the decision is made.'*

"Well Bill, this is your lucky day. I just found out that I'm going to need people to take care of a wounded Lieutenant General that insists on going home immediately. I think you'll do fine as the leader of the General's caretakers. If you're agreeable and the General is okay with this arrangement; you got yourself a ride home. What about it? Are you game?"

"You can count on me, sir. I will charm the General right off his feet."

"Well, that will be quite a feat." chuckled Major Williams. "The General has no feet to be charmed off. That's why you will have a squad of four men to carry the General's stretcher wherever he needs to go. Are you still game?"

"I'm still game Major. Let's go see the General and finalize this deal, sir."

"Good, he's right in the tent behind me. Let's go in and see him."

The Major got up and led Bill into the tent. The interior of the tent smelled like a hospital with a medley of medicinal odors. Bill had to strain his eyes to see the bulk of the General huddled on a stretcher at the back of the tent. Bill might've missed him if it weren't for the white bandages, one on his right ankle and one on his left knee. As Bill approach, the pungent smell of acid with hint of burning flesh seamed to form a cloud around the General. The General stared up with a quizzical look on his face.

"Who are you?" the General asked.

"Sergeant-Major Wilbur James Cheever sir. Formerly part of the 6th Minnesota; currently on detached duty with General Thomas's scouts" Bill replied. "I am volunteering to accompany you north, General. That is, if you accept my offer."

The General winced and reached for a bottle of laudanum situated close to his stretcher, took a swig and wiped his mouth with the back of his hand. "I can't see any reason, Sergeant Cheever, to rejecting such a generous offer."

"Great General, thank you sir. I'll make all the arrangements and be back for you in the morning."

As they left the tent the Major said," His name is Melvin Armour and he is said to be quite well off."

"Thanks Major. Could I meet my crew now?"

"Certainly, Sergeant-Major. Right this way." Williams left the tent turned left and then left again. Even in the early evening light you could see the path that had been worn through the undergrowth. The path was visible to the edge of a depression. When Bill got to where the ground dropped away to form the depression, he saw a camp at its bottom. There were 8 or 10 men cooking their food over the fire.

"Major, can I interview these men and pick any of them that I want?" asked Bill.

"Yes Sergeant-Major you can take any four you want." replied the Major.

By then Bill and the Major had reached the edge of the camp, "Attention you men." the Major bellowed. The men jumped to their feet, the remains of their dinners and utensils scattered all over the place. The men ignored this and saluted the Major.

"What can we do for you sir?" they all asked in unison.

"I need four of you men to accompany a General on a stretcher and Sergeant-Major Cheever (waving his hand toward Bill) until you deliver the General to his home in Des Moines, Iowa. After the General's home safe, you each can proceed to your homes and do what you are required to do to muster out. The Sergeant-Major will now interview each of you to determine the team he wants to accompany him on this assignment."

"Yes sir." answered the group once again in unison.

The Major saluted the men and the men saluted back. The Major looked at Bill and said "Carry on Sergeant-Major. As soon as possible, let me know the names of the men going with you so I can prepare their orders and transportation vouchers." The Major and Bill traded salutes. With that the Major headed back toward the headquarters tent.

"As the Major said, I am Sergeant-Major Bill Cheever." A gust of wind made the fire flame up and crackle filling the silence that ensued. "Is there anyone in this group not ready to go home yet? Anyone who feels that way, step out and I thank you for your time." No one budged. They all exchanged looks filled with excitement, disbelief, and joy. "I wish I could take all of you with me. I'm sure we all have reasons to want to get home, but I am only authorized to take four. I am sorry we interrupted your meal so let's finish that before we worry about who's going and who's not. Pick up your plates, utensils, and any leftovers. If any of it is fit to eat, feel free to do so. When you are ready, utensils and plates cleaned, and stored, campsite policed, gather around the fire again."

Bill chuckled as the men scrambled around picking up their dishes and food. Bill took this opportunity to find a spot for his bedroll and gear.

When the men were finish, they all gathered back around the fire. Bill said, "Let's sit down and jaw a while so I can get to know each of you better."

Bill turned to the soldier who sat down on his left. "I see from your patch you were in the Artillery. What is your name?"

"Blair Myers, sir."

"Where are you from Blair?"

"Wabasha, Minnesota, it's on the Mississippi down near the southeast corner of the state, sir."

"How old are you? If you don't mind me asking."

"Twenty-six, sir."

"One thing I want to get rid of right now is this sir crap. I am just Bill, please. Where were you stationed when the war ended?"

"A small fort in eastern Tennessee, over near Knoxville."

"Keeping eastern Tennessee out of the rebs hands was a key piece to winning the war. Thank you for your report."

Turning to the soldier on his right, "What about you? Your patch tells me you're Infantry."

"My name is Hans Halter." he said with a heavy German accent "And I come from Milwaukee, Wisconsin. I am twenty-one years old. I was stationed in Nashville on occupation duty. We did have one big battle." he said proudly. We almost annihilated the rebs under General Hood."

"I was in that battle also. Good report Hans." Pointing at a soldier on the other side of the fire," What about you Sargent? I see you are in the Infantry too."

"My name is Richard Madson and I am from Carver, Minnesota. Carver is a small port on the Minnesota River just west of Shakopee, and right next door to Chaska. I am twenty-three years old I was station in Jackson, Mississippi in the Provost Marshal's squad. I carried the telegram to General Sheridan's office describing your role in foiling the attempted train robbery. Good job, we were all impressed."

"Thanks for the compliment. By the way I have passed through Carver on my way to St. Paul. I lived in Redwood Falls on the Minnesota River. How about you Private? I see you were in the infantry also." He was pointing at the guy sitting at Sargent Madson's right.

"My parents dubbed me Peter and my family name is Bloom. I hail from St. Peter, Minnesota on the Minnesota, River. I am twenty-three years old. I was with the sixth Minnesota, Company C until we retook Jackson. Then I was detached for garrison duty in Jackson the rest of the war."

"Did we ever meet way back then?"

"I don't think so but seeing you now I remember seeing you around the camp once in a while. Also, I remember the assembly when you were awarded the citation for valor."

"That citation was a complete surprise. Do you know that the sergeant I helped was the guy who presented that citation that day? That made it especially memorable for me. Thanks for remembering."

Now pointing to the guy on Madson's left, "What about you Corporal? Another Infantry man hey?"

"David Barrett from Stillwater on the St. Croix River, I am twenty-five years old and I was stationed at Port Hudson, Louisiana. I was part of General Nathaniel Banks force that captured that stronghold and then became part of the occupying force."

"We were still carrying on the siege of Vicksburg while you were taking Port Hudson. We heard how tough a fight that was." Bill nodded at the next guy, "What about you sergeant."

" Sergeant Emery Higgins, Quartermasters Corps. I am twenty-two and I was stationed in Vicksburg the whole time. We tried to keep all you fighters supplied." He said in a defensive voice.

"Your group did a good job of that. I never lacked for ammo nor missed a meal during my stint. And you?" Pointing to the man sitting to the right of Sargent Madson. "I see you are a Sergeant in the Commissary Department."

"I am Homer Briggs from Green Bay, Wisconsin; Twenty-two years old. I got the stuff Emery sent to your unit and distributed it to the individual men. I was stationed in Memphis since I arrived down here."

Pointing to the next man, "I see from your sleeve patch you are a corporal in infantry "Your name?"

"Sam Spence from Sheboygan, Wisconsin."

"How old are you, Sam?"

"Twenty-three."

"Where were you last stationed?"

"I was a guard at the Army's Mississippi Stockade outside Jackson."

"Thanks Sam."

"Now finally, the man that looks like the prototype lumberjack. I see you are Infantry. Please fill us in on the rest?"

"My name is Duane Fish and I am from Eau Claire, Wisconsin. And guess what, I was a lumberjack and will be again when I get home."

A ripple of laughter went through the group.

"I am thirty-two and I have been working on the railroad, trying to keep it running so that Homer had the stuff you Infantry types kept losing that he had gotten from Emery who had gotten it from a train I help keep going."

A round of applause followed Duane's speech.

"Okay, now we know a little bit about each other, let's get to the business of identifying who goes and who stays. First are any of you suffering from anything that would interfere with you being able to carry one end of a stretcher with a two-hundred-pound man on it for a mile or so? Fitness for the task of carrying the stretcher is a primary concern."

Hans Halter spoke up, "I withdraw from consideration, I am still nursing a leg wound."

"Thanks for your honesty Hans. I appreciate the

sacrifice you just made for the success of this mission. Anybody else have a health problem that would interfere with doing their duty?"

"My lungs have been whistling since that winter in the swamps." said Peter Bloom.

"Thanks Peter. Anyone else had second thoughts on health issues?" No one spoke.

"Do any of you have a method by which we should select the lucky ones who get to go home?"

One of the men raised his hand. "What's your suggestion Private?"

"Length of service could be used to decide."

Another hand shot-up, "Rank."

"Those are possibilities. "Are there any other suggestions?"

"Family hardships that need attention." Sargent Briggs said, "I am not married but, I can imagine the anguish such a person would feel. They carry all the concerns of every soldier plus their family's welfare back home. Add a child or two and you have a distraction that can get you killed. Therefore, I suggest that married be the first criteria, and number of children be the second. If there are any slots left, we can draw straws for it." This suggestion won the day with unanimous approval.

Bill asked, "How many of you men are married? Show of hands please." Five of the men raised their hands. The three unwed men, Sam Spence, Emery Higgens and Homer Briggs dropped out of line.

"Do any of you have children home?"

All five of the married men raise their hands.

"Duane, how many children do you have at home?"

"I have five children; three boys and two girls."

"Do any of you family men have more than five children?"

No one responded.

"Okay Duane, step over here."

"Blair, how many children?"

"One."

"Dave, how many?"

"Two."

"Mr. Madson, do you go by Richard, Dick or Rick?"

"I prefer Dick."

"Okay Dick, how many?"

"I have a pair of strapping sons." he said proudly.

"Sargent Higgins, how many?"

"One and one on the way."

Sam Spence said, "Hey, if one on the way counts, I got a girl in a family way on my last furlough and her dad is threatening to shoot me if I don't marry her the minute I get back. So. I've got a wife on the way and a child on the way. How about those apples?"

Bill said, "Nice try Sam, but I am playing the judge on this one and I say no on the ways count. That leaves us with one contested spot. We will use the short straw method to decide this issue." Bill took two matches out of his kit and drew his knife out of its sheath. The knife sliced one match in half. He then turned his back to the group and shuffled the matches around so no one could have followed the mixing, arranged the match head so they were even and turned back around to face the group.

"Who's going to draw?" someone in the group asked.

"Hans, you and Peter get together and decide on a number from 1 to 10. You better write the number down and give the paper to Homer. Homer will be the 'Who Draws Judge'. We don't want anyone to doubt the fairness of this deal. Is the number ready?"

"Yes." Said the Who Draws Judge.

"Contestants, are you ready?" "Yes." they both said and gave their slips to the judge.

"There is no winner. Both guest 5."

"Try again, please." Once again slips were submitted to the judge.

"We have a winner. Sargent Higgins."

Bill held out his hand to the winner of the right to draw. Higgins pulled out his choice and it was the short match.

"Sorry Higgins. Blair, you will be going with us tomorrow. I hope you all agree it was as fair as we could make it."

"It was the luck of the draw Bill, that's all." Said Higgins.

"Sam, I am asking you to be "step and fetch it." Please take this list of the men leaving with me tomorrow to the Major. Find out what time in the morning we can pick up the General and what time we should report to the ship?"

Bill was sure he had four good, smart guys who would be reliable every step of the way. Just before the farewell party ended, Bill announced that he and the stretcher bearers needed to pick up the General with in ten minutes of being summoned tomorrow. "It sounds like we will have time for breakfast in the morning. We will still have assembly at six in the morning so there is no delay when we are called.""

"Mr. Madson, I'm making you responsible for getting us out of bed on time."

"You can count on me sir. I won't let you down."

"I want to thank you all for your marvelous hospitality. I am impressed with you men who accepted so graciously not getting to go home. I'm sure all of you would have been excellent companions. Good night." With that, Bill headed for his bedroll.

On his way he stopped at the camp's latrines.

They smelled so bad he almost couldn't stand it long enough to finish his business. He thought, *'Those boys from the P. O. W. camps must be suffering with diarrhea going from practically no food to fairly rich food in such a short time. This is a sad camp, between those guys I had to dangle the thought of going home and then had to jerk it away and the condition of these former P. O. W. s puts a dark cloud over any feeling of joy I have for my opportunity to get home so quickly.*

Chapter 6
Boarding the Sultana

Next morning, April 21, everything went off like clockwork. Sargent Madson had the men up by 6 AM. The squad had breakfast and finished their preparations to go. About ten o'clock, the word arrived for them to pick up their ticket at the General's tent. Within two minutes they were assembled in front of the tent waiting for further instructions. The medics had fresh dressings on the General's wounds. They also sent along a bag of stuff the General might need later. The bag was stowed at the bottom of the stretcher. The four bearers took an end of a stretcher pole and Bill led the way toward the Sultana. Their instructions said to be at the dock by 11 o'clock.

As they reached the road to the river, they joined a line of former prisoners winding its way along the road's edge. They looked like skeletons in the morning light. Some of these guys were nothing but skin and bones. Many had open sores that were festering and smelled of rotting flesh. Everywhere along the line the healthier survivors were helping the worst cases along.

Bill could not believe how bad off some of the marching men (if you could call it marching) were in. This line of former prisoners was another demonstration of the lack of civility in war. From what Bill could see from his vantage point, these P. O. W. s had gone through hell! "Do any of you guys know where this bunch of prisoners came from?"

"Camp scuttlebutt has it that they are from the Andersonville camp." said Sargent Madson.

As the squad struggled along with its burden, they had the luck to meet a farmer on his way to market with a wagon load of produce to sell. The farmer stopped and offered to put the General and his stretcher on his wagon. He said, "I can't give all these guys a lift but at least I can do this little bit of good." The squad situated the stretcher securely on the wagon, thanked the farmer profusely and fell in behind the wagon as they continued on their way to the river. With this help they arrived at the gangplank well before 11 o'clock.

The stretcher was placed on the ground at the foot of the ship's loading plank and each man shook the farmers hand along with a hearty "THANKS!"

"Sergeant-Major, would you like this newspaper? It has an article written by some reporter from New York who claims to have actually visited the Andersonville Prison after all the prisoners walked away."

"Yes, I would."

"Good luck on the rest of your trip." said the farmer as he slapped the team with the reins and drove off.

Bill tucked the paper under his arm and went to report into the ship's Lieutenant who seemed to be overseeing the loading of the Sultana. The Lieutenant assured Bill that his group would be the first passengers let on board. Thus, the squad had nothing to do except wait.

Bill opened the farmer's gift newspaper and began scanning the story written by the New York reporter whose byline name was Dan Coffee. He immediately called his group together, "Listen to this guys, it's an article about the Andersonville prisoner of war camp where these soldiers were held."

Bill read, "I could hardly believe my eyes as I gazed on the 23 acres of space enclosed in the barb-wire fence that had been the Confederate prisoner of war camp named Sumter located at Andersonville, Georgia. A small stream with its muddy banks ran through the middle of the place reducing further the available living space. Trying to imagine 42,000 men crammed in that small space was more than my mind could comprehend. I couldn't help but wonder if you could plant 42,000 turnips in that small a space? In addition, from what I've been told, the amount of food made available to the prisoners was way below starvation levels. It was obvious by looking at the camp there was no effort to minimize the prisoner's exposure to weather while the guard towers that dotted the fence's perimeter all had roofs. The creek I was told was the only source of water, for drinking, bathing and latrine. The foul water, exposure and severe crowding made for a disease playground. These extreme conditions resulted in Andersonville winning the prisoner death toll race by a convincing margin. The camp was opened in February 1864 and operated for the last 12 months of the war. By August 1864 32,000 men had been imprisoned there. By the time it was abandoned in April 1865 a total of 45,000 men had spent time in that miserable place. Of those 45,000, 13,000 died. That is a death rate of about 29%. During the worst months over 100 men per day expired. I thought as I looked at the place, I now understand why some of the prisoners crossed the Deadline to invite a Reb to shoot them down rather than continue living in those conditions."

The article continued but Bill stopped reading. "My God, spare me from a hellhole like that."

There was a chorus of "Amends" from the group.

As the former prisoners reached the dock, they were organized in rows with about 20 men to a row. Major Williams was obviously the officer in charge of this boarding operation. He kept shouting at and harassing the soldiers working in the crowd as they tried to keep the scarecrows in line.

Bill recognized Private Brass, Corporal Kramer and the Sergeant who command the camp guards yesterday as they struggled to organize and manage the crowd. Briggs, Halter, Spence, Bloom and Higgens were amongst the scarecrows also.

Medics were circulating throughout the formation trying to administer to the many who were dropping out of line or simply crumpling in it. One of the main remedies used by the medics was water, buckets full of water became buckets full of air in the wink of an eye in that press of dehydrated scarecrows. Soldiers tasked with fetching the water scurried between the pumps and the crowd in a never-ending cycle. A few of the waiting succumbed to the traumas they had been put through and gave up on life. There was a squad to take care of them also.

Mr. Fish watched the final preparation for the boarding. He couldn't quite figure out why there were four people, two soldiers and two ships crew, standing at the top of the gangplank. "What do you suppose the four blokes up at the top of the gangplank are there for? I noticed each of them has a length of rope and look there, on the rail, a bunch of extra pieces. I think those four guys off to the side are a relief team. What do you suppose is going on?"

Bill answered, "I think they are the tally crew. I saw this once when some cowboys were loading cattle onto a train. They used only two on a team, one representing the seller and the other representing the buyer. As each steer went into the cattle car these guys made a knot in their rope. At the end of the loading the ropes were compared, and the number of steers bought and sold was agreed on. Today, I believe one pair up there will count the ordinary soldiers and the other pair will count the officers. I wonder why they haven't started loading yet. There are plenty of guys in line ready to board."

As if in answer to Bill's question, some soldiers showed up with a wash tub and a stand. There also was a cart loaded with stuff that rattled and banged.

The ship's Lieutenant waved down to Bill and his group to come aboard.

Bill and the four stretcher bearers picked up the General and moved up the gangplank onto the deck. Sure enough, as their group moved up the gangplank the first pair of counters put 5 knots into their ropes. The second pair put one knot into theirs.

The ship's Lieutenant said, "Welcome aboard."

Next in the line of their greeters was an army Lieutenant with a badge identifying him as an officer in the 58th Ohio Volunteer Infantry. "Help yourself to lunch." he said as he nodded toward the group of soldiers around the wash tub. They moved over that way and sat the stretcher down. Bill, Dick, and Dave went to the chow line where each was given two mess kits. The mess kit cups were detached and filled with soup. Buns were stuffed in the mouths of the cups and two utensil jack stacks, providing a knife, a fork, and a spoon were put in their pants pockets. They were warned that the mess kit must last them the whole trip. They were then dismissed to find a place on the deck to spend the voyage. They found a sort of sheltered spot on the fantail of the Sultana. They made the General as comfortable as possible. Blair fed the General and then ate with the squad. There was nothing to do now but wait for the end of the boarding.

The passengers on the dock filled up the gangplank to be represented by knots on the tally rope, collect their lunches and seek a place on the deck to spread their bedrolls. Since Bill and his men had been first on board and had thus selected a prime location for themselves, the area around them filled up fast. The available space dwindled as the number of bodies on board increased and the search changed from looking for the best place available on deck for their bedrolls, to hunting for any space in which they could lay down. There were some arguments about who claimed what first. There was some pushing and shoving when words weren't enough. There were even a few fist fights when two hotheads clashed.

Less space meant more problems. The Ohio Infantry boys were busy trying to keep a lid on things.

Two of the ship's crew ducked behind the super-structure to get out of the wind. Bill and his squad, as well as many of the former P.O.W.s were sprawled on the deck around where the sailors stood. They ignored their audience as they lit up; the audience didn't ignore them. The smoke and smell of the sailor's cigarettes got to some of the former prisoners. These were obviously guys who had been forced to suffer through tobacco withdrawal along with the other miseries of Andersonville. They hadn't had a butt in a long, long time. The more interesting part of this get together for Bill and his group was the conversation.

The older sailor said to his partner, "Did you know we popped a steam line on our way here?"

"Yes, the black crew told me a steam engine

mechanic came on board this morning and repaired it with a make-do patch. They are all afraid of what will happen to them if the patch fails. Now we are loading over 2000 men on the old tub. That's more weight on her then we carry in three trips down the river. I don't know what the Captains thinking."

"I do, money."

"Well I guess I can't fault him for that. The bonus he promised is what kept me on here for this voyage."

"Me too!"

Their small talk continued until the glowing butts became uncomfortable to hold. To the dismay of the smokers listening, the crewmen tossed their butts over the side and parted with, "Keep safe, I'll see you later."

On hearing about the Sultana's engine problem, Bill and his squad looked at each other with a sense of dread. Each man had a private conversation with themselves that included questions like, *'What should I do now?' 'Should I chicken out and have my companions think I am a coward?' 'What happens if I don't take this chance to go home?'* Each stewed with their own dilemma until each seemed to arrive at the same conclusion. This was that they wouldn't be the first to quit but they might say a prayer that somebody else would lead the way and they could then follow.

The emotion Bill's group felt played on the faces of the other passengers who had overheard the conversation and faced the same quandary. Bill had an especially hard time with this information. The safety of the General and the four stretcher bearers were his responsibility. But, so was the successful completion of his mission. Which should come first, safety or mission. At this point there was no obvious danger, so he decided to continue the mission.

Bill's group was surrounded by this time and communications had started between them and their fellow travelers. They found out that most of this boat load of former prisoners were from Eastern Tennessee, around the Knoxville area. These Tennessee boys were proud that Eastern part of the state had remained loyal when the Western part had succeeded. An easy comradery developed quickly between the two groups.

Blair became especially popular when he used some of the General's Iodine to close, de-putrefy (you could smell the beginning of rot in the ulcerated skin lesions) and cauterize the surface to give it time to start healing. He was able to treat several guys with what he considered to be extra supplies. A bandage was the final touch applied to keep the wound clean.

Blair, because he had spent several years in the Knoxville area became especially friendly with the

Tennesseans. He asked one," Was Andersonville as bad as they say?"

"Andersonville. It's hard for me to even say the name. We all suffered so much in that place. Little or no food. Water not fit for man nor beast. The only water we had was from a little creek that ran through the center of the camp. This creek was the water we had for drinking, washing and our toilet. You had to be on guard every minute of the day and night because of the total lawlessness among the prisoners. The only safety you had was the strength of the group you could latch on to. Some guys ended their misery by overtly crossing over the deadline. They would stand there begging a Reb guard to shoot them. There were many ways to die in Andersonville, we usually buried several a day."

Blair said, "I can see it is hard for you to think about those times. I'll tell my group to refrain from asking you fellows about your time as prisoners." The new friends shook hands and parted.

Blair was as good as his word; he told all his group that the prisoners around them confirmed the facts in the newspaper story and cautioned them about the pain the former prisoners felt when reminded of the hell they had endured during their captivity.

By late afternoon, Sultana was loaded to the max on all three decks. Bill noticed that the main deck had sagged some near the end of the loading. Now there were spaces opening between the deck planks. These developments brought shivers down his spine. It didn't help Bill's feeling of dread when he noticed a group of sailors disembarking from the ship and leaving the dock area. Bill thought, *'are those rats deserting a sinking ship?'* An hour later, however, the part of the crew that had disappeared returned with a load of poles. The work gang and the poles disappeared into the hole of the ship. Immediately, Bill heard pounding from down below and felt some of the sag going out of the deck. *'Those poles must've been for shoring up the deck timbers. The deck feels much better now.'* Bill also felt better about continuing the mission. With that, Bill checked the General who was asleep dreaming laudanum dreams.

Soon after the work crew climbed out of the hole back onto the deck, black smoke started pouring out of the smokestacks and the ship seemed to be coming alive. Everyone acted like they were ready and eager to get underway.

Bill jerked his fob and dragged his watch out. It showed the time to be 7:15, *'Good'* Bill thought. *'The sooner we start, the sooner we get there. But I bet we go hungry tonight; I haven't seen any preparations to feed us.'*

By 8 o'clock the ship's boilers had a full head of

steam. They were on their way home. The Sultana's crew slipped off the mooring lines setting her free. The Captain rang a bell and put the engines in reverse. Immediately the boat started to list toward the starboard. The passengers, almost to a man gasped. When it was away from the dock the engines were shifted into forward. The list shifted to the port side. The yelp of fear was louder and more strident. Every time the Captain tacked the list would shift and the passengers would react with fear on their faces and lips. The Sultana's wake looked more like it was made by a duck than a boat as it waddled from side to side.

It turned out to be a false start because the Captain pulled her into a sheltered spot and the crew shifted passengers and cargo around to give her better balanced. When the Captain was satisfied with her trim he shifted into forward and headed back into the mighty river's current. The fourth bell of the sixth watch had just rang as they got underway again.

Chapter 7

The Voyage

The improved balance of the boat had a positive effect on the list and thus the wake. While her engines still strained to cope with the current, she was obviously doing much better than she had been.

Since Bill had nothing to do with the operation of the riverboat or have any authority to direct the boats crew, his domain was limited to himself, the General, and his squad. Bill and his group were not involved in the shift and remained in their sheltered spot on the fantail. The imposed idleness was hard on a "doer" like Bill. He could see so many guys that obviously needed help, but he had no authority to intervene on their behalf.

The General never seemed to escape from his laudanum induce dreams. He came closest to reality when Blair changed his bandages and painted the stumps with Iodine again. He was unaffected by anything happening around them.

Duane, Dick, Dave, and Blair were like most soldiers. They could drop into restful sleep at any break in the action and bounce up at a moment's notice ready for anything that was required of them. Bill shared the soldier's doze ability that his men had, plus he had the command clock ability of going to sleep with a certain wakeup time in mind and without any other prompt, wake up then. This night Bill woke up at three AM as he had planned. He checked the General, his squad and the ship. The General and his men seemed to be doing well despite the drizzle and sharp, bitter wind that had arrived out of the northwest. The superstructure of the boat was providing them a wind break and the overhang of the upper deck provided a sort of roof over their beds.

Many of the former P.O.W.S were not doing so well. The rain was light to be sure but combined with wind it meant those exposed on the roof of the upper deck as well as those situated on the western (port) side of the boat had to cope with every element of that miserable night. The combined moaning protest of these cold, wet men, the cries of those reliving a horror again in a nightmares along with the smell of rotting flesh, vomit, and feces all contributed to an aura of misery that hung like cloud over the boat.

The exposed passengers all started huddling together in search for more warmth. They formed knots of squirming bodies trying to find a little comfort in closer contact with others. This shift of weight was having an adverse effect on the boat's balance. The sound of the engines gave ample evidence of the increased strain on them.

The long, miserable night finally gave way a gray overcast day. The drizzle and wind persisted. The only bright spot was the Army had not forgotten food. The members of the 58th Ohio Volunteer Infantry came around with hot coffee, followed shortly after by two pancakes drowned in molasses. They also served seconds on the coffee. This made them instant heroes. It was around 10 AM by the time everybody had finished their breakfast.

A sailor came by and was asked, "How fast is the boat going?" His reply, "About 5 miles per hour. We should be in Memphis about two and a half days from now." The look on the faces of the passengers on hearing this news revealed their dismay. You could tell they were thinking something like 'Mercy, (or some other lament) can I hang on that long?

This morning the crew was busy with the task of cleaning the deck from last night's mishaps. The improvement in smell was greatly appreciated by all. Lunch was a nice, big, red, apple. At least there was a constant supply of hot coffee brought around by the Ohio boys.

The ship's crew circulated among the passengers asking them to move around as little as possible. Since there was really no place to move without stepping on someone, it was easy to grant this request.

Seconds became minutes, minutes became hours but every time somebody looked at a watch it seemed to be stuck in the same place it had been the last time they looked. The former prisoners handled this boredom better than others did, they had months and years of practice at this game.

By mid-afternoon, the drizzle stopped, the wind died down and the sun came out; oh, happy day. There was yet an additional change that gave their spirits a lift; the Mississippi's current wasn't as mighty as it had been. The net result was the boat's speed reached an average of 8 miles an hour or maybe even 10.

By noon on the 25th of April the Sultana was just about even with Helena, Arkansas, about 100 miles from Memphis. An hour later a small disaster occurred. One of the black crew's shovels broke. This was a disaster because it took all four members of the black crew to feed coal into the four boilers fast enough to keep the steam pressure where it needed to be.

The Captain had only one sensible choice; turn

around and return to Helena for a shovel. '*Why the hell didn't I buy those new shovels when I had a chance in St. Louis? I could kick my ass for being so frugal. I should have replaced those old shovels months ago. Now we will lose a couple of hours of time and more than likely have to pay a premium price for them.*'

An hour later they were approaching Helena's dock. When the boat was tethered to the wharf, he sent Mr. Wintringer to get four new shovels. His last words were, "Hurry back."

The passengers wonder what was going on , but since it was such a nice afternoon they didn't complain: they just enjoyed it.

Wintringer was back in a half-hour with a single scoop shovel. "This is the only suitable one they had, and they wanted 30 dollar's US for it. I showed them a 20-dollar bill and told them it was all I had on me. After some haggling, they decided 20 dollars was better than nothing and let me have it for that price."

They were free from the dock and on their way fifteen minutes later. The Captain gave his engineer a well done pat on the back. But, despite the good job done by all hands, it was about 3 PM when they reach the point where they had been forced to turn back for the shovel. Twelve hours later they came in sight of the coaling docks in Memphis. There was a line of several riverboats waiting to get their coal bunkers filled. The Sultana docked at the end of the waiting line. A big sign on the dock opposite the first ship in line announced that coaling would start again at 8 AM. The Sultana fell quiet as passenger and crew took this opportunity to sleep.

Life returned to the Sultana about 6 AM, April 26th. The routine established for passengers during the last couple of days took over again. Breakfast was served with lots of hot coffee. Molasses on cornbread was this morning's treat.

The ship's crew once again cleaned up the ugly, smelly messes left where people had been over-whelmed by the boat's motion and lost their last meal or loss of control of their bowels and did not make it to the head.

All though the passengers had been confined to the boat the last few days, they were not allowed to leave it during the stop because of the perceived difficulty related to getting them back on board in a timely fashion. They were able to move around more easily than before because their motion did not interfere with the boat's activity now. The time still dragged but it seemed to be easier to tolerate than it had been.

In the middle of the afternoon, one of the ship's officers came back from downtown with good news. General Johnston earlier today had surrender his whole army to General Sherman. It was the second largest army the Confederates had in the war. Those who heard it first were the former prisoner gathered near the gangplank. They let out a roar, clapped each other on the back and danced the jig. The word spread from there. You could tell how far the news had traveled on the boat by following the celebrations erupting in groups of passengers as they heard the news.

The jubilant scenes were repeated again later in the afternoon when the news that John Wilkes Booth had been found and killed when he resisted arrest. Spirts were high on the Sultana as the crew and passengers waited to resume their voyage.

The coal bunkers on the waiting boats took about two hours each. Only the fact that the Sultana's cargo was former prisoners of war persuaded the dock master to work his crew until her bunkers were full. It was a little after 8 PM when she cleared the dock.

During the stop, the passengers had moved around, and the boat had lost any semblance of balance. The Sultana was waddling again. Once again, the Captain had to pull into a sheltered spot while the crew tried to work their balancing magic a second time. It was about midnight when the Captain lost his patience and pulled out into the river. The ships balance was a little better but far from good. The current had gotten a little stronger, so the engines were working harder under more steam pressure to achieve about half the speed they had before their coal stop.

They struggled along for a couple of hours when everyone's sleep was disturbed by the deck shaking like it was experiencing an earthquake. Accompanying the shaking deck was a rumbling like you might hear before a volcano eruption. The rumbling stopped with a giant explosion that decimated the foredeck, the forward cabins on the first and second decks and the pilot house.

In a second the Sultana became a floating hulk headed back to Memphis. Flames and burning debris shot 50 to 60 feet in the air. The unhurt passengers from about the middle of the boat to its stern were shaken out of their shocked state as sparks and glowing embers started to reach them. A gaping hole with flames shooting out of it had replaced the front deck. The men camped there had simply disappeared. Those located around the edge of the hole found their clothes on fire. They became roman candles running around in a frenzied effort to get away from their agony. Some ran screaming to their deaths into the holes in the deck to perish in the fires below, some took a chance on surviving by jumping over the rail into the river, some ran toward the rear deck in hope that their comrades would put their flames out. This chaotic scene was made even more horrific by the odor of burning flesh. Every so often, one of the roman candles fell on the deck with their clothes still burning and they would explode like the skin on a hot dog does when it is barbecued.

The whole scene was occurring in slow motion before Bill's eyes.

The wood that had been the front superstructure came down as kindling that fed the flames from the engine room turning the bow into a magnificent, holocaust that consumed everything it touched.

The flames were spreading fast and with them panic became another grave danger. Bill and his crew were unscathed in their position on the rear deck with a semi-roof over their heads. They were all stunned and flabbergasted. Bill was the first to respond to the chaos at the front of the boat.

He immediately took command," Dick, take Blair and see if there is anything usable for a raft inside the superstructure. Dave, you and Duane look in the water for debris that could be used for that purpose. Please be careful. I do not want to make a visit to your families to explain why I didn't get you home safely."

The four saluted, said "Yes sir" and went to carry out their orders.

The screams and chaos continued unabated on the bow while Bill waited. Bill felt he should do something, but reality kept reminding him there really was nothing he could do. He had his job to finish and doing that had to be enough. He had to "steel his heart" as he had to do so many times in combat when the guy next to him took a bullet and cried out for his wife or mother. He knew that to stop fighting for any reason was a sure way to lose it all.

Shutting out the pain of the burning and dying was one of the toughest tests of Bill's self-control he had ever faced. He tried to divert his thinking by tending to the General, but the General didn't cooperate, he was fine. It seemed like forever before he saw Dave and Duane coming around the port side of the superstructure. Dave said, "Dick and Blair are bringing a bunch of lumber to the stern. We think it will make a serviceable raft for a while. We found it floating along the side of the boat. I guarded the raft while Duane found Dick and Blair. We all decided that two of us would come back to help you with the General while the other two moved the raft to the boat's stern."

"Wonderful!", said Bill.

Dave said. "You lead the way and Duane and I will carry the stretcher." Bill had to kick boards with red hot burning ends and even some with flame out of their way to make a path for Dave, the stretcher and Duane toward the stern. The procession hadn't gone far when Bill saw Dick waving from the back of the boat. He headed for Dick shouting in his best sergeant's voice, "Clear a path damn you!" This was occasionally followed by a kick if the order wasn't executed fast enough. On reaching the rail, Bill helped balance the stretcher on it. Turning he jumped on to the raft and into the water. He found Blair already in there. The two of them steadied the raft while the others loaded the stretcher and its burden.

Duane lowered himself on to the raft then reaching up for the two stretcher poles and called for Dave to slide the stretcher out as far as he could. Duane had Dick take the stretcher poles he was holding. Freed from his burden, Duane moved back to the stretcher end still balanced on the ship's rail. He and Dave maneuvered this end free of the rail and into Duane's grasp. All this time Dick's outstretched arms were bearing at least half the weight of the stretcher and General. Dick was obviously struggling with the weight resting on his outstretched arms. It took strength and dexterity on Dick and Duane's part to bring the General down safely to the deck of the raft.

Dick said, "I am sure glad that is over. I don't know how much longer I could have hung on."

Dave swung down to the raft and slapped Dick on the back. He said, "I am amazed at the strength in that scrawny little body of yours."

Bill yelled, "Hey guy's now about some help getting out of the water. It's cold in here."

Immediately Bill and Blair were pulled out. They looked like drowned kittens, wet and shivering.

Bill said, "Secure the stretcher please. We're not safe yet. Dick, grab a board and rig a tiller. Everyone else gab a board and start paddling. We want to get away from the side of this boat as fast as we can. We need to let the Sultana pass us and move down river before we can rest. So, row up stream with all your might and we may even survive this night."

Rowing upstream proved to be hard work with their board paddles, but the Sultana was now a drifting hulk under control of the current. The hulk slid by the raft and there was a most marvelous sight. On their port beam was another riverboat with its lights all aglow beckoning them. Even better, there was a rowboat a short distance away. Bill said to his men, "Yell like banshees!"

They did. To their delight and relief, the rowboat turned toward them. The rowboats crew called out "Relax we've got you now." They slid their boat alongside the raft and said, "Stretcher first." Duane and Dave handed the stretcher over. Next each of the raft's crew were helped into the rowboat. The raft slipped away and followed the Sultana down the Mississippi. The rowboat was filled with survivors, so its crew headed for the lit-up riverboat.

Bill and his squad climbed to the deck of the rescue ship on their own. That boat's crew had no trouble handling the General and his stretcher. The General was whisked away to the infirmary that had been setup in two deck cabins.

The rest of the rescued were shown to the ship's salon. A sailor was there to tell them what to do next. "You guys in wet clothes, shuck them. Heap them on the deck along with the others there. Grab a blanket to cover yourselves. When your ready find a place around the stove to warm up. We don't want to go to all the work of pulling you out of the river only to lose you to pneumonia or some other disease. Those of you who don't look like drowned kittens gather around that stove (a red-hot potbelly stove). There is hot coffee and cookies there. Please let those who took a swim get near it."

Bill and Blair did as they were told. They dropped their wet clothes in a heap on the floor and wrapped a blanket around their naked bodies. As they moved toward the stove, they saw Dick waving them over. The friends were together, comfortable and the

General was safe. The nights tragedy could not have ended better for the squad.

The survivors kept being led into the salon. The sailor repeated his directions each time a new group entered. The heaps of wet clothes got bigger and bigger. The crowd around the stove kept growing until those on the outside were getting little heat. There was little talking as each person seemed to be immersed in their thoughts of the trauma, they had just experienced.

The salon became humid and smelled like the river as the survivors and clothes started drying out. The crowding caused some to relinquish their spots and seek one of the bedrolls the crew had distributed around the perimeter of the salon.

Bill was one of the guys who opted for sleep. He claimed a bedroll in the corner of the salon and sat down on it. Before he gave in for the day, he did all he could for his drowned guns and their holsters. He couldn't do much because his ammunition pouch with his gun tools were still on the Sultana. All he could do was wipe moisture off them with the ear of his blanket. He fell asleep with his back against the bulkhead, a colt in his lap and the blanket ear still in his hand.

Historical Footnote

The Sultana sinking is one of the biggest maritime disasters in American history. It even eclipses the Titanic in number of casualties. However, its story wound up on an inside page because of all the news from events that took place on the 26th . Almost no one remembers the Sultana tragedy.

Chapter 8
Memphis

The next morning Bill slowly came awake. He ached all over. At first, he didn't recognize his surroundings or remember last night's events. Then a voice coming from far away broke through the fog in his brain. A whisper in his ear said, "Bill are you OK?" It was accompanied by someone shaking his shoulder. With this, memory came crashing back. Opening his eyes his surroundings came into focus to reveal Duane and Dick peering down at him with worried looks on their faces.

"I'm ok guys. You two seem to have come through last night's fiasco in one piece. How about Blair and Dave, are they awake and functioning?"

Dick whispered as he continued his role as spokesman. "They both woke up, groaned, rolled over and went back to sleep. Do you want me to wake them up?"

"No, let them sleep. What time is it?"

"About 10:30 AM I think, the Captain kept looking for survivors until his coal bunkers got low. That's according to one of his crew. We are headed back to Memphis now."

A shiver ran up and down Bill's spine and he realized his blanket had fallen off during his sleep. He was laying there as naked as a newborn. He struggled to his feet and draped his cold, moist, smelly blanket over his shoulders. The whole Salon smelled dank and musty with all the wet clothes and blankets. He sniffled and stifled a cough. He thought, 'I *hope I'm not catching a cold from that swim I took last night.*' As he looked around the salon, he realized there were a lot of last night's survivors still sleeping as well as some in various stages of getting up. He spotted Dave and Blair amongst the sleeping.

He was trying to remember where he had been when he shucked his clothes. Finally, he got an inkling of the location where he might find them. Sure enough, his stuff was under a pile where he thought they might be. He also found Blair's pile and moved them over to the foot of Blair's bed. While there he recovered Blair and Dick with their blankets. He shook out his stuff and struggled into the cold, wet, clingy things as best he could. "Has anybody checked on the General yet?"

"We thought that might be something you would like to do."

"Has anybody mentioned food?"

"No, but there is some hot coffee and some cookies over there." Dick said pointing at the stove.

As Bill approached the stove, he noticed it was not radiating a lot of heat. '*They must have let the fire go out.*' he thought. He called over his shoulder, "I'm going to check on the General." He stopped long enough to pour himself a cup of coffee. "Man does this smell good." He snatched up a cookie and took a bite it along with a swig of coffee and uttered a sigh of appreciation. Another survivor approached the stove. "You ready for a cup?" Bill asked the stranger.

"Sure am." was the reply, "That smells so good I could drink the pot." Bill poured the man a cup before he proceeded on his mission.

While Bill was gone, Dave and Blair showed signs of life. Dave joined his comrades while Blair grumbled and struggled into his cold, wet, clingy things as best he could. Then he joined the group gathered around the stove to enjoy a cup of coffee and a cookie.

A short time later Bill reappeared. "Good to see you two up and moving." was his greeting to them. "The General is in good hands. He suffered no ill effects from last night's doings. He will be ready to travel when we are. In fact, he has already booked passage with this ship's Captain for passage to St. Louis. The Captain has agreed to honor our travel vouchers and pick us up in Memphis in about a week. It will take him that long to get to New Orleans and back."

"Thanks for retrieving my clothes for me." Blair said, and then cracking a big smile added, "But next time could you get them thoroughly dry and pressed?"

"Why, next time I'll throw them in the river and let you swim for them. Seriously, I am so glad you all came through last night pretty much intact. Fate was with us when the piece of flotsam hit Blair in the head."

The only injury the group had sustained was a cut on the top of Blair's head and it hadn't done enough damage to need attention. He remembered being struck there by something floating down the river while he was steadying the raft. He took some ribbing about being lucky it was his hardhead that got hit.

"MEMPHIS, All A SHORE THAT ARE GOING A SHORE!" echoed through the ship.

"Well at least we don't have to worry about any baggage, we are wearing everything we own." Blair said with a smirk on his face.

"Let's go." Bill added. With that, the five

friends left the Salon and joined the crowd jockeying to get down the gangplank. For the first time they saw the name of their rescuer; it was the Bostonia No. 2. Each of the survivors said a prayer of thanks to the crew and one for good fortune to the ship.

Bill notice a bunch of sailors carrying guys on stretchers down a gangplank further toward the stern. Now and then the stretcher's occupant was covered from head to toe with the blanket signaling the start of his trip to his final resting place. The living were put in one wagon while the dead were deposited in another. When a wagon was full, off they went to their separate destinations, life or death.

Finally, the group made it to shore. The solid ground felt great under their feet. They walked toward downtown Memphis. A soldier was walking their way and Bill hailed him. "Sorry to bother you but could you tell us where we can find army headquarters or where the troops occupying Memphis are billeted?" asked Bill.

The soldier replied, "No bother at all. Army headquarters is straight ahead to the square, then take a left diagonal across the square and you should be on its steps."

"Thanks a lot for the help."

"Were you guys on the ship that blew up last night?"

"Yes, we were. It was like being on the slippery slope looking into the depths of hell."

"I'm glad you survived. It sounds like it was horrible." said the soldier as he went on his way.

Dave said, "Memphis looks like an interesting city. Look at some of these buildings. They look old enough to have been here forever. Dick agreed with Dave's assessment of Memphis.

Following the soldier's directions, they were soon in front of a building with a large sign proclaiming it to be Headquarters, Army of Occupation, Memphis, Tennessee. When they stepped through the doorway, they found themselves in front of a desk manned by a corporal who said, without looking up, "State your business?"

Bill spoke for the group, "We are survivors of last night's Sultana tragedy. We need some help and some orders."

The corporal jumped to his feet. "The Colonel asked to see all survivors as soon as they reported in. Follow me please." He turned and started down the hall behind his desk.

The men made their way past the desk and followed him. He turned into the third door on the right, stopped and said something they couldn't hear to its occupant. He then beckoned them to enter. Falling in line, they entered to find themselves confronted by a full Colonel or so his eagles proclaimed.

The Corporal excused himself and turned to head back to his desk. The Colonel said without getting up, "Welcome, it's nice to see and talk to some survivors, most of the news today has been about the dead. Are you part of the prisoners that were being transported home?"

Bill acted as spokesmen again, "No sir, we are on special assignment to get Lieutenant General Armour to his home in Des Moines, Iowa. I believe he was taken from the Bostonia No. 2 to your infirmary here in town."

"I am sure our infirmary will take good care of him." replied the Colonel. "I wonder how many survivors they have received so far. Is there anything you boys need?"

"We need just about everything. The things we have on are all our gear that survived, sir. Also, Private Myers and I need our travel orders and transportation vouchers replaced. Our originals are illegible after our swim in the river last night. Maybe, most Importantly, we would appreciate if you would, tell us where we can get some chow. We haven't had a real meal since the night before we boarded the Sultana."

"We can take care of that in about fifteen minutes. One of you get the Corporal."

Dave stepped out in the hall and shouted, "Corporal, the Colonel wants you."

Seconds later the Corporal came to the door and said, "You wanted me, sir?"

"Tell the mess Sergeant to set five more places at the officer's table, we are having five guests at lunch."

"Yes sir." and left on his errand.

"Well gentlemen, there is a place to wash up outside the side door. Take the first hallway on your left. It leads to the door. The Corporal will come for you when lunch is served. Dismissed."

About ten minutes later the Corporal led them to lunch. When they walked into the officer's mess, one side of the table was already occupied by several officers. The Colonel sat at the right end of the table while a General sat at the other end. A couple of Lieutenants, a couple of Captains and a Major were seated on the right side while the left side was vacant. The mess Sargent waved the survivors to the empty seats. Each of the men introduced themselves before the food arrived.

On the table there was water, milk or coffee to drink. A platter of fresh bread and a crock of butter occupied the center and plates with steaming mashed potatoes, a slab of roast beef and a helping of peas were served each diner by three orderlies. A fourth orderly followed with a bowl of beef gravy. The survivors sated their appetites as they were peppered with questions about the Sultana event and their escape from the inferno.

At the end they all shook hands and the officers wished the survivors well.

After lunch, the Colonel replaced Bill's and Blair's orders and travel vouchers. He also gave them orders to hand to the commissary officer instructing that officer to supply them with anything they had lost during their ordeal.

They in turn requested and received directions to the infirmary. They also were told where they could sleep until their boat made it back. Thanking the Colonel for his hospitality and concern they departed.

On leaving headquarters they made their way to the infirmary to check on the General. They couldn't see him because he was sleeping. However, they were assured he was getting stronger and feeling better.

Their next stop was the commissary where they each received two suits of new clothes. They also received new knapsacks full of incidentals, bedrolls and weapons.

Their new rifles were the tried and true Spencer Carbine. Its size and use of self-contained cartridges, seven per load, gave it an advantage over most other rifles.

Resupplied, they found their beds, spread their bedrolls and went to sleep.

Morning arrived to find the five survivors starved again. However, before finding the chow hall, they prepared themselves for the day. Their breakfast was an old army favorite known as S. O. S. This is the abbreviation for the name the troops gave this often-served army chow. The S. O. S. stands for 'Shit on a Shingle' which is actually dried beef gravy on toast.

After breakfast they went back to the infirmary to check on the General. This time he was awake and anxious to talk. He did not seem to be in the laudanum fog that he had been in all the time they had known him. His room however smelled of disinfectants, he was in fresh pajamas and looked like he had been thoroughly scrubbed.

He greeted them warmly with, "Hi, how are you all doing?

"Fine; Great; Peachy; Tops and OK were the course of responses he received to his inquiry.

"I see you received new uniforms. That must mean you are back in touch with the army. Did you find a place to hang your hats last night?"

"Yes sir." Bill replied. "We have been treated very kindly. Everybody has treated us like celebrities. It is sort of like we escaped from "Hell" and their wondering how we did that. Comparing last night's experience to being in "Hell" seems just about right to me. The most nerve-racking part of this has been being around so much Brass and having them treat us like we were worth being saved."

This brought a hearty chuckle from the General. They all talked about the previous night's ordeal. The General had lots of questions because his view of events had been seen through a laudanum fog. A little more than an hour slipped past before an orderly ask them to leave. He told them it was time for General's meds, and he needed to sleep again.

They bid the patient "goodbye" and promised him they would try to come to see him again this evening.

Before they left the orderly told them the medical staff was trying to wean him off the laudanum, so he did not go home an addict. He also said that if they could come up with something that would make the General feel better about his life in the future, it would go a long way toward his recovery. The orderly continued, "I heard him sobbing during the night about what he will be able to do in the future without feet."

This knowledge really put a damper on the good feelings they had gained from seeing the General.

They gathered in front of the infirmary to decide what they were going to do with the rest of their day. Dave and Dick said they wanted to see the town so that's what they all did. They wandered around the city like starry eyed tourists. They did find one gem. It was a little tavern near the edge of town called "Rosie's". Rosie was nice, funny and served good food. They agreed that "Rosie's" was going to be their Memphis hang out.

That evening, after chow they made their way back to the infirmary. The General looked even better than he had in the morning. The gray pallor had left his face and a faint spark had returned to his eyes. The guys shared some of the sights they had seen during their tour of the city. Once again. the orderly broke up the confab and sent them away. They were ready go to their billet, into their beds and put an end this day.

Chapter 9
Sultana Farewell

The next morning, with breakfast over the friends walked over to the infirmary to see how the General was doing. He greeted them with a cheery smile and a question about how they were doing? Each of them mentioned how anxious they were to see their families and how nice it would be to get home. This talk about getting home and how great that was going to be brought a sob out of the General and tears ran down his cheeks.

The orderly responded to Bill's call and asked them to leave. He explained that the General was in a stage of mourning where he was focused on a future without his legs and could not find a ray of sunshine anywhere in that future.

They gathered outside and Bill said, "That was pretty cruel and heartless of us to crow about our prospects in the future in front of a man whose future is so much in doubt as the Generals. Let's not do that again."

"Well it's done, and we can't take it back." said Dick. "Dave and I have decided we are going to relax and try to enjoy the rest of the morning over at "Rosie's". Anyone else want to come along?"

Duane said he wanted to look for presents for his family. Bill said he was anxious to get his '44s' checked out because of their swim in the Mississippi. Blair was kind of vague about what he was going to do but he was also determined to check out his prospects for getting it done.

Next, Blair asked, "Are we going to get back together for lunch?"

The four others answered, "Of course!"

Dave said, "I have never eaten Chinese food and there is a Chinese restaurant on the square called the Blue Moon. Have any of the rest of you tried this kind of food?"

The choice was approved unanimously. They also decided that would be a good place to meet up again.

Bill said, "What time? I would sort of like to attend the Sultana memorial service scheduled for one o'clock on the square." This suggestion was also approved unanimously."

"How about getting together again at eleven-thirty? That should give us enough time for lunch and get us to the square on time." All heads nodded approval. They split up going their separate ways.

About eleven-thirty the squad showed up in front of the Blue Moon. As planned, they entered and took a front booth. The aroma was different from other restaurants any of them had eaten in. It left the friends with a soft mellow feeling despite the big, red, fire breathing dragon that looked down on them from the wall over their booth.

Soon a young Asian girl delivered menus to them. One was for drinks and the other was for food.

Everybody was surprised when they saw their favorite beer listed as one of the drink choices. They signaled the waitress back and placed their drink order.

They start talking about their adventures while they were away.

Dick and Dave loved "Rosie's". They found Rosie to be a gruff old mother bear with a heart of gold. The two of them reaffirmed their recommendation that the group make the place its hang out while they were here.

Their beers came and they all had a swig before

Duane showed them the Mississippi River agate pendant he found for his wife. He had struck out on the kids but was pleased with the pendant. " I'll look for something for the kids again another day."

The odor from the kitchen did its thing and Bill said, "I'm hungry. Let's order. We can continue telling our tales while the food is being prepared." All agreed to this proposal. They studied the food menu. None of them knew the first thing about Chinese food and so they could not decide what to order. Bill took command of ordering as a Sergeant-Major should.

He beckoned the waitress back and, in his best, "pidgin English" said, "Missy, (pointing at her) pleasey order what you thinky we would enjoy for a first tasty of Chinese food."

She replied in perfect English, "Yes sir". She was trying to hide her laugh as she turned and headed for the kitchen door. The guy's laughed at Bill's embarrassment. The moment past as they took another drink of their beers.

While they waited, they listened to Bill's praise of the gunsmith's work on his pistols. He showed them the shine the smith had put on them.

Of course, they all consumed another drink of beer before they turned to Blair to find out what he had done.

Blair had a kind of mysterious air about him. He didn't act like he wanted to share his adventure with anyone. All they could see was the bag he had returned with. It was chuck full including a chunk of wood sticking out the top.

He was saved from further explanation by the delivery of the porcelain tea pots with delicate flowers painted on them along with the pleasing aroma of the herbal tea to distracted them. The tea pots were accompanied by dainty, matching cups. The waitress said, "This is orange blossom tea"

Next came steaming bowls of soup. The bowls it was served in were a match to the tea pots and cups. The soup was accompanied by an awkward looking porcelain ladle. The soup seemed to be a clear chicken broth that had been brought to a boil so that egg white could be dropped in it to cook. No one had a problem eating the soup. The porcelain ladle worked just like a spoon. The waitress said, "This is called egg-drop soup.

The next dish to arrive was a large platter heaped with what looked like sautéed rice. It was followed by an equally large platter covered with a pile of meat chunks mixed with red and green pieces things that none of them could identify. The meat and stuff were covered with an orange jelly like sauce. No one could figure out exactly what was in these two dishes (except the rice and pork of course) but none of them cared because it was so delicious. The biggest problem they had with this course was trying to eat it with chopsticks. The waitress identified the first platters contents as fried rice and the second as sweet and sour pork.

Of course, dessert was a fortune cookie. They enjoyed sharing their prophesied future and shared a good laugh over them.

They paid their bill including a generous tip for all her help. Each of them complimented her on the choices she had made for their lunch.

She said, "Thanky you varily much." This made Bill blush and the others laugh.

As they left the Blue Moon, they saw a podium set up in front of army headquarters. The crowd was small but growing rapidly. The friends moved over to join it.

At one o'clock, a General in full dress uniform appeared in the headquarters door. He looked the square over before moving down the steps and mounting the podium. "Ladies and Gentlemen; my fellow countrymen now that hostilities have ceased." Several of the men in the crowd scowled to show their opinion of the outcome of the war. The general gave no sign that he had noticed the scowls, he continued his speech without pause.

"Night before last we suffered a great tragedy. Over a thousand men, primarily Tennesseans, perished while on their way home to their loved ones.

We are gathered today to commend these souls to the mercy of God. We have invited the Baptist Bishop of Eastern Tennessee to give the eulogy in hopes his words will smooth the passage of the deceased into their heavenly home." Turning and motioning to the crowd of dignitaries behind him he said, "Bishop Reed, please come and commend the souls of the lost to their maker."

A tall man in a clerical robe emerged and mounted the podium. He and the General shook hands. The General descended to join the crowd.

Bishop Reed raised his arms and said, **"Please bow your heads in prayer for those who perished in last night's tragedy. Ask God to grant them a place of peace in his realm.** A hush came over the crowd. Eventually the Bishop broke the silence with his,

"Amen"

. The extent of this tragedy is best told by the official statistics. It is believed that there were 2,155 people on board, including passengers and crew. The count of survivors was 931. That leaves 1,224 people missing and presumed dead. The passengers included 1,978 former prisoners of war.

Imagine, if you can, enduring the emotional impact that months, perhaps years in the hell hole of a prisoner of war camp could have on you. Now, imagine the elation that being freed from said camp

and told you were going home. Lastly, imagine the emotional trauma of suddenly being faced with a situation that threatens your dreams and your life. Anyone who survived those mood swings with their sanity still in tack must have a strong faith in God.

MAY THE DEAD REST IN PEACE!
MAY THE LIVING USE THEIR GIFT OF
LIFE IN GOOD WORKS FOR MANKIND!
Amen!

The Bishop descended the podium and was joined by his entourage. They made their way off the square and disappeared.

There were many wet eyes in that crowd as they thought of the horror of facing the explosion and fire. Bill developed something in his eyes that made him rub them. He thought *'My God, I was there, and I could think of nothing I could do to save any of those poor souls on the fore deck. This will haunt me the rest of my life.'* He turned to his friends, and saw they were struggling with their emotion also. Blair had tears running down his cheeks. The others had their heads down studying the toes on their boots.

The crowd slowly dispersed. The friends returned to their billet without much being said by any of them. Bill wanted time to deal with his emotions and he was sure the others were lost in their thoughts also. When they arrived back at their quarters, Dick, Dave and Duane lay down for a nap, while Blair disappeared with his bag and wood and stuff. Bill went outside to oil his holsters but much of the time he spent staring into space as the images of men blown into the sky, men with their clothes on fire running into the flaming holes in the deck and men jumping into the river replayed in his brain.

The bugle call for chow aroused the nappers and brought Bill back to the present. They joined looking around for Blair. They couldn't find him anywhere. Eventually they gave up and went for their meal.

When they returned there still was no sign of Blair. The mystery of Blair's whereabouts continued as the evening wore on. Bill said, "I wonder where he is?" The others shook their heads. Just about the time the four friends were ready to launch an all-out search they heard the lost, whistling as he opened the door and entered.

"Where have you been?" said a chorus of voices.

Chapter 10
Miracles Do Happen

In answer, Blair proudly pulled a wooden foot out of his bag. "I figured the general might appreciate getting a foot back, any foot."

The friends looked the carving over. "What a great idea!" said Dave. "How thoughtful." said Dick. "How do you plan on attaching it to the General's stump?" asked Duane.

Blair said, "I hope you guys would have some ideas about how to fasten it on. First however, I've got to size the ankle to the stump. I was hoping to size it when we visited him this evening. Do you think we can still get there in time to see him? It took me a little longer to carve it than I thought it would."

"That is really a thoughtful thing you're doing Blair. The General should be delighted." said Bill.

Bill sweet talked the mess hall orderly into scraping together a plate of food for Blair.

As promised, they all walked to the infirmary to "tuck the General in" so to speak. It was a beautiful evening and they were all walking in high enthusiasm with Blair's thoughtful gift for the General. When they arrived, they found him in good spirits, sitting in a chair reading. His lower body was covered with a lap robe which hid his mangled legs.

After the "How are you?" and other small talk, Blair brought up the wooden foot. The General's amazement and gratitude were obvious. He cooperated with Blair as Blair made the marks, he needed to finish carving the foot. They had just completed their matching when the orderly showed up to put the General back in bed. The General said, "I have never introduced myself to you guys. I am Melvin Armour and I insist you call me Mel from now on. That's what all my friends do. Please come to visit any time your free".

They all said, "We will." and then added, "Good night Mel."

Their days in Memphis became a routine. Breakfast was with the army, stop to see how the Gen....err Mel was doing, then to "Rosie's". Blair matched the ankle of the carved foot and Mel's leg stump perfectly.

They came up with and discarded many ideas about how to attach the wooden ankle to the living leg. This consumed their thinking and time. Rosie and even some of the other regular customers took part in the planning sessions. At the end of the first day they hadn't built anything, but they had identified many things the coupling had to do in order to work.

The plan they devised called for a garter to be installed on the leg stump, a receptacle to be constructed on the top of the wooden foot's ankle, a pillow to fit into the ankle receptacle to protect the end of the living leg, the wooden foot installed in a stocking, the ankle socket fitted over the leg stump, the garter clips attached to the stocking holding the ankle and stump securely together. They prayed it would work.

The first step in the plan had Blair screwing four thin, stout boards on the wooden ankle at the points of the compass. Each board stuck up about six inches above the top of the ankle. The strips of wood were also there to stop the two parts from wiggling from front to back and from side to side. This arrangement they called "The Socket".

The second step in the plan had Dave constructing a cloth pillowcase that fit in the socket perfectly. When he took the cloth pouch apart, its pieces gave him the patterns needed for making the pouch out of deer skin. The images of the cloth pieces were transferred to the leather and cutout. Three sides were sewn together with sinew in small, tight stitches to make it strong, leak proof and comfortable. The remaining side was left open so the cushioning material in the pouch could be replaced as needed. Each side of the opening had been cutout with a flap of extra leather on each side. When the pouch was filled with the cushioning material these lips would be folded together and tied with a buckskin lace to make it leak proof. Lastly, Dave filled the pouch with tobacco, the cushioning material they selected, tamping in several layers of it to make it as full, hard and yet cushiony as he could. They christened this "The Cushion".

An additional safeguard was added in the form of an elastic sleeve that started at the ankle and end at the knee. This was an attempt to help the garter and sock hold the stump of the leg snuggly against the wooden ankle.

Bill hunted the town for a stocking that fit the wooden foot and garters to hold them up. The men's store had them both.

Duane scrounge up some wood and made a sturdy crutch. Dick personalized it by carving Gen. Melvin Armour on its shaft.

Bill said, "Let's pray this works."

The moment of truth came that evening. The word had gotten around that General was going to try to walk tonight. The hallways outside his room were packed with staff and walking wounded. The friends installed the foot as per plan. Then they surrounded him so he would not have to worry about falling. It was a struggle for him to get up from the chair, but he refused help when it was offered. "He's standing on his own." announced someone in the door to the crowd behind them. This started a wave of cheering. The accolades came pouring through the door in an avalanche of babble and excitement.

The person in the door next announced, "He took two steps." This started a second round of cheering.

The orderly stepped in and closed the door. "That's enough for today. He hasn't walked for a year. It will take a while to build up his strength. Great job you guys"

"Great job Mel." they all chimed in. "Maybe tomorrow we can get outside for a while. Good night and sweet dreams."

The friends felt they had been walking on air on their way over to the infirmary, on the way back they were bouncing among the stars.

On the way to their bunks someone asked, "How long have we been in Memphis now?"

Someone answered, "I think it's been about six days, maybe a little longer."

When they reached their billet, sleep overcame them immediately.

Next morning, breakfast over, they started their usual walk to the infirmary. Dave was looking at the harbor when he exclaimed, "Isn't that the Bostonia No. 2 down there?"

The rest looked and excitedly confirmed Dave's find. The shared opinion was that the boat must have docked last night or this morning.

"Dave, You, Dick and Duane head back to the billet and pack our personals in our knapsacks. Take the knapsacks, bedrolls and rifles to the infirmary. Be sure to sign us out in the office. Blair, you go to the infirmary and find when they can have the Gen......I mean Mel ready to travel. Also find out if there is a livery, we can hire to get Mel and all our things to the dock. In the meantime, I'll go to the boat and find when we can board. We'll meet at the infirmary to iron the details out. Any questions?"

They all scattered to carry out their orders. About an hour later they reassembled in Mel's room. Dave, Dick and Duane had everybody's things. Blair and the orderly had Mel dressed including his foot. They had packed Mel's stuff including any meds he might need while they were on their way. Bill had the disappointing news that they couldn't board the boat until after 3 o'clock in the afternoon. It was decided that they would pass the time in "Rosie's Bar" where they had past so much time this last week.

Blair said to the orderly, "I really appreciate all the help you have given me so I can take care of Mel on the way home. The whole hospital staff, but especially you personally have done a fine job taking care of the General. I can hardly believe the change I see in him in only one week."

The orderly replied, "I'll take some credit for the change you see and I will give some credit to the hospital staff but I know that the difference maker was the friendship you guys gave him which was expressed so elegantly in that wooden foot and the apparatus you came up with to hold it in place. You are the kinds of friends one rarely has a chance to make. Mel is so lucky to have you and I feel lucky to be able to shake your hands." With that the orderly extended his hand to each of them and said, "God's blessing on you."

The coachman's arrival ended the goodbyes. Blair had located and hired a coach to take them to the dock, instead the livery man was directed to go to 'Rosie's'

Mel struggled out of the coach on his wooden foot and crutch without anyone's help and made his way to the booth on his own. The joy of this feat was obvious in his eyes. His joy spilled over to his companions paying them handsomely for their efforts.

Blair said, "Rosie this is the General we have been

telling you about. Mel, meet Rosie, The sweetest gal in all Memphis."

Rosie put her elbows on the bar, leaned over toward Blair and said, "Me sweet lad, you are so full of the blarney I'd think you were a chip off that old Irish stone itself. You're welcome at Rosie's Mel even if you are in the company of some of the most disreputable wretches to have ever darkened my door."

The group laughed and all sat down to have a beer. Soon the conversation turned to likes and dislikes. Blair and Mel found out they both enjoyed cribbage. On hearing this, Rosie dragged a dog-eared deck of cards and a cribbage board that looked like it had never been used out from under the bar. The cribbage players were soon wrapped up in what they called a tournament. The rest of the guys entertained themselves in their usual game of darts

Lunch came and went. The cribbage tournament was tied at 3 to 3 so a rubber match was a must. All the friends and a few strangers gathered around the players, kibitzing about the playing and anything else that caught their fancy. It was approaching 2 o'clock with no winner yet. Mel had built a nine-point lead and only needed six more to win. He also had the crib to his advantage. Blair needed twelve to win. His only hope was he pegged first. Blair pegged three during the card play and had a double run for eight points in his hand. He wound up one short, in the stink hole so to speak. The winner was gracious.

Laughing, Blair said, "Next time." and took the board and cards back to the bar.

Rosie took the dog-eared cards but said, "That board hasn't been used since I brought it. You take it along for a remembrance of "Rosie's".

"Believe it, I'll never forget the hospitality you have given us this past week. God bless you and thank you for the board. It will get lots of use from now on."

The coach arrived promptly at 2:30. As the guys were collecting up their stuff Rosie shuffled out from behind the bar in the brightest red slippers ever made. (No one had ever seen Rosie out from behind the bar before).

Bill realized this was an important occasion for Rosie, so he went over to her and said, "Are you still going to be my Memphis gal even when I am far away in Minnesota?"

"You bet. You come back anytime, and I'll be here waiting for you. That goes for all of you. It is a good thing there is a lot of me so there is plenty to go around." This foray into humor got a little chuckle out of everyone. With tears in her eyes, Rosie held out her arms to each of them in turn (even Mel) and gave them a bear hug. They in turn gave her a peck on the cheek and said, "Love ya Rosie."

Mel led the parade out the door, "Goodbye and thanks Rosie." Each of the guys said as they left, "Thanks for everything!"

The excitement was growing in each of them as they climbed into the coach. They were on their way home again. Nothing could feel better right now then their thoughts of home.

At the dock, Mel paid the liveryman his due plus a handsome tip and ask him to wait until they could transfer their stuff to the ship.

Chapter 11

If at First ...

It was show time again for Mel. With the Bostonia's Captain in attendance, Mel maneuvered himself out of the carriage, walked up the gangplank followed by his escorts, and shook the Captain's hand. "Good day to you sir. How was your trip to New Orleans?"

"It could not have gone smoother, good weather makes all the difference. I see you have had some major improvements in your situation since I saw you last. In fact, I am having trouble getting my mind around the changes that have occurred for you."

"I really can't believe it myself. My escorts got together and made me a wooden foot plus figured out how to attach it to my leg. The whole set up is functioning far better than anything I could have imagined. Those guys are special. Be sure they are treated special and put it on my bill."

The Captain agreed and called crewman to show

them their cabins while others fetched their things from the coach.

Blair volunteered to act as Mel's orderly and moved in with him. These two were acting more like brothers then General and a Private. Madson and Barrett decided to share space and that left Bill and Duane together. They parted as they were led to their accommodations with the understanding, they would meet on the sun deck shortly.

When Blair and Mel reach their cabin, Blair was surprised and pleased by the harmonious blue décor of the room. He was also impressed as their personal Stewart showed them the conveniences of their accommodations. There were two double beds that could be separated by a curtain for privacy. Associated with each bed, there was a dresser, a closet and a sink with running hot and cold water. Behind a set of folding doors was a bath also with hot and cold water. A flush toilet completed the room behind the doors. The cabin also equipped with four plush chairs around a small round table. The finishing touch was a glass wall to provide a view of the river as it past. There was a door in that wall that allowed access to the cabins own veranda. The roof of the cabin was part of the boats sun deck. Blair thought, '*so this is how the rich live. I could get used to this.*'

When the steward left, Blair removed the

wooden foot from Mel's leg. Next, he removed the bandage and scrutinized the cauterized ankle stump. The stump was, of course, dark red shading toward black in some places from the Iodine. The scab seemed to be intact with no cracks or breaks and demonstrated some flexibility when Blair applied pressure to it. Blair bent down and sniffed the stump. The only odor he detected was that of the cream the orderly had put on as he bandaged it for the day. Blair's examination made him feel confident no damage had been done by the day's activities.

Mel did not demonstrate any feelings of pain during Blair's examination of the ankle stump, so Blair repeated the examination procedure on the just below the knee leg stump. This second examination had the same positive result as the ankle stump had shown.

Before Blair left the infirmary this morning, the orderly had shown him how to care for the stumps and bandage them. So, he applied the same cream the orderly had used to coat the stump scabs and wrapped them as the orderly had.

Mel said "Thanks Blair. I don't know what I would do without you."

"Your welcome Mel."

With Mel re-bandaged and their stuff stowed to

make it as handy as possible, they were ready to join their friends on the upper deck.

Mel insisted on walking up the stairs unassisted. When he reached the foot of the stairs, he grasped the stair rail with his left hand and handed the crutch to Blair. With his hands grasping the railings he struggled up the steep, narrow stairs but with the handrails replacing his crutch, he ultimately made it.

They got up there before the others arrived so Mel took a chair at a table where the Sun would warm his back and sighed with contentment at the newfound hope he had for the future. The steward appeared and Mel ordered a round of beers, a deck of cards and a cigaretto. Blair went to retrieve the cribbage board from their cabin. He arrived back just as the others arrived.

Mel said, "I presumed you might be ready to relax and enjoy a beer, so I ordered one for each of us."

The late comers said, "Mel, the cabins we're in are unbelievable. They must have cost a mint. Thanks, Mel."

"Nothings too good for you guys. Besides, the government's picking up part of this tab. Just kick-back and enjoy it."

The upper deck was flooded with afternoon sun and all got comfortable as they relaxed and enjoyed their brew. They talked about the past and their hopes for the future after they got home. Mel took part this time and seemed to have as high expectations as anybody. The conversation went on until Blair reminded Mel, they should start their game if they expected to finish before dinner.

The other four decided to take a tour of the boat. They visited the pilot house and spoke to the wheelman. They were impressed with the broad vista view of the river you had from there. When they reached the boiler room the black crew was leaning on their shovels taking a smoke break. Their faces were streaked with the telltale signs of their work, coal dust. The four boiler fires were banked leaving just enough fire burning to keep it alive but not enough to do much work. These guys were the hardest working part of the boat's crew then the boat was underway. They talk to the crew and found out there were sixteen stokers on the crew. They fed the hungry fires coal, working in teams of four in two hours shifts. This rotation of manpower kept the shovelers as strong as possible and provide ample backup if needed. They thanked the black crew for the information and moved on.

The men's quarters were in turmoil as you would expect a men's dorm to be. They did not intrude on the women's quarters for obvious reasons. The salon and other areas where passengers congregate were pristine clean in stark contrast to the crew work areas. The friends agreed it was a well-organized, smoothly functioning boat. Their confidence about reaching St. Louis this time soared. When the four tourers got back to the card players the big news was that Blair had his revenge.

Tomorrows games would give one of them bragging rights, at least for a time. At that moment two seagulls got into a squabble overhead about some tidbit. Their noise turned out to be a good thing because it alerted the friends to the bird's presence. Everybody looked up as both birds defecated. There was a scramble to escape the "shit bombs" which landed squarely on the cribbage board with a splat. Everybody but Mel laughed with relief at having escaped the bombing. Mel said with a big grin, "Sure, you leave the poor cripple to face the attack alone. Some hero's you guys turned out to be." With that, he threw back his head and gave out a gale of laughter. All the group joined him in his merriment. Blair left to clean up the cribbage board.

Mel summoned the porter and ordered another round of drinks.

The boat was scheduled to leave at 5 o'clock. Just before that time, Bill saw a courier coming up the gangplank with a yellow envelope in his hand. The courier headed for the pilot house.

Soon after the courier left the boat, the Captain hurried to show the message to Mel. The two men had their heads together in a whispered conversation.

Captain excused himself, "It's 5 o'clock and I have to get this boat under way." Then he returned in the direction of the wheelhouse.

Mel beckoned Bill to join him. When Bill arrived, Mel said, "The Captain just received notice of the possibility of trouble on our way to St. Louis. This morning a river steamer was attacked and taken by river pirates about fifty miles south of there. The passengers were robbed and assaulted. Two men who resisted were killed, the rest of the passengers and crew were put ashore and the pirates took the boat and skedaddled. The stranded passengers were picked up by the next boat to pass. Later that day the rescued and rescuers saw the commandeered boat crashed into the shore, it was still burning when they passed. These pirates were reported to be ex-soldiers from both armies gone rogue. The Captain has asked us to help defend the ship should that become necessary. I volunteered you to devise a defense knowing your experience."

"I will do my best sir. Did the Captain say how many men he thought were in the pirate band?"

"He was told the marooned passengers thought there were about a hundred of them."

"I'll need to know how many of his crew I can count on and how they will be armed. I also suggest he ask the passengers if any of them are willing to help. Tell the Captain not to be alarmed when he hears gunfire soon. My men and I were just given new weapons and we have never fired them or zeroed them. We are going to do that right now."

"At this time, he is rounding up those men he thinks will be helpful. I should have the information you requested when you get back. Would you send Blair or someone to tell the Captain I need to speak to him."

"Of course. Please excuse me sir, I have things I need to do." With that Bill turned and went over to speak with his squad. The squad split up and went to do what Bill ordered. Soon the sound of gun fire reached the General's ears. It lasted about twenty minutes and then suddenly it was quiet.

Soon after, the ship's Captain appeared with a crowd of men. The General wasn't sure how many, but each seemed armed.

Bill and his group rounded the superstructure and mingled with the assembled sailors. "Hi guys, we seem to be about to lose a night of sleep. My name is Bill Cheever and I have been given the job of organizing the boat's defense. Bill counted the available seamen and said there are twenty of us to defend the boat now. I was hoping for a defense force of at least 26. Is there any chance we can enlist six or more passengers to help?

One of the crewmen stepped forward, "I am the master mate of this boat. I will see about passenger volunteers. In the meantime, I suggest everyone eat their dinner while they can.

Bill said, "Good idea, be back here in one hour and bring the weapon you expect to use with you."

The five soldiers sat together in the ship's dining room and as they ate, they talked about how best to defend the ship if she were attack. They agreed they would need a compass defensive strategy given their lack of information about where, when and how the attack would come at them.

It was about an hour and twenty minutes before the defense force was all back. The master mate brought eight volunteer passengers with him. "I hope these guys will be enough help. If not, I can look for some more, Bill."

"Thank you master mate."

"Please call me Tom."

"We'll make do with these Tom." Bill turned and addressed the whole group. " Welcome to our defense group. You volunteers and crewmen need to stop and consider the possible danger you may face tonight. If we are attacked, we expect we will be facing a force of over a hundred veterans from both armies of the war that just ended. During this gang's attack yesterday on a boat like ours, two passengers who resisted were killed. Now, under the law, every man in the gang is considered a murderer. What does this mean to you? It means these guys are ready to kill without hesitation. I am not going to soft soap this. If you have any doubts about your readiness to kill or be killed dropout now. There is nothing worse for the men fighting around you, men counting on you for your support to suddenly lose that support during battle. That is when panic sets in and the battle is lost."

Bill looked around at the faces of the group and spotted only looks of determination. Bill thought '*Good, we're committed now.* "Ok, let's see the weapons you brought to the fight. First you crew men. Where did you get the weapons from?"

The master mate spoke up, "From the boat's 'War Chest'. They are Sharps and Hanks single shot rifles. They fire 50 caliber cartridges and because of their rolling block, lever action, breach ejection they reload quickly and can maintain a rapid rate of fire. I maintain them and I assure you they are in top shape."

"Excellent." Bill said. "Now you volunteers." Most of the passengers had 44 or 45 caliber revolvers. One had a double barrel, 10-gauge shotgun with double

00 buckshot. The shotgun pleased Bill a lot. '*Overall*', Bill thought, '*We are in surprisingly good shape*'.

He said "Ok, we should be fine with these. Our defensive organization will consist of three supporting lines. Our first line of defense will be on the main deck. One of my men with their repeating rifles will be stationed at each point of the compass. They will each be supported by one crew member. The second line will be on the upper deck where teams of two crew members will also be positioned at the compass points. I will be supporting the second line of defense with my rifle. The third and last line will be the riot squad. Master mate, I would appreciate it if you would take command of the riot squad. You and your men will be stationed in the Salon. It has the best access to all parts of the lower deck, north, south, east or west. The shotgun owner and all those with pistols and the two crew members, not part of defense lines one and two, will form the riot squad. If we are boarded, the riot squad should rush to the breach and close it up."

"No scheme for defense is going to work if the people manning it aren't super alert. Therefore, I am asking the pairs to switch off resting. The riot squad, I believe, should have at least four members always awake, one to monitor each point of the compass in case of attack and breach."

"You people on the lower and upper deck will be better off laying down or setting with your backs against the bulkhead, avoid giving your enemies a target. Don't give your position away by moving around anymore than necessary.

Last, remember we don't know exactly when they will attack, but the usual time is just before dawn. Now, decide who you are going to partner with, and which station your team is going to occupy. Next, survey the station you are going to defend. Identify any advantages it might have. After preparing your place, meet me on the stern in half an hour.

When the defense force was ready, they assembled on the stern as Bill had requested. Bill asked, "Are there any problems that should be taken care of now?"

"Dam," Duane said, "I was looking forward to a restful evening in our cabin. That's what I consider the lap of luxury." This brought a smile to the lips and chuckle from the group looking forward to an uncomfortable night.

No one had anything to say so Bill said, "Let's get to our stations in haphazard ways by acting like we're on deck for an evening stretch or smoke. Hang in the vicinity of your station and within sight of your partner. Try not to occupy your position until full dark so are enemies aren't sure if we are on guard and most importantly know where you are located. I will be somewhere in the middle of the upper deck if you need me. Are there any questions? Ok, let's take care of the danger facing us and the others depending on us. That's it, you're dismissed." Bill turned and went to his post.

The night was dark and creepy. Every sound and motion took on a sinister meaning to the watchers. The only reassuring sound was the swish ...swish ...swish of the paddle wheels as they made their rounds to push the boat along.

About 4 AM, Bill appeared at the foot of a stair-way that connected the upper deck to the main deck. He paused and stretched and said in a low whisper," How is it going?"

Blair's answer came out of the shadows, "Fine. We're both a wake." Bill wandered over to the port side and pissed over the rail. He then sauntered over to the bow flexing his arm to get the kinks out of them. "How's it going here?"

Dick's voice replied, "We're alert."

Meandering over to the starboard side he said in passing, "You guys okay?"

Duane's terse, reassuring reply, "Okay."

Bill made his way to the stern to make sure that guard post was on the job; Dave assured him it was.

Bill made one swifter round of the lower deck

before he climbed back to his post on the upper deck. An hour past with no pirates. Another hour slipped by, still no attack. Dawn came and day light flooded the deck, still no attackers.

At 7 AM, Bill went to the pilot house to speak to the Captain. The Captain was at the tiller when Bill walked in. "I think we are safe now Captain. With your permission I will dismiss most of the defense force. I will keep two man for deck patrol in case something comes up."

"You can release them all. I will send two fresh men to patrol the deck. Please convey my thanks to the men who gave up a night's sleep to protect the boat. You deserve more than thanks for the job you did Mr. Cheever."

"I thank you for that compliment, Sir. I will deliver your message to them." Bill moved off to take care of the matters on which they had just agreed.

He sent Blair to ask all the watchers to join him on the stern deck. Bill told them, "The Captain and I thank you for your sacrifice last night. We believe the danger is over and I am here to tell you how pleased and proud I am of you for standing up to the challenge last night presented. Your contribution to this boat's safety is not diminished by the fact the danger committed a 'no show'. This is the kind of victory I learned in the war is the best;

the bloodless one. You deserve the thanks of every one of your ship mates and the passengers on this boat."

As the possible peril the ship had faced last night became known to the passengers and crew, the crowd around their guardians swelled to a deck full. When Bill finished his thank you speech, the crowd broke into wild cheers and circulated throughout the defense force slapping backs and thanking them for their sacrifice. As they drifted away, every one of the defense force had a Cheshire cat grin on their face and a spring in their step.

Bill and his squad had breakfast and then slipped off for a deserved and needed sleep. No trouble showed up during the day and the squad was on deck when the Bostonia No. 2 moored at St. Louis about 4:30 PM after a safe, uneventful trip.

The General on his foot and crutch with his escorts around him was in position to be the first one down the gangplank when it was in place. The Bostonia's Captain appeared. He wished the General well and he said, "Thank you General and all your escort for your help! Thanks, from every one of the ship's crew and the passengers on this boat." When he got to Bill, he paused, shook his hand and took a rather sizable package from a crewman who was following him. He said, "Bill, I want you to take these as a token of this ships appreciation for all your help during this voyage."

"Thank you, sir. May I ask what's in the package?"

"Certainly, it is a brace of horse pistols and their holsters I acquired from an unlucky gambler sometime back. I hope they will be a pleasant reminder of your good work last night."

"I will cherish them, thank you Captain.

Chapter 12
Choo-Choo Carry Me Home

The gangplank was in place, so they left the boat behind. The cabs were lined up waiting for the rush of passengers from the Bostonia No. 2. Mel and Blair got in the first cab. Mel was really getting good at getting around on his crutch and wooden foot. The other four escorts got in the second cab. The two cabs made their way through the city to the St. Louis railroad station.

The escorts were wide eyed tourists as they saw this city for the first time. There were lots of modern buildings scattered amongst some of the old ones. The city was founded in 1763 by the French as a fur trading post. The United States brought it as part of President Jefferson's 1803 "Louisiana Purchase". That event was especially important to Mel's, Bill's, Dave's, Blair's and Dick's history because it added both Minnesota and Iowa to the U. S. A.

Dave ohed and awed at the old buildings they were passing. "I would really like to spend a couple of days in this place, it's fascinating."

"Well, we can leave you here if you like. You'll fit right in with the rest of these relics." jibed Dick.

The sightseeing ended as the cabs pulled up at the train station and told to wait. The travelers found that the next train to Kansas City didn't leave until 11 PM and would arrive at KC about 8 AM. They showed their travel vouchers to the ticket agent and received their tickets for the next leg of their journey.

They climb back in their cabs and Mel directed his cabbie to a neat, little hotel near the train station. The timing was perfect for cleaning up and having dinner. Mel was well known here because of his visits when he came to town on business. The management located three rooms for the travelers to use while they waited for the train. The group split up into its usual pairs and went their separate ways to refresh and relax before they met again for dinner.

When dinner ended, they adjourned to the lobby where Mel sat down in an overstuffed chair to enjoy one of his cigarettos. He was almost immediately surrounded by well-wishers. After greetings were taken care of, they asked why the crutch; had he suffered a wound in the war?

Mel replied that he had been hit by a spent

cannon ball rolling along the ground. No one saw it until it was almost upon them. I jumped to try to avoid it but was only partially successful. It tore off one foot and mashed the other leg. The surgeons needed to remove the foot and the mangled leg just below the knee." I have to admit, "I was pretty down until these five guys came along and made me a wooden foot and the crutch. With those two gifts I can get around well enough and I feel I still have a future I can enjoy."

"Show us the wooden foot, please Mel."

Mel looked at Blair, "What do you think?"

"I think it's your choice."

"Well it is what it is, no use trying to hide it."

Blair removed the elastic sleeve and then opened the garter snaps to release the stocking with the wooden foot in it. Next the stocking came off revealing the foot.

The crowd expressed its appreciation by its ohs and ahs.

Someone in the crowd said "Did you see the rig they used to attach the foot to the living leg? Unique. Very inventive."

A question came from the crowd, "What battle did that happen in Mel?"

"A few months before the end of the St. Petersburg siege. Around the time of the Battle of the Crater."

"Wasn't that crater thing when the Pennsylvania miners blew a large hole in the rebel defenses?"

"That was an opportunity to shorten the war but a couple of drunk and a few incompetent officers turned it into a bloodbath for the troops who were sent into the crater instead of around it. The only good thing that came out of it was the purging of the officers responsible for the screw up, including General Burnside."

The well-wishers kept showing up and marveling at Mel's foot until about 9 o'clock when Blair and the others whisk Mel back to his room to prepare for the upcoming train ride.

Despite more attention being paid to his foot then there was to him, Mel enjoyed this interlude of renewing his contacts with old friends who stop by to wish him well.

The cabs were back at the hotel at 10:30 as order. It only took about 10 minutes to get them to the Railroad Station. So, they were able to find a spot on the station's platform where they were well situated to board when the call came to do so.

The train arrived with a blast of released steam that hid the waiting travelers on the station platform from the world for a second or two. The squeal of brakes accompanied the steam blast as the engineer brought the train to a halt in position to load the waiting passengers. The train was on time and so was the conductor, "All aboard."

It was easy to find a spot where they could set together. It wasn't long before the engineer blew the whistle and released the brakes. Next came a squeal of metal on metal as the drive wheels took hold, then a couple of jerks as the slack was eliminated from the couplings between the cars. The train started down the track with a clackity-clack and the travelers were off to their next stop, Kansas City.

The next hour past in small talk about home and family. Mel said, "You are about to spend a few days with my family. I know you will be introduced to them when you meet; but I think a little pre-meeting information might be helpful to you. My wife and I have been blessed with five children. The oldest is a 21-year-old girl named Patricia after her mother. We call her Patsy. Next, we have a 16-year-old girl we named Mildred after my mother. She prefers to be called Milly just like my mother did. She is a saucy, bright eyed, life of the party type. Milly was followed by another girl. While we were happy with the child we got, we began to think our dream of having a boy might go unfulfilled. Regardless, we named her Drusilla after Patricia's mother and welcomed her to the family. Like her grandma, she chose to be addressed as Dru. She is the quiet, thoughtful one in the family. Judging by the number of boys hanging around, our girls must be fairly attractive and well liked."

"Next our wish for a boy was fulfilled. We of course called him Melvin after me. Mel Jr. is now eight years old and we know he is nothing like me. I don't expect he will every sit at a desk and run a business. He is a real woodsy, a robust youngster who likes to hunt, fish and camp out. He is itching to explore the horizon to find the unknown. The youngest is a four-year-old boy named Arthur, my father's name, when he is behaving, he is called Artie, but he is called Arthur when he is being reprimanded. He gets a fair number of Arthurs during any given day as he learns the limits of a civilized life."

The talk died out around midnight. Everybody was dozing except Dave. While they were waiting for the train, Dave had picked up a big bag of tobacco. Blair had told him that Mel's ankle cushion was getting soft. Dave unlaced the deer skin overlap on the pouch and began stuffing more tobacco in it. Then it was tamp....tamp....tamp until the bottom of the cushion was as solid again. Then he'd feed more tobacco in and repeated the tamping process again. He repeated this process again and again until the cushion was as solid from bottom to top as he could get it. He then pulled the slack out of the laces before he tied them up again. Satisfied with his work, Dave joined the nappers.

It was about 6 in the morning when the group started to stir and seek relief in the train's biffy. Only Mel had ever been to Kansas City before, so the windows were filled with faces trying to catch a glimpse of this infamous city. Now that the sun was up, they could see some of its sights. Kansas City was still a cow town in many respects. Its stockyards were the second largest in the nation behind Chicago. It boasted that the tallest building west of the Mississippi was here. As they pulled into the Kansas City station there was a sense of excitement in the group. Mel felt it because he was getting close to home. The others were feeling it because they were getting close to the end of their mission and then they would be free to go to their homes.

After leaving the train, their first stop was at the ticket window. The next train to Des Moines was scheduled to leave at midnight. They showed the ticket agent their travel vouchers and received their tickets for the midnight ride.

Outside the station, Mel said, "There is a place here I usually stay at when I am in town. It would be nice if we could stay there." They all agreed that a hotel room would be a nice luxury during such a long wait. They boarded cabs to get to the place Mel had in mind.

On arriving Mel explained their dilemma to the clerk. For such a good customer as Mel was the clerk hunted the register over until he found three vacant rooms. A bellboy took them to the rooms where they continued the arrangement, they had fallen in the habit of using. They parted making a date to meet again about nine-thirty for breakfast.

On the way to breakfast they passed through the lobby where a paper boy was hawking his wares. **"Lincoln's funeral train reaches Springfield. Read all about it. Get your Gazette here.** Blair walked over to the boy and purchased a paper for Mel. The paper was dated May 4th and described the solemn ceremony that would lead up to Lincoln's interment. While they ate, Mel read bits and pieces of the articles in it and they hash the news over.

Mel said, "Its time they let him rest!"

When they finished their meal, Mel said he was going to hang around the hotel all day to rest and visit with friends who might stop to say hello. He insisted Blair take a day off and go with the others walking around KC sightseeing. Blair asked him if he were sure he could get along without him.

Mel said, "No, I'm not sure, but I have to find out some time if I can get along on my own." Blair still hesitated a little, but Mel insistence won the day. You guys have fun and be ready to share your adventures to night on the train."

They walked downtown where they made their first visit was to a department store. Both Dick and Duane brought their boys sweatshirts with Kansas City embroidered on the front.

Next, they visited the first skyscraper out west; it was seven stories high. They took the elevator to the roof. It was a downright scary ride as it clanked and creaked its way up stopping at each floor to let riders on or off. The view from the top was magnificent, a sight unmatched in any of their collective experiences. When it was time to go down there was some talk about walking rather than trusting that rickety elevator. After some discussion, the dread of walking down the seven flights of stairs won the dread contest over the thought of riding the elevator down the seven stories to the ground. With the decision made, they climbed into the car with the operator. Again, the elevator had to stop at each floor. At each floor, the brake pads gripped the suspension cable gave out a screech that jangled the nerves. Three times the brake did not stop the car at the floor where it was supposed to stop. On each of these occasions the friends felt their stomachs bottom out a moment or two after their body's had. When the brakes failed like that, the operator had to reverse the car and climb back up to the floor they had missed before they could continue down again. Eventually the operator said, "Ground Floor" and opened the door for them.

The feeling of relief as they stepped out on the solid ground rivaled the feelings they had felt when reaching solid ground after the Sultana explosion.

They all felt the need to sit down and let their stomachs settle in. So, it was decided they would stop for lunch. Their hope was that some food would settle their rolling stomachs down. When they exited the skyscraper, they saw a little Chinese restaurant across the street. They agreed this would be a perfect place to stop for lunch. They all felt quite cosmopolitan when they ordered, without hesitation (or Pidgeon English), a duplicate of their Memphis meal.

After lunch they stopped at a type of store they had never seen before, a 5 and 10 Cent store. Here they found something for all their kids and wives. Loaded with bags and boxes they hired a cab to continue their tour. They had the cab take them to the famous Kansas City Stockyards. Its size was impressive, but the stench drove them away in a short time. There were lots more to see but they had the cab take them back to their hotel. They stopped in the lobby to see how Mel was doing. He was in casual conversation with two old friends when they joined him.

He said, "How did your sightseeing go?"

Their consensus reply was "fine". They told him they were tired and were on their way to take a nap. He said he was kind of tired himself and would join them.

On their way to their rooms, they stopped at the desk to ask the clerk to call them two cabs for 11 o'clock and to give them a wakeup call at ten-thirty.

As they walked to their rooms Blair asked Mel how his day had gone. Mel responded that he had really enjoyed talking to his friends, "It was great. By the way while you were gone, I made arrangements for our arrival in Des Moines. I ordered a coach to meet us at the railroad station at eight tomorrow morning. I also warned my family to expect us for nine o'clock breakfast." The group of friends reached the point where they had to split up to go to their respective rooms. Their goodbyes were a course of "see you at ten-thirty."

About 10:30 the bellboy made the trip to each of their rooms. At each room he knocked on the door and said, "Your wake-up call." At each room it took several raps and calls before a sleepy voice responded, "Ok, we're awake. Thank you." Within about ten minutes of the call they were all gathered in the lobby. For some of them, their previously almost empty backpacks were now straining at the seams.

This especially true for Duane with the presents for the five kids and the pendent for his wife. Luckily the pendent didn't take a lot of room. The exceptions were Bill who had a pipe knife for his dad and silk handkerchiefs for his mom and Mel who did not even have a backpack.

About 11 o'clock the cabs showed up and the travelers climbed in. There was a shared sigh of relief as they finally started the last leg of their assignment, Mel to get home and the others to get him home. They were at the station in plenty of time to be ready for the, "All Aboard" signal when it rang out. There were plenty of seats available, so it was no trouble finding a suitable place for them all to set together. Soon the engineer gave the train a few chugs and they were underway.

As the train moved a long through the rolling Iowa countryside, Mel called for a meeting of the whole group. He started by saying, "I have never met a finer group of men in my entire life then you five. I would regret it the rest of my life if I didn't try to keep you close to me the rest of our lives. I am asking each of you to take a job in my business. You will be well paid, and your families will be well provided for. Please give it some thought. We will revisit this after you have met my family and toured the business.

Duane answered first, "I don't have to wait to give

you my answer. Mel, you are one of the finest men in the world. I thank you for your kind words and generous offer, but I can't imagine a life without my family nearby or of not being a lumberjack. Therefore, I must respectfully decline."

Next Bill respectfully declined. Unfinished business in Minnesota was the reason he gave. Dick and Dave both declined for similar reasons as the other two. Blair however said he would be honored to consider it. However, the only job he would consider was that of being Mel's companion.

Mel said, "Of course you will continue as my medic and the keeper of my foot."

"Then all I need is my family's consent to join me in a new life in Des Moines."

As the train approached Des Moines, Mel became emotional about his past. He pointed out the train's window into the dark night the homestead his parents had claimed. He was born there, and his father had died there during the Black Hawk War. He proudly pointed where he shot his first deer and where he first kissed a girl. His companions acted impressed even though they couldn't see much in the dark. Mel was seeing it all in his memory. The scenes kept changing and the memories kept flowing until they reached the Des Moines train depot.

Chapter 13
Des Moines

There was a large crowd on the depot's platform. Mel said, "There is my wife and the kids. I see neighbors, old friends and some of my long-time employees there too. My GOD, this crowd is here for me." There were tears in Mel's eyes as he viewed the waiting throng. The bell rang and the whistle tooted as the train stopped with the platform of the car Mel and his friends were riding in directly in front of the crowd. The crowd responded with a mighty roar.

Blair swung down and took a place where he could help Mel if he needed it. An exceptionally large black man appeared on the other side of the steps acting like he was there to help also. Mel appeared with his crutch and wooden foot. Emotion overwhelmed the crowd as they rushed with his family to greet him. Suddenly Bill and his friends appeared and brought order and organization to the proceedings.

Mel stopped on the car's steps and clapped the black man on the shoulder and said, "Good to see you again John."

"Good to see you, Mel. When I heard how severely you were wounded, I thought I might never have the pleasure of your company again."

Blair and John helped Mel leave the train's steps and reach the depot's platform. There his wife and family surrounded him. Mel tried to hug his wife and only Blair's quick action saved him from falling. Much more under control he held her in one arm and gave her, as she gave him, along passionate kiss. This was followed by a sweet, gentle kiss of reunited lovers.

During the kissing, Dick and Dave located a parklike bench and situated it on the station deck. Blair and the giant black man led Mel and his wife toward the bench. On the way, Mel gave each of his children a one-armed hug and a loving kiss. The boys got a manly handshake too. Mel, with his wife hanging on his arm like he was a dream that might disappear without her followed their escorts to their seats on the bench.

Blair took a place just behind the bench where Mel was seated.

Bill and his men got the crowd organized into a receiving line. One at a time or in small groups the well-wishers came forward. Each had their say and then disappeared back into the crowd. The line seemed endless.

Bill and the guys (minus Blair) stood to the side in awe at the size of the turnout. The big black man came over, he said, "My name is John. I run the meat packing plant for Mr. Armour. I can't begin to express the gratitude I feel for you fellows for bringing Mr. Armour home. You guys are local heroes for the kindness and care you have given him. So welcome and make yourself at home. If there is ever anything, I can do for you, you just let me know."

"Thank you, John, we appreciate your kind words. We will call on you if there is ever a need. Likewise, we will also be ready to help in any way possible at any time we might be needed." said Bill.

The line had finally dwindled down to the last four well-wishers. Bill notice a beautiful girl giving him the once over several times. He noticed her hair was golden-brown and her eyes matched. She was wearing a brown A-line skit that harmonized with her hair and eyes. Her blouse was very feminine and tied the ensemble together. She did not flinch when he met her eyes and start examining her. Instead, she started rotating and posing at every turn to show him her best. He had never seen such a beauty before.

What impressed him most were her lovely sparkling eyes and the feeling there was a ripple of mirth just under her gaze.

He was awakened from his thoughts by a tug on his pants leg. Looking down, he was staring into the eyes of a youngster. The lad said, "Mother asked me to ask you if you and your friends would please get in the second wagon in the front of the station." He then turned and ran around the corner of the building. Bill looked back where the girl had been, but she was gone.

"Well you heard what we are asked to do, let's get it done. Dick and Dave, would you please put the bench back where you found it?"

Bill's group rounded the station and found the wagon. It seemed like everyone was waiting for them, so they immediately climbed in and found places to set. The rest of their wagon was filled with a parcel of negro children and an exceptionally beautiful woman the kids called mother. The five soldiers tipped their hats to the lady and said, "Hello." to the kids. Their wagon was driven by a strapping young man who was the spitting image of John.

The wagon in front of them was filled with Mel, his wife and his family. Blair was there as well. Two young ladies obviously John's daughters were setting at the tailgate and John was driving. The caravan seemed to be heading down toward a river that wormed its way through town.

Des Moines was bigger than Bill had imagined. There were lots of different stores to announce it was the trading center of the region. All the store fronts were a weathered gray, they all could use paint. The dirt streets were hard and smooth (relatively) showing they were watered and rolled regularly. Bill saw rake marks where a crew had worked last night to remove some ruts to improve their surface. Off in the distance was a great white dome announcing the fact that Des Moines was the capital of the State.

Eventually they turned on to a rutted path that took them down to the river. There, nestled in a bend of the river was a glade. The wagons pulled up in an area containing several picnic tables and benches. There were a couple grills with red hot coals glowing in them. Two teenage black girls seemed to be overseeing the site.

The kids tumbled out of the wagon and raced around it like attacking Indians are alleged to do. The driver helped his mother down. Bill and his group climbed out of the wagon and stood wondering what was coming next. One thing that was obvious was that roast pig was on the menu. A relatively small one was on a spit over and open fire. One of the cooks turned the spit periodically while another brushed a sauce or something on it.

Bill looked the glade over marking its features in his mind. The clear blue sky was the perfect backdrop for the greenness of the grass and leaves. Although he could not see any birds flitting amongst the trees, their songs filled the air announcing their presence.

He saw that Mel's wife and family were gathered on the ground around their wagon while Blair and John lifted Mel down. Mel tried walking to the nearest bench, but the uneven ground and the resistance of the grass were too much for him yet. Blair and John moved to his sides and carried him to the bench. Blair whispered into his ear. Mel's whispered reply caused Blair to nod in understanding and agreement.

The two young colored girls from the second wagon joined forces with the two at the grills and they all started fussing around the fires. Mel waved to Bill and the others to join him, so they did. Mel said, "All these people are anxious to meet you so get ready to be ogled"

Bill said, "We want to meet them too, so let's get it done."

Mel waved his wife over, "This is Patricia, the love of my life."

Patricia had a yellow cotton dress on that looked like spring. "Mel has written us so much about you fellows. I feel I already know each of you. I have already figured out which one of you is Bill." shaking his hand. "You gave yourself away by taking charge of the crowd and organizing everything. I also think I know which of you is Duane." Turning, she confronted Duane. "Duane, you look like a lumberman should." This brought a chuckle to everyone's lips and a smile to their faces.

Duane said self-consciously, "Yes'um. Thank you, mam."

"You other two are more of a mystery. I know you're both men of action, strong and resolute. So similar in so many ways that you leave me no clue as to which is which. Please introduce yourselves."

Dick spoke up first, "I am Richard Madson, mam."

"I am David Barrett, at your service mam."

"Now I can tell you apart. Mr. Madson do you prefer to be known as Richard or Dick?"

"Dick, mam."

"Ok, Dick Madson it is, the one with the smooth face features. Oh, by the way, all of you, I prefer to be called Patricia."

"Yes mam." Both Dick and Dave responded.

This brought a frown to Patricia's face and then a good-hearted laugh as the two culprits blushed. "What name do you prefer Mr. Barrett?"

"Dave or David, Patricia."

"Ok, Dave or David Barrett it is, the one with the chiseled face features."

"Of course, I already met Blair on the way over here. What a God-send you five have been to Mel and the family who loves him."

There was a pause while the group took in the magnitude of the blessing Mel's return was to his friends and family.

Patricia broke the silence. "Let me introduce our family. The oldest is our daughter Patricia, we call her Patsy."

Patsy curtsied and said in the sweetest voice, "Welcome all. Thank you for bringing daddy home."

Bill looked up and was swallowed whole in those eyes. Patsy offered her hand to each of them. When Bill shook it the electricity between them was obvious to all. For the rest of the introductions Bill was discombobulated by his awareness of Patsy's presence. He remembered as in a fog the rest of the family as they were introduced. He vaguely remembered the younger sisters names as they were presented, Mildred (called Milly) and Drusilla (called Dru). The pants leg puller turned out to be Mel Jr. The youngest was named after Mel's father, Arthur (called Artie).

The call to breakfast rang out. A huge platter heavy with sizzling meats was placed on the table which was now occupied by the men. The platter held rashers of bacon, along with sausage links and patties. The meats were sided by pancakes, sorghum and tubs of butter. Mel said grace and the feeding mania began. The travelers had not eaten since yesterday evening, so they dug right in. John and his son kept pace with them.

Between mouthfuls John said, "Yesterday, my crew made these especially for you fellows. We wanted to impress you with what we do at Armour Packing."

The cooks and servers were hard pressed at first to keep the supply ahead of demand. Finally, the men's hunger abated, and they gave their places at the table to the kids and women. The cooks continued their efforts until everyone had been fed. While the cooks ate everything was cleaned up by the rest of the women.

The party now moved to conversations, games and rest. Bill asked John, "When are we going to meet your family?"

"I thought we would do that at lunchtime"

"There seems to be such a strong bond between the two families that I'm convinced there is a story worth hearing behind it. Come on John, tell us what gives?"

"Well it is no secret, shortly after me, my wife

and my son arrived in America on a slave ship we were auctioned off in a Maryland slave market. We were lucky, we were all brought by the same man. Our new owner immediately started home (which I heard was in a place called Missouri). As slave owners go, he wasn't too bad, but he had two wicked men working for him. One night they got drunk and tried to rape my wife. I went wild, knocked them both out. One of them had a hunting knife in his belt and I was just about to use it to castrate them when the owner stopped me. He kicked the two out of camp because they were more about damaging his property then protecting it. Next day he got new help and four days later we arrived at his place. A couple of years past. The wife and I added a little girl to our family. Then the crops failed two years in a row, our owner was desperate for money to keep his place operating. The only assets he had to sell were his slaves. So, he sold my wife, my daughter and my son to a family down south. I now had no one left to worry about so I ran away. I ran north and reach Des Moines. I was hungry, tired, and in utter despair when Mel, Mr. Armour found me. He gave me a job, confidence and hope for the future. He paused for a breath and then continued. "I am sorry this tale is taking so long to tell but the best part is yet to come."

"Take all the time you need to tell the whole story." said Bill.

"Ok, I will. The next spring, Mr. Armour went to my former owner in Missouri and told him, "You can have a payment equal to what an adult male slave brings in today's market or nothing. His only value to you is what I 'm willing to pay. If you try to recapture him, I will run you out of Iowa and pursue you to the end of your days. The former owner capitulated. He signed my papers over to Mel. He also told Mel who had brought my family. Mel then continued down south and brought my entire family. When he got home, he made us all free.

"I knew there had to be quite a story between you two. That is the most uplifting story I have heard in sometime. I look forward to meeting your family after lunch." Bill and his men asked John about some of the details of his family's ordeal.

Next the conversation turned toward the escorts. They were asked about their past lives, where they were from and so on. After answering the questions directed at him, the conversation became just a babble in Bill's ears.

He took his thoughts down to a quiet spot on the riverbank. There he spread his six foot plus frame out on the grass. Bill was trying to figure out what was going on with him every time he saw Patsy. They were the strangest and strongest feelings he had ever experienced. '*What could be the reason for all his new, intense emotions? He really didn't see himself as an emotional guy.* A new idea clamored in his brain to be recognized, '*I think I am in love with her.*' *It's the only thing that makes sense. Maybe this is the first step in my plan to settle down on a farm and avoid conflict for the rest of my life. Patsy would make a pleasant companion throughout the years. Imagine looking across the table into those eyes each evening a dinner.*' He was hooked.

He heard a rustle in the grass and felt it move.

A familiar voice said, "A penny for your thoughts."

Bill twisted his head around and spotted Patsy standing behind him. "A penny is not enough for these thoughts. These thoughts are expensive because they are of you!

"You're thinking of me? That's funny because I have been thinking about you since dad's first letter arrived that praised you in the highest terms for the man you are. I fell in love with the hero that was bringing my father home, the man in my father's letters. What a man I built him up to be. Now you're here and you are better than my dream man could ever be. I know I am being forward and coquettish, but I know I am on the clock and have so little time to win your love. In this moment I am offering you my heart with all my love in it. I want you to know

Bill Cheever I am coming after you." With that, Patsy turned and ran up the bank, back toward the picnickers.

Bill leapt off the ground and pursued her. He called, "Patsy, wait a minute."

She heard his plea and stopped, turning to look back. He was running toward her as fast as the wind. He slid to a stop in front of her. The next set of events were a blur. Bill took her in his arms and kissed her most tenderly. He then said, "I love you too, Patsy." He fell on his knee and said, "Will you marry me?"

She pulled him erect and planted a smackeroo on him that lasted and lasted. In fact, they only broke it off when the clapping and cheering interrupt their intensity. As they looked at their friends and family, they realized everyone was looking at them.

Patsy said," Yes I will marry you, Bill Cheever."

The happy couple moved hand and hand back to the other picnickers. All the men slapped Bill on the back and congratulated him. Everyone, men and women alike, hugged Patsy and fussed over her. Bill strode over to where Mel and Patricia were setting and said, "May I have your blessing to marry your lovely daughter Patsy?"

Mel said, "I have come to trust you and respect you during our brief acquaintance. If she will have you, of course I will be delighted to welcome you to the family. Bill, please take good care of her!"

"I will sir."

Patricia said, "Nothing could make us happier."

All the bystanders whooped it up again.

The glade the lovers were in took on beauty never seen by man before. The bird's songs were prettier, the flower aromas were sweeter, and the trees and grass were greener. The rest of the picnickers didn't exist as the happy couple kissed. They were inseparable for the rest of the picnic.

Lunch of succulent roast ham in mustard sauce on freshly baked bread with lots of freshly churned butter was a winner. Blair said loudly so all could hear, "Now this is eating high off the hog. Please forgive my weak joke," he said among the laughter he spawned, "I couldn't resist."

Lunch over, Bill reminded John of his promise with a loud, obnoxious, "Harrumph!"

John said, "Do you really want to meet all fifteen of them?"

John's answer was a resounding, "Yes!" from the five former escorts."

"Ok, first, my wife, Liza, mother of my children and the joy of my life."

Liza had the warmest smile and more charm than any lady should be allowed to have. The frock she had on was simple but attractive. Patsy whispered to Bill, "She makes all her clothes and those for her family as well as for others. Liza curtsied to the men, "It is a pleasure to meet you. I hope we all can find time to get better acquainted before you leave for your homes."

Each of them bowed to match her curtsy and said, "That would be nice."

"This guy is Ezekiel (called Zeke) my African born son." John said as he put an affectionate hand on Zeke's shoulder. Zeke's handshake told of the strength harnessed in that impressive body. They said, "Hello." And he said," Glad to meet you." John continued introducing his fourteen other offspring. Appropriate recognition was exchanged between the new acquaintances. The cooks were especially praised for their effort and how good the food tasted.

It was time to call it a day. Even the kids had run out of steam. All the picnic stuff was stowed away, and the picnic site was thoroughly policed when the loaded wagons moved away.

Chapter 14

Courting

The squads mission ended as they reached the Armour's home. It was the evening of May 5th ,1865 when the family and guests climb down from the wagons. As they disappeared into the house, they shouted their goodbyes to John's family and received their response in kind. John drove the wagon with his family in it away. Zeke took care of the second wagon.

The members of the squad had let this day pass without their having a definite plan for what was coming next.

After everyone was inside, Blair said, "I had better check and re-bandage Mel's wounds. This is a lot longer than he has ever worn his foot before." Blair started up the stairs steadying Mel as he went.

Patricia said to her girls, "Let's get these guys settled. They must be exhausted after their train ride last night and the busy day we put them through to-day. Milly, show Dick and Dave to the blue room. Patsy show Bill and Duane to the green room. Both of you show them the water closet and how all the gadgets work. Gentlemen make yourself at home. Pantry raiding is permitted if hunger strikes during the night. On second thought girls, why don't you show them the kitchen and pantry on your way up-stairs? Now off with you before they fall asleep and we must call John back to help get them to bed. Oh! By the way, Blair is sleeping over near the master bedroom helping Mel. Sleep tight all."

"This way." said Milly to Dick and Dave as she headed for the back of the house. Patsy took Bill's hand and led him after Milly's group. Duane was left to tag along behind.

The pantry was explored with only a few cook-ies purloined; the wonders of water closet mystified the newbies until all the knobs and stuff were dem-onstrated. Their water closet education complete the two groups parted.

When Patsy, Bill and Duane reached the green room door Duane discreetly entered leaving the two lovers to say good night as they chose.

Patsy said, "Bill, this has been the happiest day of my life so far. I vowed after you asked me to marry you that I was not going to let you go. I now see that was a hollow vow (there was a twinkle in her eye and mirth on her lips as she said) because now is the time when bed do us part."

Bill's heart ached with joy as he gazed into those bewitching eyes. "Well we will have to do something about this separate bed thing as soon as we can!" He wrapped her in his loving arms and kissed her tenderly. The longer they kissed the more passionate they got. Finally, they parted lips and gasped for breath. He said, "It is time for you to go. Another kiss like that and I will have to kick Duane out so I can have you for myself."

"Another kiss like that and I will kick Duane out myself. I'll see you in the morning." With a laugh, she turned and hurried down the hall.

As Bill entered their room, he heard Duane chuckling, "That one is going to keep you on your toes and then some Sarge." There was a touch of sarcasm and a lot of humor in his voice

Bill couldn't help laughing himself, "She is going to be a hand full of joy to live with." He turned the gas lamps off as they hit the bed. Almost immediately they both were asleep.

Bill woke up about 4:30 AM maybe a half-hour later than his usual time. He tiptoed to the water closet and finished his morning toilet. He felt better after scrubbing his whole body with a washcloth, his hair with homemade bar soap and shaving. After rinsing everything thoroughly and toweling off he was forced to put on his grungy clothes. Finished he tiptoed back to his room.

Duane was sitting on the bed waiting. "I am going to take my fling at the water closet." as he slipped out the door.

Bill looked at his watch, it was a little after 5:30. He stretched out on the bed and may have napped a little. He sat up when an insistent knock shattered the silence. The knock was followed by a voice full of laughter, "Get up lazybones. You're wasting time that I could be in your arms and enjoying your kisses."

Bill opened the door and received a kiss that made his heart race until he thought it might jump out of his chest. Eventually the kiss ended. Patsy said, "Good morning my love. Did you have a good night's sleep?"

"Not bad considering. I kept dreaming of you and Duane kept waking me up as I tried to put my arms around you, and it turned out to be him."

"You're right. We must do something about this separate bed thing as soon as possible. I don't want anybody else getting my hugs. I love you sweetheart!" She kissed him again.

"And I love you!" and he kissed her again.

"We better get downstairs now, or we will spend the whole day kissing."

"That doesn't sound like a bad thing to me." He reached over and grabbed his gun belts and began buckling them on as he follow her down the hall.

She said looking back at him, "Come on you; we'll make time later in the day for more of that."

He followed her downstairs where everybody, but Mel, Blair and Duane were seated at the table. "How is everybody doing?" Patricia asked.

"Fine." Was the essence of the replies.

Just then Duane walked into the dining room.

"How are things with you Duane?"

"Great ma......, Patricia." This brought smiles to every face and a few chuckles here and there

"Great! Mel and I decided last night that it is time for us to show you how grateful we are for the kindness and caring you five showered on a stranger. Not only did you bring him home as per your orders, you gave him confidence in his ability to cope with life despite his mangled body. You did not treat him as an invalid but treated as a valued friend. First, we would like to provide each of you with the means shed your army clothes and resume your civilian identity. Second, we would like to throw a shindig to let all Des Moines thank you and welcome Mel home. In the hope of getting the biggest crowd possible, we thought a street dance would be best. In fact, we are convinced there should always be at least two bands playing. Perhaps the greatest inducement for all kinds of people to show up will be the free beer. We hoped you all could wait until Saturday to leave for home."

Mel and Blair joined the group and as if that were the signal the kitchen staff served breakfast. During the meal, Patricia, Patsy and Bill had their heads together in a serious discussion.

After breakfast each of the escorts was given a hundred-dollar bill. Mel said, "This is not payment for services rendered in bringing me home, no amount would be sufficient to pay that debt. This is a pure gift of love. Please accept in the spirit in which it is given."

Patricia followed, "There is an addition to our plans for Friday. In the morning Patsy and Bill insist on getting married. So, one thing you may want to buy today is rice."

After breakfast, Patsy and Bill left the house to walk downtown to shop. Bill was anxious to get out of the army clothes. Bill put his arm around Patsy's waist and gave her a hug. She looked up at him, smiled and gave his hand a squeeze. Neither of them said a word as they walked along, they were so absorbed in a jumbled of thoughts about each other, their future together and most of all about married life. Neither of them had been in a serious relationship before. As they walked along several people greeted them, but they did not respond. They were not in touch with the world around them, only with each other.

Finally, they entered the 'Farm and Fleet' store. Bill selected two pair of rider cut blue jeans, two western cut plaid shirts, and a tan Stetson. Also, an assortment of under garments. He immediately went in the backroom of the store and when he returned, he was a billboard for western wear. It's well known that clothes don't make the man, but they don't hurt either. The only sour note was his old brogans from the army.

Patsy said, "You look great from the top of your head to the bottom of the cuff on your pants. Those boots have to go."

Bill looked down at his boots and muttered, "My Atlanta shoeshine is gone, and I guess the shoes are all but done too."

"Come on Bill, I need some riding boots too"

They walked down the street to the bootmakers Shop. Bill stopped at a display of plain work boots. He picked up a pair and judged them to be sturdy.

Before he could examine another pair, Patsy said, "These are not what I had in mind. I want to contribute something we can wear to the wedding that we share. This is my gift to us." and led the way to the hand-tooled boot display. "If it's okay with you, I would like us to pick a design we can share." They picked out a pattern with intwined roses as its main theme. The cobbler promised to have the boots ready by Thursday evening.

Next, they went to a women's clothier. Patsy said she needed some things too. These turned out to be western cut shirts in a variety of colors, plaids and checks, several pair of blue jeans and a snazzy looking cowgirl hat. Her outfits would complement Bill's western garb. She also brought a riding skirt. "This is for when I need to ride but still want to look like your wife and not your boyfriend." She told Bill she still had some more things of a personal nature to get and he should take a walk.

Bill left the store as requested. Bill still had nearly half of his hundred left. He had wondered how he could get away for a while to get Patsy a special gift he had in mind. On their way over he had seen a jewelry store. Now he hurried back to it. He selected a ring set he liked and of course could afford.

He arrived back at the women's store just as Patsy was paying for her purchases. Soon the two of them were strolling hand in hand down the street. They came to a little park and sat down on a bench.

Bill fished a small, black box out of his pocket as he turned to face Patsy. He opened the box revealing the engagement ring. He said as he took the ring out of its box, "Yesterday I asked, and you said yes, today I want to put this ring on your finger so everyone will know how blessed I am."

"Oh Bill, what a sweet speech. I don't need the ring to remind me of my love for you, but I will wear it proudly to announce to the world my betrothal to you." In public but overwhelmed with emotion she kissed him. They broke off the kiss and looked furtively around to see if anyone saw them. Not seeing anyone they hurried away.

At dinner that evening there were no soldier boys as all the squad showed up in civvies. Dick said, "Boy, aren't we pretty."

The other attraction at dinner was Patsy's engagement ring. Everyone oohed and awed. Artie had the last word, "That's just like mommy's ring, are you going to be a mommy Patsy?"

Well, that was almost the last word about the ring; in the end, Patsy had that, "I hope so Artie, someone just like you."

Later that evening, Milly rushed in to inform the family that all the talk around town was that Patsy Armour had been seen kissing this stranger in the downtown park. The real mystery and the main topic of the conversations were, "Who is that guy?" This news didn't bother them much as they smooched in the hallway outside Patsy's room before the need to go to bed parted them again.

The next morning, Bill put on his new clothes and waited for Patsy to come and fetch him for breakfast. What he really waited for was his good morning kiss which he could not delivered at the breakfast table. Duane had gone downstairs and Bill was beginning to wonder if Patsy was coming when there was a rap on the door.

Bill hurried to open it and Patsy was standing there in one of her new western outfits. She asked, "How do I look?"

Bill said, "I will tell you after I've had a good morning kiss my love."

She stood on her tiptoes and gave him very loving kiss.

He gazed into her eyes and said, "You look good enough to eat if I don't get breakfast soon."

"Oh you!" She said with a grin. With that she took his hand and led him to breakfast.

After breakfast, Patsy, Milly and Drue went to Patsy's room to go through her wardrobe. Patsy had to pick out what part of her wardrobe she would take and what she would leave for her sisters. Milly and Drue were there to lobby for the things they especially liked.

Bill was there as a consultant for Patsy. His job was to tell her if he liked an outfit or not. He was on the hot seat often but avoided hot water because he learned to read what Patsy wanted to do. The requests for his opinion became fewer and fewer as the morning wore on.

About ten o'clock, Blair knocked on Patsy's door and asked if Mel could borrow Bill for a while?

Reluctantly Patsy said, "Ok."

Blair and Bill got a little time to catch up on what was going on in each other's lives.

Blair reported that his wife had agreed with the move and was preparing to join him by the end of the month. Blair and a crew of Mel's hands were going to get her and all their possessions. In the meantime, Mel and Patricia were giving Blair and his wife a house. It would be refurbished before the wife arrived.

Bill told Blair how deliriously happy in love he was with Patsy.

They reached Mel's office and knocked. Mel immediately invited them in.

Mel said, "Bill, welcome to my home when I am at home. How are you doing with my headstrong daughter? I have never seen her so happy."

"Mel, my head's in such a state of constant joy that I am having trouble putting two coherent thoughts together before a thought of her gets between them. I'm crazy in love with her and I wouldn't have it any other way."

"Well, I'll make this as fast as I can so you can get back to supervise the packing. I know your side arms have become part of who you are. I have felt bad about their bath in the Mississippi during my rescue from the Sultana. Therefore, I telegraphed home and had this rig made for you." Mel reached down by his chair and brought up a black leather gun belt featuring two holsters. There were no gew-gaws on the belt or holsters to give the wearers presence away in the dark. The only thing that might reflect light from the rig were the metallic casings of the cartridges in the belt loops and the highly polished black bone handles on the guns. The holsters and guns were arranged as Bill liked them. The left one was set up for a cross body draw while the right one was setup for a natural right-hand draw. The guns were secured to the holsters with leather loops around the hammers to keep them from falling out when riding or doing any other physical action. Each holster had thongs on the bottom so they could be tied down if a time came when that was needed. Mel held the rig out and said, "Here, try them on."

Bill thought, *I hope I never have to use a gun again. But I can't tell Mel that and spoil the pleasure he is obviously feeling about giving this special gift.* Bill took them from Mel's hand and buckled them around his waist. After he made a few minor adjustments he proclaimed, "They fit like a charm."

Bill drew the guns and tested them for balance, heft and trigger pull weight. He slid them in and out of their holsters several times to get the feel of their draw. The pistols turned out to be *Colt Firearms* new double action 45 caliber revolvers.

Each revolving cylinder had chambers for six bullets. The bodies of the guns were burnished dark iron to control possible reflection.

"Mel, these are beyond belief. What can I say except thank you! They will always be with me to remind me of your courage in meeting life head on."

"That brings me to the second reason I wanted to see you." Reaching down to the floor on the other side of his chair he brought up a Henry repeating rifle in a scabbard of soft leather. The scabbard had twenty cartridge loops along its side. "Your Sharps Carbine is a fine gun, but it doesn't have the range or the striking power one needs in wide open spaces. This is my wedding present to you. I exercised my prerogative and had my gunsmith replace the spring so many have had trouble with on this model."

Bill was fascinated with this new weapon. He took the magazine out and then worked the lever action to make sure it wasn't loaded. Next, he checked the ejection mechanism. He looked it over thoroughly and exclaimed it, "Imagine 16, 44 caliber shots in the magazine and one in the chamber, 17 shots before you have to reload. Wow, what a beautiful rifle. I believe there is a sharpshooter's scope that can be mounted on it too."

"Here is a box of 44 cartridges for the Henry and a box of 45 cartridges for the Colts. I figure a gun's not worth much without ammo. Good luck to you and Patsy. May God bless you and keep you. Oh, by the way, Mel Jr. has been pestering me for a gun. I think it is time for him to learn the ins and outs of handling one. I was wondering if there would be any problem if you were to leave your Sharps Carbine for him."

"What a great idea. Its weight and size make it an ideal gun for a young person to learn with. I wish I were going to be here to teach him. Blair, you and Mel will have to teach him the army way of dealing with guns."

"Thanks, and now get out of here so I can get back to work."

Bill left all his gifts in his room before he returned to find Patsy going back through the pile of clothes, he had thought she had decided to take with her. Patsy explained there wasn't enough room in her trunk for all of these to fit. Thus, the sorting process had started all over again.

Finally, the pile was down so it all fit. It was locked and they carried it out to the porch. Zeke was to pick it up later and take it to the express office to be sent to his parents in St. Paul.

He and Patsy had dinner with the family and then after a while they snuck away for some alone time. This continued until the "bed do us part thing."

The next day was equally busy as the details of the wedding and celebration were resolved. Late in the day. Patsy said, "I am tired of all work. I would like to have some fun this evening. There is a social and dance at the church. It would give me an opportunity to say "goodbye" to some of my friends. Would that be ok with you Bill?"

"Sure, if you don't go off dancing with all the handsome boys and leave me hanging on the wall, a wallflower in a foreign land." he said with a smirk and a wink

"First, I don't see you hanging on the wall alone. I see you more as a pot of honey attracting all the lady bees to buzz around you vying for your attention. Second. I am not taking any chances that one of those lady bees uses "black magic" to steal you away."

"Never fear you're to dear to me for that to happen." So, they picked up their boots went to the dance. Patsy and Bill danced together like they had done this every day of their lives. Patsy's friends came by in a steady stream to say goodbye to Patsy and good luck to them both.

One incident did mar the evening a little. A local guy, drunk and delusional, proclaimed that Patsy was his girl, and no one was taking her away from him. He started pestering Bill to fight. Finally, frustrated with being ignored he swung at Bill. It was too slow and awkward to be a problem. Bill grabbed the guy's arm and twisted it behind his back while getting his other arm around his attacker's neck in a headlock. It was a very polished move Bill had used many times in his wrestling matches with his Indian friends. It neutralized the guy completely. The guy's friends came and collected him while apologizing for his behavior.

Bill and Patsy left the dance soon after the scrum. When they reached Patsy's door she said, "I am so glad this is the last time going to bed will come between us." They kissed and she slipped into her room.

The next morning Bill helped Duane move in with Blair. Nothing was going to come between Bill and Patsy to night.

Chapter 15

Love and Marriage

The wedding invitations would have read that the marriage of Bill and Patsy would take place at the Episcopal Church at 10 A. M. on the 9th of May 1865 but there were no invitations sent. The original plan was for a simple, family only ceremony, but when the news got out the crush of pressure from the community forced an open-door policy. There was a crowd already gathering when the wedding party got to the church about 9 o'clock. Dick and Dave had been drafted to act as ushers. On seeing the size of the waiting crowd, John and Zeke volunteered to help. By the time the ceremony started the church was packed. There were even people outside who couldn't force their way in.

Patricia had supervised the decorating of the church. She had worked her magic on the flower arrangements which became the stars of the wedding.

Everybody who managed to make it into the church praised how beautifully decorated it was.

The Minister entered through a side door into the sanctuary. At his appearance, the organ started playing, "The Battle Hymn of the Republic" in honor of the returning soldiers involved in the ceremony. Bill, with the Best Men followed the minister through the door and marched to their places at the Altar to open the ceremony. Mel Jr., Duane and Blair had been drafted into the role of groomsmen.

Mel Jr. had on a white shirt and bow tie, his best going to church clothes. He was a stark contrast to Bill, Duane, and Blair in their new Farm and Ranch outfits. The three of them made a crescendo of color as they stood next to each other in their blue jeans and multicolored plaid shirts. To be honest, they looked more like stand-ins drafted off the street to fill in for missing members of the cast.

The organ changed its tune to the hymn, "A Closer Walk with Thee" as Dick and Dave escorted Patricia down the aisle to her seat in the first pew. Patricia was in an elegant silk dress. It was slightly off white, with a subtle pink cast to it. A beautiful corsage was on her shoulder. She stood out in stark contrast her escorts who were in their Farm and Ranch get up. Their dress did relieve some of the heat on the groom and best men in their outfits.

Milly, Drue and John's youngest daughter had become bridesmaids in the expanded production. They walked down the aisle in a procession that almost made you forget (for a little bit) Bill and his friend's clothes. Each of them had on a simple, flowery, spring dress. There was lace at the neck, the arm holes and hem. Each carried a bouquet of flowers that augmented the dress and made the apparel quite stunning. The dresses had been produced by John's wife, Liza. She had burned the midnight candle to finish them on time.

The organ broke into a rousing rendition of "Here Comes the Bride." Artie in his Sunday church clothes was waiting at the top of the aisle for this moment. As ring bearer his job was to lead the bride and her escort down the aisle to the Alter. He hesitated with a little case of stage fright as he looked at the packed church. Dave bent down and encouraged him. This got him started with the wedding ring balanced on a pillow. His struggle to keep the ring from falling off the pillow was just what the ceremony needed to dial down the tension. Artie took his place at the altar next to Mel Jr.

Following Artie were Mel and Patsy. Mel had insisted on walking Patsy down to the Altar. He was the only male in the ceremony with a suit on. He was beaming from ear to ear as he shuffled along with his crutch on one side and his hand holding Patsy's hand in his other. You could tell he was almost in tears as he reached the Altar and gave Patsy's hand to Bill, then he turned and took his seat next to Patricia. What you didn't know from watching was if the tears were for the joy of the wedding, or the joy of walking his daughter to the Altar, or the joy of being able to walk at all given the severity of his wound. The people who knew Mel best would bet without hesitation it was a combination of all three.

Patsy was beautiful standing at the altar holding Bill's hand. She had gone traditional in selecting her outfit. She wore her mother's wedding dress with her new riding boots, a blue silk hanky in her bodice and a borrowed red rose in her hair. Patsy was so stunning, that after the ceremony nobody could remember how out of place Bill and his friends looked.

Bill stood there entranced with Patsy while the Minister conducted the ceremony. He finally joined the party when the minister whispered, "It's time to put the ring on her finger Bill."

Bill reached for the ring and knocked it off the pillow. Artie said in a disappointed voice loud enough to be heard in the far corners of the church, "I didn't drop it!"

Bill immediately put his hand on Artie's head and spoke up, "Everybody here knows you did a perfect job as ring bearer today. I was the clumsy ox who knocked the ring to the floor." Mel Jr. touched Bills arm and held out the ring to him.

Bill took it and slid it on Patsy's finger and said, "With this ring I thee wed."

The minister said, "I now pronounce you man and wife, "You can kiss the bride now." Bills kiss was tender and loving. When the couple turned to the audience the minister said, "May I introduce Mr. and Mrs. Wilbur Cheever!"

The audience applauded its approval.

When the clapping ended the minister announced, "The family would like you to join them at a reception in the church basement to celebrate the marriage of Bill and Patsy. It should be ready for your pleasure right now."

A reception had been scheduled in Plan A (family only) to begin at one o'clock in the afternoon. When this large crowd showed up, John's family had gone from being guests to being caterers. Liza and the girls looked at the supplies on hand and decided that they would serve split pea soup with chunks of ham, ham sandwiches and desert. A couple of the girls found a vat in the church kitchen, filled it with water and put it on the stove to heat. Two of the older boys went to the store and brought back a sack of dried peas. Still others went to the bakery and brought all the sandwich bread they had on hand. On the way back to the church they picked up a couple of crocks of butter and an assortment of condiments. As the need for ushering died down Zeke took the wagon to the factory and loaded it with all the supplies it could hold. He was back at the church by about 10:30. His sisters had come up with quite a spread out of the supplies that were there for the now canceled one o'clock reception. Zeke was put to work slicing ham for the sandwiches. The girls immediately started working on the new supplies. Believe it or not they fed that whole crowd.

The whole cast of characters in the mornings drama ate leftovers when the crowd was gone. John's girls had done a magnificent job so that even the leftovers were fit for the finest of Royal Courts.

The prescription for the afternoon was rest and relax so they could not only survive the evening's festivities but even enjoy them. Patsy and Bill lay on the bed in each other's arms. The bed could not separate them again. They were enjoying their togetherness and talking quietly about their future. A knock on the door woke them and a voice said, "Five o'clock, show time in an hour."

The celebration started at six with Mel's welcome home ceremony. Mel climbed the stairs to the stage holding Patricia's hand to steady him. Already seated on the stage were his immediate family and the five escorts. Patsy and Bill sat together holding hands. Bill recognized many of the people who had met them at the station when they had first arrived in town plus many of the people who attended the wedding. It was an impressive turnout.

Mel held up his hands asking for quite. The crowded responded to his request and settled down. "Ladies and gentlemen, it is with a great deal of pleasure that I am here among you at this shindig. We advertised this as a homecoming party for me, but it has become much more than that. This has become a celebration of life. Let me explain why I say that. During the war, a spent cannon ball sneaked upon a group of officers as they watched a battle unfolding in a field in front of them. Luckily, all of them were able to avoid the ball except one. That one was me. The ball mangled my right foot and my left leg from the knee down. The surgeons had to amputate both my foot and my leg. I was devastated by prospect of being a cripple the rest of my life. I was wallowing in self-pity when these five guys came into my life." (He gestured toward the five escorts.) "They taught me that life doesn't end until you give up on it. They carved me a wooden foot and figured out how to attach it to my ankle. With that foot and a crutch, I get around well enough. They brought me home to the warmth and love of my wife and family. These five, by their friendship have restored my mental balance and my future. Friends can't do much more than that for each other. Would you please help me thank these five with a rousing round of applause."

The crowd answered Mel with thunderous ovation of applause and cheers. While the five appreciated the accolades, they also felt a little embarrassed by the attention they were receiving.

When the applause died down Mel said, "Thank you! Now it's time to change the subject. Today, as most of you know, the leader of this squad of soldiers married our eldest daughter. May I introduce Mr. and Mrs. Wilbur Cheever." (he motioned for Bill and Patsy to stand up) "Their courtship and marriage have been on the fast track because they are leaving for Bill's home in St. Paul tomorrow morning. Please wish them a good life together and God speed in their travels." A polite applause acknowledge his announcement.

"How go whoop it up! Enjoy the music and refreshments. Thanks for coming to our party." The crowd drifted off to start their night of merriment.

A group of people gathered around Mel and Patricia to wish him well and ask her how it felt to have him home again. Likewise, a group stopped to talk with Patsy and Bill. Blair, Dick, Dave and Duane wondered off looking for a cold beer.

The bands were at each ends of the street. One was playing square dances. The caller had a foghorn voice that could be heard for blocks around. The other band was playing waltzes, polkas and such. Bill and Patsy finally made it to the dance floor to enjoy a waltz together. Free beer had cast its spell and the throng was in a mellow mood. It was around nine o'clock before Bill and Patsy were able to slip away.

Hand in hand they walked back to the Armour house. Patsy stop at her bedroom door, "I'll be with you in a minute or two. "

Bill went to their room and was ready when the rap on the door came, "Come in."

The door opened revealing a vision of loveliness. Now Bill could see what else was in the bag when they left the women's store. The dresses' bodice was white silk, open down the front to just above the navel revealing a lot of skin. The roundness and fullness of the exposed portion of her breasts beckoned him to touch them, fondle them and cover them with kisses. The white lace covering the bodice made the vision even more alluring to him. The dresses' skirt was made of the same fine, white silk and covered with the same white lace.

Each felt a little awkward with their thoughts of what they knew was coming next. Bill kissed Patsy tenderly and they worked their emotions up to frenzied pitch before they consummated their marriage.

They lay in each other's arms, sated. exhausted and content in their love for each other.

Chapter 16
Welcome Home

Their goodbyes had been said, their tears of joy and sorrow shed, their handshakes and hugs were history now as their train moved toward St. Paul.

It had been a busy morning. Carryon bags had to be packed, breakfast eaten, and everyone transported to the train station. John and Zeke had driven the two wagons that had brought the families down to the train.

When the families got to the station, the platform was already full of well-wishers and passengers. They joined the waiting crowd.

Each of the travelers hugged the women and kids, shook hands with acquaintances and gave men hugs as appropriate. They gave Mel and Patricia special attention thanking them for their hospitality wishing them well. Liza had given each of the travelers a bag lunch, a hug and a gods speed. The travelers returned the affection she was giving them. The friends had felt a deep sense of loss as they said goodbye to Blair and Mel. Their "Good Luck" and "Good Life" wishes were from the heart as they shook hands as they parted at the train. They all waved a last farewell as they climbed the coach's steps and disappeared.

The train was coming from Omaha, through Kansas City and into Des Moines. By the time it arrived in Des Moines it was almost filled so the group could not find seats together. Bill and Patsy were together (of course) in a coach one car closer to the locomotive then Dick, Dave and Duane.

Patsy and Bill were dressed in their new western look clothes. Bill looked a little like he was going to war instead of returning from one. His new holsters and guns were situated on his hips. In his left hand he carried the Henry rifle in its scabbard. His other personal effects were in the knapsack on his back. In his right hand he grasp the bag with his and Patsy's lunch in it. He didn't scrutinize the people in the car as per his habits. His entire attention was on Patsy

Patsy leaned her head on Bill's shoulder and said, "It's hard to leave the people you love and have spent all your life with."

"Are you regretting your choice to marry me and start a new life of our own?"

The engineer blew the whistle twice and released the brakes. The drive wheels screeched on the rails until they took a hold and the train lurched a couple of times before it moved smoothly down the track on its way to St. Paul.

Over the din Bill heard, "Oh no! Please don't get that idea. I've never been happier in my life than I'm this moment with my head resting on your shoulder and knowing you will always be there for me. Last night was fantastic, you were so sweet and gentle that I fell in love with you all over again."

"Good, my master plan for keeping you with me for the rest of my life is working." he said with a satisfied smile.

"How long will it take to get to St. Paul?"

"About ten hours I think."

The door on their car opened and the conductor entered. "**Tickets please, tickets.**" As he collected tickets, he announced there has been a new development in the war over night. "**The Confederate President, Jefferson Davis was captured by a Union cavalry outfit in Georgia last night. His wife and what remained of his cabinet were captured with him.**" With that he finished the ticket collection and left the car.

The passengers broke out in individual conversations that filled the car with a babble of undecipherable noise. As the excitement waned, so did the noise and people returned to their previous conversations.

"Do your parents know you're coming home today; with a new wife?"

"Yup, I wired them yesterday right after the wedding and they wired their congratulations back. I would have told you about it, but things were moving so fast; I couldn't find time for that. I did have them rent a room in a nearby hotel for tonight. I am not ready to take any chances on anything coming between us again." They both chuckled at their little shared joke.

"I am sure mom will have a meal ready for us. We more than likely won't be able to get away to go to the hotel until sometime late tonight. I am not worried about mom and dad liking you, but I am a little concerned about what your opinion of them will be. They are pretty old time."

"I am going to love them. After all, they brought you into the world for me." They kissed in agreement. Their conversation continued. It delved into all the unknown nooks and crannies of their previous lives. They had a lot to learn about each other since their courtship and marriage had been in double time. They started with the many aspects of what each wanted out of life/marriage.

About noon they opened the lunch bag to see

what delights awaited them there. The appetizer was a small tray of Deviled Eggs and some crackers. The entrée was ham between fresh baked slices of bread lathed in that fit for a king mustard sauce and dill pickles on the side. Dessert was two wedding cup-cakes, one with her on it and the other labeled him. The feast was fully sampled and appreciated. After lunch they returned to their hopes and dreams of the future.

Suddenly it seemed the conductor's call of, **"Five minutes to St. Paul."** caught them completely by surprise. They gathered up their carryon stuff and were ready when the train came to a stop at the station. They joined the line waiting to exit.

Eventually they made it to the station platform where they met Dick, Dave and Duane. It was time for parting again. Bill and the three of them had shared multiple trials and formed strong bonds of friendship that would last their lifetimes. Still their parting was the traditional round of hand shaking, well-wishing and I'll see you again.

Dave left for the streetcar depot to catch a ride to Stillwater. Duane entered the station to find out when his train to Eau Claire would be leaving. Dick, Bill and Patsy walk around the station together. Dick found a bench where he could wait for his ride to Carver. They parted after another quick goodbye.

Bill and Patsy left to look for their ride. Bill spotted his dad parked at the curb in front of the station. Dad was in a spiffy surrey, fringe and all, and a nice-looking team of Bays. Bill wondered where he had gotten that rig. As soon as Bill and Patsy were in the coach, Bill said, "Patsy this my dad, James Cheever, dad, this is Patricia Armour, my wife."

Bill's dad snapped his whip over the bays, and they pulled into Kellogg Boulevard. "Pleased to meet you Patricia," dad said over his shoulder, perhaps with a little more edge than he intended.

Patsy said, "Pleased to meet you Mr. Cheever. That was awkward for me. Sir, how would you prefer I address you? I would like to be called Patsy myself."

"Please call me dad or pops Patsy, if those are not too uncomfortable for you."

"Pops or dad it is then. Thanks for accepting my state of confusion and clearing it up for me."

Bill, seeing this as a meeting going wrong broke into their conversation, "Are you still working at that stable?"

"Actually Bill, I bought it about a year ago." They were now climbing up Summit Avenue past a large Catholic Church."

"That's great! How is the business doing?"

"Just great! I've been able to get sound horses from some of our old neighbors out in the valley and sell them here at a nice profit. Here we are." The surrey came to a stop in front of a neat little house with an office attached. Behind the house, a sprawling stable and plenty of pens were visible.

"You and Patsy go in and say hello to ma. I'll put the team away and be right in."

Bill jumped down and then helped Patsy down. They walked hand and hand toward the front door. Patsy said, "Sorry Bill! I don't think I made a particularly good impression on your dad."

"You did fine. Just try to relax and enjoy. If you get uncomfortable pinch me and we'll get out of here A.S.A.P. I've known dad gets a little uptight around strangers. He'll be fine when he gets a chance to sort it out."

"Thanks Bill. I'll be ok." Bill knocked on the door and it flew open and an exceptionally large woman flew into Bills arms. She dwarf him as she covered his face with kisses and said, "Thank God you are home safe and sound from that terrible war." She had an impressive stature, over six feet tall, broad shoulders and impressive stout body. She needed to find several feed sacks with the same print on them if she were going to make a sack dress for herself. She wore her gray hair in a bun. At night when she let her hair down it reached below her knees. Her face showed the ravages of time with its many creases.

Turning to Patsy she said, "Is this the girl who captured your heart and wouldn't let it go? I can see why, she is beautiful. Come in my dear, welcome to our family."

"Mom, this is my wife, formerly Patricia Armour. She prefers to be addressed as Patsy. Patsy, this is my mother, Nellie Cheever, I've never called her anything but mom so I don't know what she would prefer to be called."

"Well, I like to be called mom. It makes me feel important, like I still have my job in life. If you don't mind, I'd like you to call me mom."

"I would love to call you mom. Thank you for accepting me in your family."

"I wonder where that old man is, dinner is ready."

""I'll go look him up." Bill said as he stepped out the back door. He saw a lantern light in one of the stalls. He headed that way and found dad rubbing down one of the bays. "Hello dad. Has the other one had his rub yet?"

The other bay was munching on hay patiently waiting his turn. "Not yet son."

Bill grabbed a gunny sack off the stall fence and started rubbing him down. With the two of them pitching in they finish in a minute or so. "Shall we go in? Mom says dinner's ready."

"Just a minute. I hope I didn't hurt Patsy's feelings.

I was a little sharp with her. I'll blame it on driving in downtown traffic but there really isn't any excuse. She seems like a sweet, sensitive girl."

"She is dad. But she is also one of the strongest and most resilient people I've ever met. She won't hold it against you if you don't continue with it. My advice is that you apologize to her, not me. That might do you some good that talking to me won't."

They had started walking across the yard as they talked and now stopped at the bench on the back porch. There was a bucket of water, a wash basin and a bar of homemade soap on the bench. Hanging on pegs above the bench were towels made from rough cloth. The water was cold and bracing as they scrubbed their face, their hands and toweled off. Cleaned up, they entered the kitchen.

The aroma was of good, old fashioned food with a hint of baking smell for seasoning. A covered dish was being kept warm on the back of the stove. Mom came to the kitchen door and beckoned them into the next room. Patsy was there with a rosy face. Bill thought she's had a chance to wash up too.

When Patsy saw Bill's dad, she emit an audible "Oh!" then tried to hide her surprise. He wasn't a big man when compared to his son or wife but anybody who had ever work with him would testify, it was nearly impossible to keep pace with him. Today he was dressed in his finest. Clean bib overalls with a red bandana in his bib pocket, denim shirt and polished brogans. His bare head was almost that with only wispy, white hair on it. His face was strong and clean shaven. The skin on his face was wrinkled and about the color of well-tanned leather. The feature of his face that people remembered and was surly what Patsy had reacted to was his empty left eye socket.

Patsy apologized, "I am sorry, I was taken by surprise."

Bill cut in and said, "I should have told you about it, but I'm so used to it now I forget it."

"Forget it Patsy, you're not the first to react to it nor do I expect you will be the last. Accidents happen and this was just that. I was working at a sawmill one day when an errant wood chip flipped off the saw and stuck in my eye. The sawmill doctor removed the damaged eyeball and sewed the lids together. The only time it is a bother any more is when the empty socket cries for its missing eyeball and I have to wipe it with my bandana."

The missing eye trauma over, Mom stood at the table with her hands on the back of the chair closest to the kitchen door. She said, "Jim and I usually sit on this end of the table, next to each other so we can talk but for this meal, I thought maybe we should all set opposite each other so we can all talk to one another."

She then waved Bill and Patsy to sides of the table while dad moved to its end. Everybody but mom sat at their designated places. Mom disappeared into the kitchen. Soon Patsy joined her.

The table was set with what Bill knew to be mom's best dishes. They were the China porcelain dishes with a petite flower pattern. They were only used when the guests were important people. Their presence on the table was a definite tell of the high importance his mom and dad were placing on the return of their son and the meeting of his new bride.

"May I help you?"

"Would you mind serving the coffee?"

"Not at all."

"Careful, it's pretty heavy."

Patsy lifted the pot, "This is a load." she said with a grunt as she disappeared into the dining area. On returning she found a bowl of warm buns just out of the oven to deliver while mom took the covered dish off the stove.

Bill looked at the covered dish and said, "Mom, you didn't?"

"Yes, I did. What would your homecoming be if I didn't make it special with Shepherd's Pie?" Mom said to Patsy, "This has been Bill's favorite, special meal since he was a youngster. I don't remember how it started but somehow it's become the meal I always fix when he returns from being away." The cloth came off exposing a golden-brown layer of mashed potatoes. As the mashed potatoes were pierced by the spoon, a medley of mixed garden vegetables came into view with just a hint of the ground beef layer it covered.

Mom said, "Patsy, have you ever had Shepherd's Pie before?" This started the small talk for the evening.

Chapter 17
Catching Up

"Not that I can remember. This is delicious. Will you give me your recipe so I can try to keep this wonderful tradition going?"

"I certainly will. I'll write it out and have it for you next time you come by. Do you like to cook?"

"Yes, I do. I haven't had much of a chance to cook because at home we always had a kitchen staff."

As they ate, Patsy's satisfied their curiosity about her life before Bill. They asked her about her likes and dislikes; her hobbies; her friends; etc.

Mom said, "We really appreciate you sharing all of this with us. I hope you would forgive us if we asked questions that seem pushy or nosy. Our only nosiness is our desire to get to know you better. "

Bill added, "That helped me too. We've never talked about that part of our previous lives."

Patsy's reply was "I didn't mind at all. I appreciate your interest."

Mom replied, "I have a feeling that you are going to be a blessing in all our lives. I think it's time to have dessert. Patsy will you refresh our coffee please?"

"Yes mom." She smiled as she realized the growing bond between her and Bill's mother.

Talk stopped while the table was cleared, and apple pie was served.

During dessert, Bill asked, "What about the family back in Pennsylvania. Has anyone been killed or hurt since Bud's son Jacob died fighting General Lee's army at Antietam?" asked Bill.

Patsy broke in, "I didn't know you had family in Pennsylvania. How many brothers and sisters do you have Bill?"

"I have three brothers and five sisters. Mom do you know how many grandkids and great grandkids there are now?"

"There are 72 grandchildren and 24 great-grandchildren, with a couple of more on the way."

Dad took over to answer Bill's question, "Yes! Paul's son Bob was killed in a futile attempt to stop the Rebs from robbing the bank during Lee's Gettysburg campaign. After killing Bob, the Rebs mauled Paul when he wouldn't give the robbers the combination to the bank vault. His clerk saved his life by giving those Rebs what they wanted. It took about a year for Paul to recover. Even now he has a limp."

"The last two family casualties both occurred at Gettysburg, they were Burr's sons, Jack and Ralph. In early afternoon on the second day of the battle for Little Round Top, General Hancock was riding along the Union defense line when he found a gaping hole in it. A whole division had been advanced out of the line to take up weak, exposed positions in a wheat field in front of where they should have been. There wasn't time for Hancock to move them back into the line because the rebels were already attacking and rolling the out of place division up.

The General found the only men available to plug the gap was an undersized regiment of about 270 men under a Colonel Colville, commander of the 1st Minnesota Volunteer Regiment. The General explained to the Colonel what he needed. He ordered the Colonel to take his regiment and perform an act that amounted to suicide. He was to take his 270 men and stop a Brigade of about 2500 Mississippians from getting up Little Round Top until the general could find enough men to plug the hole in the defense line. The General pointed out that holding the Rebs or not would decide who would win the battle. Colonel Colville led those Minnesotans in a gutsy charge that stopped the Rebs in their tracks and the line was plugged. Ralph was killed as his Pennsylvania regiment took part in the counterattack to plug that hole in the Union defensive line. Jack was hit by a snipers bullet shortly before Pickets charge on the third day of fighting. He has fully recovered now."

Dad asked Bill how he managed to get transportation home so soon after the end of the war?

"Just dumb luck that almost became a disaster." Bill told about the train robbery attempt and his meeting with Mel, how he picked the squad to carry Mel's stretcher and the horror of the Sultana tragedy. He lauded the work of his squad in finding the raft of debris, the effort they put into loading Mel on the raft and the joy they felt at the sight of the Bostonia No 2.

He talked about Blair's carving of a wooden foot for Mel and how that foot helped Mel have a more positive outlook for the future. He told them John's story and all the other events that occurred in Des Moines, including Patsy and his quickie courtship and wedding.

In the end, the conversation turned to the Sioux War. Bill asked, "Where were you two when hostilities broke out?"

Dad told their story, "We were in our bed sound asleep. It was right around dawn when we were awakened by banging on the front door. Somebody was shouting, Getup! Getup! The Indians are revolting against the whites! Mom and I jumped out of bed. While mom dressed, I pulled my pants on and went to the door. I opened it and there was Fox Feather with the one you call Erect Bear. I asked them, what was going on."

"Fox Feather told us that a bunch of braves and chiefs were headed toward the government warehouse to demand the past due payment for the land they had ceded to the settlers."

At this point in his tale dad editorialized; "This money had become a major factor in the financial support of the Minnesota Sioux tribes. I knew the payment was due in the spring but the word going around was that the government was having trouble getting it together because of the expense of financing the bigger war, the war you were fighting in. The most ironic thing about this whole situation, as we learned afterwards, was that the money had arrived at Fort Ridgely the day before the Indian's ultimatum and the start of the Sioux uprising."

"Fox Feather went on to tell us the Indian chiefs didn't care why the payments weren't there as promised, they only cared that their people were starving. He said the chiefs were fed up with the stalling that had taken place the last couple of months. The chiefs had been to the upper agency often during the spring and summer and their pleas had been dismissed every time. They had tried to reason with the traders and Indian agent to release the supplies their people needed so desperately, promising the payment would be made when the money arrived. The traders refused."

Dad editorialized again; "It's interesting to note that the lower agency tribes made the same request and the traders there distributed the supplies. Still the uprising spread to that agency as braves from there entered the war."

Before dad continued the story, Bill asked, "Weren't there soldiers guarding the warehouse?"

"There were." was the response he got. "This time that won't matter." Fox Feather said, "The chiefs promised their hungry people they would take the supplies if they weren't given peacefully."

Dad took a sip of coffee before he continued. "Fox Feather told us, he, Erect Bear and Bold Otter had a powwow of their own. They decided they were honor bound by the oath they made to you when you left for the war. They said they had sworn they would take care of us if we should need help. Their concern for our safety had brought them to our door that morning. They had decided that the only safe place for us was St. Paul. They said they were committed to escorting us to a place where we could reach that haven. I asked where Bold Otter was, and Fox Feather said he was watching their back trail to avoid being taken by surprise. He told us to get what we needed and could carry a long way. He also urged us to make it fast because they did not know when war parties would be sent out. He asked if we had moccasins. We said we did, and he said we should wear them. A careless or young brave might not recognize a moccasin print made by a white, but no one would miss a shoe or boot print."

"Your mom picked out what she thought we should save, and we divided the burden evenly for carrying. We all hurried through the door and Bold Otter joined us. Fox Feather took the lead with mom and I next, Erect Bear followed us to help if the need should arise and Bold Otter came last so he could watch our back trail."

"We hurried north at a rapid pace. An hour later, we came to the steep bank down to the Redwood River. We were several miles west of the falls, but Fox Feather led us to some rapids with big rocks that let us cross without getting our feet wet."

Bill injected the comment, "I have crossed the river at those rapids."

Dad continued his tale. "An hour or so later we came to the Minnesota River Valley. Our guides led us on a long walk diagonally down the slope to the riverbank. They chose this spot because they knew some canoes were hidden there. We were sweating by now as the cool of the early morning gave away to the noon day sun. Under the direction of Fox Feather, mom got into the middle position of one canoe. I was told to take a paddle and sit in the stern of a second canoe. Then Fox Feather and Bold Otter pushed off in the canoe with mother in it and began to paddle across the river. Erect Bear pushed off our canoe and took the bow position so he could power and steer it at the same time. My job was to simply supply as much power as I could muster. The Indians paddled mom across, and erect Bear and I followed. We landed and put our crafts with some others already stored there. I felt safer with the river behind us and forest all around us to hide in."

"However, Fox Feather did not hesitate. He immediately led us away from the river and up the river valley's slope. At the top of the river's bluff the trail entered a dense forest, He taught us to walk on the trails fringe of grass, gently pushing hanging branches of the bushes growing along the trail aside rather than walk on them or in the middle of the trail. I know mom and I were slowing your friends down, but they adopted their pace to ours without one indication of irritation. As the sun dropped down to midafternoon Fox Feather changed our direction by gently pushing a bush's branches up and tip toeing around its base to its other side. He motioned us to do the same. He then set out on a zig zag path away from the trail we had been following. He found a well camouflaged hollow under some trees and called a halt until night."

"I believe this halt was for me and mom because we were beginning to stumble along. Your friends took out some jerky and we each had a piece to gnaw on. Your mom and I went to sleep and didn't wake up until Fox Feather shook us. We each received another piece of jerky to eat while on the trail."

"We trudged along the trail until early morning light. We had reached the edge of a clearing. From where we were, we could see the spire of a church in Olivia. Fox Feather did not enter the clearing. Instead he wove his way about halfway around its edge and then left it behind as we moved a little north of east."

"I asked Fox Feather why we didn't stop for supplies. He said as far as we know we are not missed nor are we on anybody's mind. The scouts might be watching the towns so we would be taking a chance of being detected if we went into it. "

"A few miles after we passed Olivia, Fox Feather stopped at a shade tree surrounded by brush. Around the base of the tree was a depression that would keep

us out of sight unless someone were looking directly down on us. He told us we would rest here until
dark."

"Mom distributed some rolls she had brought
along and each of us had a piece of jerky provided
by your friends. We slept comfortably until dark and
then started out fresh with another piece of jerky to
gnaw on."

"The moon was past its zenith when we reached
Hutchinson and turned east-south-east toward
Carver. We were sure we could catch a riverboat
bound for St. Paul there."

"The woods were thick, but a road had been
cut through the forest, so we made good time. We
stopped to rest at daylight. We weren't worried about
the Indians anymore, but we were concerned about
some trigger-happy settler seeing our guides and
opening fire first and asking questions after it was
too late."

"At darkness we started out again. I think it was
about three o'clock by the time we reached a point
near Carver. Fox Feather said, just keep following
this trail and you will come to a valley with Carver at
its bottom. It shouldn't take you more than an hour
or two to get there from here. Please tell Bill when
you see him, we did all we could for you."

"I told them I certainly would tell you of their

help. I thanked them and said to them, you have been true friends to are son when we, his parents needed it most. I clasped forearms with each of them and said thank you. Mom gave each of them a kiss on the cheek. In parting I said, "May the sunshine light your path and warm your back all the days of your life."

"Our guides left us then. They told us they were going north until things quieted down. Mom and I waited until full daylight before we walked to Carver's wharf to hitch a ride down the river. We landed safe and sound in St. Paul, thanks to your friends."

Dad continued, "After the uprising ended, Mom and I appeared before the war tribunal to vouch for those tried and true friends of yours. They were acquitted of any wrong doings. The war tribunal recommend that over three hundred braves and chiefs hang for the crimes they allegedly committed during the uprising. President Lincoln reduced that number to forty. Thirty-eight of them were hanged together in Mankato on December 26, 1862. The two Dakota chiefs condemned but not hung with the other 38 escaped to Canada after the war. They were captured this summer and are now awaiting trial at Fort Snelling. They are Shakopee also known as Little Six and Medicine Bottle."

"Acts of Congress in February and March 1863 revoked all treaties between the United States of

America and the Minnesota Sioux Tribes. This means the Federal government usurped the land the Indians ceded by canceling the payments they agreed to pay for it. In addition, the two strips of land along the Minnesota River that were the reservations have now been confiscated. "

"In May 1863 over 1,300 women, children and acquitted non-combatants were sent on river boats and barges down the Mississippi and up the Missouri to a place in South Dakota that has been designated, Indian Territory. This Indian Territory stretches from the Canadian Border in the north to the Red River in Texas to the south and from Nebraska to the mountains. As you might remember, Indian Territory has consistently been pushed across the country in front of the wave of settlers. Where the exiles might be now is anybody's guess."

"That is ridiculous," said Bill. "With all the chaos and barbarism in the War Between the States, only one notable Confederate leader has been tried and executed. That is the man who was the commandant of the infamous Andersonville P. O. W. camp, Captain Henry Wirz. Some obvious criminals such as General Nathan Bedford Forrest who was in command at Fort Pillow when his troops murdered every Negro in the fort's garrison, some after they had surrendered, is free to continue spreading his hate to the people of the South. Both the Sioux uprising and the North/South war are glaring examples of the uncivility of every war. I guess it should be an expected result that even civilized people are capable of uncivil acts in war."

"Amen." The chorus replied.

"On a happier note, now that the hostiles in Minnesota are a thing of the past, what are you and mom thinking about your future?"

"Now that the uprising is over, and the valley is safe your mom and I don't know what to do with our old place. We still hold the deed for it. We went back once to salvage anything of value that might have survived. Nothing had been disturbed. However, the Carlsons, the next place west was burned to the ground and the family massacred."

Bill said, "I remember them. They were always giving the Indians trouble about using that old trail to the river."

"By the time, the hostilities were essentially done, we had established ourselves here. I can't imagine us ever going back."

Dad had been watching his audience getting sleepier and sleepier. He knew Nellie had a fretful day worrying about this evening. Her relief that it gone off well allowed her to relax and she was getting sleepy. He also notices Bill and Patsy yawning behind their hands. He thought, *'They have had a long eventful day with Patsy's leaving home, the ten-hour train ride and the stress of our meeting each other for the first time'*. He said, "I am tired. I must be getting old. I haven't talked this much in years. Our conversations did make me remember a letter from the army that came for you about a week ago. I'll get it for you." He went into another room and came back shortly with an envelope. "Here, some midnight reading for you. I left a horse and buggy out front for you to use. Your hotel is a new one. Just go south on Snelling until you reach Grand Avenue. You can't miss it"

Goodnights were said. Bill and Patsy found the hotel right where they were told it would be. Bill left the rig with the hotel's hostler and joined Patsy in the hotel lobby. After checking in they found their room with their luggage waiting for them. Patsy said, "It has been so long since our last kiss that my lips are having withdrawal symptoms."

"Well look out babe because here comes a smack-a-duesy." With that he grabbed her, squeezed her and planted along, passionate kiss on her lips until she was gasping for air. "There are your lips complaining now?"

"Only that those are too few and far between."

"Well we will have to take care of that as soon as we find out what the army's after now." He ripped the envelope open and started to read.

"Dear Sergeant–Major Cheever.

*It is with great pleasure that I write you regard-
ing money you earned by your decisive action
on April 20, 1865 near Tuscaloosa, Alabama
on the train from Atlanta, Georgia. On behalf
of a grateful Government and the Mississippi,
Alabama & Georgia Railroad, for causing the
death or capture of the majority of the Bart
Simpson Gang. The rewards you are entitled to
collect are as follows:*

Bart Simpson	*Railroad:*	*$1,500*
(Leader)	*Government:*	*$1,000*
Sally Fields	*Railroad:*	*$1,500*
(Lady in Red)	*Government:*	*$1,000*
John Crow	*Railroad:*	*$750*
(Member)	*Government:*	*$500*
George Apple	*Railroad:*	*$750*
(Member)	*Government:*	*$500*
Paul Small	*Railroad:*	*$750*
(Member)	*Government:*	*$500*
Angel Ramos	*Railroad:*	*$750*
(Member)	*Government:*	*$ 00*

Total: $10,000

Show this to the paymaster at any U.S. Installation to collect your reward.

Signed: Captain U. R. Rich, Provost Marshal, Tuscaloosa, Alabama.

"Patsy, we are RICH!" exclaimed Bill" or at least we will be after tomorrow. Now I know why I thought I knew that guy when he entered the train. I and my men chased that gang around northern Georgia for several months without success. It seemed that every cracker delighted helping him avoid us."

"This calls for a celebration." He promptly grabbed her and said, "We'll start with the kissing problem and work our way up to other things." And they did!

Chapter 18
Now What?

The next morning, they had breakfast together in the hotel coffee shop. Breakfast over Patsy returned to their room to unpack her trunk. With his reward letter and orders in his pocket, and just in case, his Colts in their holsters on his hips and the Henry in the gun rack behind his head, he got in the buggy and left for Fort Snelling. He crossed the Mississippi at the Mill's Ferry in Minneapolis and took Minnehaha Avenue south along the river. The river bluff and valley were heavily wooded, and the trees were in full leaf. It was a beautiful drive. He reached the Fort about an hour after leaving the ferry. He was stopped by the sentries at the gate. After they assured themselves of his identity, they gave him directions to the Commandant's Office. It did not take long for a Sargent there exchange his orders for his discharge papers and a voucher for three months back pay. He was also given directions to the pay-master's office. However, the paymaster did not have 10,000 dollars on hand, so Bill was told to wait while a detail went to fetch the needed cash. He was told the money should be there in a couple of hours.

Bill asked around and was given directions to the rifle range. He planned to use the two hours there to familiarize himself with his new guns. The range was a short way by buggy. The range master saw no prob-lem with his plan and assigned him a spotter.

It took a little time to get used to the double ac-tion mechanism of the colts, but familiarity finally became the norm. Next, he fine-tuned the hammer and trigger pull weights. Last, he filed off the front sight. Most times a pistol is a close-range instinct aimed weapon. Usually there is not enough time to lining up the sight, on a target before you take your shot. Only practice hones the instinct to shoot a pis-tol and hit your target. He ended his work on the 45's by drawing and firing three cylinder loads from each. He was satisfied his performance with his new pis-tols was every bit as good if not slightly better than it had been with his old 44's.

A large added advantage the 45's had over his old 44's was reloading time. With the 45's, exposing the chambers and slipping in the six manufactured cartridges took a fraction of a minute. The old 44's reloading was more complex and time consuming. With those you had to clean the old unburnt power and paper out of the cylinder, then you had to charge the cylinder with fresh powder, paper, shot and ram the cartridge home with the built-in ram rod. No matter how much you practiced it took considerable time to load the six cylinders in one pistol by this routine. With pistol practice done, Bill cleaned, oiled and reloaded them.

Next, he took the Henry from its case. He tweaked its balance a little. He filed a few parts he thought were interfering with the lever loading action. He made the loading action as smooth as a baby's butt. Next, he removed the magazine tube from the rifle's butt and loaded 16 shells in it. He then levered open the chamber and put a 17th bullet in it.

After signaling his spotter, he fired a three-shot group. His target spotter signals a tight pattern, but a little high and to the left. He made a few more adjustments and then fired another group of three. The spotter signaled this group was still a little left of the bullseye. Few more adjustments, three more shots and a check brought the satisfaction of three in the ring at 50 yards. He walked back 50 more yards and shot another grouping of three. Once again, the spotter signaled three in the ring. Again, he walked back 50 yards. Again, he scored three in the ring. He moved back yet another 50 yards. He knew that if a gun shoots true at 200 yards it will shoot true at any distance within its range. After 200 yards, accuracy becomes almost totally a function of the shooter's skill. So, at 200 yards he shot his last two cartridges and levered open the breach to insert another bullet so he could finish the last group of three. The spotter signaled another three in the ring. He was sure now he could hit any target the Henry could reach.

Bill had just finished cleaning, oiling and reloading the rifle when a Private from the paymaster's office came to tell him his money had arrived. He stored the gun in its case and whistled to get his spotters attention. Then the spotter looked his way, Bill, gave him a "Thumbs up!" for his help. He followed the soldier back and collected $10,039 .

After he had the money in his pocket he headed back to the hotel. When he arrived, he immediately deposited the money in the hotel's vault.

With his receipt in hand, he burst into the hotel room dancing a jig and handing Patsy the paperwork. "I am no longer obligated to the government and I bring you riches beyond belief."

Patsy looked at the papers with a look of disbelief on her face and pout forming on her lips, "I suppose now everyone will say I married you for your money!" Then she took his hands in hers and they danced around the room laughing. They ended their dance on the bed kissing. And yes, kissing led to other things just as it is supposed to. After the kissing had its desired effect, the passion was sated, and the dreamy aftermath faded they lay in each other's arms and talked. Bill said, "Now that we can do most anything we want to, what would you like to do?"

"I would like to settle down somewhere and live a normal life with you."

"What does normal mean? Have kids, a house, a garden, neighbors; that kind of normal?"

"I would like all those things accept I don't really want over the fence neighbors; I prefer the down the road type. I would like room for livestock if that's what we decide. Good hunting and fishing nearby would be a plus."

"I know just the place if you will consider it. I suggest we visit the Redwood Falls place I grew up on. It has all the things you listed, plus a small town a handy distance away."

"That sounds ideal. Let's do that as soon as possible."

"Ok. Let's go talk to mom and dad to find out what they think about it."

It took a little while to straighten things out, so they felt presentable. They called for their buggy and it arrived almost immediately. On their drive back to the stable they were excited about the prospect of having their own home.

When they reached the folks home Bill tied the horse to the anchor stone and they knocked on the door. Mom opened the door and said, "There you two are. We wondered what you were up to this fine day. Come in." She gave each a hug as they passed. "I've got some coffee ready on the stove. I'll heat up the leftover Shepherd's Pie and we'll finish the apple pie left from last night. Bill, take the horse and buggy out to the barn and fetch your father for supper."

Bill left but was back shortly with dad in tow. The meal was ready, so they sat down and ate their fill. Table was clean and coffee cups full when, 'out of the blue' mom said, "Your dad and I talked last night. We agreed that we would never consider returning to the Redwood Falls place. Our home is here now. We wondered if you two would consider accepting it as our wedding gift to you. We have never heard what you are planning for your future but if it fits in it, it's yours."

Bill and Patsy exchange astonished looks. Bill said, "Were you two listening in on our thoughts this afternoon? We talked and decided Redwood Falls would be a great place to live. That is a very generous gift."

Dad chimed in, "Then it's a done deal. I'll stop at

the courthouse tomorrow and have the deed trans-ferred into your names. Congratulations, you are about to become homeowners."

"This is our lucky day." said Bill. "Remember that letter you gave me last night? That was a voucher for reward money that was on the heads of those train robbers killed near Tuscaloosa. It amounted to ten thousand dollars; I picked it up this morning when I went for my discharge."

"That is wonderful." said mom.

"Weren't their others in evolved in that fracas who should be entitled to some of that?" asked dad as he wiped his eye socket with his kerchief.

"I can only speculate that I was the only one identified by name and address because of my army records. Whatever the circumstances I've got the money.

"From what I've heard, you deserve it." said mom.

Patsy finally got into the conversation with a question, "Do you know what shape the house in Redwood Falls is in? Does it need any major repairs before we can move in and be comfortable? Mom, will you help me figure out what supplies I should take along when we go there?" They talked into the night about the future, their hopes and dreams.

The next morning after breakfast, mom and Patsy started compiling a list of staples Patsy would need in her new kitchen. The list was a long one. It contained everything you could imagine for the kitchen and every cleaning whatchamacallit ever dragged into any house in the world. Bill and Patsy's loaner rig would be mom and Patsy's transportation for the day. It was tied to the anchor stone in the front of the house for their convenience.

Dad and Bill decided finding an appropriate wagon for their trek to Redwood Falls would be their first priority. Dad hooked up a small roan mare to a buckboard for this day's search. They were ready when dad's two hired hands, Clem and Jack, showed up for work. Dad introduced them to Bill and gave them some last-minute instruction for the day.

That done, Dad and Bill entered the house for a few last words with their wives and a loving kiss. Their goodbyes said, they headed out to visit all the wagon manufacturers, dealers and stables they could locate. By late afternoon, they were very frustrated with their complete lack of success. Then, as luck would have it, they spotted a sign tacked to a fence:

Conestoga Wagon for Sale
Inquire Inside.

The sign was faded and weathered as if it had been hanging there for a long time.

Bill said, "Could it be possible the wagon hasn't been sold yet? That sign has been there for a long time."

"It can't hurt to check. Conestoga is usually a big, sturdy wagon that are built for the purpose you have in mind."

"Let's check it out. It won't take awfully long to find out if it's still available." Bill turned the buckboard into the opening in the fence and to both their surprises the wagon was right there in front of them. It looked to be in good shape except for the canvas cover. The cover was tattered and torn. A little further up the lane was a neat clapboard house. The two would be buyers climbed out of their buckboard for a closer look at the prize. It was obviously old but seemed to be in good enough shape. Bill walked up to the house and knocked on the door.

A voice from inside said, "Coming, Hold your horses." A middle-aged man appeared in the doorway. "What can I do for you gents?" He was of medium height, a little overweight, dressed in bibbed overalls and no shirt covering the top of his short sleeve summer long Johns.

Dad said "We have some interest in your wagon. It seems you have had some trouble selling it if the condition of the sign is any indication."

"There is nothing wrong with the wagon, it's

been in the family for at least 50 years. My great grandfather brought it soon after he landed in Boston and used it to move his family to Rochester, New York. Grandpa used it to move to his family to Chicago, Illinois. My father used it to move our family to Milwaukee, Wisconsin and I used it to get my family here. I was saving it so my son could marry and migrate to Colorado, but he won't need it. He was killed at Appomattox Court House an hour before Lee's surrender took place. Have you looked it over? It's been used but not abused. What do you think of it?

Both Bill and dad said, "I'm so sorry for your loss."

"Thanks for your condolences." I can almost endure the pain now. I will feel a lot better when I don't see this reminder of him every day. Most of the people who looked at it before thought it was too big for their needs."

Dad said, "When was it moved last?"

"Oh, I don't remember. It's been a long time. I haven't had a team of horses for a long time."

"Do you know when the axles were greased last?"

"No but I do know the axles were replaced just before I moved here from Milwaukee."

"Ok, here is the deal I am offering you. I'll buy the wagon for $150 with the condition that I get to take it to a repair shop, and have it brought up to snuff including the canvas. Any cost for the repairs comes out of your $150."

"That is not a great deal, but I really just want to get rid of it now that the kid is gone. You will have to move it to the wagon shop, I don't have the means to do that."

"Not a problem. We'll be back tomorrow morning for the wagon. I'll give you $75 then and the remainder after the repairs are done. What about the harnesses? Do you still have them?"

"Yup, but they haven't been oiled in a long time."

"In the hope they are salvageable I'll give you $5 for the lot."

"Okay! It's a deal. I'll round them up and have them in the wagon tomorrow morning."

Bill said, "Again, sorry about your son. War is such a fickled business. There is no rhyme or reason to what happens or when."

"It sounds as if you have experienced war yourself."

"Yes, I have."

The three shook hands and parted.

Chapter 19

Preparations

Now that the main requirement was fulfilled, they were free to hunt for the other things needed for the trip and after they arrived at the farm. They would have to at least one team of draft horses to pull the loaded wagon and they wanted a pair of riding horses, one for Patsy and one for Bill.

On the way home, Bill and dad stopped at a friend of dad's wagon repair and planned for the inspection of the wagon and the estimated cost to fix any defects.

At supper that evening the four of them shared their day's adventures. The evening ended early after a stressful day and the expectation that tomorrow would be more of the same.

In the morning, Bill rode one of the Bays and led the other while dad followed in the buckboard pulled by the same little roan mare. They hitched the

Bays to the Conestoga and soon dropped it off at the repair shop. The harnesses were transferred to the buckboard and Bill rode one of the Bays and led the other back to the stable.

When he arrived, he hooked the Bays to the buggy for the women to use and tied them to the anchor stone in front of the house. He and dad would use the roan mare and buckboard for their transportation.

They visited their wives in the house to see how they were doing. The ladies said they were making good progress. A goodbye smack, and the men were on their way.

Dad pulled the buckboard up to the barn and they unloaded the harnesses into a stall. They left to start their search for riding horses.

Their luck continued this morning. The first place they stopped at was the stable of a close friend of dads. His friend had this barrel-chested gelding. He was a dark chestnut color which wasn't flashy but would serve to camouflage him if there was a need to hide. His head was too large for his neck and body thus killing any thought of calling him beautiful. Bill saddled him and took him for a short spin around the paddock. The horse was chock full of energy. When he looked at the horse's teeth to assess its age, he noticed it had an intelligent look in its eyes. Bill and the horse seemed to bond immediately.

The dealer offered the horse to Bill at a friend's price and included all the usual western style tack that Bill had used on his test ride. The sale was completed with shaking of the hands and the passing of cash. Oh, and bill of sale

While Bill was making the purchase, dad was snooping around the stable and spotted a pair of Percherons. He asked his friend, "Joe, when did you start dealing in Percherons?"

"I don't usually deal in them Jim, they're actually here as part of one of those transfer deals. I am supposed to find someone going to Walnut Grove in southwestern Minnesota who would be willing to take them back there. They were part of a rental deal that allowed a family to bring their household goods to Minneapolis when they moved here. Do you know anyone that might be interested in taking them back home?"

"Yes, I do. Bill and his wife are leaving in a few days for Redwood Falls. They're taking over our old homestead and plan on making it their new home.

The three of them talked over the details of the transaction and in the end, Bill accepted the job for three dollars per day wages plus a dollar per day expenses. Bill left Joe's place riding the gelding and leading the Percherons. Dad drove the buckboard. On reaching the stable they turned the gelding, and the Percherons into the pasture with the Bays and the rest of dad's herd. The horses immediately joined the herd in their grazing and romping.

Bill and his dad looked at the pile of tack and decided their roaming was over for this day. All this leather should be inspected and oiled to make sure it was in top shape for the trip. They add the roan to the group in the pasture and pitched into the pile of leather. They had made a dent in the pile by the time mom and Patsy returned with their buggy full of boxes.

Mom went in the house to fix dinner while the guys and Patsy unloaded the buggy, added the horse to the herd of horses and went in to clean up for dinner.

During dinner they shared the progress they had made in their preparations thus far. Bill and dad said they hadn't found a suitable horse for Patsy yet and they weren't sure when the wagon would be ready to roll. Patsy and mom were sure they would finish their preparations tomorrow. That is all but packing the wagon.

Once again, the evening ended early after the hustle and bustle of the second day with the expectation that tomorrow would bring more of the same. While Patsy and mom cleaned up after the meal, Bill and dad brought in the horses and bedded them down for the night. They also gathered up all the tack and stored it until they could finish it in the morning.

Patsy and Bill said their good nights and returned to the hotel for some alone time. It seemed that they had just finished their loving when the alarm gave out its get up call. They finish their morning rituals and called for their buggy. The swaying of the carriage as the horse trotted along made it difficult for the two of them to stay awake. Suddenly they became aware that they were in front of the folk's house. They climbed down from the carriage, Bill tied the horse to the stone, and they went in for breakfast.

Immediately after they were through eating, Bill and dad returned to the unfinished pile of tack and re-commenced the cleaning and oiling process. Mom and Patsy cleaned up the breakfast debris and then rechecked their list to see if they may have missed anything.

The two men finished the leather cleaning and oiling at the same time as the women came out of the house to continue their shopping. Their two carriages started down Summit Ave. toward downtown St. Paul together. They split up as they neared downtown each giving the other a parting wave.

Bill and dads first stop were to check on the Conestoga. They were told by the foreman they could pick it up this afternoon. All it needed was a new canvas and axle grease. The canvas had been delivered late yesterday afternoon and would be installed this morning. However, the foreman did suggest they buy an axle jack so they could grease the axles every day they were on the road.

Bill asked, "Will you show me how the jack works and how best to grease the axle?"

"Sure." the foreman replied. "Let's go over to your wagon and I'll demonstrate on it. When they reached the Conestoga, he took out a long funny looking pole. "Here is how it works. You put this slab of extremely hard wood under the axle. Then you tip the handle of the jack up until you can slip the "Y" under the axle. By lowering the handle, you bring the "Y" up until it cradles the axle. If you notice the stem of the "Y" now makes the pivot point for the lever and when you force the lever down the axle goes up. The weight is off the wheel and you can remove it, slather the axle with grease and reinstall the wheel. The jack is removed by reversing the installation process. Any questions?"

"Okay, well take one of those. Does the hard wood slab come with the pole?" Bill asked.

"Yes, and an axle nut wrench also."

They paid the bill for the repairs and jack and said they would be back for the wagon before six o'clock.

From the wagon shop they went back to the

former owner of the Conestoga and paid him $50 and explained the canvas had cost $20 dollars and the axle greasing $5.

It was already 10 o'clock so they stopped for some coffee and a roll. As they sat down at the counter in the little cafe, the counter man said, "Hi Jim, I haven't seen you in a while. What you been up to?"

"Tony, this is my son Bill. He just returned from fighting the Rebs. We've been busy outfitting him and his wife for their move to our old homestead near Redwood Falls."

"Well it's nice to meet you young feller. What do you want to eat?"

"Nice to meet you Tony. I'll have one those luscious looking cinnamon rolls and a cup of black coffee."

"What will it be for you, Jim?

"The usual Tony."

Dad's usual turned out to be a caramel roll and a glass of milk. He said, "Best pastry in town. You haven't heard of any saddle horses for sale that would make a good mount for a lady have you Tony?"

"No, but I did hear there was a little spread just northwest of Rogers on the way to St. Cloud that is trying to get rid of their livestock. The rumor is that they are going to build an addition to Rodgers on the land. Progress, bah, before you know it there won't be any farmland around here. It will all be houses. Then what will we do for food?" Tony shook his head in discussed.

Dad didn't say anything. He told Bill later that use of the land for anything, but growing food was Tony's big crusade in life even though he lived in the city. Bill and dad finished their rolls, said goodbye and escaped the unsolvable conflict in Tony's mind.

Back in the buckboard dad asked, "Should we give the Rogers area a look see."

"Why not? Our prospects here at this time are little and none." The road bordered the Mississippi River as they made their way west north west toward St. Cloud. The road was in good shape, well-traveled so they made good time. They crossed the Mississippi at the little burg called Elk River and proceeded southwest to a wide spot in the road known as Rodgers. Here they asked if there was a ranch around that was selling off its livestock. They were told to take the trail north about a mile and they would find signs and the ranch.

A short time later they found themselves in a ranch yard looking at the string of horses the ranch had for sale. There was one neat little pinto mare that caught Bills eye, but he played a cool game." Isn't that Pinto a bit small and delicate to carry a full-grown man through a hard day's work?"

"I wouldn't know about that. She belonged to my daughter who loved her dearly. She has speed, stamina and a loving disposition."

"Well I have a couple young'uns that have been clamoring for a horse. Dad, look her over and see what you think."

Dad nodded and began his close examination of the pinto.

Bill looked the rest of the string over and found a reason for passing on each one in turn. Finally, he said, "I am sorry, but I can't find one of theses that meets the standard I was hoping to find."

"What about the Pinto?"

"She seems to be in good shape and would be fine for the kids, but it sounded like your family places a sentimental value on her which usually means a higher than market price. I am in no hurry to fill the kid's whim, so I guess I'll have to pass on her too."

"Wait a minute. I haven't given you a price yet. Market price for a neat little filly like her would be about $75 at an auction."

"Yah, but the auctioneer would take $25 of that for his fee and the horse would come with a health certificate from a veterinarian"

The seller threw up his hands in disgust and said, "Okay, okay, $45 and I'll throw in the gear your kids will need to ride her."

Bill felt a little guilty about the lies, but this was a horse deal where truth stretching was the norm. Ten minutes later they were on their way home with the saddle and stuff in the box and the Pinto tied behind the buckboard.

When they got home the wives were not there so they decided they would go and get the Conestoga from the repair shop. They had just gotten the harnesses on the horses when Nellie and Patsy showed up. Patsy was all excited over a bed the women had found. It was a large four post with canopy and netting. Patsy said the mattress and spring were super comfortable. Patsy said with her most mischievous grin, "Bill, you know a good bed is the foundation on which families are built. This bed will be a great place to build our family."

"Why you little minx. Are you trying to bribe me into buying this bed? Well you can relax; you have already won your case."

Bill and dad sat on the back edge of the buckboard box leading the Percherons and Bays while Patsy drove to the wagon shop. The horses were quickly hooked to the big wagon and then it was on to the bed shop. With help. Patsy's bed was set up in the Conestoga. It fit very nicely in the back with ample airflow to make it a comfortable place to sleep. When they reached home, they all agreed that they needed sleep more than food. Tomorrow will be a busy day with loading the wagon and having everything ready to leave the following morning. Good nights were said, and the couples separated until they would meet again in the morning.

Chapter 20
On Their Way Again

The deed was in Patsy's care. They were on their way to a house Patsy had never seen but Bill knew well.

All their earthly possessions were loaded in the Conestoga wagon. Hitched to the wagon were a rental pair of gray Percheron draft horses Bill had contracted to take to Redwood Falls. They looked like they could pull the wagon to China and back all by themselves. They were the wheel horses. In addition, the fine-looking team of bays that Bill had enjoyed driving the last couple of days were harnessed as the lead team of the four-up. Bill had insisted on buying the Bays. He said they would be their going-to-town-team.

The big wagon was filled with everything the four of them could think of for making Bill and Patsy's new house, into their new home. Tools, dishes, trunks and a multitude of boxes holding this, that and another thing. The two riding horses, their saddles and bridles stored in the wagon, were hitched behind it.

They had moved everything out of their hotel room and paid the bill yesterday. Last night they had slept in the wagon. It would be their home during the trip and while they made the house livable. Sleeping in the wagon also gave them a chance to test the bed they had purchased for their bedroom. The bed worked fine if you know what that means.

During breakfast, dad had taken a piece of paper and sketched them a map for the path Fox Feather had taken when rescuing them. (Carver, Hutchinson, Olivia and Redwood Falls).

After they finish eating the four of them moved outside to wagon and horses which were ready to go. Bill kissed his mother and shook his father's hand. Patsy gave both parents a hug and kiss. Goodbyes finished; the travelers swung up into the wagon seat. Bill took the reins, gave his parents one last wave and drove out of the yard. Patsy continued waving goodbye until they passed out of sight. Then she said, "I love your parents Bill. They are such kind, loving people."

"I'm glad you like them. I know they both love you." They became quiet as they thought about the past and the future. This did not last long as they became aware of their surroundings and each other.

It was a glorious day, clear blue sky and a gentle breeze to cool and soothe the travelers. Bill and Patsy were in happy mood as they considered what this trip would mean to their future.

They had made an early start in hopes of reaching the ferry at the Mississippi to avoid a long delay before it was their turn to cross. Their wishes were granted, the traffic moved along, and there were only two rigs in front of them at the ferry.

After crossing the river Bill took the Minnehaha trail, he had taken the other day to Fort Snelling.

Patsy breathed a sigh and said, "What a beautiful sight! So green and peaceful looking. Minnesota seems to have a lot more trees than Iowa."

"I never thought of that, but I think your right."

There was some small talk now and then but most of the time they were silent as they took in the scenery. Bill suddenly turned left off Minnehaha on to a trail that led east.

"Where are we going?"

"You'll see."

Soon a roar announced a falls in the distance. Next, they caught a glimpse of the Mighty Mississippi through the trees. Bill parked the wagon where they had a clear view of the roaring falls. A board stuck in the ground had "Minnehaha Falls" carved on it. The creek was full of water from recent spring rains, so the falls were spectacular, so they decided to take their morning break here even if it was a little early.

Bill took care of the horses while Patsy got the snack and oil cloth out. She spread the cloth on the grass and place some cheese and fruit on it. They had their snack with the roar of the falls in their ears. About ten o'clock they were back on the trail again.

Bill pointed out Fort Snelling and where the Mississippi and Minnesota converged. Just about where they passed the joining of the rivers, they turned right onto the Shakopee Trail. This trail cut several miles off their trip. The trail went across the peninsula made by a big bend the Minnesota made to join the Mississippi rather than following the riverbank. The Shakopee trail was where they started the westward part of their trip.

After an hour or so the trail returned to the north bank of the Minnesota River at the Shakopee ferry. There was a picnic area at the ferry, so they stopped for lunch. As they were finishing lunch the stagecoach to Shakopee, St. Peter and Mankato pulled up to the ferry. All the passengers vacated the coach. The lead and swing teams were unhooked, and the wheel team pulled the coach on the barge by themselves.

The passengers got back in the coach and the

ferryman, helped by the stage driver hauled the boat out into the river. The river on this shore is a broad backwater with little current to battle so the ferry made good time for most of its crossing. There was only a short distance near the far shore where the men had to battle the swifter crosscurrent of the main river.

Bill and Patsy overheard another bystander explain to those gathered around him that the Shakopee Stage Station was just across the way on top of the far bank. The travelers would have their lunch there. During lunch, the teams would be changed, the coach cleaned, and a new driver would take over so that when they were ready, they could immediately enter the stage and be on their way.

Bill and Patsy didn't wait to see the rest of the crossing. Their trail broke away from the riverbank and up a steep cut. The horses had quite a struggle pulling the big wagon and its load up that steep hill to the top. Bill thought, *'thanks dad for your advice. I don't think we would have made it without the Percherons'*. At the top, the trail leveled off onto a plateau. The horses had a much easier pull here and they made good time for the next few miles. This part of the trail was cutting across another peninsula made by a big swing southward by the river.

When they reached the end of the plateau the

trail dropped down into a small valley that was part of the riverbank. The trail left the western edge of the small valley and proceeded along the riverbank and across a small creek. Almost immediately after crossing the creek they found a side trail which had a stake with two arrows pointing up it. The top arrow had "Spring Road" burned in it. The second arrow had "Artesian Well, One Quarter Mile" scratched in it.

Bill said, "I think we should give the horses a breather and a drink. I know I could benefit from stretching, walking around and a drink of cold water myself. How about you Patsy?"

"That sounds like a splendid idea."

Bill turned on to Spring Road. The small valley on the right of the road and the hill on the left from which the road had been cut were densely wooded. About a quarter mile up the road was a pipe with a steady flow of bubbling water coming from it.

There was a flat area in between the pipe on the right with the creek just behind it and the hill on the left. This made it easy to park the wagon and team as well as being able to turn around when ready to leave.

Bill got down with a tin cup in his hand. The pipe made it easy to get water, so Bill took a drink. "Wow is that good! Here try some." He said as he handed a cup to Patsy.

Patsy took a mouthful and chirped in delight.

"Can we take this with us?" she said with a mischievous grin on her face.

Bill responded by throwing a cupped, hand full of water at her, "Well you can take that with you at least."

What followed was a short water fight that ended in a truce that was sealed with a kiss.

Bill thought the horses had cooled enough to be allowed a drink of cold water, so he filled a pail and allowed each horse to drink a limited amount. As they left the spring Patsy said, "I hope the guy who installed that pipe knows how grateful all us wayfarers are to him."

The big wagon with its hard-working team pulled back onto the river road again, heading west to Chaska. The trail followed a natural bench as much as possible but in several places the roadbed had to be dug out of the bank to connect the natural bench parts. Now and then they caught glimpses of Shakopee's spires and even some of its buildings across the river.

About the same time as they passed Shakopee, the trail reached level ground that continued to Chaska and Carver.

Carver was the first planned stopover on their trip. It owed its existence to some rapids in the Minnesota River. At Carver, the river curved, changing from a north flow to an east flow on its way to the Mississippi. Except in the high waters of spring the bigger river boats couldn't make it over the rapids at Carver so they docked there, had their cargoes unloaded into wagons and portaged around the rapids to be reloaded on narrower, shallower draft packets more suited for upriver navigation.

Produce from the farms around Carver was brought in to fill the big, emptied river boats for transportation to St. Paul and Minneapolis. Carver, being the friendly, generous village that it was, provided a free improved campground area for the farm wagons waiting their opportunity to unload. Bill pulled their big rig into a convenient spot. While Bill took care of the animals, Patsy took care of getting the camp ready for the night plus making their suppers.

After the meal was done and the campsite back in order, they walked into town to see if they could find their quarry. A grocery store looked like a place that might know where they could find the object of their hunt. Patsy waited outside while Bill went into inquire. Soon Bill came out and pointing in the direction of the river. He said, "This way."

Patsy asked, "How far is it?"

"It seems like the common distance estimate here is not far." The not far estimate was appropriate this time as Bill stopped in front of a neat white bungalow with red trim. "This is it." They walked up to the door and Bill rapped on it. At their rap they heard muffled steps running somewhere inside it. Soon the door opened and a young man of about ten years was standing on the other side of the screen. "What do you want?"

"First I would like to know if this is the home of Dick Madson."

"That's my dad." The lad said proudly."

"Is he at home?"

"Yes, he's out back chopping wood."

"Would you please tell your dad that Bill and Patsy Cheever have come to visit."

"You're Bill Cheever? My dad really thinks you are great!" Patsy squeezed Bill's arm. "I'll get him right away." As he started running toward the back of the house, they could hear him yelling, "Mom, mom he's here, Bill Cheever's here to see dad." A door slammed in the back of the house. The door in front of the visitors was filled with a new young man. He gave them the once over and disappeared. The back door slammed again, and footsteps approached.

Dick said with emotion in his voice, "I certainly didn't expect to see you again, especially so soon. Have you tired of civilization already? Come in and meet the family." He opened the screen door and ushered them into the setting room. His wife was standing in the door that must lead to the kitchen. "This is my wife Jane and my two boys, gesturing to the bigger, older one, Seth, name from my dad and Sam, name from Jane's dad."

"Nice to meet you." Patsy and Bill said in unison.

"I have heard so much about you two I fell I know you already." Jane said.

Seth grabbed Bill's hand and shook it and said, "Hello, glad to meet you." Then with a burst of emotion, "Dad says you are the best leader he has ever worked for." This made all three of them blush, Seth, Dick and Bill. Sam said "Hello." and then confirm Seth's report about their dad's high regard for Bill as a friend and a leader.

Jane said, "You two go play somewhere else. We adults want to talk about old times. Patsy would you mind helping me in the kitchen while these two old soldiers tell their war stories?"

"Good idea Jane, I'll be there in a second." She then walked across the room and hugged Dick.

"It is so good to see you again. Your family seems like they fit you. They are all nice like you." She turned and disappeared into the kitchen in Jane's wake.

Dick said he had gotten his old job on the docks back and that he and the family were regaining their former easiness with each other.

Bill explained to Dick the opportunity of a home he and Patsy were pursuing.

Dick said, "You are going to become a farmer? I would never have imagined you as that."

"Well, it sounds like an ideal life after the turmoil of the last few years."

Their conversation changed to their companions of the last few weeks. Bill told Dick of his and Patsy's visit to Dave and his family in Stillwater. Bill reported Dave also had his job back and was settling back into his family life. Bill also had news of Blair via letters from Patricia to Patsy. Blair's wife and child had arrived in Des Moines and things were going quite well for them. Blair was looking for wood to carve a leg for Mel, but nothing has worked out yet. It seems the problem is weight. A leg carved out of the available woods would be impossible to manipulate. I think he's about to give up and fashion a peg leg for Mel

At that point Jane and Patsy rejoined them. The two of them seemed to have hit it off immediately. They came armed with coffee and cake. The evening flew by. It seemed like they had just arrived when Bill announced it was time to go if they were going to get an early start tomorrow. The goodbyes were the hardest part of the evening.

The two travelers were asleep the minute they hit the bed. Exhaustion kept them apart this night.

Chapter 21
A Place to Call Home

Next morning was all business, except for their good morning kiss and Patsy asking, with mirth in her eyes and a smile on her lips, "Is the honeymoon over?"

Bill's reply was a chuckling, "We will see about that, later." as he slapped the reins on the wheel team's rears and they started on their second day on the trail.

Patsy snuggled her head on his shoulder and said, "I sure hope not."

"You make it awfully hard for a guy to think about his driving."

"Good!" and they drove along in silence, comfortable in their love for each other.

It was another gorgeous day. The team was rested but they hadn't gone far when the trail started its climb out of the river valley. The trail was rutted from previous traffic and the team was having some trouble finding good footing. Things got better as they reached the top of the steep hill and found themselves on a little bench which led to a more manageable slope. The trail went up this slope and disappeared into the forest that marked the edge of the valley. The trail in the woods was level as far as they could see which wasn't far when you came right down to it. The team settled into its travel gait and they started making good time. Now and then they came upon a clearing that held a house, a barn and a good crop starting to show itself in the field.

Sometimes the branches would form a canopy over the trail blocking out the sun. Most of the time they could hear birds singing and see woodland animals scurrying around doing what animals do when they are scurrying around.

Occasionally they would meet a wagon headed for Carver. Pleasantries would be exchanged, news past on and well wishes expressed as they past.

About mid-morning they came on a little glade with a creek running through it. Bill suggested this would be a good place to take their break. Patsy agreed so Bill pulled in. He took the sickle out of the wagon and cut them a small clearing in the tall grass. While Patsy rustled up a snack, Bill took the horses two at a time down to the creek for a drink. When he brought the horses back, he put their halters on so they could eat the lush grass he had cut.

Soon the break was over, the horses hitched again, and they were back on the trail. It continued primarily as path through the woods with an occasional clearing with the usual house, barn and cultivated field. Everything was going along smoothly and as the sun just past its zenith, Hutcheson came in sight. Bill pulled the rig into a shady spot for their noon break. Both took care of their chores and they were ready for their afternoon jaunt to Olivia.

Bill asked, "Have you ever driven a team Patsy?"

"Not very much. Usually I used a one-horse hitch."

"Okay, you drive this afternoon and I'll ride with my head on your shoulder."

Patsy climbed up onto the driver's seat, took the reins in her hands and waited for Bill to climb aboard. As soon as he was seated, she slapped the reins on the Percherons rears, and they started out at a trot.

Soon however, she had them down to the ground covering walk that all teams seem to share. As the afternoon went along, Patsy became more and more comfortable with her job. At their afternoon break Bill asked Patsy if she wanted him to take the task of driving over again. She declined. She said she wanted to know how it felt driving when you were tired.

"Okay, let me know when you have had enough. If we can camp near Olivia tonight, we will have an easy drive home tomorrow."

"Home does that sound good. Well, I guess for me, home is anywhere you are because that is where my heart will be." She stopped the team, turned in her seat and gave him a sweet, tender, loving kiss. "Olivia you say?" as the reins urged the teams forward again.

As evening approached, Bill said, "We can make a choice here. We can camp here tonight and still make it home late tomorrow or we can go on to Olivia and be home around noon. Which do you favor?"

"Both have advantages and disadvantages but I'm anxious to see what we've gotten ourselves into; I would prefer to get to Olivia today."

"Olivia it is then." Just before darkness they pulled into a campsite on the edge of the town. The western sky was brilliant red against the darkening sky. They were both kind of stiff and sore as they hit the ground and started their chores. Soon the evening routine set in, the discomfort of the days ride in the wagon were forgotten and the chores were done before they ate supper. A quick policing of the campsite was followed by a race to get into the bed. Patsy won the race and was waiting for Bill with open arms when he crawled in. The two lovers were content to just lay in each other's arms and dream beautiful dreams. Exhaustion had come between them again.

The morning was as glorious as the sunset had predicted. Each of them was now old timers at what they had to do to break camp in the morning, so it wasn't long before they were on the road again. The trail and its surroundings remained the same except they past more and more farmsteads as they again approached the Minnesota River. When they passed the town of Morton Bill said, "The Redwood Ferry is not far now. The ferry is the only way to get the wagon across the Minnesota."

The trail became an incline as they approached the river. It was about noon when they pulled up to the ferry's loading ramp. The ferry was on their side of the river and ready to go.

Bill knew the operator, so he jumped down and said, "How are you Pete?" The men shook hands.

"You're back from the war and look none the worse for wear and tear, that's good. Is this young lady your wife? Bill introduced them.

The ferry operator said, "Welcome to Redwood Falls mam. Bill, are your ma and pa coming back from St. Paul?"

Bill shook his head no.

"That's too bad, they are fine folks. We are going to have to unhitch these fine-looking Bays. We'll take those two big guys and the wagon across first. Then we'll come back for the Bays."

Bill released the singletree from the Percherons and led the Bays away. He also untied the two riding horses from the back of the wagon and tied them a long side the Bays.

The ferryman led the Percherons pulling the wagon on to the ferry. The freeboard of the ferry became precariously low.

Bill said, "Patsy, I'd feel better if you waited and crossed with the Bays and riding horses." He held up his arms to help her off the wagon. After Patsy made it to shore, the ferryman and Bill began pulling the rope through the pulley system which now brought them to the opposite bank.

Bill drove the wagon off the ferry on to the shore and tied the team to a tree. Then it was back across for Patsy and the Bays. By the time the whole business was done it was just past one o'clock. Bill handed the operator dollar and a half.

"Sorry Bill, but I have to charge you for three trips across. Company rules."

Bill grumbled a bit about highway robbery and dragged out another three dollars and forked it over. They said goodbye to the ferryman and moved off down a trail marked Ferry Road.

Soon Ferry Road became Redwood Fall's Main

Street. The road was bordered with a cluster of buildings that made up the main part of town. The buildings had signs on them that you would expect to find on the main street of any small town.

On the other side of town, it became Ferry Road again. They were on the last leg of their trip with no more obstacles between them and home. Bill let the team determine their own pace. Bill told Patsy, "The Redwood River runs west to east across this plateau. When it gets close to the Minnesota it drops down to its level before they merge. The falls and river are a little bit north of the town. He said, "We'll ride over and see it someday soon. The falls are really very pretty."

West of town the road angled a little south of west through more forest. As they moved along the road, Bill started pointing out historical spots from his childhood and teen years. They shared several laughs as events and antics of his life were revealed. Patsy smile and gripped Bill's arm tighter as he told the stories of his youth. She thought, '*I didn't think I could love him more than I did when I first met him but as learn more about him my love just grows and grows.*'

Eventually they turned into a little used side trail and after a few miles through the woods they came to an overgrown trail that went right off the main trail. Bill said, "This is our driveway." Shortly after they turned on to the driveway, they reached a clearing and stopped, "This is it." Bill said.

They sat there in silence, looking at their new home. The clearing ran paralleled the main road they had been following and contained a modest size log cabin, a log outhouse and a log barn. The house was just across from where the driveway entered the clearing, the outhouse just behind it and the barn was to their left against the trees that fringed the clearing on that side. The side of the clearing opposite from where they were sitting was also a fringe of trees and underbrush. Bill said, "Behind that fringe of trees is stream that runs from the house pass the outhouse and the barn providing good drainage for wastes."

The tops of poles visible in the grass in the area between the house and barn. The tops of the poles gave them a clue about the layout of the pens for managing livestock. The driveway entrance they were on entered the left side of the clearing if you gaged direction by the front of the house. There were ruts clearly showing the drive passed in front of the house, made a loop back to exit through the entrance gap.

Bill snapped his whip and they moved into the clearing following the ruts to the front of the house. The wagon stopped there.

The largest of the pens included the front of the

barn as part of its enclosure. This pen's gate was open. Bill said, "Patsy, would you mind taking the riding horses and follow me?"

"Not at all."

Bill quickly unhitched the bays and led them to the open gate. There he stripped the harnesses off and hung them on the fence. The Bays moved hesitantly into the pen. Patsy followed his lead with the saddle horses. The horses joined in an exploratory run around their new corral. Bill unhitched the rental team, stripped off their harnesses and added them to the others. All six horses seemed happy to have all that lush grass to chomp on.

Bill had some trouble closing the gate. He had to lift the open end because it had sagged over its unused years. Also, there was a high-pitched scream to tell him of its need for oil. He thought, '*There will be lots of little jobs before we get things shipshape*'.

"Come on Patsy let's check out the house". Holding hands, they walked up to the front door. To the left and the right of the door there were windows. Bill stopped on the porch and said, "May I carry my bride over the threshold?"

"Of course." she said.

He picked Patsy up and she lay her head on his shoulder as he reached for the doorknob to enter their soon to be home. He kissed her with a loving tenderness. "Welcome to our home. May nothing but good times visit us here." He put her down and said, "I see hard work before we get this place up to snuff."

"Are you afraid of a little hard work Mr. Cheever?"

"No mam, not at all."

They stood just inside the door and looked the front room over. It looked like it took up half the length and half the width of the house. In addition to the widow in front next to the door, it had two windows in the left wall. The end wall featured an oversized fieldstone fireplace. The right-hand wall stopped short of the end wall providing an entry to the right side of the house.

It was obvious no one had lived here for several years. The fireplace still had ashes and scorch stubs of wood that had not been completely consumed during its last fire. Cobwebs were everywhere. Dust was piled on every flat surface.

They walk to the opening in the right wall to find it opened into the kitchen. The cast iron stove was on the back wall. The stove showed a little rust which would require a little elbow grease to remove. That at least could be put off for a while. There was a double sink with a pump alongside in the countertop. A window over the sink was sandwiched between wall cabinets. The front part of the room had a side window and a front window. There was a table and four chairs in there too.

A rag had been shredded and strewn all over the kitchen floor signaling mice inhabitants. More evidence of the mice was their footprints in the dust. Piles of dust and cobwebs were the dominant feature of this room also. The kitchen windows had tattered curtains on them.

Next to the stove a hallway ran to the back door. Also, there was a door in the left hallway wall. When they opened the door, they found a large room with two windows in the opposite wall. In the common wall with the living room was a neat small fireplace backing the front room one. The dust and cobwebs were everywhere again but they had come to expect that.

Next, they looked at the bedrooms located off the hall to the back door. They each had a window and little else. Like the front rooms, about all they needed was cleaning.

At the back door, Bill showed Patsy a nook where a kerosene lantern usually hung for use if you needed to venture outside at night.

The back door swung open revealing a tattered piece of screen that needed replacing. Thankfully, the frame was solid. They found the path to the outhouse overgrown and the back porch needing new planks.

Bill pointed out a shelter on the outhouse wall next to its door, "When I was a kid, there was always a lamp burning there through the night, every night." Bill said, "I suggest we continue that tradition." Patsy nodded in agreement.

"I need to see about water for the horses now. If you are up to it, moving the cleaning supplies into the house would be a big help in the morning."

"Of course." Patsy replied, "That makes perfect sense." There was a little bite in her words.

Oops, Bill thought, '*I have to resist being too much of a sergeant*'. He and Patsy moved around the house to where the wagon was parked. He filled a canteen with water and headed for the horse pen. Patsy took an arm load of cleaning supplies and headed for the house.

The corral gate worked a little better, but he had only opened it enough to let himself in. The horses gave him the eye and then went back to their grazing. He remembered where the watering trough and pump were located so he went right to them. He poured about one third of the canteens water down the pump rod and let it set soaking the gasket. While it was soaking, he walked the fence picking up the harnesses at the gate and hang them in the barn on his way back to the pump. The fence looked to be in good shape.

Upon reaching the pump again he gave the handle a few tries. There was a little resistance which ended almost immediately. Encouraged, Bill poured another third of his water down the pump shaft and went to inspect the barn. It seemed to be in fair shape. The hay mow looked to be at least half full and the building appeared to be in good shape.

He went back and poured the rest of the canteen's water in and then tried the pump again. He was rewarded by a trickle of water from the pump's spout. Each stroke of the handle brought bigger and bigger gushes of water until the pump was fully operational. At first the water was rusty but that soon cleared up. He filled the trough full. Then he pulled the bung and drained it only to refill it again with fresh water. Happy that chore was done, soaked with sweat, he started for the gate. Looking back, he was rewarded by the sight of the horses crowded around the trough enjoying their first drink in their new home.

When he entered the house, he heard joyous singing from somewhere in the back. He found the singer in the master bedroom fighting the cobwebs with a broom. He startled her with a "Hey there, what are you doing?"

"Oh," she exclaimed, "You gave me a start. I was enjoying my thoughts of our future together here. I decided that we hadn't really arrived home until we were sleeping in our own bed in our own bedroom, so I started to make that happen." She hurried across the room and they shared their first kiss in their soon to be love nest.

Bill chipped in and the cleaning proceeded at a rapid pace, the cobwebs were gone, the windowsill and glass were clean, the floor swept and mopped with soapy water. Even the log walls had been swept clean when Bill said, "Shall we bring in the bed?"

"Lets!" So, they did. "Now I feel like we have reached home. My heart's content because it dwells where my love dwells."

"Welcome home my love. It's getting dark so let's knock it off for the day. I want to hold you in my arms, kiss your sweet lips and perhaps if the spirit moves us, consummate our new home."

"Good idea, but aren't you hungry?"

"Yes, for you, my soul food, the other stuff can wait." And it did.

So, Bill and Patsy officially took possession of their new home during the evening of May 18,1865.

Chapter 22
Redwood Falls

I n the morning they were famished. Patsy made them a breakfast of ham and scrambled eggs with toast and jelly for sides. The old cast iron stove worked fine the rust could wait just as Bill had surmised. Bill cleaned the tabletop and the counters while he waited. The sun was streaming through the window making the kitchen a bright, cheery place. *'Another day of great weather'* Bill thought.

After breakfast, Bill rounded up the riding horses and saddled and bridled them. The gear was the type usually found in the west. Now that the strain of getting the stuff they needed to make a life out here was behind them, Bill wanted to put an end to the arrival part of their trip, so he put halters with lead ropes on the Percherons. They were taking them to the livery stable

Now that they were home and Bill paused to

reevaluate his mount. It had long legs and a barrel chest that made it look like it could run forever and still be able to run on.

He also took a look at Patsy's pinto. It was a great looking mare. It had shown it had stamina by keeping up on the long trip out here. It should have surprising bottom carrying a light load like Patsy. That pinto should be able to go a long way, fast. These two should fill the basic need of stamina and speed.

When Patsy joined him, she had that happy, impish look in her eyes. A look he loved but also signaled mischief. She looked at the pinto like she had never seen it before and said, "I simply can't expect a horse to carry me unless we're on a first name basis. In order to have a first name relationship, the horse needs a name. I think I'll call her Patches. Now it's your turn to come up with a name for yours."

Bill had more difficulty coming up with a suitable name for the gelding. He and Patsy came up with some awful, some funny and some weird before they settled on Butch. After it was all over neither could tell why they chose Butch as the name for the gelding. All they would say when asked was the whole deal was one big hoot.

Finished with the naming, they each grabbed a lead rope for one of the Percherons and swung into their saddles. They shouted with glee as they galloped out of the yard on their way to Redwood Falls. The trail headed north through a mixed forest until it merged with a trail that showed heavy use. It ran east and west parallel to the Redwood River. They took it to the east.

A sign at the edge of the road reminded them that this trail was named Ferry Road. At the edge of town another sign renamed the trail Main Street. They found the Blacksmith/Livery Stable on the north side of the road between Lincoln St. and N. Halverson St.

The livery was their first planned stop, so they pulled up and tied Butch and Patches at the hitch rack. The Percherons were led into the barn but there was no one in sight. "Bill yelled, "Anybody here?" They looked around to find someone to accept the rentals back and pay Bill the money owed him for delivering them.

A young man came from nowhere and said, "May I help you?"

"We need to have someone take these two back." nodding at the Percherons, "And settle my bill for delivering them."

"I'm the hostler so I can take the horses, but you will have to talk to Mr. Schroder about the pay. I think he will be here in a minute or two."

""What is your name son?" Bill asked.

"Michael Schulze, sir." Michael was about Bill's

height but looked to be 20 to 30 pounds heavier. He had a pleasant face with red cheeks and lots of dish water blond hair on his head. Bill took an immediate liking to the young man.

Michael took the Percherons leads and turned away.

Bill stopped him with a sharp, "Michael, we want to leave our horses here for a few hours too. Please take off their saddle and bridle and let them run."

"Ok sir."

"My name is Bill, and this is my wife Patsy. We should be back for horses early this afternoon. Tell Mr. Schroder we'll pay the rental and boarding fees then."

Michael took Patch's and Butch's reins and moved toward the back of the barn.

Bill and Patsy walked across the dusty main street to the wagon makers shop. The sign over the door said, Hans Krautmyer, Wagon Master.

A man was sitting at a desk near the back of the little office when Bill and Patsy walked in. Bill asked, "Are you Mr. Krautmyer?"

The man replied, "Yes I am."

Bill said, "My name is Bill Cheever, and this is my wife Patsy." We were wondering if you could make us a two wheeled cart that could be easily attached and pulled behind a saddle horse.

The owner said he had seen such a rig in St. Louis, and it would take him about two hours to assemble it. He was quite sure he had all the parts on hand. He asked, "Do you want a rail around the bed with a tailgate in it?"

Bill nodded his head yes.

"The rail and gate will take another hour at least and will be unpainted."

"Okay we'll be back about one o'clock to pick it up."

"I'll get right on it and thanks."

The couple took a left diagonal back across Ferry Road to the east side of Halverson to a solid brick building with a sign that reads "Redwood County Bank and Trust." It only took a few minutes to open an account and deposited most of what was left of the reward money. The teller said, "Welcome to Redwood Falls folks and thank you for putting your trust in us."

"You're welcome, have a good day." As he turned away, Bill saw a man peering through an office window into the bank lobby, the window had a small plaque in its corner that announced this was the bank president's office.

After leaving the bank, they proceeded east along Main, passed Emmon's General Store, crossed Swain St., past the gunsmith's shop, crossed Gould St.

and angled across to the courthouse. It took a little searching to find the "Register of Deeds" office. They had a short wait as the clerk finish with another customer. The clerk beckoned them and soon the deed was registered. They were now officially homeowners in Redwood County.

Their courthouse business done; they retraced their steps to Emmon's General Store. Here they brought every kerosene lamp the store had in stock, two five-gallon cans filled with kerosene and a funnel. They also bought two boxes of stick matches, paint supplies for the wagon rail and five, five-gallon cans of whitewash for the log walls of their cabin. Two long handled straw like brushes for applying the whitewash completed their shopping. Oh, except for one last splurge, two pieces of hard rock candy for the ride home. They asked Mr. Emmons to hold their stuff until they picked it up that afternoon. As they stepped out of the store Patsy pointed across the street and said," Look Bill, can we find out if my sister's namesake can cook?"

Bill looked across the street at a sign with 'Milly's Diner' on it. "Of course."

They walked over and as they approached some very fetching aromas assaulted their noses. As they walked through the door, Bill gave the room a thorough look over. He recognized the banker setting at a back table talking business with a stranger. Besides the banker's table there were two women at another table in the middle of the room.

Patsy and Bill sat at a table against the wall where Bill could watch the door and see the room behind him in the window. His old habits were still with him. A hard-bitten woman who look closer to fifty than twenty stopped at their table and introduced herself," I'm Milly, you must be new in town since I've never seen you before."

"Hi Milly, this is my wife Patsy and I'm Bill Cheever. Nice to make your acquaintance."

"You the folks that went to St. Paul during the uprising and didn't return after it was over?"

"No, those were my parents, but we are the owners of the property now."

"Well, if you ever decide to sell, please look me and my husband up. We love the place and are ready to buy."

"I don't think we will be selling but we will keep you in mind." Patsy said.

"Well then I better make some money so I will be ready if you do. You want anything to drink? Coffee comes with the meal. The Mulligan stew is especially good, I made it myself."

Patsy and Bill look at each other and said in unison, "Coffee and stew."

"Good choice." said Millie and she headed for the kitchen.

"This Milly is definitely not my sisters name sake." she said with a grin.

"I agree." He said with a laugh. Soon she was back with the coffee, cream and sugar. "I don't leave these on the table anymore. The cream sours and the sugar disappear like an army of ants were the clients." she returned to the kitchen.

The banker and this companion got up and left some money on the table for their meal and walked by them on their way out the door. Bill thought it strange that banker hadn't at least nodded his head on his way by, given that they had just made such a substantial deposit only this morning. Bill thought, *'they might have been talking about us because he had caught them glancing their way several times. Or was he being paranoid because of his recent war experience when everything was sinister and threatening'.*

Millie delivered the food and said, "I wonder who the gent with the banker is? I haven't seen him before either. Ornery cuss, all he did was growl when I said howdy stranger. I hope he gets a belly ache from the green apple pie he ate. Enjoy your stew." and away she went. She came back in a while with two pieces of green apple pie. "Would you eat these for me? I can't keep them around here if they're going to make my customers ornery." They both told Milly that the pie and stew were delicious. Bill paid for the meal and Patsy asked if she ever shared her recipes.

"I'll make copies and have them for you the next time you're in town. It has been nice to get acquainted with you two. Enjoy my dream home and do come again."

Bill and Patsy headed back to the wagon shop to see how their special wagon was coming along. It was setting out in front of the shop. The wagon box, bed and wheels were like any other two-wheel cart. The tongue was the strange part. It stuck up in a large arc resembling a goose's neck. The end of the gooseneck pipe had a larger pipe on it. The larger pipe had three bolts threw it. Each bolt had a crossbar on its head so you could tighten them without needing a wrench. While they were inspecting their wagon the shop owner joined them. "What do you think of her?"

"Wow." said Bill.

Patsy said, "How do you hitch it to a horse?"

Mr. Krautmyer said, "Why don't you get yours and I'll show you."

"I'll get them," said Bill and he hurried away toward the stable.

Patsy kept the conversation going by asking question about the Redwood Falls area. About fifteen

minutes later Bill reappeared with the saddled and bridled horses.

He said to Patsy, "I finished all of our business at the stable, so we'll be ready to go home soon after we're through here. Okay Mr. Krautmyer show us the rig"

Mr. Krautmyer reached in the wagon box and took a bundle out. He opened it up and spread the contents out on the wagons rail. "Okay, here we go. Which horse do you want this on?"

Bill point to Patsy's pinto.

"Alright, here is how this rig is supposed to work. In order to put the hitch on the horse, it needs to be unsaddled." So it was. "The saddle blanket goes on as usual. This separate piece of blanket snuggles up to the main one on the flattest part of the hunches. The panel with the ball on it I call the load panel. This load panel goes on the extra swatch of blanket." He lay the load panel on the swatch. "These two side panels attached to the load panel and hanging down the sides are what I think of as the stabilizers."

"The Load panel has two straps on it." He picked up the back one as he talked, it had a ring at its end. "This straps length can be adjusted. You slide the ring over tail and pull it up to the tail's root, making sure you don't move the load panel." He grabbed Patch's tail and stuffed its hair into the ring, slid the ring up until it was snug against the horse's body. This unaccustomed monkey business at her rear made Patches shy away a little. "I'm sure she will get over that once she gets used to it." he said as grabbed the load ball and cinched the ring tight on the tail's root. "The front strap lays out a cross the saddle blanket. It will be attached to the saddle horn later."

"The stabilizers each have two straps on them. The strap on the bottom functions as a girth for the apparatus." He reached under Patches and caught the right-side strap by its ring and slipped the end of the left strap into the ring and cinched it tight. He grabbed the load ball and gave it a pull and push to make sure the girth was secure enough.

"The strap on the front of the left stabilizer is the load strap. It is broader to reduce the pressure on the horse's chest. It is laid out along the left side of the horse, across the chest, and down the right side where it attaches to the ring on the right stabilizer and then it's cinched up."

"Next the saddle is put on as usual and the load panel's front strap is tied off on the saddle horn."

"Last the wagon tongue pipe goes over the load ball, the bolts are tightened, and you are ready to roll." He had demonstrated each move as he talk so Patches and the strange wagon really were ready to go.

"Ok, let's put this deal to bed. Patsy, I'll meet you over at Emmons."

"Come into my office and we will close it out."

Inside Bill said, "I know you didn't come up with this in just one morning. Tell me how long you have been working on this hitch idea?"

"I saw something like this in St. Louis about four years ago. What I saw was a wagon hitched to a bicycle. I've been working on the idea off and on since that time."

"I imagine this is your test case. So how much are you asking your guinea pig to chip in for the privilege of testing your prototype?"

"Would one hundred fifty dollars be acceptable?"

"I will agree to that amount but with the proviso that if it doesn't work out, I get all my money back and you take back all your surviving paraphernalia."

"Ok. It's a deal."

"You write out the contract just as we agreed, and I will stop back with your money on my way out of town. I've got to get to the bank now." He turned and walked out the door. When he got to Emmons everything was packed in the wagon and Patsy was ready to go,

Withdrawing the one hundred and fifty dollars from the bank took about ten minutes. The wagon dealer had the papers ready so the exchange of money for document took a minute or so.

"Thank you for the opportunity to serve you Mr. Cheever."

"Thank you, Mr. Krautmyer. It has been a pleasure." Bill left the wagon shop, Patsy was waiting on the street for him, mounted on Patches with the strange wagon attached behind. Bill swung on to Butches saddle and by two-thirty they were on their way home.

On arrival, their purchases were carried into the house. The new wagon was unhitched and parked by the corral fence. The horses were unsaddled, rubbed down and their bridles replaced with halters before being led to the corral and turned in with the bays. The Bays galloped over to greet there friends.

Bill and Patsy got right to work filling the new lamps with kerosene and strategically placed inside and outside the house. That done, Bill and Patsy took out the new brushes and started white washing the walls in their bedroom. They worked together through the afternoon and evening stopping only long enough for a sandwich. In the end they were pleased with the effect the white walls and the lanterns had on turning drab into pleasing.

It was now time to pursue the pleasure of each other's company. They hurried through their going to bed rituals and met in the middle of the bed for the joys of marriage time.

Chapter 23
His Name Is Bill Cheever

The next morning Bill was out by the wagons when he heard a bunch of riders go by out on the road. He was trying to decide if he should paint the new wagon. The sky was still overcast threatening more rain. He had been out there about twenty minutes when he heard another bunch of riders on the road, but these turned into the driveway. Bill spotted a star pinned on the shirt of the lead rider. The group pulled up around Bill. Star said, "I'm Deputy Sheriff Williams from Redwood Falls. Have you seen or heard a group of riders go by this morning?

"There was a group out on the road about twenty minutes ago or so. Why? What's going on Deputy?"

"The bank was robbed, and the Sheriff killed this morning. We are a posse sent out to catch the crooks." The Deputy was a nice-looking guy with a lean, fit looking body of average height and weight.

His demeanor was competent, confident and decisive. Bill thought, *I can count on this guy if it comes down to a fire fight*.

"Do any of you have experience in hunting desperate men who are willing to kill in the wink of an eye?"

Nobody answered.

"This is not like going on a rabbit hunt. These rabbits are desperate to get away and they are thinking all the time about how they can kill you and make their escape. I just finished three years in the Union Army chasing this type of scum. Also, I have a personal stake in this. I deposited a substantial amount of cash in that bank yesterday. I don't take kindly to being broke again. If one of you wouldn't mind saddling the big Chestnut gelding over there, I would be most appreciative. It would save us precious time.

A tall, lanky guy with an easy going looks about him if the way he set in his saddle was any indication said, "I can do that. Where will I find the tack?"

"It's in the barn. In the meantime, I'll get my weapons."

Bill gave Patsy a heads up about what was taking place and then rejoined the posse carrying his Henry rifle in its scabbard, a brace of horse pistols and his colts on his hips. His horse was saddled and ready to go, so they did.

The rain last night made the hoof prints of the group in front easy to follow as they continued south. Bill thought *these guys are doing nothing to cover their tracks. That could only mean one of two things, either the group wasn't the bank robbers, or they were trying to lure the posse into an ambush. Of the two possibilities, only the ambush would spell disaster for us.* So, Bill concentrated on the possibility of an ambush.

"Do any of you have any experience with tracking and getting around soundlessly in the woods?" he asked the group as they moved along in the wake of the riders ahead.

"I do." said a guy who Bill took to be the youngest member of the posse.

"Would you mind riding point for us?" asked Bill.

"No problem at all." replied the young man as he spurred his horse to gain a lead on the group.

About a half hour later the posse came up to the man who had volunteered to take the point. The Deputy said, "What did you find out Zeke?"

"The group we have been following left the road here. They're still not doing much to cover their trail. I followed it a couple of miles until it came to a rock moraine. The trail continued through a gap in the rocks. That gap looks like the perfect place to set a trap, so I came back to warn you."

"Good job Zeke. I and my Indian friends used

to practice tracking each other in this area. I remember that moraine. It ends a little bit north of the gap. Let's follow the trail until we are in front of the gap and then we can decide what to do next, remember, no talking, hand signals only."

The trees, primarily saplings, that let a lot of sun reach the forest floor, so it was covered with bushes and spots of grass. They had to weave around a lot to get where they wanted to go but they made good time despite it. It hadn't changed much since Bill had seen it last.

When the gap wasn't far from where they were, Bill raised his arm in a signal to stop and put a finger across his lips for silence. He didn't think they had been making enough noise in the wet underbrush to warn anybody of their presence, but you never knew. He had the posse dismount and gather around him. He had them hunker down and whisper with their mouths aimed at the ground. This precaution assured that the sound of their voices would be absorbed by the ground and the wet plants before it traveled far. He said, "The gap is a short way up ahead so it's time to talk over the plan I have in mind. I would like to position Deputy Williams and three men in front of the possible ambush site. I and the other man will circle around to the rear of the position and if they are there, the two of us will attack from their rear.

The natural reaction to being attack from the rear is to change your front. When that happens, Deputy Williams' group attacks from their new rear, we have them in a crossfire and that usually means a short successful fight. One caution. Be sure to identify the positions of your friends and your foes. You will be firing at your foes in the general direction of your friends. Zeke, I would like you to accompany me on the move to the back of the ambush place?"

Sergeant-Major Cheever was in full command now.

Zeke said, "Am I volunteering again? No need to answer because I accept your invitation."

"Thank you!" Bill said with a twisted grin. "Before I go, I need to place Deputy Williams' group. Zeke, see that bunch of trees over on the left?"

Zeke nod his yes answer.

"I'll meet you there as soon as I have placed these men. Don, if you and your guys have slickers, I suggest you use them for camouflage. This will also make the wait more comfortable for you." The Deputy nodded his head, stood up and pulled his raincoat out of his saddle bag. Two of the other men followed suit. The last man said, "I don't have a slicker with me." Bill went to his saddle bag and after a little searching took out his and flipped it to the man.

There were so many suitable places with cover and

good fields of vision in front of the gap in the rock ridge the trail ran through that Bill had his blocking force in place very quickly. Looking back, Bill had trouble locating the hidden men even though he had placed them.

He met Zeke and they made their way around the end of the ridge and behind the gap. Bill saw seven horses tied to a Picket line stretch between two trees. Bill thought '*Zeke's instincts and my memory were right on.*'

Some movement to the left caught his attention. Sure enough, five men were huddled around a smokeless fire drinking coffee.

Bill thought, '*seven horses, five at the fire which means two lookouts.*' Bill started looking the ridge over trying to locate the lookouts when a voice came from the top right side of the gap, "Hey, bring some of that coffee up here!" That yell was joined by another from the left, "I could use some of that too." What appeared to be the youngest man at the fire filled two cups with coffee and started for the lookouts.

Bill pointed at Zeke and raised his left arm, then he pointed at himself and raised his right arm. Zeke nodded his head in understanding. Bill stood up behind a tree and yelled, **"Drop your guns, this is a posse from Redwood Falls and you are all under arrest!"**

The startled men all turned his way and the right-hand gap guard started to raise his rifle to his shoulder when Bills bullet knock him down. Bill felt the compression and the bang from his left and watched the left-hand lookout crumple to the ground. Four of the five around the fire broke for the gap in the ridge, the other outlaw ran toward the horses. Bill's next shot brought him down halfway there. Zeke had knocked down one of the gap runners also. Now sounds of shooting came from the other side of the ridge. It stopped almost as soon as it started. Soon three guys with their hands in the air came through the gap, followed by Williams and the other three posse members, all with their guns out covering the advancing crooks. Bill and Zeke entered the clearing and Zeke continued to join his friends; Bill went to check on the guy who had made for the horses. It didn't really surprise him when the dead man turned out to be the man, he had seen with the banker yesterday. From there he went to the line of horses and rummaged through the saddlebags. Most of them contained only the personal stuff of the rider but one had about five thousand dollars cash in an envelope. Bill pocketed the envelope. He headed back to the group and said, "Do you have enough pairs of handcuffs for these prisoners deputy?"

"No, I only have one pair."

"Okay. You posse members keep your eyes open and your guns ready. Did you check the prisoners for weapons including their boots? If you haven't done it yet pair up for the search. One checks while the other guards. Be sure to check those two up on the moraine too. Do it now."

The body searches turned up a hideout gun in a boot, a knife in another boot and a throwing knife in a sheath under the neck of one's shirt.

"Now that we know they have been secured, search them for any papers and such. Have the survivors drag the dead over to the horses. Get these survivors to load their dead buddies on the horse they rode in here." Sure enough, the banker's friend was loaded onto the horse whose saddle bags yielded the envelope of money.

"Deputy, we are going to arrest the banker as soon as possible. He was in on this robbery. I'll explain when we get back to town."

Leading the outlaw's horses, they made their way back to their mounts. Everyone climbed on and the posse with their prisoners made their way back to Bill's place. Bill got out a length of rope and the three living crooks were bound hand and foot.

While the posse was tying up the prisoners, Patsy made a tray of ham sandwiches and a big pot of hot coffee for them.

Over lunch Bill introduced Patsy to Deputy Williams, and Zeke. Then he said, "Don, you'll have to do the honors with these other guys." as he gestured toward the three other posse members," I haven't had the pleasure yet."

The Deputy obliged by pointing to the man who had saddled Butch this morning, "This long drink of water is Al Flannery. He is a HK Star brand cowboy.

Patsy and Bill said, "Nice to meet you Al, welcome to our home."

"Next to him is Hugh Mitchy who works at the 'Star Bright Saloon'. Hugh had impressed Bill 'with *his dogged determination to get things done right.'* He was a small man, about 5'5" and 130 pounds. He seemed to be slow in movement and possibly mind.

The Cheevers said, "Welcome Hugh."

"Last but not least as I have often heard it said, Paul Hoffstead. He is a security guard at the bank."

Paul had a paunch and look to be 20- or 30-pounds overweight. He was seriously out of shape. His complexion and actions in this morning's engagement were ample proof that he did not spend much time outdoors. Bill thought *'he is too heavy for that horse he's riding. He'll kill it if he rides it long and hard.*

"Welcome to our home Paul."

"Now that they were all acquainted," Bill said, "I want you all to know how impressed I was with how each of you handled this morning's operation. Now I think it's time to get those crooks in to their new home in the city's jail.

Bill said, "Don, I think Patsy should come to town with us incase her testimony is needed in the arrest of the banker."

Don nodded in agreement.

Bill said, "Al would you mind saddling the Pinto for Patsy. The rest of us will help her clean the kitchen while you do that."

Al got up and left without a word. When the Cheevers and posse came out of the house, Al was lounging in his saddle, holding a lead rope with Patches ready to go on its end.

Soon the four dead robbers, three living robbers and the five posse men with Bill and Patsy were on their way. It was quite a cavalcade that approached Redwood Falls. At the edge of town in a fringe of trees Bill had the bunch hold up. He told Zeke to ride to the back of the bank and to stop anybody from leaving that way. He told Paul to hold the dead and captured robbers there for at least 15 minutes before coming into town. Then he and Deputy Williams rode to the front of the bank, dismounted and entered. They walked over to the teller's cage and asked for the bank president. A clerk went to summon him. The clerk came back with a puzzled look on his face, "I can't find him anywhere."

Zeke entered from the back of the bank pushing the scoundrel in front of him. "Look who I found sneaking out the backdoor."

"Good work Zeke." Bill walked over and searched the banker's pockets. In the breast pocket of his coat he found a similar envelope to the one he had taken of the robber leader.

Bill handed both envelopes to the clerk with the instructions to count the money in each but be sure to keep the money in the envelopes it was found in. When the facts were laid out for the banker, he confessed.

Patsy came in and after one look Bill whispered, "How are you doing?"

She whispered back, "Not so well."

"Where are the three surviving crooks?"

"They are locked in jail."

"What about the dead?"

"At the Doc's office."

He whispered, "I will get us out of here pronto. Deputy Williams, you seem to have everything in hand, so I am going home. You can catch me there if you need me for anything."

" Thanks, Bill. I'm not sure how things would have gone without your help but with it we are all safe, they are all caught and the money's back in the bank. Things can't get much better than that." He reached for Bill's hand and they shook.

As Bill and Patsy stepped out the banks door the big crowd assemble in the street greeted them with a cheer, and somebody yelled," There he is!" A second spontaneous cheer erupted. "A voice in the crowd said, "Who in the hell did you say he is? I can't remember ever seeing him before."

"His name is Bill Cheever."

Bill grabbed Butch's reins from the hitching rack and forced his way across the street to where Patches was at the hitch rack in front of the jail. They mounted and rode out of town.

Chapter 24

Man of Action, Not the Plow

They walked their horses all the way home to make the ride as comfortable as possible for Patsy. Her women's sickness kept them apart this night, but it could not dent the love they shared. Cuddling in each other's arms can sometimes be perfect bliss between lovers. Patsy said, "I was so worried about you this morning. What a great relief it was when you rode back into the yard."

Next morning Patsy insisted on making breakfast but after that she put Bill's concern to rest by sitting at the kitchen table sewing curtains for their bedroom. The cloth Patsy had chosen complemented the quilt Patricia had given them. The 4"x 4" quilt squares featured a yellow flower on a light purple field. Each flower square was separated from all the other similar squares by 4" strip of Royal Purple cloth. The area of the quilt squares and purple strips matched flat area of the mattress. The perimeter of the quilt square field was finished with a two-foot Royal Purple skirt.

While Patsy sewed, Bill whitewashed the logs in the back hallway. This emptied the first of the five-gallon cans they had brought at Emmons. Bill thought, *'One down and four to go. We're making progress. Our bedroom is almost done since we painted it the other day. All we need to finish it now is the dresser from the wagon and hang the curtains when Patsy finishes them.'*

It was just before noon when both projects were done. Bill hung the curtains while Patsy remade the bed with the spread on it. The room was shaping up.

The drawers from Patsy's chest of drawers were spread out on the floor along the wall waiting for the cabinet to be brought in from the wagon to hold them.

Bill brought in a small bedside stand to hold a "last light out lamp." Next came several boxes of odds and ends that were stored in an extra bedroom. They were making progress toward having the big wagon empty. Their greatest need now was a wardrobe.

Patsy yelled, "Lunch is ready."

Just as they were cleaning up from lunch, several horses were heard coming into the yard. Bill went to see who was there. He recognized the deputy sheriff, the wagon maker, Mr. Emmons, the postmaster and several other men he had seen on their trips to town.

The deputy knocked on the door. Bill opened it, "Hi Deputy Williams. What brings you and your friends here today?"

"We have a proposition to make you. May we come in to discuss it with you?"

"Certainly. Please come in gentlemen.", he said with a somewhat embarrassed chuckle. "I don't know what we'll do for seats. We haven't gotten that issue resolved yet."

Patsy came from the kitchen carrying a chair. "Welcome to our home! I'm Bill's wife, Patsy. There are three more chairs in the kitchen. I see four five-gallon cans that we can use in this emergency."

Mr. Emmons still wearing his apron said, "Bill, it looks like you have already been wrestling with a whitewash can. Any chance we could use that as a seat too?"

Bill said, "I'll use that one in case it still has wet paint on it." He retrieved the can from the hallway.

Three elderly men in business suits Bill and Patsy didn't know retrieved the kitchen chairs for their use. Mr. Emmons, Mr. Krautmyer and Carl Schroeder, and another stranger sat on the four unopened white-wash cans. Deputy Williams stood leaning against the wall next to the entry.

The middle of the three elders sitting in the chairs stood up and made the introductions. "I'm Judge Peter

McKay, this guy on my right is Mayor Harvey Clayton and on my left is Postmaster Harry Thomas.

The postmaster said, "I brought your mail for you." handing a package and several envelopes to Bill.

"Thank you."

Across from you is Alderman John Emmons, Alderman Hans Krautmyer, Alderman Carl Schroder and Alderman Pierre La Bouef. Of course, you already know Deputy Sheriff Don Williams. We are here to offer you the job of Sheriff of Redwood County. As you know our former Sheriff was killed in the line of duty. This leaves the county unprotected which is an intolerable situation. What do you say about this offer, will you accept?"

"Well gentlemen, I take this as a very complementary offer. However, I didn't come back here to enter a war again. My wife and I are here to resurrect this farm and start a family. Most day-to-day law work would bore me to death. A clerk is all you need for most of it. I would say a sheriff's office of four deputies and a clerk should be enough to keep the county safe. Having worked with Deputy Williams I would recommend him as your person to run the day to day operations of the Sheriff's Department. Another person who impressed me the other day was Zeke. I don't know anything else about the department to comment further."

Harvey Clayton spoke up, "We agree with much of what you just said but what we are looking for here, to go along with the day to day operation of the office, is a name that will make outlaws think twice before they tackle a town protected by a lawman with a reputation like you have now."

"Reputation? Where did I get a reputation from?"

The Postmaster, Harry Thomas, replied, "Their happened to have been a reporter from the St. Paul Pioneer Press in the crowd the other day. He did a little research and ran across the stories of your exploits on the train, on the Bostonia No. 2 and your superlative war record. His article ran in every newspaper in the state and the Upper-Midwest. Reputation, you have an awesome one."

"My God!" Bill said, "I didn't expect that. Well here's the rub, I wouldn't mind being part of investigations, apprehensions and prosecutions but I'm not thrilled with the Idea of being involved in day to day petty and mundane operations that are part and parcel of policing a town day to day."

"That might work." Said the judge. "That would give us the reputation we seek. Let us take that idea and gnaw on it for a while. We have taken up enough of your time today. We'll leave you and Patsy to talk it over. Please let us know."

"Patsy and I do have lots to consider before we

will be able to make our decision. Don, I hate to impose on you, but before you leave would you mind helping me carry in a dresser from the wagon?"

"Sure Bill. No problem."

Bill and the deputy went out to the wagon and had the dresser in the bedroom in a minute or two.

"Thanks Don."

"Glad to help. Think the offer over carefully Bill. I think we would be a good team.

"I will, you can count on it."

Goodbyes were said all around and the town's delegation rode out of the yard. As soon as they were alone Bill said, "You were pretty quiet. Cat got your tongue?"

Patsy replied, "Actually, I was trying to figure out how such an obligation would impact our lives. I don't do well without people around. It has been great here so far because I have had the love of my life around most of the time but what would I do if I were alone for a couple of days?"

"This is a serious issue that requires deep thought. Let us retire to our thinking spot. Will you accompany me to our couch for some quiet time and deep thought?"

"I'll race you to it!" She ran into the bedroom flopped on the bed.

He was right behind her.

"Come on slowpoke I'll make room for you!" She opened her arms and he slid right in. They snuggled and talked for an hour or two before dropping off to sleep to wrestle with their own thoughts of the future.

About seven Bill got up to answer nature's call. He was still anguishing over his newfound desire for his future and the lingering appeal of the dreams they had shared thus far in their short-married life. The one unquestioned part of any existence for him was Patsy's presence, happiness and comfort. He wondered if she had drawn any conclusions herself. He went back into the house and found her working in the kitchen getting food ready for dinner.

While waiting, Bill remembered the mail delivered by the postmaster. He sorted through it. There was a letter from Patsy's mother for her and a letter from each of her sisters. He received letters from Mel, Duane, Dave and Blair. There was also a seed catalog from the farm store in town.

They ate dinner while talking about the future. Patsy was worried about the loneliness and lack of friends she was experiencing in the rural life. She had come to realize that she didn't need to live in a town or city, but she did need to live close enough to be involved in the hubbub and support one could find in a town. She felt out of place on the farm.

Bill was becoming aware of his growing discontent with the idea of being a farmer. He was surprised about the change in his attitude toward violence and killing. He had become aware that circumstances and motivation drew the fine line between preservation, protection, aggression and greed.

When he was young, he had rebelled against the killing of farm animals. His dad had been patient and explained that if chickens didn't lay eggs for their breakfast and make a fine Sunday meal, we wouldn't bother raising them nor would anybody else. Since chickens can't survive on their own, there would be no chickens on Earth. Those farm animals died to provided food for the family table.

During the war, he had come face to face with the need to take another person's life for abstract reasons. He vomited after killing his first Reb in the battle at the Big Black River bridge, but he had come to the realization that sometimes killing was a necessity. The Reb had died because he was fighting to keep a great evil alive. Bill's war experience gave him a sense of being a man of action, not a man of the plow. Bill was now aware of why you might have to kill, not wantonly, but purposefully.

In the end, they agreed that the sheriff's job might be just the thing and decided to check it out in the morning. They agreed that their start had been worth it because they had gotten to know each other better and had a better feeling for who they were and who they wanted to be.

Later that evening Bill answered the letters he had received. His friends all seemed to be doing well in their return to the role as citizen, father and husband. His letter to them summarized the events that were taking place and the quandary he was in with the offer of the sheriff's job. In Mel's letter he told about his struggle with the idea of being a farmer.

Patsy was busy answering her mail. It seems her sisters were enjoying her clothes and the social life in Des Moines. Her mother said she was missed but they were all pleased that she was so happy and settled down with her own home and all.

Finally, they climbed into bed to cuddle up in each other's arms. This night things didn't work out so well. Both tossed and turned the night away as they struggled with thoughts of the future. By morning each had resolved their personal dilemmas. They agreed they would at least listen to the job offer. They thought they needed to know the scope of the job, understand the impact the job would have on their personal lives and what the financial compensation would be. They decided they need to get those questions answered immediately.

Bill saddled their horses and they rode into town

while the dew was still heavy on the leaves. They tied Butch and Patches at the hitch rack in front of Millie's Café and went in for breakfast.

"Hello you two. What are you doing in town so early?" Millie poured coffee in their cups from the pot she was carrying in one hand and put the cream she had in her other hand in the center of the table. Next, she dug in her apron pocket for the sugar and placed it alongside the cream. "Bill, you certainly let it be known when you arrive in a place. All the talk around here the last couple of days has been about you and the number you did on the bank robbers. Who is this Bill Cheever? It is the most asked question in the county these days!"

"There were five others involved in catching those crooks, I could not have done it alone."

"Well," Patsy said, "one thing we came for was to find out how serious you were about buying our place?"

"I am dead serious; my sons and my husband Ed are fed up with working for others. They are eager to put their sweat into something we own. Have you changed your mind about selling the place?"

"We are not sure yet, but we have added a *maybe* to our thinking." Said Bill.

"Have you gotten so far as thinking about a price you might be asking for it?"

"No, but I have decided on a short stack of pancakes with lots of butter and syrup, two eggs over easy and bacon." Replied Bill.

"I'll have a bowl of oatmeal and light toast, please."

"Coming right up."

Bill took a sip of coffee and proclaimed, "Millie does serve good coffee."

They finished their breakfast, paid their bill and said, "We'll let you know as soon as we know anything more about the house."

They entered the courthouse wondering where the Judge's office would be. A sign told them it was on the third floor. They walked up but to their dismay, after looking at every door, they still had not found the Judge's place of business. Frustrated and wondering what to do next; they went down to the second floor and resumed their hunt. The result was the same. They finally found it in the back corner of the first floor. The door was ajar, so they went in.

"Hello. How may I help you?" said the gray-haired lady behind the desk.

"We would like to talk to the Judge about the position of County Sheriff. I am Bill Cheever, and this is my wife Patsy."

"Oh, it is so nice to meet you. You have been the big news around here these last few days. I'll tell the

Judge you are here." She arose and entered the door on the wall behind her. Patsy and Bill heard voices but not words. The door opened and the Judge appeared, "Come in Patsy, Bill, I am really happy to see you two. Thank you, Doris that will be all. Have you come to any decision yet?"

Bill said, "We have decided to hear the details of the offer before we make our final decision."

"Can you give me an hour to gather the rest of the council members, so everyone is on the same page as to what we promise you?"

"Yes, we will be at Millie's, let's say at 10 o'clock to hear the details of the offer and hopefully make our decision."

"Ok, I'll see you at ten."

"Before I go, satisfy my curiosity," said Patsy. "The sign in the front hallway says your office is on the third floor but its hidden here on the first floor, what's the deal?"

"Sorry Patsy, I've been down here for over two years now and never thought to change the sign. My rheumatism got so bad; I couldn't climb the stairs anymore. So, I pulled rank and usurped this first-floor office. "

"Well Judge, changing the sign might be a good thing. People might deem it a courtesy if they didn't have to traipse all over the building looking for you."

said Patsy with a grin. With that they left the Judges office.

Bill and Patsy filled the time by browsing around the various stores to scope out what each offered that they might need. On a whim they each brought a bathing suit. They agreed that the summer was getting warmer and a dip in the river might feel good from time to time. At ten o'clock, they arrived at Millie's.

It didn't take long to iron out the details. The city fathers had made up their minds that they wanted Bill, and nothing was going to deter them from their decision. The County had foreclosed on two houses, one in town and one just outside of town. Ether of these would be rent free as part of the compensation of the job. In fact, the county would invest $1000 to refurbish which ever one they chose. The salary would total $400 per month plus expenses. Also, during the winter, one month paid vacation was included. Deputy Sheriff Williams was going to be employed by the city as Town Marshal to take care of the day to day problems that would come up.

Bill's only demand was that the County provide him four deputies under his personal command. This sparked a heated debate that wound up granting him the right to recruit four deputies at two hundred a month plus expenses. The argument that won the

NEIL GILLIS

day was that even four was meager coverage of an over 800 sq. mile area. Bill's plan was to incorporate Town Marshals with the Sheriff's Deputies to make a strong network for law enforcement everywhere in the County.

By 12 o'clock the deal was done, and an introductory dance was scheduled for next Friday night, oh, and Bill was officially sworn in as the Sheriff of Redwood County with a star on his chest to prove it.

Bill thought, '*It was about a month ago I, the squad and the General were boarding the Sultana. I hope this deal doesn't wind up being a disaster like that one did.*

Chapter 25

Starting Over

With Bill's acceptance of the Sheriff's job, he and Patsy's priorities for the day changed. Satisfying their curiosity about the two houses offered with the job became the next item on their day's agenda. They found the in-town house on a quiet, shady street near the edge of town down by the river. While the area was beautiful, the houses' layout and size were similar to their present house. There was a small barn out back for the horse but no place for them to graze. Several flower gardens were scattered around the house and yard. There was also a vegetable garden. All the gardens were overgrown with weeds. After taking everything into account, they agreed it would do as a temporary place until they could find better.

It was a pleasant ride out along the Redwood River to the other property. They found the house without any trouble. It had been built on the side of a hill overlooking the river which at this point was curving south thus giving the house an eastern facing front. It looked majestic sitting up on the bench in the hill with a grassy sloped running down to the road where Patsy and Bill sat on their horses giving the place the once over.

On the right side of the house, the hill continued to rise about ten feet to its top. On its left, the hill dropped down about ten feet into a swale. The barn was located at the bottom of the swale. A trail ran up to the barn with a spur to the hitch rack in front of the house, to which Bill and Patsy now tied their horses.

It was obvious to both that the house and barn could stand a paint job. The front of the house was covered by a three-season porch. All the screens needed to be replaced and one window on the house that looked out on the porch was broken. The screen door to the porch needed re-hanging. There were double hung windows in the walls on each side of the entry door. The entry door needed a Bill swift kick to get it open. The door opened into a spacious sitting room with an eye-catching stone fireplace in the back-right corner. It had double windows in the left wall. that matched those in the front wall. The right-side wall was a post and lintel arch leading to the dining room. The back wall of the front room had a door in it. On exploring what was behind this door they discovered a pleasant smaller room with the same double windows in the side and back walls. A second doorway led to the back hall and door.

Next, they returned to the dining room which had the same double window arrangement as the other rooms. There were two doors in its back wall. The one in the center of the wall led to the kitchen. The kitchen featured the usual big cast iron stove, the counters and cupboards you would expect. The sink in the back counter was serviced with a hand pump and had a window over it. There was a preparation table in the center of the room and an icebox next to the doorway which led to the back-center hall with its door to the outside.

On returning to the dining room, they opened the second door. This door was located next to the wall that backed the fireplace. It led to the back-central hall also. The main feature of this back-center hall was the stairs to the upper level. Patsy and Bill climbed the stairs and were greeted by a second central hall leading back to the front of the house. At the top of the stairs was a door on the right which opened into a bedroom. Across the center hall at the top of the stairs was a door to a second bedroom. Each of these bedrooms had potbellied stoves for heat in the winter and the double window arrangement they had seen downstairs. The hallway to the front of the house ended in two more doors leading to two more bedrooms. Each room had its own fireplace around the central chimney from the downstairs fireplace. Patsy looked at Bill and said, "This has the makings of a mansion why would anyone let this go for taxes?"

Bill replied, "Let's go look at the stable and the paddock, then we will find out why it has gone unclaimed."

They returned downstairs and headed for the back door. Tucked under the stairs was a wood box handy to the outside door. On opening the outside door, they found a large porch. A long side the porch was the entrance to the root cellar.

The stable was down in a swale to the left of the house. This would provide excellent drainage away from the house. The pasture was full of tall grass, the fence looked to be in good shape and the stable was fitted with stalls including a box stall. Bill said, "I don't know what more we could wish for in a house?"

"I can't think of a thing."

"Are you ok with this then?"

"Yes. With a few improvements this would become the house of my dreams."

They rode back to town to find out the story about the property not being kept by the present owners and close the deal if possible. The County tax office was ready for them. The story behind the house being taken for taxes was a tragedy. "During the uprising, on its first day, when emotions were highest, the entire family was ambushed and killed on their way to town. No kin have been found to claim the property. After one year of extensive searching with no result, the County had no choice but to take it over.

"Well!" said Bill "That is really sad, but the former owners can look down with pride at the house they built. We intend to give it as much love as the previous owners did. We are going to accept the County's offer and make it our home for the duration of my tenure as Sheriff. Are there papers we need to sign?

The papers required a little explanation before Bill and Patsy were ready to sign them. About a half an hour later they were tenants in the house on the hill.

They stopped a Milly's for a sandwich and to tell her they were selling. The county assessor had told them $800.00 would be a fair price.

As they rode out of town Patsy said with a chuckle, "Does this mean no swimming?"

That night, with their wet bathing suits drying on a line stretched between the eaves and a nearby tree, Patsy wrote a long letter to her mother about the events and changes taking place in their lives. Bill wrote a short note to his father and mother telling them about his new job and explaining why he would like to sell the homestead. He asked their blessing on the proposed sale.

It was hard for them to find peace this night with so many things going on in their lives. Even snuggling in each other's arms didn't bring the calm that it usually did. Finally, exhaustion took over and they dropped into a fitful sleep.

The next morning, Patsy and Bill rode into town. The weather was continuing to make Minnesota look and feel like Eden. They stopped at Milly's for breakfast and to talk about her offer to buy their place. Patsy said, "Could you and your family stop out this afternoon. You can look the place over, and we can talk about the deal."

"We can't do that today; Ed is on a job this afternoon and tomorrow."

"What does Ed do?" Asked Bill.

"He is a handyman. He does a lot of different odd jobs."

"He sounds like the man we are looking for. We want to hire somebody to fix up our new home. Does he do carpentry, remodeling and painting?"

"Yes, he does. For an opportunity like this, I think we should make the effort to come out your way this evening."

"Oh, by the way, Milly, we checked around some more and it seems $800 is more than just a fair price it's a slightly below market price for our place. You and Ed talk it over and maybe we can close that deal this evening also."

"We will see you about 6:30 then."

Patsy and Bill mounted and rode to their new home for another look around. They made a list of all the repairs and changes they would like to have done. Then they rode home again to wait for Milly and Ed.

It was about 6:15 when the Saunders arrived. Ed was a block of a man, stout, strong and capable looking. The sons, Tom and Jack were duplicates of their dad. Milly looked like a twig in comparison to her men folks.

Patsy had found a nice bed of rhubarb hidden behind the tall grass near the corner of the corral fence so she had made a pie for the evening thinking they could all enjoyed a product grown on the farm before getting down to business. The pie was a nice way to start out the evening. After the pie, the boys went off to look the fields over to find out what needed to be done to get in some kind of crop during the remainder of this year's growing season.

The adults gathered in the kitchen with their coffee to work out the details of the contract to buy and sell the farm. They agreed without any haggling that $800 was a very fair price for the property. They also agreed that the living quarters, the barn and home corral would not be vacated and turned over until the new property was ready for occupancy. The exception was that corral and barn would be used jointly with the boys being responsible for its up-keep and care of the stock. Further, the buyers could immediately start farming the property including harvesting and selling the hay crop, plowing and planting. The buyers were to immediately deposit $100 as a good faith escrow in the bank. The re-mainder will be paid by work on Bill and Patsy's new property at $5.00 per day or cash at the choice of the buyer.

Next, they went over Bill's and Patsy's list of things they would like Ed to do. At the end they all shook hands to seal the deal.

As Millie and Ed were climbing into their buck-board Bill asked them if they knew when the former Sheriff's funeral would be.

The answer they gave was tomorrow at 10 A.M. With that the drove off to look for their boys.

Patsy and Bill discussed their plans for the time between now and when they could move into the new place permanently. They decided Patsy should look for something to keep her busy during the week when Bill would do his sheriffing. If Bill need to be gone overnight or on a weekend, she would go with him.

They put in another restless night and were up early the next morning to prepare for the former Sheriff's funeral. It was going to be a hard day with lots of questions to answer for which they had very few answers. They arrived on time and joined the gathering crowd. The ceremony was more like a farewell than a burial. The burial was scheduled for later in the week in Rochester, Minnesota, his hometown. They left for home as soon as they could get away from the crowd.

On May 25th Bill started making the rounds of all the Town Marshalls in the county. Within nine days, he had visited all of them. His message was the same at each stop, cooperation. The conversation started out with the question from Bill, "What can the county sheriff's office do for you?" The conversation always ended with a short list of what the sheriff's office would hope the Town Marshall would be willing to do as part of the Redwood County Law Enforcement Network Bill was trying to build.

The county board followed through on their plan to hold a shindig to introduce the new sheriff. Signs popped up all over the county announcing:

**All County Residents are Invited to a
Meet and Greet with the New County Sheriff
Being held Friday Night in Redwood Falls,
It will Feature a Potluck and Dance!
Friday June 3, 1865, 5:30 to 10 at the County Hall**

On Thursday, June 2nd the news circulated around the county that Kirby-Smith had surrendered the last Confederate Army still in existence turning Texas and western Louisiana over to Union control. The American Civil War was over.

Friday night Patsy and Bill arrived at the county hall at about five PM. They enjoyed the potluck dinner. Patsy contributed two rhubarb pies to that feast. They were even able to get in a few dances together before a steady stream of well-wishers started to monopolize their time.

Several people asked Patsy what she was doing scooting around town with that strange green wagon attached to the back of her pinto pony. The gooseneck hitch always caught everyone's attention.

Patsy explained she was the City's "Welcome and Get-Well Ambassador." As Welcome Ambassador She went around to newcomers with samples from businesses advertising their goods. As Get-Well Ambassador she takes lunches around to shut-ins so that the City can be sure they are getting at least one

hot meal a day. Most people ask where the meals being delivered come from? The answer they got was,
from the church basement where a different group of
volunteers make them fresh every weekday.

Bill noticed the sparkle was back in Patsy's eyes
as they kibitz with the folks.

The bays pranced their way home without much
guidance from the driver or his companion. Bill and
Patsy were too wrapped up in each other to care
about the world around them.

Bill parked the buggy and took care of the bays.
When he made it to the bedroom Patsy met him in
that provocative outfit, she had worn on their wedding night. Bill was so taken in that he could not
control his emotions. He was only partially undressed
when the dam of self-control broke, and he rode with
his boots on.

Once was not enough to sate the fire burning in
their souls. They recoupled again and again before
exhaustion overcame desire and they slept in each
other's arms.

Saturday morning arrived and it heralded one
of those beautiful July Minnesota days, not too hot,
not too humid, exactly right for being outside. When
Minnesotans think of outside on such a lovely day,
they think of water and picnics. Patsy got a lunch together and they decided they would ride over to their

new house and see if there was a good swimming hole in the river with a place to picnic.

When they stepped out of the house, Bill notice all the changes that were taking place. The grass in the yard around the house had been cut. A small stack was curing in the front yard. The grass around the pen, under and in the fence and in the pen, itself had been cut and stacked. Bill said with a smile, "It looks like the Saunders are operating on that old saw, 'Make hay while the sun shines."

They were pleased with the energy the Saunders were putting into working the farm.

They saddled up and galloped out of the yard on their way to the Redwood River. As they rode, they enjoyed the woods and the beautiful day. They crossed Ferry Road and saw no one and shortly came to the bank of the river.

Riding down river they had to make a detour around a good-sized swale. There were shrubs and trees masking the shore from their view, but they were alerted to trouble by shouts and screams from the direction of the river.

Bill turned Butch toward the commotion. The horse and rider slid down the bank to the floor of the swale. The floor was solid, so Bill urged the gelding to pick up speed. They broke out of the underbrush on to a sand beach. There were several kids on the beach pointing out toward a log floating away down the river with a small boy entangled in its branches. Bill again urged Butch for more speed. Butch responded with an all-out burst that overtook the log in a flash. Bill angled Butch into the river as close to the log as he could get. He then made a shallow dive out of the saddle that brought him up to the trapped youngster. Working quickly, he freed the boy from the tree's grasp. Butch had kept abreast of the log, so Bill caught a stirrup and hung on as Butch pulled the two of them to shore.

In the meantime, Patsy and Patches had arrived on the beach and Patsy was working to calm the kids down. When Butch got Bill and the youngster on the riverbank, Patsy grabbed the boy and hugged him both to reassure him he was safe and to give him as much warmth as she could. Bill rummaged in the saddlebags for the towels they had brought along. He gave them both to Patsy, one to use as a blanket and one to dry the soaked kid off.

Then Bill dug in his bags for rags to dry his guns and holsters. When he was finished wiping them off, he draped them over Butch's saddle to dry. When Patsy finished drying the boy Bill took the wet towel and dried himself as much as he could. With the excitement over, things slowed down to a normal pace.

Patsy suggested they all share lunch, so nods of agreement turned to smiles of contentment. Patsy being a prototype woman had packed enough lunch for an army. Everyone ate their fill and there were still leftovers. The afternoon passed with the Cheevers and the kids getting acquainted while swimming and frolicking on the beach.

Bill found out that the boy in the tree was named Bill also, William Flowers. He was called Billy by his friends. His father had been a Corporal in the First Minnesota and was killed during its suicide charge that saved Little Round Top from being captured by rebels on the second day of the battle of Gettysburg. Little Round Top was a strategic part of the Union's defense line that day at that time.

Billie's father was one of the estimated 618,222 soldiers killed in the American Civil War: 359,222 North and 258,000 South.

Billy told Bill that he and his mother lived in an old warehouse that used to belong to the Sioux Traders. The traders simply abandoned it after the uprising started and never returned because their business disappeared when the Indians did.

Billy said several other women and their children whose husbands had not survived the war lived there too. Billy said there were also men living there with war wounds that made it difficult for them to find work.

Bill and Patsy had never heard of this side of Redwood Falls' society, but they knew immediately they were going to find out all they could about it.

Chapter 26
We Want to Help

The people living in the warehouse with Billy and his mom are victims of war that do not appear in any statistical description of war. The total number of people Nationwide whose lives were altered by the American Civil War as collateral damage must have been staggering.

Bill and Patsy knew they wouldn't be able to help all the forgotten victims, but they thought it would be worth their while if they could even help a few of them. Bill remembered what the farmer who stopped his wagon on his way to market in Vicksburg and told the stretcher bearers to put the General's stretcher on his wagon said, He had said *'I can't give all these poor souls a ride but this little bit I can do.'*

This reminded Bill of his belief that, *'The Sioux uprising could be attributed to the War Between the*

States also. A government totally immersed in its survival forgot its obligation to another Nation putting the Minnesota Sioux into a situation of starvation and despair. The Sioux responded by trying to take what they believed they were owed sparking a war they had no chance of winning and thus they lost everything. All the Sioux who survived the war; the women, children, old people and good guys who help whites survive the hostilities as Fox Feather, Erect Bear and Bold Otter did for his parents were exiled and thus became collateral damage of the war. If one looked you could find the forgotten casualties of war almost anywhere in the Nation. Bill thought, '*I wish there were some way I could help them too. but helping Billy, his mom and the others here in Redwood County, Redwood Falls and vicinity will have to be enough for now.*'

Bill asked Billy if all the kids on the beach lived in the old warehouse. The answer he got was no, only he, Jamie and Louise lived there. The rest of the kids lived nearby and were friends from school.

As the afternoon waned, Bill said to Patsy, "I would like to meet Billy's mother and look over the situation they are living in. Will it be ok with you if I ask him if I can give him a ride home? Oh, by the way Louise and Jamie live in the warehouse too. I thought I'd take Billy and Jamie on Butch with me and Louise could ride with you."

"Sure, I know I want to help those people and your plan seems to be a good way to get started. So yes, let's do that."

A little later Bill asked the group. "When do your folks expected you home?

Someone asked, "Is it 3 o'clock yet?"

Bill took out his watch and proclaimed it to be ten minutes to three. Billy's school friends said they needed to go get the cows in for milking. Each one of them stopped and got a hug from Patsy, told her how good the lunch had been and how much fun they had this afternoon. After saying goodbye to Patsy, they each went over to where Bill was and told him they were glad he was the new sheriff and how glad they were he had been here to save Billy. They all waved goodbye when they got to the top of the swale's bank and then disappeared.

Bill asked the remaining three if it would be ok with them if Patsy and he gave them a ride home?

"Yes," was their answer.

Patsy mounted Patches and Bill helped Patsy get Louise up behind her. Louise put her arms around Patsy and hung on for dear life.

Bill lifted Jamie up in front of the saddle horn on Butch's saddle and then mounted. He had Billy stand on a convenient tree limb while he put his right hand under his armpit, said "jump" and swung him on to the saddle behind him. "You guys ready, hold on, here we go."

The horses had no trouble getting out of the swale. Bill asked Billy what direction they should go. He pointed east in the direction of the old abandoned Lower Sioux Agency site.

The ride was a bit uncomfortable in a way but fun in another way. They skirted around Redwood Falls and continued east until they pulled up to the hitch rack in front of the warehouse.

The warehouse was built out of fitted native stone, mostly gray in color. This was the warehouse the traders had used to store supplies meant for the treaty payment. There were bullet pockmarks in the rock walls of the building and in the heavy plank wagon doors. There was a people entry door with its windowpanes gone to the right of the wagon doors A rug hung over the window hole to keep the weather out.

Bill supposed, *'This damage must have been done on that first day of the uprising when the attackers were trying to dislodge the defenders. As he remembered the story he'd heard about this warehouse, the attackers broke off their attack here too join in burning the agency's other buildings. This gave the defenders time to sneak away across the Redwood Ferry. When the Indians returned to the warehouse, they found it undefended, so they took the stored goods and left without further damage to the building.*

Bill swung Billy down by his arm, so he was almost touching the ground before he let him go. Next, he swung Jamie down and then dismounted himself. He then walked over and lifted Louise off Patch's back so Patsy could swing out of the saddle unhindered.

Bill said, "Billy, would you mind asking your mother if she could come out and talk to us for a few minutes? "

"I don't know if I should. Are you going to tell her about the stupid thing I did at the river?"

"No, that is strictly between us. We just want to make sure you're safe here for the time being"

Billy said, "Ok." He, Jamie and Louise disappeared through the warehouse door.

About five minutes later Billy returned with a rather large, woman with a soft motherly look about her. She had on a faded floral pattern apron, a flour sack dress. Her brown hair showing signs of graying. It was done up in a large bun on the back of her neck. The side of her face was scarred with a large burned patch spreading down from her hairline across her ear, down her cheek and down her neck disappearing under the neck hemline of her dress. It looked like the kind of scar you get when you have been scalded by boiling hot water.

She had a puzzled, somewhat concerned look on her face. "What did Billy do now?"

"Nothing." Bill said, "Mrs. Flowers, "I am Sheriff Cheever of Redwood County and this is my wife Patsy. We heard of your circumstances here and we want to help you and the others living here as much as we can. I was in the war like your husband, but I was lucky and survived. My wife and I are going to try to make people around here realize there are some amongst us who gave more than others and still need help to get back on their feet."

"That's good of you Sheriff. It would help a lot if you could help us find work. No one wants to hire a scary, scarred old woman or someone with a useless leg or a guy with one arm. Having such a person hang around would be bad for business, they say."

"Getting jobs will be our third priority. Our first priority is to make sure you are all safe and healthy. Our second one is that you are getting enough to eat on a regular basis. Once those two issues are solved, we will put our full effort into finding jobs for as many of you as we can. I would like to return tomorrow with my wife Patsy and Doc Simmons. While the doc is finding out how healthy each of you are, Patsy will work with you to arrange a menu for next week. I will talk to each person so we can match each person's experience with the jobs we find. Do you think that would be ok with you and the rest of the group?"

"I can't see why anybody would complain about that. We all know we need help."

"Patsy, why don't you and Mrs. Flowers make a list of kitchen staples they could use now?"

"Would it be alright if Corea McHugh worked with us? She and I have been sharing kitchen duty."

Patsy answered that enquiry, "Of course that is ok."

By 5:00 o'clock the list of needed kitchen supplies was ready and arrangements for the next day visits were in place. As the Cheevers left for their ride home, they heard a voice call out, "God bless you!"

They rode to Redwood Falls to check with Doc Simmons on his availability for tomorrow's visit. He promised he'd be at the warehouse at 9:00 sharp. Bill checked with the county tax office to see who the registered owner of the warehouse was. It turned out to be the Federal Government. On their way home they stopped to see how the new house was coming along.

As the house came into sight, they were delighted with the impression it made. The cool green grass hill leading up to the mellow yellow house with cream trim made the view a masterpiece worthy of hanging in an art gallery. They just caught Ed and his crew shutting down for the day. So, Ed showed them the fixes he and his crew had made thus far. Most of the items on the list they had given Ed were fixed. Ed said, "You can start moving in anytime. Most of the remaining work is outside."

Bill replied, "We'll start moving some time later this week. Thanks Ed, great job. We have several things going on so it might be awhile before we see you again."

Patsy prompted Ed to, "Please say hello to Milly and the boys for us."

Bill added, "Those boys are doing a bang-up job on the haying."

"Yaw, they have already sold it to the livery."

"Great, we'll see you soon Ed." With that they mounted and rode away.

They reviewed their day over coffee that evening. After taking it over they decided to hire Mrs. Flowers as their housekeeper at twenty-five cents per day with room and board for her and Billy. They would also see if any of the men knew horses and would be able to handle taking care of Butch, Patches and the Bays at the same wage as Mrs. Flowers. Billy would be paid a penny a day plus miscellaneous help on outside expenses like school and clothes.

Now that they had some idea of what they wanted for the future they lay down to rest. Patsy asked

Bill, "Do you think we are over sexed having intercourse almost every night?"

Bill looked at her thoughtfully for second and then said, "It's not the sex that matters to me, what matters is the total togetherness feeling while we are coupled. I love you so much, I just want to be as close to you as I can get as much of the time as I can."

"That was beautifully put and all though I had not formulated the words, you captured my feelings exactly."

"Good night my love." But sleep didn't come until their loving was complete for the day.

Next morning, they met Doc Simmons at the warehouse. He said before even getting out of his buggy, "No one can really be healthy living in a place with no ventilation or sunlight. You either must put windows in this place or move them elsewhere if you expect to keep them healthy. I'll give them a thorough examination and then report back to you."

After his examination Doc Simmons reported one of the vets had a serious health problem. Frank Stanley had TB and needed to be put into the county sanitarium immediately. Doc said he'd take Frank with him when he left. He was sure he could get him into the sanitarium that afternoon. He said, "I better be able to get him in, after all I am on the Board of Directors for the place and I am quarantine him as of right now. Max Sharper needs dental surgery. I know a couple of the best dental surgeons in the country. I'll see if they will take Max's case on an experimental basis. That leaves you 11 able bodied adults and five children to nurture. I don't know how you'll do it but good luck in your efforts to help and God bless you for trying. Come on Frank, we have to get you some help pronto." Doc's whip cracked over the buggy team and away the team went in a well synchronized trot.

Bill had talked to the adults individually throughout the day. Three of them had worked as farmhands. Each of these were hobbled by leg wounds. One guy had been a clerk of court in Hennepin County but when he showed up with an arm missing at the elbow, the county judge wouldn't even give him a chance to show what he could do. Another guy had been shot in the mouth. He was having trouble with his speech, opening his mouth and biting. He needed specialized help before anything else. There was one guy who interested Bill. He professed to be good with horses. He had a stiff leg and some back pain if he lifted too heavy a load.

The last guy living there had owned a hardware store which had gone broke because of neglect while he was away. When he got home, he was told a different story. This story started with a fast-talking sharpie who sweet talked the guy's wife into selling off all the merchandise they could and then the building. The last anyone heard, the sharpie and wife were living it up out west somewhere. His main wound was loss of pride and self-confidence. His war record told a story of bravery and tenacity.

The interviews over, Bill and Patsy had coffee and talked about their day. Patsy said, "I offered Mrs. Flowers the housekeeping job and she accepted. I would like to move her and Billy in as soon as we can provide bedroom furniture for them."

Bill said, "Good, I hired one of the guys as a deputy sheriff, one as a clerk to run my office and I found one guy I think would be a good horse handler for us. I will hire him if that's okay with you."

Patsy nodded her approval. "Are you ready to go home?

"In just a bit. I'll meet you at the front door, He went and offered Hal Marks the horse handler job, which he accepted. The deputy Bill had hired was the jilted husband, Grady Mensch. Bill was impressed with his war record and believed he only needed a chance to gain his confidence back.

He also hired Charlie Cahill, the ex-clerk, to run the sheriff's office for him. Last, he offered the farmers, Casey Cox, Lee Storm and Chris Smith a chance to farm the land that had come with the new house.

It was a sweet deal for them and for the castoffs. Bill and Patsy would take care of all the initial cost to get started and any cost overruns and in return the farmers would supply produce to the Cheevers and to the warehouse kitchen. They were thinking about it and would decide in a few days.

He explained the farm deal to Patsy on their way home. Patsy and Bill were pleased with the day's progress, one woman, her son and three men employed and three other men pondering an opportunity to get back to farming. Not bad for a start on their help campaign.

Chapter 27

Progress

B illy's mom, Emma, was in the kitchen of the Cheevers new house getting breakfast for the family. The family had grown these last few days. First to come were the Flowers, Billy and Emma. Next was Hal Marks. Hal had a special gift for handling horses. Patches, Butch and the Bays loved Hal and Hal seemed the love them. Bill liked to watch as the horses responded to his kindness. Billy was doing fine learning about horses from Hal.

Bill was especially pleased with the way things were going for those forgotten victims of war who were barely surviving in the old warehouse a week or so ago. When people in the county learned about the forgotten casualties of war living in their midst, they opened their hearts and purses to them.

One morning after Bill and Patsy had started their word of mouth campaign, an eight-burner used wood stove showed up in front of the warehouse door, stove pipe and all. The same day Ed's crew installed it in the area now called the kitchen.

Two days later, a new washstand with wash tubs was delivered from Emmon's General Store including a clothes wringer.

A menu of meals for the week hung next to the stove. The group was now getting nourishing food on a regular basis. Jamie's mother, at the same wage as Emma, became boss of the kitchen. There was now a steady flow of cash donations to allow this extravagance. It also allowed Jamie to be employed as helper and janitor with much the same deal as Billy had from the Cheevers.

Other improvements included an icebox and weekly ice delivery donated by "The Harris Ice Co". The addition of the cold storage had a significant effect on the quality of the food served.

Each person now had their own cot equipped with a mattress, mattress sack and sheets. Sleepers also had a pillow, a pillowcase and a wool blanket in standard army brown with USA stenciled on it. The cot and all the things that went with it were donated by the garrison at Fort Ridgely. A great use for the surplus, now the war was over.

The most significant improvement came a couple of days after Doc's examinations. A flat bed wagon loaded with five piles of something hidden under a canvas tarp pulled up in front of the warehouse. Riding on the edge the wagon were six men in work clothes. The men jumped down and removed the tarp exposing piles of prefab double hung windows. These were a new innovation on the building market. Each had a screen and a storm accompanying it.

The wagon's driver got out and took charge of the crew. Using chalk, the foreman laid out where the first window should go. It was to the left of the wagon door between the door and the corner of the building. This window would be in the dining area of the kitchen. The foreman moved around the corner and marked a place on the wall 10 ft. from the corner. The outline of the window opening straddling the middle of the 10' from the corner mark. This window would also be in the dining area of the kitchen. He then moved another ten feet to mark the corner of the planned kitchen. The stove pipe exited the building in the middle of this last ten feet of the designated kitchen. From there on a window was sketched in the middle of every ten feet of wall. The ten windows on the wagon would provide two windows in the kitchen and eight ventilated, healthy living spaces.

Each pair of workers took crowbars, sledges and stone bits off the wagon and proceeded to turn chalk outlines into window openings. It took three days open nine holes and install nine windows. On the fourth day one pair of workers finished the tenth window while the other four cleaned up the rock debris from their work.

No one ever found out who the good Sumerian was that footed the bill for the windows, but Bill always thought it was Doc Simmons in cahoots with Harvey the lumberyard owner. The lumberyard did use the installed windows as hype for this prefab new product.

Perhaps equally important to the warehouse occupants was the number of jobs their members had gotten. Of course, the largest part of these jobs was provided by Bill and Patsy. Besides hiring Emma, Billy and Hal to work for them, Bill had managed to get the county to hire the former court recorder, Charlie Cahill to run his office and keep the records. In addition, Bill employed Grady Mench as one of his squad of deputies. Grady was the veteran with the good service record whose wife and new paramour had liquidated his business and stole all the cash. Still further, the farmers, Casey Cox, Lee Storm and Chris Smith were going to work the land on Patsy and Bills new place with a very favorable sharecropping agreement.

The word of this refuge was getting around to groups of needy in Redwood County and the surrounding territory. A trickle of newcomers was showing up every day in need of help.

While Bill was pleased with progress, he and Patsy were making regard the castoffs of war situation, he was not pleased with his pace of setting up the sheriff's office. He needed deputies and he needed them fast.

He was planning on spending this day on making his pitch to Zeke. He knew Zeke usually ate breakfast at Milly's about 9 o'clock and he planned to ambush him there. About 8 he mounted Butch and rode into town. He stopped in his office to find out if Charlie had any messages for him. "Hello Charlie, anything happening that I need to look into?"

"You have several telegrams you might want to check out."

After looking through the telegrams, Bill said, "You remember that request we sent to the War Department asking for ownership of the warehouse? Well the War Department says that request has to go to 'The Bureau of Indian Affairs'. Take care of that will you. Also, I want you to do some detective work for me. I want to know every piece of property in the county that the county believes is abandoned and/or unoccupied. Can you handle that?"

"Sure can. what do you need if for?"

"I'm looking for places people might be using that the county isn't aware of."

"When would you like to the list?

"Yesterday would have been a good time but realistically I'll check back with you at the end of the week. I have some business to take care of now. I'll stop back before I leave town. By the way, where is Grady?"

"Out buying a horse and a gun at county's expense." He said with a smirk.

"Good, we're not only understaffed we are equipment poor. Find out if you can if the last sheriff had any county stuff, like horses, guns and handcuffs stashed away. I've got to go now."

Bill entered Milly's right after Zeke and some young guy he was with. "Mind if I set and jabber for a few minutes Zeke."

"Not at all. This guy is an old friend from the war. Bill Cheever meet Terry Ham from down Kansas way. He is a little cheeky but an exceptionally good man in a fight."

"Thanks for the big build up Zeke, sorry sheriff but Zeke gets a bit full of himself on occasion. I read about your exploits in the St. Paul Pioneer Press and Zeke confirmed how skillful you were in the field. In fact, you are the reason I showed up here. I plan to use Zeke to get to meet you."

"Well, that mission is accomplished. Just a minute Terry. Milly, sorry to keep you standing there with that heavy coffee pot. You can unload some of it here in my cup."

"Mine too." said Zeke.

"Oh well I don't think it will soil my reputation too much to be seen drinking with these two, so I'll have a cup also."

"Thanks guys. I was about to hand this pot to one of you and leave for a nap." Milly filled the cups, put the cream on the table, and dug the sugar out of her apron. She put the sugar next to the cream and said, "Holler when you get ready to order breakfast." She turned and strode her way back to the kitchen.

"Why did you want to meet me, Terry?"

"Frankly, I would like to learn the profession of peace officering. I believe the best way to learn something is to do it and the best way to do it is with the best. If you aren't the best, you are pretty damned good."

"Thank you for the compliment. This is quite a coincidence. I'm here to ask Zeke to become my chief deputy. If he says yes to that proposal, he will have the say as to who's hired as deputies. Zeke what do you say?"

"Let me think on it for a while. I'll stop over after breakfast with my answer."

Bill called out, "Milly, you have two hungry paying customers here. See you two soon." With that he took a dime out of his pocket and put it on the table next to his empty cup and walk out the door.

When Bill arrived back at his office Grady was there waiting for him. "Did you want to see me sheriff?"

"Yes, how are things going so far?"

"Everything is pretty much up in the air right now. I am waiting for some loose ends to be tied up, so I know what I'm supposed to be doing."

"That should become clearer by the end of the day. Did you find a gun and horse that suited you?"

"Yah, the gunsmith had a used holster rig with a Colt .36 caliber Navy Revolver which is the pistol I am most familiar with. He also had a Sharps Carbine which he says is going out of style, so we got it at a bargain. He through in a scabbard for the Sharps."

"Are six pistol shots enough for you? I've always found that a second pistol full gives me an advantage in a running fight."

"I usually carry a 6" hideout for extra firepower."

"I do too but I have never been sorry for too many shots and several times I moaned about to few."

"Right I'll think of that when I get my first pay."

"Don't wait for your first pay. Draw what you need from Charlie and get properly heeled. That means another revolver and holster for your waist and a holdout gun for your boot or wherever you keep it. Wait a minute, here comes the word for which I've been waiting."

Zeke and Terry push open the office door and entered.

"Well?" Bill asked.

"You've got yourself a couple of deputies."

Bill stood up and shook their hands. "Welcome aboard. I'd like you to meet Grady. Grady meet Zeke and Terry. Zeke is your boss when I'm not here. You guys are three fourths of my deputy force." The deputies shook hands all around.

Bill yelled, **"Charlie, do we have any more chairs?"**

"Yes sir, in the back." was Charlie's reply.

"You guys will have to get your own chairs. You'll understand why when you meet Charlie."

Zeke and Terry found the chairs without a problem and were soon back. "Good thing my pant seat is worn shiny, it's ready to become a permanent dust cloth anyway." Terry said.

Bill ignored Terry's complaint or more likely, attempt at humor and said, "I think we should get to know one another better first. I'll start. I was Sergeant-Major Wilbur James Cheever in the army. My service record tells that I fought with Sherman at Vicksburg, Jackson and Chattanooga. Also, all through the Atlanta campaign. When Sherman went to the sea, I went to Nashville to serve under Thomas. Under Thomas, I led a group that hunted down bad guys in Georgia and elsewhere. Some reporter from the Pioneer Press wrote a story which made me a notorious good guy and that's why I'm here. The town fathers wanted a notorious good guy to scare notorious bad guys away. Grady, what about you?"

"I was Sergeant Grayson Whit Mensch. I served in the Army of the Potomac from first Bull Run through Lee's surrender to Grant at Appomattox. I went to war in the First Minnesota but served in several other units after the First disbanded after Gettysburg. I re-enlisted three times to keep killing those gray traitors." Grady was about five foot five inches tall and maybe 190 to 210 with a fringe of gray hair around his bald head. His gray beard was trimmed to a mutton chop style. His hat was a battered army issue Stetson looking thing with the emblem of his last regiment on it. His shirt, vest, pants and boots were part and parcel of his scruffy look, but he had a sparkle in his eyes that hadn't been there a few days ago.

"Zeke, what is your story?"

"I don't have an army service record. My name is Ezekiel Harp Evers. I was in the war before the War

Between the States started. Back then it was a war between slavery and freedom. The first man I killed happened when I was defending my parent's home from some Missouri Red Legs. We escaped but our farm went up in flames. I help my folks get to Iowa and then went back to fight the Missouri bastards. I, like many Kansas fighting men, ended up in the Jayhawker irregulars, fighting guerrilla style. We did things that were as outrageous as the Red Legs had. When Yankee troops started chasing Jayhawk marauder groups because of their atrocious behavior, I went to Iowa to find my folks. I regret some of the acts of violence in which I have been involved. My shield of self-forgiveness for those acts has been the violence that was the Missouri-Kansas border during those years. " Zeke stood close to six feet tall and looked like he didn't have an ounce of fat on his body. He had a pleasant face and wore nondescript clothes that let him melt into almost any background. The thing that was most outstanding about his face his was his piercing dark blue eyes.

Bill said, "Wow! That area was such a mess in those early years. By the end, the Jayhawkers did the right thing and became part of the Union army and part of the bigger fight. Terry what about you."

"My story is like Zeke's in many ways but different in some important respects. I was not home when the Red Legs came to call. They killed pa. They raped ma and my little sister before they killed them both. Before they left, they drove off what they could, and killed what they couldn't. Of course, they made a big bonfire out of the house and barn. I joined the Jayhawks to get revenge. I have spent every day since then killing every Missourian I could get my hands on. I am soaked in the blood of my victims. Finally, I had to find a way to curb my blood lust, so I came up here to my uncle and aunt's place to get away from my all-consuming hatred. I finally realized I had become a monster like the Red Legs and now I want to protect people instead of killing them, even if they are Missourians." At the end of his spell his face was twisted into a terrible grimace. It was easy to see Terry still struggled with his memories and his fight to forgive and forget his former enemies. His day to day countenance, however, was happy go lucky. His face was pleasant with a smile and cheerful expression. His clothes were attention getting with his red shirt and blue suspenders. He toped these off with a black Bowler hat. Wisps of reddish, curly hair escaped from under the hat.

"So, we all share a common bond, we have all killed another person. I hope we can put our past behind us and serve this county as a force for peace not chaos." Bill said.

Bill took thee badges out of desk drawer and said, "Please stand up and repeat after me, I, (your name), swear to uphold the laws of Redwood County to the best of my ability, so help me God." He then pinned the badges on the shirts of his deputies.

Chapter 28

A Sheriff's Work

B ill now had three deputies and it was time to go to work. "Thank you, guys. I'm so pleased to have your assistance. Remember, we still have room for one more deputy, so if you run across someone you think would fit in our group, let me or Zeke know, and we'll take it from there."

"Now, please sit down and I'll tell you what we are facing. It seems there has been sporadic horse rustling over the last year or more. It appears to be relatively small in scope at first glance. I know by reading the previous sheriff's reports that one horse disappeared in Redwood County during the last six months, two in the last year. The horses that went missing were never found even though an extensive search was conducted. Today I received a telegram from the sheriff of Meeker County asking us to keep an eye out for a Roan horse with a white blaze reaching from its chin down to the bottom of its throat. This made me start thinking, so I looked through all the files I could find. As I read them a pattern of missing horses started to take shape."

"In our county and the surrounding counties about one horse goes missing every three months. Distance between where the thefts occur and the time lapse between thefts taking place in the same vicinity are being used to make the thefts appear random and unconnected. They are trying to make the law men in this state believe that each theft is being done by different individuals. It is my belief that a single person does the stealing in each area but each of these individuals are only one tentacle of a larger operation out of the Minneapolis-St. Paul Area. Instead of a horse per three months or so the pattern shows one or two per month. I'm going to have my dad snoop around up there for the center of the octopus while we look around here to see if we can find our tentacle. I believe our guy is holding the horses he steals in a remote location not necessarily in the county but close. I'm thinking the place the horses are spirited to maybe one or more of the homesteads vacated in the Indian trouble and never reoccupied by its owner."

"Our horse stealing investigation dovetails with another problem I want us to chase. I have found a nest of survivors, collateral damage of the recent war, existing in wretched conditions. Grady was one of those until I brought him to work here. Grady you can tell them about that or not another time as you please. The survivors are living in a building vacated during the Indian uprising. One of the ladies living there has a burn scar on her face made by several applications of boiling water. Grady, do you know anything about Emma's scarred face?"

"I don't know how Mrs. Flower's face became scarred; it was that way when I got there. I do know that every week they, Mrs. Flowers and Mrs. McHugh go around and ask everybody if they have any money for rent."

"Well I just received a telegram from the Marshall at Milroy reporting that a member of such a group was killed by a henchman of a man demanding the group pay rent for the premises they are occupying. It seems this bunch is expanding its collection area. They have also added murder to their methods of persuasion. When an old soldier said, "NO!" They shot him several times in front of the group to impress them as to what would happen if they continued to resist."

"Terry and Zeke, I would like you to ride down to Milroy and check in with the Marshall. Find out what his story is and then get the story from the remaining members of the group. Tell the group they would be welcome here where they would be under our protection. You guys are free to pursue these bad guys just as you did with the 'Red Legs'. They are killers now."

"Grady, I would like you to stick around the warehouse in case the rent collectors return there. See if you can get anyone to tell you about the rent and the rent collectors, especially when they expect them to return. I am sure now that the burns on Mrs. Flower's face were part of the persuasion technique they used on the group when they first tried to collect, and Mrs. Flowers resisted. Those three creeps have got to be stopped. I want their hides nailed to the wall, now. I want you to go undercover at the warehouse Put on your old clothes if you still have them. Do not show your badge or wear guns on your hips. They would not be what the others would expect on you. Always keep your hideout hidden. It's the only fire power you will have available. Don't under any circumstances share why you are back. Tell them you became the forgotten man. Tell them you left, and you don't think the sheriff even knows I'm gone. Tell them that you waited and were not given a badge, a gun or a horse. Tell them you had started to feel as "Useless as tits on a bull" so you left. Tell them it made you feel like you did when you found out you had been tossed by your wife and be sure to act that way too. Do not share what you are really up to with anyone."

"Go out to my house and leave your horse with Hal. Have Billy hide the rest of your stuff. The only gun you'll keep is the hide-out. Have Billy use Patches to take you to a clump of trees where you're not insight of the warehouse but you are within easy walking distance. Walk in like you walked from town at an easy pace so you wouldn't get hot and sweaty."

"All of you be careful, we know these guys will kill. Grady, you be especially careful. You are going to be among friends. The temptation will be to share the burden of your secret with someone you trust. Do not expose yourself to anybody. There is nothing harder for a person to keep then a secret they have sworn to not tell. Failure to keep your secret to yourself could mean death for you."

"All of you, remember these guys are ruthless. When you make an arrest, don't trust anything the person your arresting is saying. They are primarily talking to distract you. In fact, don't let them talk or move unless you specifically order them to. Shoot them at the slightest provocation. I don't have hand-cuffs for you yet so acquire some pigging strings and use them until we have better equipment. Now guys get to work, and I am really glad to have you with me."

The three deputies got up and departed without a word. Grady saw Charlie and then walk toward the gunsmith again. Terry and Zeke took the trail to Milroy. The Redwood County Sheriff's Department was fully engaged in protecting the county's citizens again.

Bill left his office and went to the city's jail to talk to town Marshall Williams. Williams needed to know what was going on in the county so he could better protect the town.

Bill opened the door and said, "Hello Don you got a few minutes?"

The Marshall answered, "Sure Bill, sit down. What's up?"

Bill told him about the horse rustling and the rent collectors. "The only clues I have on these rent collectors are the one that seems to be the boss is a small man while his thugs are big men."

"I'll keep an eye out for them and an ear out for information on both situations. How are things going for you?"

"Pretty good right now. I just hired some deputies. You know one of them. Zeke has signed on as my chief deputy. I was impressed with him when we chased those bank robbers. Well I better get back to the office now, I still have a few things to do before the end of the day."

"Before you leave, I have been thinking of hiring a housekeeper. You wouldn't have one of those casualties who would take on the job

"Are you a bachelor Don?"

"No, but my wife is not very strong and can't keep up with the house and the kids."

"Do you want someone part time or full time? Drop in or live in?"

"I never thought that deeply about it. I'll talk it over with my wife and let you know what would work best for her."

"I'll check and let you know. Bye Don."

"Bye Bill."

After returning from the jail, he had Charlie telegraph the information he had to every town Marshall in Redwood County plus all the surrounding counties.

Then he sat down to write out a wire to his dad.

Dear Dad and Mom (stop) Hired three good men as deputies today (stop) We have a couple of cases we are working on. (stop) Dad, I could use a little help on one of these. (stop) A horse disappears here about once a month. (stop) I have put feelers out to other county sheriffs, and I have returns from five counties around the State that are having the same problem. (stop) I imagine these horse thieves to be like tentacles on an octopus. (stop) The horse thefts are supposed to look like random acts in a localized area, not a statewide crime ring. (stop) I am convinced the body of this octopus will be found in a large volume horse trading area, i.e. Minneapolis or St. Paul. (stop) Would you look around among the horse dealer's and see if there are any that are doing stuff that might be considered suspicious (stop) If you find anything, just file it away under your hat and wire me (stop) I will come up and check it out. (stop) Do not take any chances. (stop) I don't want to tip anybody off that we are investigating a statewide ring. (stop) Love, your son Bill. (end)

Bill took the scribbled telegram to Charlie and said, "Send this please. I am going home now, See you tomorrow." When Bill got home, Billy was setting on the front steps looking kind of forlorn. Bill stopped and said, "Why the long face, kid?"

"Please don't get me wrong Bill, I love what you and Ms. Patsy have done for ma and me, but I do miss the friends I had at the warehouse."

"Sure, you do. What a dunce I have been. Stranding you out here with no way to get around. Tell you what, take Butch down to the stable, pull his saddle and give him a good rubdown. A short drink and a quarter cup of oats. By the time you get that done I'll be ready to see about that transportation problem you have. Get Hal to help you."

Billy jumped up, "I will be ready in a jiff." Taking Butches reins he disappeared around the corner of the house in the direction of the stable.

Bill had to chuckle over the immediate change the idea of shopping for a horse had on the kid. He rounded the house to the back door and called out, "Patsy I am home."

"Patsy is not feeling well today." said a voice from the kitchen. "She is upstairs resting. Have you had lunch today?"

"No, I didn't have time at noon and haven't thought of it since."

"You sit right here, and I'll get you a sandwich and a glass of lemonade."

"That will be perfect because, as sheriff I have some questions for you."

Emma made a roast beef sandwich on fresh baked bread with butter and salad dressing on it. She put it on a plate and served it with a tall glass of ice-cold lemonade. She sat down and said, "What could I possibly know that would help you with your work as sheriff?"

"Emma, I have been wanting to ask you, since the first day I met you. How did you get those scald marks on you face? It looks like there were at least three applications of scalding water poured on to make that scar. Please tell me your story. "

"I'd rather not. I would just as soon forget that awful day I was scalded."

"Emma, the answer to the question may shed some light on a case we are pursuing. Your answers may help us to stop this kind of thing happening to others."

Emma puzzled over the sheriff's comment for a moment before she said, "It happened shortly after the first group of us started living in the warehouse. One day these three men showed up demanding rent from us. The rent they said was a quarter per week per person. I complained that we didn't make enough to pay that much. They said they didn't care how we got the money, but they would be there every week to collect. Then they said that we already owed three weeks rent because we had been staying there that long, I blew my top. I started swearing at them and waving a broom around. The ugly little man with his pinch spectacles on his nose and his bowler hat said we'll collect the first three weeks rent in pain. **'Grab her Dirk.'** he shouted. The two gorillas with him forced my head down on the table. Ugly took the kettle of boiling water off the fire and poured about a cup of it on the side of my head. I screamed in pain. The little guy said in a loud voice, **'that's one week,**

this will make two and poured a second cup on the same spot. I was nearly out of my mind with pain. I am almost sure I screamed again. I really didn't feel the third cup because I was already out of my head with pain. That is all I remember until I woke up on the floor with Mrs. McHugh dribbling cold water on my face. The three showed up every week for several months. Then they changed the payment to monthly. This month's payment should be due next week. That's it, I had never seen any of them before nor have I seen any of them except on rent collection day."

"How much will this month's payment be?" Bill asked.

"Let's see, there were eighteen of us before you started your effort to give us a life. So, the rent will be $72.00 this month."

"Ok, don't say a word to anyone about our conversation. I am sorry about your pain and sorrow, but you and Billy are safe now. We'll see what we can do about Mr. Ugly and his two thugs. One more thing, you said Patsy has been sick in the morning. She hasn't said anything to me about that."

"She said she didn't want to bother you. You have enough of that already. Frankly, Bill, in my experience, sickness of this kind is the first sign of being with child. I am not sure yet but that is a possibility."

"That would be great! God, I hope so. I am going to see her right now."

The back-screen door slammed and Billy, all excited, came into the kitchen. "Everything is done!"

"Well, there are some changes in our plan. I decided Hal should go with us. After all, he's the horse expert. So, take Patches and Butch back to the barn, get Hal and hitch up the Bays. I'll be waiting for you when you get back."

Billy looked disappointed but did what he was told. Bill ran up the stairs to check on Patsy. As he entered the bedroom, he thought she looked pale laying on the bed. He said, "Hi, how are you feeling sweetheart?" as he walked over to the bed and sat down beside her.

"A little under the weather, I feel I may be coming down with the flu. Don't kiss me. I don't want you to get sick."

"Some risks are worth taking if the reward is big enough. One of your kisses is reward enough to face any peril." with that he bent down and gave her a "smack-do" (a miniature smack-a-dozee) "You rest now. I am going out with Billy and Hal horse hunting. I figure Billy needs transportation."

"We should have thought of that sooner. Good luck."

"See you at dinner, bye" and he was gone.

Chapter 29
Preparations

When Hal, Billy and Bill reached town, Bill had Hal drop him off at the bank. "You two go down to the livery stable and look over the horses they are offering. I'll get some money and be along in a few minutes." Bill walked into the Bank and withdrew $200 from his account. Next, he walked over to his office, "Hello again Charlie. Are you making any headway on your detective work?"

"Not much. I've been busy over at the telegraph office sending all those messages you ordered sent. That's done. Why are you back in town this afternoon?"

"I've heard there is a way to mark money, so the marks are invisible unless you put the lemon juice on them. Have you ever heard that?"

"Yes. In fact, I found some of it in the former sheriff's desk. Just a minute and I'll get it for you."

Charlie went into the storage closet and came back in a few minutes with a small bottle with a label on it that said, "Invisible Ink". He also had a second bottle which claimed that a drop or two of it would reveal messages written in that ink.

Bill gave Charlie $72.00 and told him to mark each bill with the invisible ink. "I think the word, "Got-cha" would be appropriate. Put it in the same place on each bill and make a list of the bills noting their denomination and serial number. Put the money in an envelope and put the envelope in the middle drawer of my desk, please. I'll be back in an hour or so to pick it up. Good night Charlie. I'll see you in the morning."

Bill left the sheriff's office and walked across Ferry Road to the gunsmith's shop, then he walked west along the road past Emmons and the bank to "Schroder's Blacksmith and Livery". Out behind the livery he found Mr. Schroder, Michael Schulze, Hal and Billy. Michael was holding the reins of neat looking, medium size gray mare with a white blaze starting just above her eyes and ending just below her nostrils. Hal said, "I looked her over Sheriff. She's 2½ years old, sound of limb and wind. Billy can mount her with a little struggle, and he controlled her fairly well while on her back."

"Hello Mr. Schroder, Michael. Michael, have you

ever been up on this horse? Do you know anything about its speed and stamina?"

"I ride all the horses to keep them in shape. This horse is fast given the length of her stride and I have never had her play out or give up no matter how hard I push her. One thing I like about her is her travel gait. She covers distance fast with an easy lope."

"Billy, will this be a satisfactory mount for you?"

"Yes, I think she is perfect for me now and when I grow a little more."

Bill whispered to Hal, "How much do you think she's worth?"

"I think $35 to $40." said in a whisper just loud enough for all to hear.

"Mr. Schroder, how much are you asking for this half-pint?"

"Well Sheriff I had to pay a premium price for her. I paid it because I thought she would catch the eye of some young lady and her doting father would pony up a few extra dollars to satisfy her whim. I don't think I could let her go for less than $75.00."

"This isn't my daughter and I'm not a doting father, but I am a man with money (he flashed the roll of bills from his pocket) and a desire to buy a small horse this afternoon for this young man. I'll give you $30.00 for the horse."

"God, if I made deals like that I'd have to move my family out to that warehouse where your forgotten casualties live but I'll tell you what since you are new in town and the sheriff and all, I'll give you my best offer without all this haggling. $65.00 for horse, saddle, blanket, bridle and halter."

"Well we are getting close to a deal. I'll tell you what, I'll come up $20.00 if you come down $15.00.

"So, you are offering me $50.00 for the horse and all the trappings we've mentioned."

"That's right, cash on the barrelhead, right now." Bill flashed the wad of bills again.

"I'd go hungry if everybody I dealt with were as stubborn as you. I can't believe I am saying this but ok, it's a deal." They shook hands as the $50 appeared and disappeared. Mr. Schroder took out a piece of paper and wrote out a bill of sale and handed it to Bill who turned and handed it to Billy.

The gray had all the equipment included in the deal already installed on her except the halter.

Michael went in to the stable and came back with a rope halter which he gave to Billy.

Bill said, "Thank you, it's been a pleasure." He and Hal got in the buggy and Bill told Billy to meet them at his office. The buggy started down the street while Billy grabbed the saddle horn and with a combination pull and jump managed to get his foot in the stirrup and swing into the saddle. He followed the buggy down the street.

When they got to Bill's office, Bill excused himself and retrieved the marked money from his desk. Back in the street he told Billy they were going to the warehouse so he could plan to meet his friend's tomorrow. He told Hal he had to go out there to talk to Grady about why he left town without letting him know what was going on. He also gave Hal the $72.00 of marked money and told him to tell whoever was going to pay the rent this month to use this money for it. Explain that by next month we'll have a regular system for paying it that will be fair for all. Tell them I'm footing the bill because we didn't have time to figure out how it should be paid.

Hal agreed on doing what Bill asked.

When they reached the warehouse, Billy met with his friends, Hal slipped the money to Mrs. McHugh and Bill met with Grady where they clashed in load voices about Grady's leaving and communicated in whispers about their findings and plans. Grady had found out that the rent collectors were expected tomorrow afternoon. Bill told Grady about the money and that all he expected from him was information.

Bill said, "Do not confront these guys unless they are going to hurt someone. See if you can discreetly get a look at them and study their features, especially any discriminating characteristics and marks. I'll be close by in case there is trouble. When they leave sneak down to the ferry landing as quickly as you can; I'll be there with our horses and your guns." Bill ended their fake fight with, "Don't bother coming back, I'm through with you."

Bill came out and hollered, "Hal, let's get out of here. Billy are you coming?"

"I'm coming." Billy yelled back.

The three of them were soon on their way home for supper.

Patsy was feeling better and joined the family for supper. It was pleasant having them all together.

As Bill and Hal expected, Billy was all excited about his horse and couldn't stop talking about her. Patsy asked Billy what he was going to name her. Billy said he hadn't given it much thought but agreed it was something that needed to be done sooner rather than later. The name chosen was "Ghost" shortened from the real favorite, "Gray Ghost".

After dinner Bill told Hal to have Grady's horse saddled and ready to go at 11:30 in the morning, including his handguns and rifle.

Bill and Patsy retired early feeling the necessity to talk about the future. What if Patsy were with child, how would that affect their lives? They were both kind of clueless to the baby birthing process. So, the next thing they need to find out was if she was pregnant and if she is, what rules does she have to live with until she gave birth. Dr. Simmons should be able to provide the answers to both those questions. They decided that Patsy should go to the Doc's office tomorrow alone to have the doctor's full attention and seek confirmation of pregnancy and other information. Their plans made they fell asleep in each other's arms. They slept with concerns about what they didn't know and delighted with the prospect of having a child to share.

Hal insisted on sleeping and spending most of his time in the barn with the horses. So as usual he arrived with Butch already for Bill to jump on and get on his way. Breakfast over Bill did just that. On his way to town he wondered, *has 'Doc. heard from his dentist friends. Max Sharper was having trouble keeping his weight up trying to eat with his shot-up mouth.* Bill also wondered *how Zeke and Terry were doing in Milroy.* Bill's main thoughts *were about the rent collectors and if his plans for them would work.*

By the time Bill got to his office, his head was clear of stray thoughts and was in its honed action mode. He pulled Butch up at the office hitch rack and looped his reins over it. He stopped in the office to see if Charlie had anything for him. Charlie handed him a note from Doc Simmons saying, Next

Saturday I need to have Max in St. Paul for an examination of his mouth. I will be taking the boat out of here early Thursday morning with Max. Can you arrange to have Max at the Minnesota River Docks by 8:00 A.M. that morning? If not let me know, I'll need to make other arrangements.

Bill asked Charlie if he could rent a horse and buggy on Wednesday evening to go out and get Max from the warehouse, get him a room for the night and make sure he was at the dock by 8 the next morning. Charlie said sure. Bill took out a $20 bill and gave it to Charlie for expenses. He asked Charlie if he could let Doc know that Max would be there ready to go. Again, Charlie said sure.

The telegram was from his father, Son (stop) I have had some concerns about one horse dealer who jumped from a small-time operation to the leading volume dealer within a few months (stop). His name is Ray Delevan. (stop) He always seems to have prime stock to sell. (stop) You might want to come home and look at his operation (stop). Jim Cheever (end).

Bill thought, *it would be nice to see the folks and Patsy could talk about having a child with mom.*

Bill left the office and walk over to the Judge's. The Honorable Judge McKay was in, but his clerk wasn't. Bill knocked on the door and the Judge called out, "Who is it?"

The reply he received was, "Sheriff Cheever."

The Judge in turn said, "Come in."

Bill opened the door and let himself in. The Judge greeted him with, "Hi Bill. How is the job panning out?"

"Pretty good, Judge. In fact, I'm here to ask for a Court Order that I would like to use today."

"What would you like to order, who would you like to order and why?"

"I would like to have the bank hold all deposits for the rest of this week and next until my clerk can check the bills for an invisible mark we put on a certain set of money. My clerk well go to the bank at the end of each day and check the deposits for the day to see if any of them contain the marked bills. The money will never leave the bank and the bank will have the OK bills immediately available for circulation."

"OK, we have what you want to order and who you want to order now why do you want this order."

"There is a scam being run on some of our most vulnerable citizens. These citizens are the forgotten victims of war. Many of these people have banded together in small communities living in abandoned buildings. There is a band of thugs going around to these communities demanding rent. If the occupants resist, they use force to obtain compliance, up to and including murder. This little ploy is an attempt to smoke out the mastermind of the scam."

"OK Bill you will get your court order. I should have it ready about 11 o'clock. You or your clerk can pick it up."

"Thank you Judge. Someone will be here to get it."

When he got back to his office, he instructed Charlie on what was going on and gave him his instructions for the bank operations. Then he said "Charlie, I'm going out for the rest of the day. If anybody asks for me, tell them you don't know where I am."

With arrangements made for the bank part of the scheme, Bill mounted Butch and headed home. When he arrived home he immediately checked to find out if Patsy had gone to the Doc's. Emma said she had gone but wasn't back yet. Next, he had Emma make him a sandwich and pack him a lunch for later with at least two of everything in it.

While Emma made the lunch Bill had requested, he walked down to the barn to fetch Grady's gear.

Hal said he had checked everything over including the guns. The guns were loaded and ready for action.

Bill went back to the house to pick up the lunch and tell Emma to tell Patsy not to worry if he was late tonight.

The only question on Bill's mind now was would his plan for taking out the rent collectors work.

Chapter 30
First Blood

After delivering his message to Emma, he mounted Butch and with Grady's horse in tow started off toward town. After he was away from the house, he turned on to a little used path through the woods. Not long after leaving the road the path crossed several groups of flat rocks. Bill exited the path across the rocks. From there on he made his way through the woods and around several clearings, skirting Redwood Falls all together and winding up in the thickets overlooking the Redwood Ferry.

After looking around a little bit, he found a small glade with ample grass and tied the two horses so they could graze.

With the horses taken care of he made his way along the bank of a small riven with a creek at its bottom. Along the creek bank, he found an ideal place to be able to see but most certainly not seen. He settled in to watch the comings and goings at the warehouse. Ghost was tied at the hitching bar but there was no other activity now.

Bill looked at his watch; it said 12:30. *I don't expect any action until late afternoon or evening.* Bill had been on many of these lookouts over the last few years. He had developed a method of super awareness within a shell of calm and relaxation. He could wait with the best of them.

About 3 o'clock, Billy came out and mounted Ghost and rode off toward home. After his departure, everything returned to its previous inactivity state.

Around 5:30 a pack of dogs appeared in front of the warehouse, looking east and barking at something yet unseen by Bill. '*I wonder where the dogs came from*'. Using his binoculars, he scanned the eastern horizon. Some movement in the trees at the far edge of the clearing caught his eye. He looked again and was able to pick out three horses and their riders. Soon the riders broke through the fringe of trees into the clearing. The two big men were on nondescript roans. The little guy had on a derby hat and pinch-nose spectacles and was riding a magnificent dapple-gray.

They did not hesitate but rode directly up to the warehouse, tied up their horses and barged in without knocking.

Bill levered a shell into the chamber of the Henry. After about 10 minutes Bill heard a shot coming from inside the building. The first shot was followed by a second one. The door burst open and one of the big guys came out holding his shoulder. He was followed by derby hat and specks. Following on his heels was the third rent collector with a gun in his hand. The three mounted and as the third guy topped his mount Bill took him out with about a 300-yard shot with the Henry. The other two took off like bats out of hell in the direction from which they had first appeared. Grady appear in the doorway and took another shot at the fleeing riders.

Bill thought, *'Dam, the plan wasn't going to work.'* Bill came out of his hiding place and yelled as loud as he could. He started running toward Grady, yelling and waving his arms. Grady saw him and took a few steps towards him before he stopped. Grady waved back to let him know he had been seen.

Bill was a little out of breath by the time he reached the front of the warehouse, but he soon recovered. "What happened? Why all the shooting in there? Was anybody hurt?"

"Nobody was shot inside except the one I winged, and he rode away. I don't know if anyone else was hurt. I haven't had time to check since I chased those bastards out the door. I do know Jamie was back-handed and knocked headfirst into the stove."

"I'll go check the damage inside while you check the condition of the guy that's down and collect his guns and horse." Bill entered the warehouse and found Jamie's mom seated in a kitchen chair holding Jamie in her arms. "How is he?"

Mrs. McHugh said, "He is going to have a goose egg on his head where he butted the stove but it's not bleeding or anything. He'll be alright. Grady's action kept the rest of us safe."

Grady entered and said in a loud voice, "**Well, we draw first blood, one wounded and one dead!** I tied his horse to the hitch rack. Bill, you should have seen Jamie go after Dirk when he started dragging his mother toward the stove to give her the same treatment they used on Mrs. Flowers. He was fearless and ferocious in his attack until Dirk caught him with that backhand."

"Grady, do you have your badge on you? Let me have it will you? I'll give you a new one tomorrow."

"I have it right here in my pocket." Grady said as he flipped the badge over to Bill.

"Jamie, I'm asking you to become a Life Long Honorary Deputy of the Redwood County Sheriff's Office with all the privileges and responsibilities of that job. Do you accept this offer?"

A weak, "Yes sir." issued from Jamie where he was huddled in his mother's arms. "For bravery in the face of the enemy I make you my honorary deputy. Bill put the Star into Jamie's hand. I'll let your mother pin the badge on you when you're feeling better.

Grady, I'm going to get our horses. Have all the people here look at the dead crook in case someone has some information about him." Bill mounted the dead man's horse and rode around the copse of woods to the glade where he had staked out Butch and Grady's horse. They were standing with a full contented look about them. Bill cinched up their saddle girth. It took a couple of extra tugs on each girth to get them to pass gas and allow the cinch to be drawn tight enough to make them safe to ride. Bill mounted Butch holding the reins of the other horses. He started his ride back to the warehouse. On reaching it, he tied the three horses to the hitch rack and entered.

An excited Grady met him at the door. "Bill, we're in luck! One of the newcomers recognizes the dead bozo. He says he has seen this guy in Morton on numerous occasions."

Bill said to Grady, "Calm down, we'll get to that next but first tell me what happened here today." They re-entered the kitchen and sat down at the table. Mrs. Betters served coffee to the adults and sat down with Louise on her knee.

"Well, when they busted in, I was sitting in the kitchen drinking coffee. Mrs. McHugh, Jamie McHugh, Mrs. Betters and Louise Betters were in the kitchen also.

Little pig said in a high screech, "**You got the money?**" Mrs. McHugh said, "**Yes**" and went to the cupboard to get it. Little pig had followed her and grabbed the money out of her hand. "**This is only 72 dollars; rent has doubled with all the improvements that have been made to this place.**"

Mrs. McHugh sputtered, "**But that is all we have!**"

Little pig said, "**Are we going to have to take the rent out in pain again? Speaking of that, where is old scar face hiding out today? Maybe she would be willing to donate the pain in your place. Dirk!**" Dirk's the guy who got away and the one who held Mrs. Flowers when they scalded her. Dirk grabbed McHugh and started dragging her toward the stove and hot coffee pot. Jamie came to his mother's aid. He attacked Dirk ferociously, kicking, biting and hammering with his fists. Dirk backhand Jamie and sent him sailing head-first into the stove after which he crumpled unmoving to the floor. I decided this had gone as far as I could let it go. So, I drew my holdout and shot Dirk in the shoulder. Unfortunately, it was the only shot I had. Dirk ran for the door blocking the third man's possible lines of fire. Little piggy's race to the door obstructed the gun man's chance to fire back again. I of course didn't care if I hit piggy, so I shot again but missed both. By that time, all three were outside and you know the rest. By the way, that was a nice shot, I reckon it was about 300 to 350 yards and hit him just below the shoulders in the middle of the back. He was dead by the time he left the saddle."

"Now, what did you say about the dead guy?"

"There is a guy who showed up around a week or so ago needing help. Of course, he was welcomed as everyone is. Well, when he looked at the dead man, he said he was sure he had seen him several times in Morton."

"Can I talk to him, is he here now?"

"Sure, I'll get him." Grady returned in a short time with a little man by any standard.

"This is Phil Qual, he's the one that says he has seen the dead man in Morton."

"Hi Mr. Qual. My name is Bill Cheever, Sheriff of Redwood County. May I ask you some questions about the dead man?"

"Yes Sheriff, I'll tell you everything I know."

"Where in Morton have you seen him and what was he doing. Any other details you remember would be helpful."

"Most of the time I have seen him picking up

groceries at the general store. There is only one in Morton. I have never seen him in town at night. I have seen him leave town on a trail that heads north toward a vacant homestead that is said to be haunted. As far as I know, no one goes near there. There are stories of weird noises and creepy happenings out that way. One of the stories is about a guy who wandered out that way and was never seen again."

"When he comes to town, does he ride or walk?"

"Well he walks into town, but he rides to town on a roan fleabag. I know because one night I didn't have any place to sleep so I crawled under this big evergreen. I was awakened in the morning by a commotion nearby. Peeking out from under the tree I saw that guy tying the roan to a branch and heading to town. As soon as he was out of sight, I got out of there. When I got to town, he was coming out of the store with a gunny sack of groceries."

"Does Morton have a town marshal?"

"Not right now. The last one got run out of town by the lawless bunch that runs the town now."

"What about town's people? Are they part of the corruption or are they citizens that lived there before the lawless bunch moved in?"

"Most of them are longtime residents."

"How many bad guys are holding the town hostage?"

"I think six, they can usually be found in the saloon from early in the morning until late at night."

"How long have you been living in Morton?"

"I have been living near there most of my life."

"Would you be willing to return to Morton and help us identify the bad guys and the good guys?"

"Sure, no one pays any attention to me anymore. They all think I'm daffy. I'm invisible to most and they simply ignore me."

"Good, we'll pick you up tomorrow morning. Can you ride a horse?"

"It is very difficult given my size."

"Okay then we'll bring a wagon for you to ride in. Mrs. McHugh, I want Jamie to go to see Doc Simmons. A blow to the head like he just experienced can have serious consequences. I don't want to take a chance with Jamie's future. Hal will be here as soon as possible with a wagon to take Jamie to town. Jamie, how are you feeling son?"

"I'm having problems with seeing things, they are all fuzzy and I'm not hearing very much."

"You rest and Hal will be back to take you to see Doc Simmons just to be sure you're okay. Grady, are you coming with me?"

"No Bill, Mrs. McHugh has invited me to dinner. I'll see you tomorrow in town."

"No, I will pick you and Mr. Qual up here about

7:00 in the morning. By the way, what's the story about that pack of dogs that signaled the coming of those jerks?"

Mrs. McHugh replied, "As far as we know they are strays. When our food improved and we started having scraps, the dogs started showing up. The pack has been growing ever since."

"I'll be darned. Well they were helpful today. Oh, that reminds me, Max needs to be on the Minnesota River docks to meet Doc Thursday morning at 7 AM. Charlie will be here Wednesday afternoon to pick him up and take him to town. If you could make sure he's ready it would help a lot."

Heads nod to say, "Max would be ready."

"I have to go get Hal now." Bill immediately mounted Butch and rode "hell bent" for home. His only thoughts now were about Jamie's wellbeing and what Patsy had found out today. Ferry Road wasn't busy, so he made excellent time. The glow of the lights in the windows of the house made a very welcoming picture as he rode up to the barn. Hal answered his call. Billy was with Hal and took Butch's reins as Bill got down. Bill explained what he wanted Hal to do. Billy asked Bill if he could go with Hal. He said he was worried about his friend Jamie.

"You can take care of Butch while Hal hitches

the Bays to the wagon. Have you two had anything to eat?"

"Yes, mom fed Hal, Patsy and I because you told her you would be late."

"Good I'm going to eat now. I'll see you two when you get back." Bill hurried to the house and as he rushed in, he yelled, "Patsy, I'm home!"

His wife's voice came from the kitchen, "We're here Bill." Bill entered the kitchen in a rush to find Patsy and Emma sitting at the table with cups of coffee in their hands. "Well?" Bill said with an unnaturally excited voice for him, "What did Doc say?"

"He said there is no doubt about it, I'm about a month pregnant. Can you believe it, we are actually going to have a baby."

"**Hallelujah**!" Bill yelled as he gave Patsy a joyous smack-a-dozee. "Oh, Emma, Billy is going to town with Hal. His friend Jamie was hurt today, and they are taking him to see the Doc. I'll tell you all about it if someone will find me something to eat."

"How about a big bowl of Milly's stew?" Emma said with a smile. "We have been trying out her recipe this afternoon."

Emma, Patsy and Bill filled the time while waiting for Hal and Billy to arrive home with news of Jamie's condition, talking about the ups and downs an ins and outs of pregnancy. Midnight past and there was no word yet. It was about 1:30 when the guys came through the kitchen door. Nobody had to ask how Jamie was doing, Billy blurted out that Doc was sure he would be okay. Doc did keep Jamie with him over night just in case something unforeseen occurred.

Hal and Billy were late because they had gone by the warehouse to tell Mrs. McHugh and Grady what Doc had told them about Jamie's condition.

With the good news about Jamie, everybody scattered to their beds. Before Hal left the house, Bill told him to be at the house about 4 o'clock in the morning with the Bays hitched to the wagon and Butch tied behind.

Bill fell asleep immediately still fully clothed and his guns handy. Patsy had a harder time calming down given all that was taking place in their lives right now. Not the least of which was the peril she knew Bill would be facing tomorrow. Eventually sleep did come for her.

Chapter 31

Retribution

At 4 o'clock Bill tried to slip out of bed in an effort to not disturb Patsy, but that didn't work. She woke up and insisted on a goodbye kiss. Bill gave her a warm hug and a loving kiss before parting the bedroom as he strapped his guns on.

He found Hal out the back door waiting for him in the wagon with Butch tied on behind. Bill climbed in and Hal moved the horses and wagon as noiselessly as he could about 500 yards from the house before he let them pick up their pace and reach their travel gait. It was a little before 5 o'clock when Hal pulled up in front of the Sheriff's office, they were startled by low light shining in the office window.

Bill said," What's going on here? I didn't expect anybody to meet us here." Bill hopped down and that's when he noticed the gun in Hal's waist band. Bill thought, *'once a soldier, always a soldier'*. They cautiously approached the office door with drawn guns and then burst in.

Terry Ham reacted by going for his gun which was a handy distance away. A second later the doorway to the inner office was filled with Zeke, in his hands were his colts.

"You boys expecting company?" Bill said.

"No, but that's a problem for anybody who shows up and disturbs our sleep; we shoot first and ask questions after the answers, don't matter."

"Well, believe it or not and in spite of all the bullshit about how you handle being caught with your pants down, I am so glad to see you I could kiss you both."

Terry's response was, "Maybe being caught by surprise is bad but does such an offense deserve the worst penalty known to man?"

"I'll answer that and lots more over breakfast at Milly's."

After everyone washed their face in the cold water from the office pump and dried off with some clean rags from the storeroom, they all looked better and felt ready to meet the day. The short walk to Milly's cleared the last of the cobwebs out of their heads. Milly's was busy this morning with the crew from a Minnesota River Packet that had mechanical trouble last night. The trouble had to be fixed before it could return down river.

The Sheriff and his men found a table and enough chairs for them in the back corner of the café. Milly wasn't doing the waitressing this morning. She must have been busy elsewhere. In her place was a saucy little redhead that caught Terry's eye.

His eyes were fixed on her any time she was in the room. When she served their coffee, Terry asked, "Would it be impertinent if I asked you your name?"

"No, not at all, my name is Elizabeth Schulze, my friends call me Ellie."

"Are you any relation to the hostler down at Schroder's Livery?"

"Yes, he is my brother. We just got here a few weeks ago to help Aunt Geraldine and Uncle Carl with their work. Their getting on in years and no-body is hiring in Pine City. Sorry but I better see to the other customers before I have a riot on my hands. By the way what is your name?"

"Terry Ham, thanks for asking."

Ellie took their breakfast order and refilled their coffee cups before flashing a sweet smile and move back a amongst the other tables filling coffee cups as she went.

Bill said with a grin on his face, "Ok Terry, now that your social hour is over can we get down to business?"

Bill asked Zeke if they had found out anything

in Milroy. Zeke replied that they confirmed that the descriptions match those Bill had given them of the rent collectors who visit the warehouse. The shooters name was Dirk, and the leader was a short man wearing a Derby Hat and pinch-nose spectacles. The third man was big, around six feet tall with a lower jaw that stuck out beyond his upper one making his face look funny.

Bill said, "I believe you just found out there are more than three people in the gang. Yesterday I killed the third guy at the warehouse, and he didn't have the problem you just described." Bill went on to fill Terry and Zeke in on the details of what had been going on while they were away. During his spiel their breakfast was served and eaten. Bill paid the tab.

As they got up to leave Milly's, Terry looked around for Elly, but she was nowhere in sight.

Bill told Zeke and Terry he wanted them to do a reconnaissance tour of Morton while he and Hal picked up Grady and Mr. Qual at the warehouse and then they would meet them there. They rode out of town sticking together until the Redwood Ferry Road and Lower Agency Road split and took each group on their separate ways.

Grady and Mr. Qual were ready and waiting when Bill and Hal reached them. Bill got off the wagon and retrieved Butch from the back of it. After

Mr. Qual was perched in the wagon seat, Hal started back to the ferry. Bill and Grady mounted and followed behind.

When they reached Morton, Bill sent Hal and Mr. Qual down the main street trolling for Zeke and Terry. Their mission was to bring the two deputies back as well as having Mr. Qual check it out for any changes since he had gone away. They soon returned with the deputies.

Bill told them to hold their reports about the Morton operation until they were through looking into the mystery of the haunted homestead. With Mr. Qual's guidance, they moved as a group around the sleeping town and onto the trail their guide pointed out as the one, he had seen the dead rent collector travel. Bill told Grady to watch their back trail and sent Zeke ahead to ride point and scout the haunted area. About three miles later, Zeke showed up with some bad news and some good news. The bad news was that the trail ahead and the surrounding woods were booby-trapped with devices that made noise when their trip wires were disturbed. The good news was that he had discovered a corridor through the traps that allowed him to make his way to the clearing in which the buildings were located undetected. From the end of the corridor he had been able to sneak around to the barn. He found three horses in it, a nondescript roan, a shaggy ill kept gray and a magnificent dapple-gray.

Bill said, "It looks like we may have gotten lucky and caught all three of the gang members we know of here together. Let's get this operation finished before these guys scatter for whatever they plan to do today. Zeke you take the lead. Hal, where we leave the trail, park the wagon and wait for us. When we reach the clearing, Zeke, you and Terry try to get around to the barn. How long do you think it will take you to get from the end of the corridor to the barn?"

"No more than 5 minutes."

"Okay, during that five minutes, Grady and I will try to sneak up to the front door. If we can get there unseen, we will breach the door and carry the fight inside. If we are spotted before we get to the door and the fight starts with us outside, you two attack from the rear of the house. We will meet in the house when the fight is done. Any questions?" Nods of understanding finished the conversation.

The attack party moved down the road about a half mile before Zeke called a halt and said, "This is where we need to go into the woods to skirt the noise makers."

Bill helped Hal find a suitable place to hide the wagon while the attack force was gone. His instructions to Hal included going back to Redwood Falls if

Bill and the others had not returned by noon. If we're not back by noon something will have gone radically wrong. Hunt up Marshall Don Williams and tell him everything we have been up to this morning. Ask him if there is anything, he can do to end this business.

Bill and his men followed Zeke into the woods far enough so their tethered horses couldn't be seen from the trail. They continued on foot stepping in Zeke's footprints until they reached the clearing with the house and barn in it.

Bill fished two sticks of dynamite out of his pocket and gave one of them to Zeke. He also gave Zeke a small bag of sticky clay. "I wasn't sure of how stout the doors on this place would be, so I took the precaution to be ready for anything. The clay will let you stick the dynamite close to the door latch. The dynamite has a short fuse so be sure to get in a safe place as soon as the fuse starts burning. I wanted to be sure we could get in when we wanted in. If you hear my dynamite go off come running from the barn. The explosion will be our signal that we have breached the door and should be in the house. Now get to the barn as fast as you can. Grady and I will be in a position to blow the cabin door five minutes from now."

The four lawmen exchanged their good luck

wishes, then Zeke and Terry started out in a trot. They kept to the fringe of the woods as they made their way around the clearing.

Bill and Grady decided to approach diagonally to the corners of the front wall of the cabin. There was only one small window in the front of the cabin and no windows at all in its sides. Bill took the corner closest to the door as his objective. He would set the charge and enter the cabin first. Grady's objective was the opposite front corner of the building. When the door was blown, Grady would cross to the door entering after Bill and acting as back up. Each laid out in their mind the path they would take to their objective. They exchanged good luck wishes as they started their approach.

Bill got to his corner first. He took out the dynamite and clay. He stuck the clay in the crack of the door where the latch entered the jam and buried the dynamite in it. This only took a couple of minutes. He took a quick look to make sure Grady was in place. Grady gave him a thumbs up and Bill's internal clock said it was show time. He flicked the match with his thumb nail, and it burst into flame. When the flame touched the fuse and the fuse started burning, Bill jumped back around the corner and plugged his ears.

The explosion shattered the latch and blew the door wide open. It hung there on one hinge.

Bill ducked through the door looking for targets. Both men in the room were stunned and seemed unable to give any resistance.

Grady followed Bill through the door and took control of the two prisoners. He got them to stand braced against the wall. One was Dirk with his wound and the other was extended jaw.

Bill went to the door that seemed to lead to the kitchen. As he reached the opening a bullet buried itself in the door frame close to his face. During his glance into the kitchen he saw a big iron stove with a big saucepan on it. Bill flopped on the floor and peek around the corner. He saw the feet of a man crouched on the other side of the stove. The guy was perfectly safe from any bullets reaching his hiding place.

The saucepan however gave Bill an idea. The smell identified the boiling liquid as meat broth. Bill had also seen a bunch of cut up vegetables on the table. Bill thought, *they must be making soup.* He put his right handgun in his left hand and drew his left handgun with a cross draw. He took one last peek from his prone position to make sure he had the details correct. Then he raised up to a crouched position and launched himself across the door opening. As he crossed it, he fired both guns into the stove top right where the saucepan edge rested on the burner. The bullets propelled the pan to the edge of the stove where it teetered for a split second before tipping over the edge.

A shriek issue from behind the stove and the man stood up dropping his gun as he tried to get the scalding broth off his head and face. It was little piggy, the name given him by Grady yesterday. His head and face were covered by the hot broth. His right eye was full of the scalding liquid and the odor of burning flesh started to fill the room. His head and face started to look like boiled lobster. It was enough to make a grown man cry, and it did as the little pig bawled out his pain.

Bill knew he was showing a weakness, but he just couldn't control himself as he blurted out, "Now don't you think this is perfect retribution you little bag of shit?" Even though he felt some shame for his words while he watched the little man suffer, he felt really good for getting that emotion off his chest. He threw a rag into the little man's face, found the man's gun and opened the back door to signal Zeke and Terry to join them.

All three of the prisoners were searched and their hands and feet bound with pegging strings. They were seated against the back wall in the main room.

The house and barn and surrounding area were searched to be sure no one else was lurking around to surprise them.

Terry volunteered to go for the wagon and horses. He claimed that if he didn't do that he might as well have not bothered coming along because he had gotten to do dam little else.

Bill was satisfied they had captured the whole gang and extracted just retribution for the rent pain payments little pig had extracted from his victims.

Chapter 32
Revelations

B ill and the other two started searching the house for any evidence it might contain. Despite what they thought was a very thorough search they found nothing. When Terry, Hal and Mr. Qual arrived they joined the hunt also. Terry found a ladder and decided to look in the rafters. He was rewarded by his discovery of a letter size green metal box tucked up behind one of them.

They opened the box and found all the evidence they could possibly have hoped to find. The box contained evidence that this gang was part of the horse stealing ring and that the ring operated out of Ray Delevan's stable in St. Paul. Documents showed that this gang had delivered three horses to the ring in the last four months. Each horse had been stolen from different counties in the surrounding area. It also provided proof that the Morton occupiers were part of this gang. The most surprising revelation in the box was the name of the gang's mastermind. Every one of the posse looked at the information in disbelief. There was no doubt, the man they were after was Judge John McKay.

"Now let's go to work on the three guys we have in custody and see if we can squeeze some useful information out of them. Grady and I will work on Little Piggy, Zeke, you and Terry see what you can get out of Dirk and Hal, you and Mr. Qual talk to lantern jaw. We will share what we find out later."

When Zeke and Terry confronted Dirk, he immediately asked when he could see a doctor. Terry replied, "Don't worry, you'll survive to hang."

Using guile and pressure, Zeke and Terry got Dirk to tell them how he had been recruited into the gang. His story was, "I appeared before the Judge on a relatively minor charge but with a rap sheet that was a mile long. The Judge threatened to lock me up and throw away the key unless I would join his band of businessmen, as he called them. If I joined his group, the judge would put me on probation. I would be free as long as I was considered a member in good standing. As a member I would receive my cut of the profits of our activities. All the gang members I know have gotten there by appearing in the Judge's court. Now will you take me to a doctor?"

Zeke replied, "In a little bit. There is no emergency, the bleeding has stopped."

In the meantime, Bill and Grady found Little Piggy on the floor, in the corner of the front room, rolled up in a ball, sobbing his heart out. Bill and Grady might have felt sorry for him if they weren't aware of Mrs. Flower's burns and the threatened scalding of Mrs. McHugh. His burns covered most of the right side of his face, including his scalp and neck. His right eye was completely closed, his eyebrow and lashes were missing. There was no way to tell what shape the eyeball was in.

Bill asked him, "Do you have any clean cooking grease in the house?"

Piggy sobbed out his answer, "There is a can of lard in the cabinet over the pump. Grady retrieved the lard and held the can while Piggy spread a thick layer over all his burned area. He seemed more at ease by the time he finished, and his sobbing had stopped.

Bill asked, "So, what is your part in this organization?"

"I'm the operations manager, second in command to the boss." Piggy proudly admitted. "I was the first one to be recruited by the Judge." Bill and Grady recognized immediately that Little Piggy was proud of his status in the gang.

They went to work stoking up Piggy's ego to

a fevered pitch. He was so busy telling what a big, important man he was that he did not realize he was spilling the beans about the gang's history and operations.

The story he told mirrored Dirk's recruitment scenario. Soon after he agreed to the roll the Judge had in mind for him, Dirk and Frank came on board. Piggy said Frank was the rent collector Bill had shot at the warehouse. According to Piggy, he was to run the operation and the other two were to provide the muscle for the rent collection scheme. At first the Judge's only criminal plan was to press the homeless and the helpless into paying rent for occupying vacant properties. The Judge thought this would be a low risk source of extra money for his retirement. It never became the gold mine he had hoped it would be.

So, when the judge heard from a friend about the horse stealing ring, he became interested. He was impressed by their mode of operation. Spreading the stealing out over a large area and spreading the frequency in any one area over long periods of time, he felt this would make it a fairly low risk operation. He thought there was a small chance the police would ever put two and two together and realize it was a ring of horse thieves instead of individuals operating on their own. He believed the Law would never mount a large-scale effort against individuals. The Judge decided to opt in. This improved the bottom line but still left the gang with an inadequate steady flow of cash to finance their daily operations.

So, the judge came up with the Morton operation. It was undertaken as a test case. The risk was small because the Town Marshall was weak and there were no heroes living there or so their scouting around indicated. Eliminate the Town Marshal and the nearest law was the county Sheriff located up in the middle of the county near the towns of Renville and Danube. True, Redwood Falls and the Redwood County Sheriff's Office were close, but the Redwood County Sheriff had no jurisdiction in Renville County. The Town Marshall ran for his life after he was savagely beaten in a fist fight staged to look like a personal altercation. The Marshall never had a chance. Dirk was his opponent and he had been a prize fighter in his younger days.

The gang moved in and started collecting the monthly protection premiums from the people of Morton. Of course, the gang made sure everyone knew they couldn't do without that protection.

The Morton operation changed everything for the gang. It provided the needed steady cash flow for operating capital. Life was good. Everything started coming up roses.

Piggy explained how the gang's income was laundered and distributed. At the center of the scheme was some worthless Canadian Mining Stock. The Judge had gotten scammed years ago before he had found out 'if it sounds too good to be true it probably isn't true'. He signed these stock certificates over to his clerk's, invalid mother who lived in Montevideo. Doris deposited the certificates in the Montevideo Trust Bank in a deposit box she rented in her mother's name. As far as the bank is concerned these stocks were priceless. Near the end of each month a courier from the mining company's lawyer shows up and deposits a tidy sum in the deposit box. This deposit was advertised as being the dividend from the stock certificates.

When Doris made her monthly visit to her mother, she arrived on Friday afternoon and went immediately to the bank. As her mother's executor, she would withdraw the money under the guise of her mother's need for expensive care. That night she would distribute the money as per the Judge's instruction. So much for her mother's care, so much for her part in the scheme and so much for the gang.

The gang got its split of the money via Dirk. On those once a month visits by Doris to her mother, Dirk showed up and spent Saturday night with

Doris. Dirk knew this was just an errand for the gang with a little bonus of sex thrown in for good measure.

However, Doris thought it was true love. She lived for those Saturday nights. Sunday morning Dirk left with his libido stroked and the gangs cut of the months take. Monday on her way back to Redwood Falls the stage had a scheduled rest stop in Granite Falls that was long enough to allow Doris time to deposit the rest of the money in a lock box rented to Fanny and Frank Gore. The signatures for the box were in the handwriting of Doris and the Judge but only Doris had ever visited the bank in person.

Under extreme duress Piggy revealed that Dirk was supposed to visit Doris on Saturday night of this week.

Bill immediately saw away to bring the marked money in to play. If they could apprehend Doris as she exited the bank in Montevideo and found the marked money in the cash, she had just withdrawn it would prove that the money was not from the Canadian mine but from the rent collection scam.

The lawmen got together after they finished their interrogations. Zeke and Terry shared their findings. Bill and Grady followed suit. Hal and Mr. Qual had nothing to add except that Lantern Jaw was a new recruit and knew little about the gang.

Bill said, "Piggy told us that Dirk's next trip to

pick up the gangs split is this coming Saturday night. Zeke and Terry, would you go back and see if you can get Dirk to confirm that?"

A short time later the two came back and Zeke nodded his head in the affirmative.

When the sharing was done, Bill said, "Now it's time to move on to our Morton operation. Mr. Qual, has anything changed in Morton since you were there last?"

"Not that I could see."

"Zeke did you and Terry find out anything of interest on your recon?"

"We found out the gang has made the 'Red Garter Saloon' their headquarters, their hang out and their residence. In general, they eat together, breakfast at seven, lunch at noon and supper at six. During the day two of them man the jail, two of them roam the streets and two of them hold down the 'Red Garter.'"

"Do you think we should go for the two street roamers first?"

"That would be my choice" said Zeke. "Then I would go after the two in the 'Red Garter' and let the two in the jail come to me."

The others nodded in agreement and Bill chimed in, "That seems about right to me. Hal, we'll load the prisoners in the wagon, and you take them to the edge of town and hide there. Don't take any chances with them. They're tricky and ruthless. Use Mr. Qual to move around and to make sure you are not surprised by anyone. If we're not back to get you by 7 do what we talked about this morning." After the wagon was loaded and the prisoners secured the four lawmen mounted and rode off in direction of town. Hal followed.

Chapter 33
Roundup

It was about 12:30 PM when Bill and his men pulled into the trees on the north edge of Morton. Bill said, "Let's tie our horses at different hitch racks in town and casually circulate until we know for sure where our targets are. Grady, you take the left side of the Red Garter and I'll take the right."

Bill selected a hitch rail one block north of Main Street in front of a building with a sign proclaiming it a cobbler shop. Then he strolled over to a spot from which he could observe the back of the 'Red Garter' with only a small chance of being seen himself.

Terry moved down Main Street to the jail. After tying his horse up, he took a chair on the sidewalk in front of a diner called 'Hoppy's'. The aromas reminded Terry that he hadn't had a bite to eat since that early breakfast at 'Milly's. His stomach growled in protest of his fasting. He longed to go in and get some food, but he knew that would jeopardize his chance of tracking the bad guys if they come out of the saloon. The thought of food reminded him of that red headed waitress, he would have to check her out soon. His memory of her pushed his thoughts of food to the back of his mind.

Zeke tied up in front of the grocery store and walked in to see what he could see. While in there he brought an apple. Back on the sidewalk he took a bite out of it with an elaborate display of pleasure. He was playing to his audience, Terry, who he saw across the street. Taking another bite, he strolled across the street and down the walk. As he passed Terry, he dropped the half-eaten apple in his lap and kept going.

Grady tied his horse next to Bills and moved to a position where he could see the back and the side of the saloon Bill couldn't see.

With the watchers in place, all they could do was wait. About 1:15, two guys came out the front of the saloon and crossed to the jail. Shortly after the first two appeared, two more came out. They said something to each other which none of the watchers could hear and then they split up.

Terry followed the guy who was walking west along Main Street because he knew Zeke was to the east. The guy showed no signs that he knew he was being followed. In fact, the guy looked like he was completely absorbed in his errand, what every that was. Terry watched as the guy climbed the outside stairs to the banks upper story and enter the door at the top. Terry went to find Bill at the back of the saloon. When he reached Bill, he told him of what he had seen.

"I wonder what the attraction up there is? Go back there and watch to see if he comes out. I'll go ask Mr. Qual if he knows what's up there. I'll find you as soon as I know what it is." Each of them left to take care of their assigned task.

Bill had no trouble finding Hal and Qual. Bill said, "Mr. Qual, what's the attraction over the bank?

Mr. Qual said, "That's where Molly and her girls work."

"Have you been up there?"

"Yes, I've done some odd jobs for Molly up there."

"Can you describe the lay out of the place?"

"There isn't much to it. Only five rooms. Two on each side of the center hall and one at the end. The room at the end of the hall is Molly's. The room on the right at the end of the hall is sort of a combination lounge and kitchen for Molly and her whores. The other three are workrooms for her girls."

Armed with this information, Bill returned to find Terry. On the way he collected Grady from where he was still watching the back of the saloon. When they found Terry, Bill had him go look up Zeke and bring him back. If Zeke has a better target come back and get us. Soon Terry and Zeke returned. Zeke said the other guy was obviously collecting the current premiums from the victims which should keep him busy for a little while.

"Ok, here is a plan I think might work. I think we should go up those stairs like a bunch of drunk cowboys looking for a good time. I don't expect any opposition at least until we get inside so no guns until we are in the door. Grady, you overpower the greeter and keep her quiet. Terry, you take the two right hand doors and Zeke you take the two left hand doors. Don't let anybody come out of those rooms. I will bust into Molly's room and hopefully catch this jerk off guard. Any comments?"

Zeke said, "Grady and Terry should be able to control the hall and the two of us should assault the stronghold." The rest of the group nodded their agreement with Zeke's suggestion. That sealed the deal.

"That's it then. Let's get this done."

The drunk act started as they emerged from the alley where their meeting had occurred. Terry said to Grady, "Do you still think you can get it up ole timer? How long has it been since you had your ashes hauled?"

"Old doesn't mean impotent, sonny. We'll let the

ladies decide who's the stud and who's the dud when our romp is done." The banter continued until they reached the top of the stairs. Bill tried the door and it was locked so he banged on it.

A voice from inside said, "Who is it?"

Bill answered, "Just four cowboys looking for a good time honey!"

"Well you came to the right place sweetie!" as the key turned in the lock and the door swung back. The perfume odor came to the men like physical blow to the chops.

They stepped in passing the greeter and started milling around in the hall. Grady was the last to enter and their hostess had turned her back to the door making it easy for him to put her in a head lock and stifle her attempt to shout by stuffing his hand-kerchief in her mouth. She tried to spit it out, but Grady's free hand prevented that.

The others pulled their guns. Bill and Zeke moved quickly down the hall to Molly's room and without breaking stride crashed the door in. A skinny white ass stared back at them and his private parts hung down between her legs. His pecker was buried in her mop of pubic hair.

Bill snapped, "See if you can find his guns."

Zeke found them on a chair rolled up under the guy's clothes.

"Give him his clothes. Get dressed punk."

The Punk rolled off Molly and stood up. All the spunk had gone out of his pecker and it dangled forlornly until it was mercifully covered by his clothes.

Molly got out of bed, closed her Boa collared, ornate robe and tied the sash. Next, she looked in the mirror, made a few repairs to her makeup and fluffed her hair. She appeared to be ready for her next customer.

Bill left the crook under Zeke's watchful eye and herded Molly into the hallway with the other ladies. He had the women line up against the wall.

Then he said, "I want you to go about your business this afternoon as if none of this took place. You can remember it tomorrow but not today. If this gets out before tomorrow, I will know it was one of you four who squealed, and I will come back and arrest you on all kinds of charges. You will want to tell everyone this secret but don't unless you want to face 'all hell' before the sun sets this afternoon. Got it?"

The women nod their heads "Yes." as if their heads were attached somehow.

"Ok men, let's get to our unfinished business." With that they left the brothel. When they got to the bottom of the stairs the prisoner's hands were tied.

"Okay, Grady, take this guy to the wagon with the others. Be sure he is searched and hogtied before you leave to find us. We'll be searching the eastern part of town looking for the premium collector. Get back as quick as you can." Grady took the bad guy and jerked him toward the woods north of town.

The other three spread out to broaden their search area. Just as Grady found them, they found their quarry. He was in a women's dress shop. His hand was out in the traditional "gimme gesture' and the woman behind the counter was in tears as she handed him some money. He counted it, made a mark in a book he was carrying and turned to leave. As he walked through the door, he was greeted by four guys, two on each side, with their guns pointing at him.

Bill said, "Keep your hands down. Give me that book. Hook your thumbs in the very back of your belt. Zeke get his gun. Terry take that money back to the lady and tell her not to say anything about this to anyone. You (gesturing toward the premium collector) come along peacefully. Terry, come down to the 'Red Garter' when you're done, we'll be waiting out back."

Terry reentered the store to do the good deed. The rest of the group disappeared between the buildings. They stopped long enough to search their catch and found a wad of cash, a holdout derringer in his boot and a throwing knife up his sleeve.

"Grady take this guy to the wagon and tie him up tight. Tell Hal to bring the load of prisoners to the back of the saloon in a half-hour unless he hears gun fire when he arrives. If there is shooting tell him to head for Don Williams in Redwood Falls as fast as he can. Hurry back! We're going in as soon as you and Terry are back."

Terry caught up just as they reached the saloon. They had to wait ten minutes more for Grady to return.

Grady said, "That wagon is getting awfully full."

"Well it's destined to get a lot fuller if we are successful here." said Zeke.

"Zeke you and Terry go through the front door acting like two thirsty hands who just rode into town and stopping for a drink. When Grady and I hear your voice, we will come through the back door. We should have those two in there between us. No shooting unless it is necessary. Any questions? Ok let's do it."

Zeke and Terry dusted their pant legs and boots so they would appear like they were fresh off the trail and disappeared around the building.

Grady tried the back door and found it was unlocked. It opened into a storeroom. There was only one other door in the room, so they moved to it. It `was also unlocked. They snuck a peek through the second door and found that a floor to ceiling rug/ tapestry formed a pseudo hallway between the back wall and the bar room. They slipped through the door and quietly took positions at each end of the hanging partition. They were in a great position to back Zeke and Terry when they make their move.

It wasn't long until they heard the stomp of boots and Terry's voice saying, "Boy is a beer going to taste good after that ride."

An unknown voice said, "Hey, you yahoos, can't you read. The sign outside says we're closed"

Terry's voice said, "Why? Do I have to read something to get a beer in here?" Bill and Grady moved into the barroom with their guns ready. If Terry and Zeke saw them, they did not react and give their presence away.

Besides the four lawmen, there were three men in the room. Two were setting at a table with beers in front of them. The third was behind the bar. The guy doing the talking was one of those at the table. He was a grizzled old coot with a mop of gray hair on his head and a straggly gray beard to match. The yellow suspender straps, plaid shirt and bib overalls made up his attire. He looked more like a prospector then a crook.

The second guy at the table had a baby face. He was dressed in fancy clothes you might expect a gambler to ware. He didn't look like he had been wearing long pants enough to become a hardened outlaw.

The guy behind the bar had a shiny bald head, with prominent sideburns and a waxed handlebar mustache. He was wearing a white shirt with pinstripes in it. A starched white apron covered his lower body.

Bill knew instinctively that if there were trouble it would come from the kid, not the old coot. At this point Bill decided to make Grady and his presence known to the others in the room,

"Hey guys, just so you know there are four sides to a room and this room has law on two sides of it. You are all under arrest. Don't make a move or all hell will break loose. We have you covered."

The guys at the table and behind the bar shifted their attention from the front to the rear of the room. The coot put his hands in the air. The youngster tried to get on his feet as he clawed for his gun. He didn't accomplish either act as he took two bullets in the chest, one from Zeke and one from Terry. He was dead before he hit the floor.

The bartender used the distraction to reach under the bar only to be shot in his shoulder by Grady.

Zeke immediately moved to the door. As he looked over the batwing doors, he saw the two crooks in the jail make a break for the horses tied to the hitch rack in front of it. He shot the first one as the guy swung into the saddle.

The second guy had untied Terry's horse and was trying to mount when Terry let out a sharp whistle. His horse bucked, sending the crook flying to the ground where he lay dazed on to his back. Terry was there with his gun on the crook's nose by the time the guy's eyes focused again.

Hal arrived with the wagon right after the chaos ended. The two dead men were laid out in the jail. The bartender's shoulder was bandaged to stop the bleeding. The three new captors were added to the wagon's load.

This gang was all wrapped in a ribbon, neatly tied in a bow and ready to toss in the clink.

Chapter 34
Loose Ends

H al was given Butch to deliver Mr. Qual back to the warehouse and then return home to tell Patsy and the rest that everyone was okay.

Bill wasn't going to get home anytime soon because he was driving the wagon load of prisoner to Renville. Technically this posse had no real legal standing in Renville County. Since this bunch had been apprehended in that county, they had to hand them over to the proper authorities as soon as possible.

This also worked into Bills plans. It kept the Judge and Doris in the dark about the noose that was tightening around their necks. It was about 10:30 when Bill pulled the wagon up to the Renville County jail. The night jailer listened to an abbreviated version of the events that led to the wagon load of bad guys and sent for the Sheriff. The Sheriff showed up after a while and of course the story had to be retold. With knowledge of the facts, the Morton crooks were booked and locked up.

With their Renville business done, Bill dispatched Zeke and Terry to Montevideo to inform and enlist the help of Chippewa County Sheriff in the arrest of Doris Friday afternoon.

Bill and Grady left for Redwood Falls. When they were across the Minnesota River they split up, Grady to the warehouse and Bill to home. By the time Bill, the wagon and the Bays reached home only the Bays were still awake and they were showing signs of exhaustion. Bill's head was bouncing on his chest, he was fast asleep. As the team pulled up in front of the barn Bill was jarred out of his sleep. His first thought was to *'leave the Bays and go directly to bed,* but on second thought *he knew he would never forgive himself for neglecting horses like that.* He climbed down and unhitched the wagon. As he finished unhooking the team, he felt a tap on his shoulder, it was Hal telling him to go to bed and he'd take care of the team. Bill thought '*I should argue about this, but he could not think of a word to say'* so he said nothing. Instead he staggered up the hill, entered the house and climbed the stairs.

Patsy lay in bed, wide awake. She couldn't sleep because of the emotion that had built up as she waited for Bill. She didn't let on that she was awake until Bill crawled into bed. As he lay his head down, he felt Patsy's arm around his neck and then she was hugging him to her breast. All the pent-up emotion burst out. She started sobbing in response to her relief and whispered, "I love you so much. I don't know what would happen to me if I lost you."

"You're not going to lose me, loving you is the most important job of my life."

It is amazing how being in the arms of the girl you love banishes fatigue and replaces it with the fire of passion. This turned into a grand homecoming. The next day was lost in exhausted sleep and the warmth of each other's company. Emma served them breakfast in bed. They got up long enough to eat a light lunch and then crashed into each other's arms again. Finally, the fatigue and emotions were sated. They broke out of the warmth of their embrace and dressed for dinner.

That evening Bill composed a long telegram to the State Police detailing the horse stealing syndicate's operations.

The next day Bill rode with Billy over to the warehouse to check for himself on how Jamie was doing. He was so pleased when Jamie said he was fine, no lingering effects.

He also made sure to shake Mr. Qual's hand and

thank him for his help in Morton. "I don't believe we could have pulled it off without you. Thanks again for your help."

He spoke to Grady and found out he was moving back to the warehouse permanently. Bill said that was fine if he checked in at the office every day for his instructions.

Bill left the warehouse and rode into town. He stopped at the jail to speak to Don Williams. He outlined for Don the evidence they had collected that related to the Judges involvement as the mastermind of the crime ring operating in Redwood and surrounding counties. Don had a hard time accepting the idea the Judge was a criminal, but the evidence Bill presented could not be denied. Bill outlined his plan to arrest the Judge tomorrow. right after his clerk left on the stage. Bill said, "I hoped you would come with me so no one can challenge the validity of any evidence we might find."

"It will be my pleasure. I think the stage leaves at nine, how about meeting here at 8:30 so we can watch her go."

"It's a deal. See you tomorrow at 8:30. One more thing Don, have you and your wife decided on the housekeeper you asked about a while back?"

"Yes, I don't think we have enough room for a live-in, so it would have to be a drop-in."

"What days do you have in mind?"

"We were hoping for Monday, Wednesday and Friday."

"When should they start?"

"Tomorrow wouldn't be too soon."

"I'll try to make that happen. What time should they arrive?"

"How about nine o'clock?"

"Good."

Bill left Don's office feeling good about the arrangements now in place. His next stop was the livery stable. Carl was in his office. "Carl, I need a horse and buckboard for the people at the warehouse tomorrow. You got anything like that to rent?"

"Yes, you are in luck. I'll rent you that rig for two dollars a day."

"Isn't that pretty high?"

"Here we go again. How much are you willing to pay?"

"If the horse is sound and the wagon solid, I would buy it outright. But I don't have Hal here to look the horse, so I guess that's out."

"What if we strike a bargain which becomes final only after Hal okays the horse?"

"That sounds like it might work. How much do you think you need for the wagon, the horse and the harness?"

"I was thinking 50 bucks."

"Well, all I have on me is $35. I guess that means that $35 is all I can offer."

"This time, I'll go down $10 if you go up $5."

"It's robbery but it's a deal. Can you have it harnessed any ready to go in an hour?"

"Sure."

Bill dug in his pocket and brought out a wad of bills. "Oh! I guess I had more than I knew I had."

"Why was I so sure you'd come up with the money after we agreed on the price?"

"I guess I'll have to change my tactics when I negotiate with you in the future. He peeled off $40 and handed them to Carl. "I'll see you in an hour." He walked over to his office to see if Charlie had anything for him.

The only thing Charlie had was a note from Doc Simmons about Max. The note said the dentists were making some progress with the jaw but doubted Max would ever be able to talk again. Max had lost too much of his tongue to make articulate sounds.

He left his unsent draft of the message to the State Police in his desk and returned for the wagon.

On his way out of town he stopped at Milly's and asked if Ed would be around tomorrow afternoon. She said she thought he would be here. Bill said, "I have another job for him."

With Butch tied to the back of the wagon he made his way home for Hal's inspection of the horse. Hal okayed the horse, so Bill continued to the warehouse to talk to Mrs. Betters about the William's job offer. She agreed and said she would show up there tomorrow morning at nine. Bill enlisted Grady to be sure Mrs. Betters knew how to drive the horse and buckboard.

With all the arrangements in place for tomorrow, Bill and Billy rode home together.

Bill arrived at the jail the next morning at about 8:15. Don had just arrived so the two of them found a place they could watch the loading and departure of the stage. About 10 minutes before nine, Doris showed up and soon after she climbed into the coach. At nine sharp the stage pulled out. At about ten minutes after nine Bill and Don walked into the Judge's office and arrested him. The Judge seemed almost relieved as they escorted him to jail. Some people stared at the procession, but nobody tried to stop them or ask questions.

Soon they were on their way back to the Judge's office. There they started going thru his files and correspondence. There wasn't much new evidence but a few things that collaborated things they already knew. They did find a packet of letters from a lawyer named Al Fenton postmarked Olivia. They agreed that there was something strange about them and decided to investigate this Al Fenton further. During the search they also became convinced that the Judge started his life of crime shortly after his wife died.

Bill took the materials they had found to put it with the other stuff they had. He now sent his telegram to the State Police since there was no one left to be warned in Redwood Falls about the roundup of the criminal ring. Doris was the only one still at large and she was on the stage to Montevideo.

Bill's second telegram went to the Sheriff of Renville County asking that he check out a lawyer thought to be living in Olivia by the name of Al Fenton.

About a half hour later he got a reply. There is no lawyer named Al Fenton in Renville County. However, there is a ne'er-do-well by the name of Al Benton who liked to act like he was a lawyer.

Bill replied immediately asking that this Benton be held in connection with the gang being detained in the Renville jail. The Sheriff's reply came back, "Will do."

Saturday morning, Bill was in his office when Zeke and Terry rode in. Zeke told their tale. Yesterday afternoon Doris showed up at the Montevideo Bank and Trust as expected. They and the Chippewa County Sheriff had nabbed her as she exited the bank. When they reached the jail, Terry used Charlie's list to compare the serial numbers of the marked bills to those of corresponding denomination. He found all $72. When he tested them with the lemon juice and they all told the same story, "Gotcha". Doris was locked up and the three law men went to Granite Falls to confiscate the Judge's lock box. The Chippewa County Sheriff took the safety deposit box back to Montevideo while Zeke and Terry rode directly to Redwood Falls. The round up was over as far as the Redwood County Sheriff's department was concerned.

Early Monday morning an Investigator from the State Police came to Bill's office. His name was Captain Clayton Mahoney. He was well known throughout the State for the excellence of his police work. He and Bill reviewed the materials collected by the Redwood County Sheriff's Office. Inspector Mahoney was impressed with the case it made against Raymond Delevan and his crew. Mahoney said he and the State would take over the investigation and prosecution of the case. Mahoney assured Bill that the good work of he and his deputies would receive proper credit for their efforts.

By the next weekend, the St. Paul Pioneer Press ran the entire story of the Judge and his gang of thugs. The byline was the same reporter that written about the apprehension of the bank robbers last spring. Bill's fame took another leap in public opinion.

About a week after the newspaper article was released, Bill was working late trying to complete the after-action reports required by the State. About 8:30 he finished the last one. He straightened the papers on his desk, blew out the lamp and left the office to get Butch. As he bent over to lock the door a shot was fired, and a slug hit the eaves a yard above his head. His training took over and he hit the ground while drawing his gun. He looked into the darkness but could see nothing. A second shot rang out followed by a curse. Bill had seen the flash of this second shot, so he knew it had not been fired at him. A voice called out of the darkness, "Don't shoot Sheriff. It's Michael Schulze and the guy who was lying in wait for you is down."

"Michael what the hell are you doing in the alley behind my office?"

"Saving your ass. I'll explain when this bird is in a cage."

Bill hurried toward the sound of Michael's voice and found him standing over an unmoving body. Bill said, "Lets drag him over to the jail before he gets his senses back."

Each of them grabbed a foot. They dragged the shooter unceremoniously from the alley to the street and then across the street to the jail. All the way he was bleeding from the bullet wound and his head was getting a thumping from the rough ground.

Bill knocked on the door and said, "It's the sheriff. Let us in."

A face Bill didn't know appeared in the door's window, so he flashed his badge. A key grated in the lock and the door swung open. On the other side of it was an older man, kind of chunky, dressed in bib overalls. The gun belt around his waist looked totally out of place but the gun in his hand looked like it belonged. He relocked the door and said, "Who is this guy?"

Michael answered, "A guy who was waiting in ambush for the Sheriff."

"Do you have a cell we can put him in?" asked Bill.

"Yah, follow me." as he moved toward the cell block. He pointed at a cell with an open door. Bill and Michael dragged their burden in, picked him up and flopped him on the bed.

"Do you have a first aid kit?" asked Bill.

"Yup, I'll get it."

"Then go get Doc Simmons."

"I'll bring the kit back." said Michael as followed the jailer out into the main office. Michael hurried back and gave the kit to Bill while Michael was gone

Bill had cleaned the bullet wound and since he had bandaged many wounds on the battlefield, he worked efficiently to stem the flow of blood to a trickle before it stopped all together.

Just as Bill finished, Doc Simmons walked in. He examined the wound and said, "Nice bandage, if you ever get tired of being sheriff, I could use an assistant. You guys might as well go home, this guy isn't going to wake up anytime soon. What did you hit him with a sledgehammer?"

"Just the barrel of my gun." Michael said.

"Well you have given this guy one hell of a headache for his effort.

When Bill and Michael got outside, Bill said, "Come over to my office, I want to hear your story about what happened this evening."

When they were seated in the office, Michael said, "I was out walking with my girl this evening and we ducked into the alley to share a kiss or two. We were trying to avoid a scandal. Right after we finished the first kiss, I saw this guy sneaking around in the shadows behind your office. I saw the glint of his gun in the moonlight and figured he was going to ambush someone. As he jockeyed for position, I became convinced he was after you. So, I sent my girl home and tried to keep the guy in sight so I could intervene if necessary. When you came out the door he moved, and I lost my target. I shot over your head to warn you of your danger while I moved to find a new shooting lane. I saw him when he turned to look my way. I winged him and ran to where he was to pistol whip him. I was thinking you might want to question him. It wasn't quite as stupid as it sounds. He was down and obviously stunned."

"Well I am certainly glad you were there. Thanks a million! "I'll be here at eight in the morning if you're interested in what he has to say."

"I'll see you in the morning" Michael said.

They shook hands and parted.

The next morning Bill arrived at the jail to find Michael waiting for him. They walked into the Marshal's office together.

"Hi Don, I hope you won't mind Michael Schulze joining us this morning. He has a vested interest in this guy's story. Have you ever met Michael before?"

"No, I have seen him around the livery a few times. Michael, it is nice to meet you." They shook hands. "That was great work last night."

"It is a pleasure to meet you also."

Bill asked, "Can we question him now?"

"No need unless you are looking for something, he hasn't told me already."

"Tell us what he said and then we'll decide."

"He read the article in the St. Paul paper which

told of the great shot you made; about 300 yards I think it said. The guy you killed was his older brother. He was looking to avenge his brother by killing you."

"Does he have any more siblings at home who might want to still pursue this vendetta?"

"No, he and his older brother were cast out of their family years ago because of the Godless path they had chosen."

"That sounds like the end of it then."

Chapter 35

The Aftermath

A week later Bill received the news that Delevan's livery had been raided by the State Police. They had captured all the known members of the gang working at the livery except Delevan. They had also identified four more tentacles and arrested the gangs that operated them. In a building, hidden away, out of sight on the back of the livery's property, 10 of the more recently stolen horses were recovered and returned to their rightful owners.

Two unanswered questions remained. First why had Ray Delevan not shown up at the livery on the morning of the raid as expected and two, where was he?

The first question was answered when an internal investigation turned up a mole working at Police headquarters. The second question took care of itself when Delevan was arrested near St. Cloud while trying to escape to Dakota Territory.

On studying documents found during the raid six more horses were confiscated from their buyers as stolen property and returned. This tied the last ribbon found by the Redwood County Sheriff and his deputies into a strong bow for the courts to prosecute.

Bill, Zeke, Terry and Grady were kept busy during the next month or so traveling around the State testifying at trials. Michael Schulze was hired as the fourth deputy. He was a great help during the time while the rest of the force was occupied with testifying at trials. In case after case the evidence was so overwhelming that guilty verdicts were quickly voted by the jurys. In every case the convicted were sentenced to Stillwater State Prison for the term of their incarceration.

There were two exceptions. One was Dirk who had been sentenced to be hanged by the neck until dead. Since he had killed a veteran of the 'Army of the Potomac' he was being held in the brig at Fort Snelling until his hanging. It was scheduled for November 30th at the Fort. The second one was Doris. She was serving her time in the Shakopee State Women's Prison.

All the outlaws who had been shot recovered. Little piggy would never see out of his right eye again, the eyeball had boiled in its socket. Judge McKay lasted only a little more than a month in prison before he escaped through a hole in the wall of his own making. He committed suicide by hanging himself in his cell. He left a note full of remorse and pleas for forgiveness of his wicked acts.

The County and surrounding areas were peaceful now that Bill's reputation had been backed up by action. Still the deputies were kept busy visiting town marshals to assist if needed and to keep Bill's creation, The Redwood County Lawmen's Association alive and functioning.

Unexpectedly money started pouring in. First was the long-awaited reward for the apprehension of the bank robbers last spring. Next came money collected by the people of Morton in appreciation of their deliverance from their extortionists. This was followed by a sizeable sum from the Horse Breeders Association. Still more arrived from individuals who had posted rewards for the return of their animals. It was divided equally among the men involved.

The warehouse community was thriving now that the rent collector menace had been eliminated. More and more of the homeless and helpless were showing up as word of this sanctuary spread across the area.

More windows were added to the outer side of the building making more living spaces and plans were a foot to fix up the second level to make even more living space.

Bill and Patsy were elated at the progress and vitality these once downtrodden people were putting into regaining some of the 'good life' the war had robbed from them.

Improvements of the living conditions in the warehouse seemed to never quite keep up with demand but they never lagged far behind either.

Bill had Ed build a shelter for horses with five stalls in it. Only the buggy horse was kept there now but they expected there would be need for more.

Mrs. Betters had become a valued member of the Williams family. Louise was making herself useful playing with the William's kids.

Max had returned from Minneapolis and although he couldn't talk, he could eat and was regaining some of the weight he had lost.

Jamie didn't seem to have suffered any permanent damage from his run in with the stove.

Perhaps the biggest news from there was Grady's engagement to Mrs. McHugh. Bill congratulated Grady on his break from his past to looking forward to the future.

"Thank you, Bill. The chance you gave me to be your deputy was the break I needed to regain my self-respect and confidence; without that I was nothing going nowhere. Cora is a fine woman, solid and dependable and she can cook. Our relationship doesn't have the fire and passion of first love or young love but in many ways it's better. It is warm, comfortable and enduring."

"And you get a fine son in the bargain. Jamie is a great young man."

"No date has been set for the wedding but I'm not waiting to start acting like a father and a husband. Tomorrow Jamie and I are going to shop for a horse, so he has the freedom and independence like you gave Billy. I believe having something to love and being solely responsible for its care is a life lesson every young person should have."

"Amen brother, amen."

Mr. Qual had become a valued and respected member of the community. Each weekday morning, he hitched the horse to the buckboard and drove around doing all the errands that needed to be done. His earliest run each day was to get all the employed men to their jobs. His second run was to haul all the youngsters to school. On Monday, Wednesday and Friday on his way to school he took Mrs. Betters to the William's for her job. Mr. Qual stayed at school for the lessons. He was proud as Punch with his progress in the 1st grade.

Bill's life settled into a pattern. Each morning he

rode into town to have coffee with his deputies to discuss past and current events, the conditions they found as they canvased the county and planning future operations. During his visits he took care of the correspondence the office received. Bill was still Sheriff of Redwood County, but he was now also a man of leisure with little business to bother him.

Chapter 36
For the Good Times

B ill and Patsy made good use of Bill's leisure time. They joined Redwood Falls social activities with 'gusto'. It started when they attended a square dance put on by the church. They followed this by going to a potluck dinner a few days later. At both events they were treated as guests of honor. After the potluck they were deluged with invitations from all over the county to various events and parties. Hayrides, Polka Parties and Potluck Dinners to name a few.

Since it was fall, there were lots of get together with harvest themes. Apple picking, dunking, pressing and cider drinking all had their day(s) on the social calendar. Corn on the cob roasts were also popular. One unique event was the 'Chamber of Commerce Annual Wheat Shocking Race.' Bill of course was drafted to be a contestant in it. He was teamed with Don Williams. They were dubbed, 'The Peacekeepers.' Neither Bill nor Don had ever worked a wheat field and thus knew nothing about shocking wheat.

(For any of you city boys and girls not in the know, harvesting wheat in 1865 was a multi-step process. First a reaper-binder cuts the wheat, binds it into bundles and drops the bundles in a row behind it. The second step is where the shocking comes in. Someone must pick up a bundle on a pitchfork and make it stand up using the cut stems as the base. Next as many bundles as possible are leaned against that center standing bundle to make a teepee of wheat called a shock. The shocks purpose is to let the wheat dry out before it is thrashed. The last step then is to feed the dried bundles in to the 'Thrashing Machine' to separate the wheat from stems and other plant parts.)

Bill and Don made a valiant effort but lost to experience despite their superior cheering section led by Patsy, Mrs. Williams and including Mrs. Betters, Louise, the William's kids, Billy and Mrs. Flowers. The good food and laughter cheered up all including the bruised egos of the vanquished.

As Halloween approached pumpkins were carved and displayed while the insides became soup, pies and such. After Halloween winter set in. When the river froze over, Ice skating became the activity of the moment. When a blizzard came and lay down a blanket of snow, skiing and tobogganing also took their places on the social agenda.

The approach of Thanksgiving shoved all other activities aside. Patsy and Emma helped by the ladies living at the warehouse and Milly were busy preparing a feast for the multitude of people they were inviting to join them for the traditional dinner and celebration.

Bill and the men under Ed's direction constructed plank tables and benches which crowded the front room and dining room. There wasn't a smidgen of unoccupied space in either room.

The kids had a great time decorating the place. They let their artistic side rule the day. There were red, white and blue streamers everywhere. Nowhere in the two rooms was there a single spot that was unadorned. Even the tables were covered with bright red paper.

The only discord in the decor occurred on the day of the feast. Each person was asked to bring their own dishes, so the tabletops became a potpourri of colors, sizes and shapes as each family and individual placed their dishes at their chosen spots at the tables.

One of the tables in the dining room held the dishes of the host family, Bill, Patsy, Mrs. Flowers,

Billy and Hal. Doc Simmons place was next to Patsy. Charlie the clerk who ran the sheriff's office was situated on the left end of the bench opposite the sheriff's family. Next came places for the deputies, Zeke, Terry (with his girlfriend, Ellie) and Michael (with his girlfriend, Anne.)

Grady, Mrs. McHugh, and Jamie's places were at the next table. Also, on the same side as their friends at the next table were Mrs. Betters, Louise and Mr. Qual's selected places. The residence of the warehouse had grown in number, they filled three tables.

Don Williams with his family and Don's deputies and their families filled a table.

Milly, Ed and their sons were accompanied by Ed's work crew and their families filled another table

The rest of the tables were filling up fast with a conglomeration of people the Cheevers deemed would be alone or unable to provide a celebration of their own.

When the cooks signaled that everything was ready, Bill in his best Sergeant-Major voice asked that everyone sit down and listen up. "I and our country have a lot to be thankful for as 1865 draws to a close. The terrible war between slavery and freedom finally ended." Applause and cheers broke out from the listeners. Bill continued, "One year ago I was chasing Rebs around Georgia. I never gave Redwood Falls a thought back in those days. I didn't know even one of you then. But fate has been kind. First, I met the love of my life and then we moved here and found a place and people we love. Now I would like to have each of you to join me in a prayer of thanksgiving for our country, our community and our families. Oh, also would please include a wish for a healthy, happy little Cheever that is scheduled to arrive this spring." There was a ripple surprise across those assembled as this last line sunk in. "Now, let each of us pray in our own way for the blessings we received in the past and for the hopes we have for the future." Bowed heads and silence invaded the room. Finally, Bill said, "Amen, Now let's eat."

At these words, the kitchen door opened, and a procession of kids and mothers covered a close by table with all the wonders of the culinary world that the women had created this past week. The aroma emitting from the food wetted ever one's appetite as they waited their turn to choose the delights, they would eat this day. This was the 'Horn of Plenty' in spades.

The 'Horn of Plenty' table was ravaged as it sated the appetites of the diners. As time wore on people became drowsy, put on their coats and stopped to thank Bill and Patsy for their hospitality. They also congratulated them on the expected addition to their family.

The household took a week to recover from Thanksgiving. Now the decorations were gone, the tables and benches were stored, and everything was back in its rightful place. Even the kitchen pots, pans and order had been restored. Life could now return to its normal pace.

Bill and Patsy had decided to spend the week prior to Christmas with Bill's folks and then travel to Des Moines for New Years with the Amours.

They rode the stagecoach to Mankato then changed coaches for the trip to St. Peter. They stayed in comfortable accommodations in St. Pete but had to get up early to catch their ride to Shakopee and then to Minneapolis and St. Paul. Dad picked them up at the stage station in St. Paul and took them home. Mom was overjoyed to see them. The evening meal was no surprise to any of the diners.

The week was busy but rewarding. Patsy and mom spent hours talking about childbirth and care. Dad and Bill reviewed all the action of the previous fall including the Delevan take down. Christmas Eve they exchanged gifts and well wishes as the travelers prepared for their train ride to Des Moines the next day.

The train left right on time and seemed to be flying down the track. Bill and Patsy found out the train crew was from Kansas City and were trying to get home for a late Christmas dinner with their families. For whatever reason they were in Des Moines and hour early. The train's telegrapher had wired ahead and all the families expecting passengers on the train were notified of its early arrival. All passengers holding tickets for K.C. and beyond were contacted and told to be at the depot early.

Zeke's black, smiling face greeted them as they swung down from the train. It was a relief to find out that their early arrival was expected, and they wouldn't have to wait for their ride. This was a great start to their extremely successful visit.

A week and a half later the travelers were back in Redwood Falls. They were tired but pleased with reconnecting with their families. Patsy was especially tired from carrying the extra weight of the baby. She was also feeling awkward as she worked around the ever-increasing bulge of the child growing inside her.

While Bill and Patsy were away the weather had turned to Minnesota nasty. Nobody in their right mind ventured out unless it was absolutely necessary. Hal had abandoned his place in the barn for a room in the house with a Franklin stove near his bed. Billy had a few chores to attend to after he got home from school. The most important of these was keeping the wood boxes full.

Bill returned to having his daily meetings with his deputies. Zeke had taken care of everything that had come up during Bill's absence, so the meetings were mostly social. Peace and order prevailed in Redwood County as far as the Redwood County Sheriff's Office was concerned. The meetings were mostly review of gossip and assignment of duties. Bill was usually home by lunch time.

Occasionally, on a better than average day, Bill would hook the Bays up to a sleigh he had brought. He and Patsy would go into town to shop, or to a neighbors to visit or just for a ride around to enjoy the weather and each other's company. Patsy was now big with child and following Doctor's orders to not overdo physical activity. Bill drove the sleigh very carefully to keep from jostling her in the ruts, potholes and ice ridges. In the evening, the family would gather around a roaring fire in the front room fireplace. Patsy and Emma usually kept busy making things for the baby. Bill, Hal and Billy spent their evenings playing competitive games like chess, poker and cribbage. The bonds between these three were getting stronger every day.

Still the best time of the day came when Bill and Patsy lay in the loving comfort of each other's arms. Occasionally they would share a giggle over an action the baby would take in Patsy's protective pouch. The baby's reassuring heartbeat was also a source of joy and pleasure for them.

Finely the weather broke, and the first hints of spring appeared. The weather kept improving and near the end of March the trees began to show the first signs of buds. Once and awhile a tulip could be seen with its bud waiting for the right moment to burst open into its full glory.

About the middle of April while Bill was at his morning meeting with his deputies at Milly's, Billy rushed in. He said, "You better come quickly. Something is hurting in Patsy's stomach. I already told the Doc and he is hitching up his buggy now."

"Take over Zeke." he yelled over his shoulder as he raced out the door and mounted Butch with a running start. Butch sensed his rider's urgency and broke into an all-out run as soon as Bill found his seat. Down Main Street and out Ferry Road horse and rider flew.

Somewhere in his dust was Billy and Ghost. Bill didn't give them a thought. All his thoughts were for Patsy and their child. Bill made a running dismount at the back door and rushed up stairs to Patsy's side. Now that he was here, he couldn't think of a thing he could do except hold her hand and encourage her with his voice. Emma was on the other side of the bed trying everything she could think of to keep Patsy comfortable.

Five minutes later, Billy showed up but all he could do was stand respectively back out of the way. Ten minutes after Billy, Doc Simmons showed up. He immediately asked Bill and Billy to leave the room so he could concentrate on his examination.

The exiled pair went to take care of the horses that they had abandoned on their arrival. When they came out the back door there were no horses in sight except Doc's who had a feedbag on and was munching on some oats. The two hurried down to the barn expecting Hal had taken care of theirs as he had taken care Docs. They had been correct in their surmise of the fate of their mounts. Hal was there giving Butch a good brisk rubdown. Billy took over that task for Ghost.

Bill walked up to the house to see if there was any news. As Bill tiptoed into the bedroom Doc took him by the shoulders and steered him to a chair. "Bill, I'm so sorry, the news is all bad. Take a deep breath and get a hold of yourself, Neither Patsy nor the baby survived."

Bill's eyes became blurry with tears. He pushed Doc aside as he bolted to the bed and fell to his knees. Patsy's lay on her back. Her hair was arranged in a wreath of brown around her head. Her face was very pale, you might even say ghostly. The quilt was pulled up to her chin. The baby was cradled in Patsy's left arm and only its head was visible above the blanket. The baby's head was very red, and its face was contorted.

Bill's cries of anguish filled the room. Suddenly all became quiet. Bill said in a very controlled voice, "rest in peace my love. You will be missed in my world, but it has been blessed by all the good times and good deeds you brought to it. Someday soon I will join you and our son to spend an eternity together." Tenderly and lovingly he put his arm across her and the baby, embracing them both. Then he kissed her so tenderly and lovingly that it broke every heart of the watchers in the room. With that he stood up and started blindly toward the door.

Doc grabbed his arm, "Do you want to hear my thoughts about what happened here, Bill?"

"Not now Doc, maybe some other time."

.Bill's mind was berserk. *'What is there left to live for? The best part of my life, past and future, lies there dead, out of reach of anything I can do or say. How will I ever be able to pray to the God who took them away? I have got to get away and find a place to grieve but where will that be?*

With tears in his eyes and his heart on the floor he stumbled out the door of the bedroom he would never enter again, down the stairs he would never tread again and out of the house he would never call home again.

Chapter 37

The Quest

B ill stood on the dock alongside the 'Minnesota Queen', a side wheel, river packet that would carry his life and his future away from him. A week had passed since the death of the baby and Patsy. The coroner's autopsy had found the baby's cause of death to be the unlikely wrapping of its umbilical cord around its neck as it made its turn for birth. The baby had fought the strangling cord and lost. In its struggles, however, it ruptured the cord and Patsy bled to death.

Bill still couldn't come to grips with the sudden loss of all he held dear. He looked into the crate he was standing beside, at the bundle wrapped in a tarp shroud, laying on a bed of ice. He felt numb, devoid of all feeling. He wrenched when the crew continued filling the crate with ice. The ice would preserve the Earthly remains of his wife and the baby she would be holding and protecting through eternity. They were heading for their final resting place, the Amour's family burial plot in Des Moines.

Bill thought, '*I was told in Sunday school that the Lord moves in mysterious ways but for the life of me I cannot see why he would need to call Patsy away from her Earthly existence so abruptly. I was also told he was a kind and loving God. Right now, I don't feel loved. Right now, I feel Patsy, our baby and I are victims of his wrath. Will I ever lose this bitterness I feel toward him? Will I ever be able to pray to him with genuine love as I have been doing since I was a kid?*

He knew he had to get away from here as soon as possible. Everywhere he looked he saw Patsy and was reminded of the good times they had shared. Then his thoughts would be pulled into the scene that haunted him the most. He would be back on the train depot platform in Des Moines seeing again the beautiful girl giving him the once over. The girl with eyes that almost devoured him whole right then and there.

He had been preparing his escape for the past week. A couple of days ago he had gone out to the house that was home no more. He had Billy bring his stuff to the barn. It was hard enough to be close to the house he and Patsy had come to love. There was no way he could have mustered the strength to enter it. When he saw the house all his thoughts were filled with the memory of Patsy's white face in its wreath of brown hair, laying in the bed they had shared holding the baby they had wanted so much. She was beautiful in his memory, like the angel she had already become.

In the barn they sorted through his belongings, carefully putting them in go, no go piles. This proved to be hard for Bill because it was so reminiscent of when Patsy had divided her clothes up with her sisters before she came to Minnesota after their marriage. Out in the barn he could at least put his grief aside enough to sort, organized and loaded the horses.

The guns were the most noticeable part of his paraphernalia. Of course, he wore his Colt 45's in their holsters on his gun belt. The gun belt held 36 cartridges to reload each of his two six-guns three times. So, when the pistols and belt were filled, he had a total of 48 shots available. The remainder of the box of pistol shells along with shells from a previous box were stored in a special pouch in one of his saddlebags giving him another full reload for each Colt. Over his shoulder-across his chest was a bandoleer with loops for forty, forty-four caliber cartridges for the Henry. The Henry's scabbard also had 20 more cartridges on it. The Henry when fully loaded had sixteen shots in its magazine and one more in the chamber. This gave Bill a total of 77 rifle bullets at hand when needed. The horse pistols were fixed in front of Butch's saddle. Each of these were loaded with black powder and buckshot. Behind Butch's saddle was the bedroll containing his ground tarp, slicker and blanket. Also, back there would be a pair of saddlebags. One of the bags would be loaded with the grub sack, fry pan, utensils and coffee pot. The other one would carry Bills extra clothes. All this weight plus saddle, the tack and Bill would rest on Butch's brawny back.

Patches was the only reminder of Patsy he was taking a long. She was going to be used as his pack horse. Her load included the other part of his armory. A two lb. keg of black powder. Two, one lb. bars of lead. A bag with a lb. of buckshot for the horse pistols. A twelve-gauge, pump shotgun, was hanging in the pack where it would be easy to get at. Bill had often used the shotgun when hunting ducks and pheasants. It would add firepower at close range. Its magazine held 8 shells regardless of the size of the shot. Bill added a case of 50, 12-gauge shells to Patches load. The shot Bill chose was buckshot of course. This time he wanted enough striking power to stop a man, not a bird. In addition, Patches would carry a backup box of shells for the Colts and another for the Henry. The other gun Patches would carry was one Bill acquired just a couple of weeks ago. It came with quite a story attached. The story as Bill told it went like this.

"The guy who sold it to me stopped at the sheriff's office a few weeks ago to report two deaths. None of them had occurred in Redwood County but the guy figured some lawman should know what happened. He told me he and a couple of friends had snuck into Indian country to hunt Buffalo. None of them had the slightest idea how to go about it. However, they figured it couldn't be too hard if savage Indians could do it. After a couple of days, they found a small herd grazing in a bend of the Missouri River. So, they left their horses and started to crawl toward their prey. The Bulls standing on the outside edge of the herd put their heads up and sniffed the wind. Whatever they smelled agitated the bulls and they snorted loudly. All the herd was now on its feet and milling around. Almost as if a command had been given, they all broke into a run in the opposite direction from where the three hunters were hidden in the grass. That was when things got dicey.

Unfortunately for these guys a small band of Indians had spotted the same group of cows, calves and bulls he and his friends were stocking. Therefore, when the herd stampeded it went right through hidden Indians. The guy said he knew some of them got hurt and he believe at least one was killed. They were mad as hornets. He said he learned something else that day. Indians do not leave their horses behind. They were mounted and after the friends almost immediately. The three wannabe buffalo hunters scattered. The guy in my office got lucky. Being closest to the river during their advance he made it over the bank. A few hundred yards upriver was a large snag of driftwood. He went into the river and by using the driftwood was able to pull himself to the middle of the pile. He said it was a great hiding place with air and a view of the shore. Soon four braves showed up and searched the wood pile and the riverbank in both directions without success. Finally, the four got together for a talk and left. The guy in my office said he stayed put despite how cold he got from being in the spring water. All that night the wails of his friends were heart wrenching, but they served to keep his resolve to stay in hiding and endure the cold. About noon the next day, after not hearing anything all morning, he snuck out of his hiding place to find the Indians gone and the mutilated bodies of his friends dangling from a tree. He said he threw up at the sight of what had been done to them. He cut them down and dragged them to the riverbank. There he found a broken off branch among the driftwood and scratched out a grave in the riverbank for those two souls Then on the chance that their horses hadn't been found, he walked back to where they had left them to start the hunt. Finally, he had some good luck. All three horses were still there. He removed the hobbles and made a bee line back to civilization. He said he wouldn't go back to Indian country if the only other choice was '**HELL**'.

I said, "Have you figured out what went wrong that day?" He shook his head no.

"Well in case you ever are trying to escape or sneak up on someone or something be sure to keep the wind blowing from them to you. Now you should be able to figure out why the herd ran toward the Indians and not you. I handed the man a pad and pencil and said, "I will need to have you write that all down. Include anything you remember about the Indians. Be sure to include your name and those of your friends."

"Sheriff you wouldn't know anyone in the market for a Buffalo gun, would you?"

"Do you have it with you?"

"Yes, it's out in the scabbard on my horse."

"I'll take a look at it while you were writing out that report."

"I also have 50 brass shell casings, a cleaning kit and shell reloading tools to include with it."

The gun was a Sharps 50 caliber Buffalo / sniper's rifle. Bill was familiar with this type of gun from his war experience. The 50 brass casings were a big bonus. Bill, like most snipers, had his own blend of powder and weight of lead he liked to shoot. Bill's mixture of powder was smokeless and clean burning, Bill thought *'This gun is an absolute gem. I would guess it hasn't been fired more than half a dozen times. I wonder how much he is going to ask for it. This gun with all its extras is all one would need for long range artillery.'* When Bill re-entered the office, the man was just finishing the report.

Bill took the pad from him and glanced at it. "Address and sign it please."

The guy took the pad and pencil back and signed it, Jim Fogle. Austin, Minnesota. Bill took the pad and pencil and stuffed them in his desk drawer. "Okay Jim, have you decided what you want for that Sharps cannon?"

"Really I just want to get rid of it. Do you think someone would take it right now for $50?"

"I feel honor bound to tell you it is worth a lot more than that."

"Not to me, every time I notice it, I hear the screams of my friends and start blaming myself for the stupidity I showed by going along with the bravado the three of us built up until none of us could escape with our self-image intact."

"I can't give you $50 for all you have there, but

THE FORGOTTEN CASUALTIES OF WAR

I will offer you $100. That way I can keep a little of my self-respect for not taking total advantage of you."

"It's a deal." and they shook hands.

Bill still felt a little bit guilty because the Sharps was one hell of a bargain. It was now stored in Patches load.

Bill's thoughts moved on to the other things he had done to prepare for this day.

He had written to Mel and Patricia to inform them of the deaths and apologize for not keeping Patsy safe as he had promised he would.

He had turned the sheriff's office over to Zeke with the county's blessing. Zeke and all his deputies were rehired. The county had insisted Bill's name remain listed as the Sheriff of the county in hopes that his reputation would deter bad men from trying to operate here. The county board thought this important enough to pay Bill $100 per month for the privileged.

Bill planned for Hal, Billy and Emma to live in the house rent free. In fact, he named them caretakers with a payment of $100 per month for maintenance.

He got Don Williams to take over guardianship of the warehouse and its occupants.

Now, with a last look into the crate where the tarp shrouded occupants were now covered with ice,

Bill turned and walked off the dock. Michael had agreed to accompany the crate to St. Paul where he would meet Bill's dad. Arrangements had been made to replace the old ice with new. The two would then ship it on to Des Moines for burial. These were the arrangements requested by Mel and Patricia.

Butch and Patches were tied to the wharf waiting patiently. They both nodded their heads and snorted at Bill's arrival. Bill took Patches lead rope and mounted Butch. They were both fully loaded and ready to go. The little cavalcade trotted out of town on Ferry Road. Bill looked neither right nor left or acknowledging any of the many shouts that arose from the people on the street. He was through with Redwood Falls as far as he was concerned.

His quest to find peace in a world without Patsy was going to be channeled into his desire to find out how his Indian brothers, Fox Feather, Erect Bear and Bold Otter were doing.

Chapter 38
Have You Ever Seen...?

I t was a fine day, springtime warm, the world turning green and bird songs serenading him from the trees along the trail. Bill should have been enjoying the beauty that surrounded him, but he hardly noticed it. His mind was consumed with his lost hopes and dreams. He was almost oblivious to the passage of time, distance and the toll his pace was taking out of Butch and Patches.

Finally, he got his thoughts in line with reality and became aware of his surroundings. His pace became less urgent and more in tune with the travel gaits of the horses. He realized he would never hold Patsy in his arms again, but he could always seek her presence in his subconscious mind. He decided that was better than losing her completely. With the recognition of his path forward and acceptance of reality, peace came to his soul.

He started studying his surroundings and decided he was near the Redwood County line passing into Lyons County. Marshall couldn't be much further off to his southwest. He thought, *'It's time to stop for the night and see if the packs need any adjustments.'* With this thought he started looking for a likely spot to camp. First, he found a little spring where he and the horses drank their fill and he refreshed the canteens. Then he moved on west a little further until he spotted a stand of pines a short distance to the right of the trail. He thought, *'Pine needles don't hold tracks very well. I can hide my trail in those pines and then circle so I can watch my back trail.* Acting on his thoughts, Bill soon found the right set of circumstances so he could accomplish the tasks he had planned for this night.

He took care of the horses first. Patches showed her happiness at being free from her pack by romping around the glade they were in, including rolling on her back and wiggling to scratch it. Butch was equally happy to shed the saddle, bridle and other items he had been carrying. Bill pull halters on them and staked them out so they could graze.

Next, he scrounged around picking up very dry, small pieces of wood he could find until he had a substantial pile. He cleaned the pine needles out of a small depression in the forest floor and lay a small fire in it. The sticks he had picked up burned hot and with almost no smoke. While this first bunch of wood burned down to a bed of red-hot coals, he got a chunk of ham and a heel of bread from the grub sack for his dinner. While he ate, he kept feeding sticks from his pile into the glowing coals. When he judged the fire to be hot enough, he got out the hooked rod he used to hang the coffee pot over the fire.

Tonight, it wouldn't be the coffee pot hanging on it, tonight it would be a lead melting pot hanging there. He took out one of the bars of lead, ten shell casings and the other equipment for loading the Sharps shells. He cut about half the bar into small chunks and put them into the hot pot for melting. While the lead was heating, took out the Sharps two bullet molds and prepared them for the molten lead. When all was ready, he poured 45 grams of the lead into each mold and set them aside to cool. He added more lead to the pot and more wood to the fire before he cracked the molds open. He repeated the process four more times until the pound of lead had turned into 10 slugs. The finishing touch was to remove the mold marks and make the slugs smooth as possible.

With the slugs prepared and cooling, he took a shell casing and installed a percussion cap in it. Then he added 145 gains of his special smokeless powder and a fast burning, ash less paper wad. Last came the slug. It was fitted and crimped into place. Soon he had added 10 bullets for the Sharps to his arsenal. He decided to wait until after he zeroed the gun before he committed to this bullet as the right one for his purpose.

By this time, it was dark, and the woods had gone quiet except for an occasional rustle in the under-brush as a night hunter looked for their next meal. He yawned as he spread his ground tarp. He slid into his blanket sleeping bag and pulled his slicker over him to keep the next morning's dew off his blanket. Sleep came immediately

Morning came quickly and Bill was up at first light and checked on the horses. They were fine. Next, he built a small, hot, smokeless fire from his left-over sticks. He filled the coffee pot with water from a canteen, added a scoop of coffee and hung in on the hook to perk. He cut a slice of ham and a cou-ple of slices of bread from his supplies and flopped them in the frying pan that had been heating over the fire. The bread became toast soaked with the ham's fat. This was a hearty meal to start what would be a two-meal day.

Erasing the evidence that someone had camped here took a little extra time, but he thought it was worth it. It had been a long time since his last scout-ing expedition, and he wanted to regain the level of expertise of his army days. Soon everything was in order and he rode out of the pines and back on the trail heading west.

They traveled for about an hour or so until they arrived at Marshall. Bill went into the hardware store and came out with three, one-pound lead bars, a package of shell papers and a sack of powder. They left Marshall at a leisurely pace in a southwest direction toward Verdi. An hour or so later they came to a large meadow a ways off the trail. The meadow had everything that horse and rider could want. There was a little clearing in the grass by the creek. Someone had put a picnic table in the middle of the clearing for the traveler's use. There was also a fire ring close by.

Bill loosened the pack, the saddle and staked the horses out to graze and water. He took the Sharps rifle out of the pack and looked it over. This was the first time he had looked at it with a critical eye. It was a Sharps Shiloh Model which could handle a variety of loads and bullet weights. He thought, *'I bet the shells I filled last night are going to be perfect for my purpose.'*

He took some targets with sticks so you could press them into the ground and started walking. At what he thought should be close to 300 yards he set up three targets. Then he traced his path back to his starting point. He took a bullet out of a pouch, flipped up the breechblock slipped a shell in the chamber and replaced the block. Using the table as a shooting platform he rested the swing down rod to help steady the 9.5-pound rifle with its 34-inch barrel. He checked the direction and force of the wind before he bent down to line the guns sights at the middle target. Satisfied with his aim he pulled the cocking trigger which moved the gun's hammer into the ready to shoot position. He rechecked his aim before squeezing the second trigger releasing the hammer on to the cartridge's percussion cap thus igniting the shell's powder which propelled the lead slug toward the target. He gave a satisfied grunt when the target disappeared. He walked out to the target and found he had hit the bullseye. He repeated the process at 700 yards and at 1000 yards with the same result. He cleaned the rifle and stored it with the seven remaining loads on the right side of the pack under cover. Bill was ready for war if that become necessary. He gathered up the horses and set out again.

The country was changing as they moved west. Fewer trees, more prairie and covered with the tall prairie grass so common across the western North American Desert, as some called the land between the Mississippi River and the Rocky Mountains. Still there was plenty of animal activity to be seen and heard as he moved along the trail. The Meadowlark song was a constant reminder of the great weather they were enjoying.

He topped a rise and below was a vast plain still in its early spring colors, lots of yellow with splotches of rusty red. Some of the shrubs around a watering hole added a bright green contrast to the otherwise drab scene. A little way north of the watering hole was an immense, stark white building shining in the late afternoon sun. Bill took the white building to be the Verdi Trading Post. It was the only building in sight, if you ignored the unpainted, sun bleached building that appeared to be the trading post's outhouse.

There were five horses tied to the hitch rack and a wagon parked next to the loading dock on the eastside of the building. Two men were loading a variety of materials and supplies into it. They stopped long enough to give Bill the once over as he and the horses moved to hitching rack in the front of the store. Before he tied them up, he gave them a drink from the nearby water trough. Then he loosened their girths a notch or two. When the horses were taken care of, he entered the door to the bar.

Four men were sitting at a table with cards in their hands, money on the table and a glass of whisky in front of each. Close by was a bottle, promising a refill when needed. These guys were all toting guns with holsters tied down.

Bill headed toward the bar when a voice stopped him, "Want to get in the game stranger?"

Bill looked back at the players table. The spokesman was a lanky, thin guy in a loud, blue, silk shirt and gray Stetson. He was standing on the other side of the table. The other three players had pushed their chairs back from the table. Bill assumed their move was to clear themselves to back the spokesman if it came to that. "No thanks. I just want a cold beer and I will be on my way."

"I'm afraid that won't do. We wouldn't want you to go away from here with a story about how unfriendly we were when you stopped in and since your guns aren't tied down and the loops are on their hammers, I don't know how you can refuse our kind offer."

"Well I wasn't sure how friendly you five boys were going to be. Five little boys, when they think they have an advantage might do the dandiest things, so I brought along a friend just in case."

All five of the would-be robbers shifted their attention to the door to see who his friend was. When they realized no one was there they looked back at Bill to find they were covered by a rifle that had suddenly appeared in Bills hands. "I want you to meet

Henry, but I don't think you want Henry to meet you. Barkeep are you part of these jerkoffs?"

The bartender's hands shot into the air, "God no!"

"Good, keep your hands up, come around the bar, sit in that chair and put your hands in your lap where I can see them. Now don't move or you will pay with your life. You by the bar, take your right-hand gun out of its holster using two fingers of your left hand to grip the butt. Now throw the gun in the spittoon by your feet."

One of the guys around the table shifted his weight as if to make himself more comfortable. "Hey wiggler, wiggle back to the position you were in a moment ago. I don't care how uncomfortable you are, but I do care if you move and you should care about that also."

"Now back to our friend at the bar. Get rid of your left-hand gun exactly as you did your right one, then take off your boots. Hand them to the barman. Thank you!"

"Now barkeep, check in those boots for hidden weapons. Remember I am holding you responsible if a weapon appears from one of them after you have checked it.

Now each of you other four, throw you gun belts with guns still in their holsters over the bar. Be careful, any poor throw in my direction and you will have to catch a bullet from Henry. A barrage of guns and belts followed this command but none of them flew in Bill's direction. Not all of them made it over the bar either but all of them were far enough away from their owners to satisfy Bill.

Did you get the boots checked?

"Yes."

"Good, hand them back to mister barfly. Now barfly take your boots over to that far wall behind your buddies and face the wall. Stand your boots up in front of you. Now brace yourself on the wall, body straight and at least two inches between your heels and the floor.

"Blue shirt, your next. Pull off your boots and throw them to the barkeep. When you get your boots back join your buddy on the wall. So, the ritual went until all five of the would-be jokers were leaning on the wall in their stocking feet.

"Ok, barfly, we'll start with you. Bend over and put your hands in your boots and then walk your feet back until the two inches between the heels and the floor are back. When the five were bent over, Bill said, "Keep your heels up your weight on your hands. I have a clear picture of your straining asses, so I'll know if your weight shifts. Barkeep I've waited far too long for that cold beer."

The bartender hopped up, grabbed a mug, pulled

a beer and set it in front of Bill. After his first swallow he said, "Now that's better."

There were some stamping and slapping sounds from the front porch. Bill shifted a little to keep all that mattered in the room, including the front door in view.

The batwing doors swung open and a large man in faded bib overalls, a plaid cotton shirt and brogans on his feet stepped in the room. He had a straw hat in his hand and his face was streaked with rivers of sweat and dust. He wasn't wearing a gun. Bill said, "You look like you could use a cold beer. First ones on me. Barkeep, two beers. My name's Bill Cheever. What's yours?"

"I'm Dan Blocker, owner of the -DB ranch a few miles south of here. What's going on over there?" the newcomer nodded toward the wall of butts as he took a swallow of his beer.

"They were anxious to be jokesters, so I taught them a new joke. You boys laughing yet? Do you know them?"

"I know of them. You're not the first they have bullied. Usually it's a rigged contest that costs the victim all the cash they have on them. What happened here?"

"They saw my six guns were not ready for quick action and thus insisted I join their poker game.

They were so sure I was a pigeon, five to one and no visible available weapons that they didn't notice I had brought Henry to the party. Henry took control of the situation and they were eager to partake in a new joke. Now I'm not sure what I should do with them. They're most likely going to hold a grudge because of their treatment today. However, they never got a chance to do anything unlawful before the table turned on them. I think a good walk might give them time to think about their misdeeds and cause them to drop their bullying ways. Barkeep pick up those guns and gun belts behind the bar and give them to me please. Ok, jackasses along the wall take your hands out of your boots and put them in your pockets leave your boots where they are and move out the door."

The five ruffian's horses were standing peacefully along the hitch rail. Each had a saddle gun as part of their rig. While keeping careful watch on his prisoners, Bill untied each horse from the hitch rack in turn, unloosened its saddle girth and pulled the saddle horn until the whole rig was on the ground. When all five horses were free, he sent them scattering with a three-shot volley from his left hand six gun. He waited until the horses had disappeared to the west before, he started the five jokesters down the eastward trail. They were warned not to turn and look back until they had crossed the trails ridgeline. As the jokesters trudged away in their stocking feet, Bill collected up all their abandoned hardware, emptied them one by one and flung the ammunition out into the tall prairie grass. The guns were then dumped unceremoniously into the muddy pond behind the building. All the other gear was piled on the porch.

As Dan, the barkeep and Bill stood watching the exodus he asked, "Has either of you ever seen a Sioux about my age wearing a foxtail in his hair where most Indians wear a feather. He would most likely have been accompanied by a big, by any standard, brave and a scrawny twitch of a one?"

Dan shook his head no.

The barkeep said, "Yah, every summer in the middle or late August a band of Sioux of most every size and description show up here to trade. Fox Feather is their obvious leader."

"Well anybody who lets me know when they arrive will earn themselves a handsome reward. I'll keep in touch in the meantime. Now it is time for me to find a roosting place for the night. See you gents soon."

"Hey, wait a minute Bill. How about coming home with me for a hot meal and a warm bunk for the night. I'll even throw some grain and a good rub down for your horses into the pot for the pleasure of your company."

"Dan, you silver tongued devil you. How could anyone refuse such a magnificent offer.

Chapter 39
Time to Heal

The days and weeks had flown by since Bill met Dan and accepted his invitation to supper and overnight stay at the -DB. In the morning Dan offered Bill a place to stay while he waited for his Indian friends to show up at the Verdi Trading Post. Bill accepted with the proviso that he would work like every other hand who received room and board as part payment for their work. A deal was struck between the friends that had Bill signed on as regular -DB hand for the season or until his awaited Indian friends showed. Bill buried himself in the hard work, cowboy comradery and nurturing of the Blocker family.

It was now going on three months and Bill was as fit as a fiddle. He had put on a little weight, all muscle. He had also honed his rope and riding skills to a fine edge of perfection. Even his emotional state had improved although most of his idle time was spent with his memories of Patsy. He remembered those eyes most of all. They could be full of mirth; they could be full of love or they could be full of deviltry. They were a direct read of her state of mind. The memory of her wreath of brown hair around her white face as she lay on the bed with their baby in her arms disturbed his dreams less and less.

His feelings toward God had also undergone scrutiny during this time. Finally, after deep consideration of all he knew about life and death, he concluded that God doesn't orchestrate the lives of individuals. God created the conditions that support life, the mechanism to create life and then sets the individual free to play the tune they please. Life is full of hazards that individuals can encounter without any involvement of God. In battle, who lived or died seemed to depend on the path of the bullet, not the choice of God. He and Patsy had decided to have a baby and thus setup the circumstances that led to the disaster of her death. Were they wrong to have challenged death to bring new life into the world?

Dan's family was a shining example of why people looked death in the eye, accepted its challenge and decided to have children anyway. He and his family were good people. They worshiped a God of tolerance. Their genuine caring for each other and for everyone they dealt with in their daily lives was an impressive statement of their relationship to their God. Their way of life was a major factor in restoring Bill's faith in God.

In the valley below where Bill was setting on Butch was the -DB herd of cattle being gathered for market. That would mean a trail herd to Sioux City, Iowa and the end of the cowboys' work year. To be sure, some of the hands would drift south to see if they could catch on with a southern ranch for the northern winter. Many of them however would stick around these parts existing on the poke they had built up this summer.

Bill wasn't sure what he should do, wait here in hopes of his friends showing up or go down to the Missouri River to look for them. As if in answer to his question, he spotted a rider coming toward him. He waited patiently for the rider to arrive. It was the bartender from Verdi, "Hey Bill, your Indian friends showed up yesterday. Their leader, Fox Feather, said you could find them at the Vermillion Bend of the Missouri."

"Thanks, come with me and I'll get your reward." The two of them rode back to the ranch where Bill got a twenty-dollar bill out of his stash. He handed it to the barkeep and asked, "Have those poker players showed up at the bar since I refused their invitation to play?"

"Nope, Oh, I guess you could say they were back at least once. A few days after that fiasco their stuff all disappeared from the porch."

They shook hands. "Well thanks again, this means a lot to me." Bill shouted as the barkeep rode away. It took over an hour to collect his stuff and repack Patches load. Then came the difficult part. Riding Butch and leading Patches he stopped at the ranch house. Dan's wife gave him a hug and said, "Come back anytime." The kids all came to say good-bye. Dan shook his hand and they exchanged man hugs and it was over. Bill head west to the Dakota Territories.

After several days of travel, he was riding along the Big Sioux River, in mid-morning when he heard gunfire in the distance. It seemed to be off to his right over the river valley hills. He turned Butch toward the sound and urged him to increase his speed. He topped the riverbank hill and stopped. From there he had a panoramic view of the battleground. Five men were laying in the grass on the brow of a hill shooting at someone or something hidden in an arroyo off to the west. Once and a while the five received return fire from those in the arroyo. As Bill examined the scene with his binoculars, he saw two bodies stretched out in the grass in front of the arroyo. From their bodies position it was obvious they had been running to reach the cover their friends enjoyed. The other revelation his closer inspection revealed was that those five attackers were the jokers from Verdi. That settled it for him.

He put the horses back below the top of the ridge. The Sharps and the remaining seven cartridges came out of Patches' pack. He then wiggled his way back to the crest. The conditions were ideal he was about 1000 yards from his targets. The wind was blowing directly from them to him thus it would have little if any effect on his bullets path. It also meant the targets probably would not hear the sound of his shots. He set the Sharps up on its rod support and took aim, made a couple of adjustments, checked the aim again. He seemed satisfied but then he wet his finger and test wind direction and strength. Another twist on the rifle's sight, a last check and he was ready.

He lined up the hombre he remembered as blue shirt, the apparent leader of the gang. He squeezed the cocking trigger, shifted to the shooting trigger and squeezed off his shot. Blue shirt slumped where he lay. The four remaining jokers had puzzled looks on their faces as they looked around and at each other. All they knew was the Angel of death was behind them. They hadn't heard a shot and there was no telltale puff of smoke. The wind took care of them.

Bill in the meantime had opened the Sharps breach and inserted a new round. His targets were still looking around wondering what had just happened.

The barfly was his next target. And he died still not knowing what was going on. The last three jokers stampeded toward their horses. None of them made it. Indians on horseback came boiling out of the arroyo to cut them off and cut them down.

The Sharps was back in Patches pack when Bill rode over the hill to join the Indians gathered around the bodies of the two the Sharps had struck down.

One of the Indians was Fox Feather. He said, "So, brother, you are the Angel of Death that visited these two and scared the other three into the open so our braves could send them to the white man's fires of hell." Bill was struck with the change in Fox Feather. It wasn't the way he was dressed that was different. He still wore his trademark fox tail in his jet black hair. It was attached where most braves would have feather dangling. Around his neck was a bears tooth necklace. Bill had been there when he killed that bear. His doeskin vest was decorated with chips of gems and shells. His chest had several totem images tattooed on it. His leggings and moccasins were decorated to match his vest.

"Yes brother. It is the least I could do to repay you, Erect Bear and Bold Otter for the kindness you did for my parents in their hour of need."

"Speaking of Bold Otter. He was struck down on our retreat to the arroyo. He was watching our back as he always did but this time he did not escape. I must go and see what fate the Gods have dealt my brother."

Bill realized then that the difference he noted in Fox Feather was how he deported himself. He was a man who accepted responsibility and carried that responsibility with aplomb and confidence.

"My I come with you? He is my brother too."

"Come."

They found Bold Otter laid out on a Buffalo robe with the medicine man performing a ritual over him. Bill thought Bold Otter did not look good. His five foot three inch body looked even smaller then usual. Bill knew from experience no one packed more fight in a 150 pound frame then Bold Otter. His intelligence and sharp senses made him a valued asset and friend. He could get us laughing and keep us laughing with his humor. *I'm going to count on his indomitable spirit to pull him thought this crisis.'*

Bill stood respectively by as Fox Feather looked at Bold Otter's wounds. His lower leg had been broken by a bullet threw his left calf. The most dangerous wound was in his back. The bullet was still in there and there was no way to know the extent of the internal damage but with one look Bill knew the bullet had to be removed if Bold Otter were to have a chance to survive.

The tribes bone setter set the bones in his leg and put a splint on it. He was moved to the medicine teepee that was in the center of the village that had sprung up. Here the medicine man continued his chants and dances to keep the Evil Spirits away. In front of the tent Fox Feather and some of the tribe elders met to determine what they should do in this situation. Bill was allowed to join the group as Fox Feather's friend and as the tribe's savior this day. After much discussion, the council decided the tribe would camp here for a week or until Bold Otter died.

Bill didn't speak at the council but as soon as it broke up, he asked Fox Feather for a private powwow. He asked if it were possible to talk the medicine man into letting him remove the bullet from Bold Otter's side. He said that from his war experience he knew their friend would not last a week with a bullet in him. He said, "There are risks in any operation that things can go wrong but compared to the almost certain death that waits if the bullet isn't removed the operation is a worthwhile chance at life."

"The medicine man is enormously proud and

guards his part of our tribal life jealousy. I do not think he would willingly allow anyone to tamper with the sick or the dying. We must think of a way to get Bold Otter the help he needs while letting the medicine man save face."

"Is there any way we can get him away from his tent for an hour or more?"

"This afternoon the tribe will have to mourn the brave that was killed in today's fight and prepare for his burial tomorrow. I will order mourning to start immediately as well as preparing for tomorrow's burying. I will also call for a dance of thanks to our Gods for our victory today. That would be an expected event after things came out as they did. That should work to keep the whole village occupied for most of the night. Further I will make the Shaman the leader of our victory celebration since it must have been his medicine that brought you to save us. This will keep him occupied as long as the dancing lasts."

"There is only one other detail to iron out. I will need one person to help me. A strong person who can hold Bold Otter, so he doesn't move under the knife. I was thinking Erect Bear would be perfect for that task. Where is he? I haven't seen him all day."

"He is out hunting with five other braves. A few buffaloes would make the winter pass easier. He should be camped a few miles west of here."

"Actually, that is perfect. I am going to ride out of camp this afternoon to find that hunting party. The reason you can give for my leaving is that I am going to tell Erect Bear about the serious wound our brother received in defense of his village. This eliminates both me and Erect Bear from being expected at the party. When the party starts, we will sneak into the medicine tent, perform the operation and disappear until tomorrow."

"That may work. It is certainly worth a try."

Bill put his part of the plan in action shortly after their powwow and rode west on Butch. As he rode. he thought about his Indian brothers. Fox Feather was the thinker and leader, Bold Otter was the sly one always watching your back and foiling any attempt of foes to surprise you. Erect bear, whom he was seeking, was the Hercules of the bunch. Bill had never been able to beat him in a wrestling match; he was just to strong to be thrown. He stood about six and a half feet tall and weighed upwards of two hundred fifty pounds. His body look like it didn't have an ounce of fat on it. Despite his size, he could be gentle as a lamp in situations that called for being gentle. Bill thought, *'I love all three of these guys.'*

Fox Feather initiated had the tribe crier ride through the village, **"It is now the time to mourn**

our fallen brave. Remember his courage in today's fight in your chants and prayers. Sometime in the afternoon, Fox Feather announced the evening's victory dance to start at sundown with the Shaman as the special celebrant because his magic brought help to save them.

The evening's festivities got underway at their appointed time and an hour later Bill and Erect Bear slipped into in medicine lodge to find Bold Otter burning up with fever. While Bill honed his knife to a keen edge and purified it in the fire Erect Bear slipped out for some cold water and a cloth to make a compress to cool Bold Otters forehead and a stick for him to bite to help endure the pain.

They were ready now so Erect Bear pinned Bold Otters' shoulders and arms so he couldn't move. Bill probed until he found the slug. By pushing the slug with his finger and clearing a passage with his knife Bill was able to extract it. Then knife was heated red hot and the wound was cauterized. Bold Otter would have given them away with a scream under the hot knife if the stick held in his mouth hadn't stifled it.

The friends stuck around as long as they could putting cold compresses on Bold Otter's head and watching the wound to make sure it had been completely sealed by the hot knife. When Bold Otter dropped into a sound sleep and his fever was gone his brothers slipped back out of camp. They would show up tomorrow filled with praise for the medicine man and what his rituals had achieved.

Chapter 40

The Indian's Dilemma

A blizzard howled across the Dakota Plains and rattled the boards on the shack where the four friends sat around a roaring fire, a white man's fire. The fire kept their fronts warm but did little for their backs because the walls acted like a sieve to the wind more than a barrier. Thus, they all looked like the hairy behemoths whose skins they wore to keep out the cold.

Bold Otter had recovered from his wounds except for a slight limp and the ugly scar the red-hot knife had left where the bullet entered. His recovery had been quite remarkable, and the medicine man was enormously proud of his great accomplishment.

Erect Bear's buffalo hunt had been successful, and every lodge had an adequate supply of jerky and pemmican to last the winter.

The tribe had been enriched by the horses, guns

and other valuables found on the bodies of the five dead attackers. These made things okay right now but what about the future? That was the topic of discussion around the fire.

"Are you and your people sure you want to return to the land you lived on before the exile was imposed?" asked Bill.

"That is what we have heard from many sources. We will have to ask the People to confirm that is their choice." replied Fox Feather. Erect Bear and Bold Otter grunted in the affirmative.

"If that is their choice it will take time and hard work to achieve that goal. The National Government will have to lift the exile ruling and restore the reservation land. There are several problems that will need to be solved before we can hope the government would even consider granting those favors."

"What problems do you see standing in our way?"

"I think the dilemma for the tribe will be they must blend in to the 'Whites World' when outside the reservation. This means accepting/adopting some of the Whites ways in order to minimize the recognizable differences that immediately identify your people as Indians. I believe the more they resemble the Whites in dress, appearance and actions the easier it will be for them to live in harmony with the Whites. That is the bottom line. The People and Whites living in harmony with each other. I see no problem in the People living as they always have within the boundaries of the reservation but any time, they travel outside of it they should attempt to not stand out any more than necessary. To achieve that goal, they must look and act as much like Whites as possible. I know that **SUCKS** big time, but it will help our cause immensely. Do you think the People will accept that challenge? Do you think they will be able to do that without losing their own unique identity and pride?"

"That will be a bitter pill to swallow to be sure but if they are truly sincere about moving back to the land of our Fathers, they will see the wisdom in this edict."

"I think there may be a small chance of the land being returned but I see no chance that the payments for the ceded treaty land will be resumed. Therefore, the People must be able to show how you will be able to live among the whites and support yourselves."

"Yes, I have thought on that dilemma myself. Our old ways are gone, never to return. We must learn new ways if we are going to live in peace where they control. Do you have any thoughts on this my brother?"

"I have thought long and hard on this problem but until this last summer I was completely baffled by it. Trying to fit any part of your free former life into the stable life the White's live is like throwing water on a fire to make it burn. I know that trying to build a new life based on hunting and fishing wherever and whenever you please are a pipe dream that will never happen again. I also believe that the sedentary existence of a store clerk, a laborer or any job that requires day after day repetition of the same task does not fit the nature of my Indian friends. I believe work that has challenges, dangers and basically takes place outside would be a better fit for your braves. Throw in a horse to ride while they are doing their work and I think/hope we will have employment that your young men and old alike will be good at and may even get to enjoy."

"What marvelous job do you have in mind?"

"Cattle ranching. Last summer I spent about three months working cattle. Believe me. It was hard work but never boring. I spent most days in the saddle doing a variety of tasks. The tasks were challenging to me and my horse. What do you think of the idea or do you have a different vision?"

"We three have talked about what the People could do to make their way peacefully in the country of the Whites. Farming was the only thing we could come up with. I think that our thoughts were bound by our past when some of the people actual became farmers under the Whites urging."

"I would guess there will still be opportunities to farm for those who want to farm."

"Ranching sounds like an opportunity sent from 'The Great Father' to his children on Earth. Is there anything else you think we should think about?"

"Yes, I recommend you establish a strong plan for how you expect to govern the Reservation and the people who live there."

"That is something we three have talked about also. First, we need a chief, someone the people will follow. Since so many of the elders were hanged at the end of the hostilities the people have been looking to me for their leadership. We will have to put the question to the people to name their leader and the members of the tribal council."

"When can we do that?"

"As soon as the weather will allow a powwow of all the tribe."

"Good the sooner the better."

The talks continued all afternoon and into the night. The only interruptions were to pile more wood on the fire. Finally, the friends curled up in their robes and slept.

About a moon went by before the weather modified, and the people started spending days outside. Nights were still too raw to hold a powwow, but the time was fast approaching when that critical event could take place.

Then, as if by magic, the rains of April vanquished the snow, brought spring flowers and green grass to the prairie and eased the hardships of winter imposed on the people. Spring had sprung, Fox Feather called for a council of all the people.

The Grand Council started by building a large bonfire. Then the women and girls of the tribe danced around it in costumes that honored the greening of Mother Earth. There were costumes that represented flowers and other plants that were now pushing through the prairie soil. When the dance neared its climax the men, in elaborate finery, lots of feathers in their hair, decorated deerskin leggings and beaded vests joined in a frantic courting ritual finale. The drums fell silent on cue and the dancers fell to the ground in exhaustion.

After a short rest, the tribe crier rode through the camp shouting, **"Hear ye, hear ye, the Grand Council is about to begin. Attend and speak your mind or forever hold your opinion of what is decided there."** The people moved quickly to the assembly area around the dwindling fire.

Fox Feather rose and addressed the throng in a voice that reached far beyond the outer fringe of the

488

crowd. "My fellow tribesmen. Since our chiefs and elders gave into the pressures of the warrior cults and the cries of the hungry, our tribe has been without a chief. This situation must be resolved if we are to survive as a People. You have all seen how a chicken acts when you remove its head. It still moves but without purpose or results. Tonight, we must decide on some important issues about our future, the first of these is who is to lead us? Do any of you have any favorites you would like to be Chief?"

"Gray Wolf stands to speak to us. What say you Gray Wolf?"

"I am the oldest member of the People left alive after the hangings and hardships have taken so many of our elders. I believe on this occasion we don't need the wisdom of a grey hair who knows the past. What we need is a young Buck who can cope with the Whites who will certainly control our World in the future. During these last years of exile and survival we have laid the heavy burden of leadership on Fox Feather. He has responded by carrying that weight admirably. I can think of no reason to change the leader we elected by our actions. I support Fox Feather for Chief." Gray Wolf sat down.

"Is there anyone else who has something to say? Fighting Elk speak your piece please."

"I, Fighting Elk, rise in support of Gray Wolf's suggestion. We have all benefited from Fox Feather's leadership over the last four years. I like to hold on to a good horse when I find one." There was suppressed laughter from the crowd. "Fox Feather has proved himself to be a good leader and we should make him our permanent Chief."

"Does anyone have a different suggestion for Chief?" No response. "Does anyone want to speak in opposition to the proposal?" Again, no response. "Seeing no one standing I will call for a show of support. Will everyone who accepts Fox Feather as their Chief please stand up. The crowd arose in mass. " The people have spoken. I, Fox Feather, accept the mantle of leadership as per your wish."

The crowd responded with a mighty cheer, "Yip, yip, yip."

This is how Fox Feather became the youngest Chief ever in the Sioux Nation. Fox Feather said, "I thank you all for placing your trust in me. Your wellbeing became my major concern with your vote of trust."

An outburst of approval swept over the crowd. Two Young maidens carrying the Chief's ceremonial feather headdress approached Fox Feather who put his symbol of authority on for the first time. The howls of approval started again and continued until he raised his hands in a gesture calling for silence.

"Now, on to other important concerns. The next item on our list of decisions is where we should try to make our place in the World. This decision is critical to giving the tribe clear goals to pursue over the next couple of years."

The powwow continued until most of the main questions were answered for the present time. Ten braves were elected to the tribal council and thus became sub-chiefs. Bill was one of these at Fox Feather's request. His job on the council was to guide the Chief in relationships with the Whites. Returning to their former Minnesota lands was the tribe's choice of where they wished to live. The need to imitate Whites was debated for a long time until finally the tribe accepted the necessity for doing everything possible to eliminate friction between the two races. The tribe then formulated and adopted a strict code of conduct for off the reservation decorum. Cattle ranching was accepted as the economic opportunity the tribe would try. The last item on the agenda was acceptance of the rule of law on the reservation and the appointment of Bold Otter as chief of police with Erect Bear as his main deputy.

By the time all the business was finished it was late and the crowd scattered to their beds.

The friends met for a minute or two in celebration of the results of the powwow and then found their beds. Sleep came quickly for all of them.

In the late afternoon, a week later Bill and Fox Feather with four other Indians rode up to -DB ranch house. Bill dismounted and rapped on the door. In a moment or two Molly Blocker filled the doorway and said, "Bill it is so good to see you!" as she gave him a big hug of welcome.

"Hi Molly, is Dan home?"

"No, he's down at the bunkhouse settling some of the new crew in. I'm sure he'll be home soon. Ask your friends to step down and come in. I have some lemonade to cool them off."

Bill waved at his companions who responded by sliding off their horses and hesitantly approaching the house.

Molly said, "Welcome to our home. Come in please." This was accompanied by a welcoming sweep of her arm.

They were setting at the big, round, family table, each with a cold glass of lemonade. The condensation on the glass was evidence of just how cold their drinks were.

The screen door slammed followed by a shout, **"Bill, where you been and what have you been doing? I knew you were here the minute I saw Butch.**

Dan stormed into the room and headed straight for Bill. Bill hardly had time to stand up before he was engulfed in Dan's bear hug. "By golly I'm so glad to see you. Shortly after you left here last fall a group of cowboys ran across sign that five White men had been killed in a scrape with a group of Sioux. It was right on the track you were following so I thought it possible that the worst had happened to you."

"Dan, if you slow down a minute, I'll tell you what really happened at that site. But first I would like to introduce you and Molly to my friends. First this is Fox Feather new Chief of a tribe of Mdewakanton Sioux and an old friend of mine. He and two other braves led my parents to safety at the beginning of the Sioux uprising. Next, we have two young braves that we will call Sam and Charlie for simplicity's sake.

They have volunteered to live with a white rancher for a summer to learn how to handle cattle. Guess which white rancher I hoped I could place them with. At the end of the summer they are expected to return to the tribe to teach others the cow punching skills they have learned. Since these two know nothing about cow handling, we don't expect them to be paid in money, their pay will be the experience they gain."

Dan raised his hand in a traditional stop gesture and said, "If they ride for the -DB they will be paid whatever the other riders are paid and that is the last thing I want to hear about that."

"Okay, if you insist. Last we have two escorts, Gray Wolf and Fighting Elk."

Dan flashed the salute Indians use then meeting people and said, "Welcome to our home." He pulled the chair out from the table next to where Molly was sitting and took a seat.

Molly excused herself and retired to her kitchen. Soon she was back with a pitcher of lemonade and a glass for Dan. She filled Dan's glass and then refreshed everyone else's drink.

Bill told Dan about the fate of the five jokers. Then he brought up the main reason for their visit. Bill said, "We would like you and your boys to teach these two the cowboy's jobs. "Will the crew have trouble working with Indians?"

"Well they better keep it to themselves if they want to work here. In this house and on this ranch, we are all equals in the eyes of the God we worship."

"Ok then. I have one other item on my list. I would like to buy ten heifers that are going to drop calves this spring.

"I'm sure we can come up with those for you."

The business completed Bill suggested they show Sam and Charlie where they will bunk and introduce them to the crew. Dan led the visitors into the bunkhouse and introduce everybody to everybody. Bill knew a couple of the crew from his time on the ranch. He greeted them with a handshake and personal hello.

Introductions over, the new hands and visitors selected bunks for their stay. Sam took the lower and Charlie the upper in the area near where the rest of the crew was located. The visitor's bunks were a short distance away. Out of deference to their age Bill and Fox Feather took the uppers so that Gray Wolf and Fighting Elk could have the lowers.

Finished finding the sleeping arrangements for their stay, the visitors returned to the ranch house for dinner with the family. The conversation around the table continued until bedtime. Bill led his friends back to the bunkhouse and they were all soon fast asleep.

The next few days were busy. Sam and Charlie started their cowboy education. The heifers were rounded up and a price set. Bill and Fox Feather rode over to Ruthton to have money telegraphed from Bill's account in Redwood Falls. As they sat on a bench waiting for the money, many people paraded by to see the strangers. They and their business became the talk of the town. The telegram transferring the money to the Ruthton Bank arrived around one o'clock. Fifteen minutes later. The attractions had left the bench and Ruthton behind.

About forty-five minutes later, Bill said to Fox Feather, "We have two guys trailing us."

Fox Feather replied, "There were three but one rode around us. I assume we will see him ahead of us along the trail."

"Well, I'd rather takeout the two behind us rather than wait until the three of them spring their trap."

"That makes sense my brother. Do you have a plan?"

"Well sort of. I've been thinking that we need to turn the tables on the two behind us. When we get to an open spot where they will be sure to see us, I'll act like I've got to take a shit. I'll get off my horse and hand the reins to you. Then I'll act like I'm getting ready to drop my pants. I'll unbuckling my belts and unzipping my barn door as I head for the woods. When I get into the woods, I'll make my way as quickly as I can back to those guys and ask them why they are following us. You sit patiently on your horse until I brace them and then hurry to us to back me up."

Fox Feather nodded his head in agreement. He remembered how Bill had won every foot race when they were young. On a couple of occasions, he had out run every man in the village on fox and hound day. Not only was he fast but he could hurdle significant obstacles that might block his path.

Soon they came to a perfect spot to execute their ambush. Bill dismounted and as he started for the trees made all the appropriate moves to drop his pants. A little over three minutes later he reappeared behind the followers with his guns covering them. Fox feather closed the trap as planned.

"**Hands up!** You, tall and skinny, keep your right arm in the air and use two fingers of your left hand to lift the pistol out of its holster and drop it on the ground. Ok short and hefty do the same thing as Long John just did. Now let's ride a way."

"This will do. To complete phase two of defanging you, use both hands and remove your boots. We will start with you Long John, the right one first. Good, now drop it. Now the left one. Shorty, it's your turn. Ok boys explain why you are following us."

The two looked at each other and shrugged. The taller of them said, "We weren't following you, we just happened to be going your way. You have no call to brace us"

"And you just happen stop when we stopped. Where is your friend on the sorrel horse waiting to dry gulch us?"

"What friend on what sorrel?"

"The man who left you a few miles back and headed off to the right, away from you. Now let's try again. Where did your friend on the sorrel go?"

The answer he got was, "We don't know."

"Ok, Long John get off your horse. Take off your hat and shirt. Give them to me. Bill took off his shirt and hat and said, "Here, put these on." as he handed them to their captive. Long John did as he was told. At the same time Bill put on Long John's stuff. Bill took Henry from the scabbard and said, "Now get on my horse and give me the reins to yours." Once again, the captive did what he was told.

Fox Feather said, "I remember the game we are playing. I will keep a sharp lookout and keep this guy between me and the best cover."

Bill tied both Shorty and Long John's hands to their saddle horns and one of their feet to their stirrup with the pigging strings he always carried now. Everything was ready as they could make it, so they rode on. Long john was in the lead with Fox Feather slightly behind him. Staying close but out of sight, shadowing these two were Bill and Shorty.

About a half-hour later, Fox Feather gave out a low-pitched whistle that was what they had used to signal danger when they were kids. The whistle had barely died out when Bill heard the bark of a rifle and the thunk of a bullet. As Bill and shorty gained a line of sight to the scene, they saw Fox Feather's pony with its rider hanging on its side using it as a shield racing toward some cover on the opposite side of the trail from where the shooter seemed to be. Butch with Long John still tied in the saddle, was racing back toward them. Long john was slumped in the saddle. The ruse had worked. Bill whistled and Butch came toward him.

Bill cut long john's ties, lifted him out of the saddle and laid him on the ground. He was dead. Butch and the saddle were covered with blood, but Butch hadn't been scratched. Bill cut Shorty down and tied him face down on the ground. He then selected a position from which he could fire at the shooter while still having some cover himself. His first shot got the bushwhackers attention and he started getting return fire. This standoff dragged on for a half-hour or so before Fox Feather's victory howl issued from the hill where the shooter was hiding. Fox Feather emerged from the woods waving a scalp.

Soon Bill was on his way back to Ruthton to report the attack to the authorities. He was leading Butch with long john draped across the saddle, the bushwhacker's horse with his burden and shorty's with their prisoner on it. Fox Feather continued to the –DB with the money for the cattle.

Bill arrived back at the ranch late that night and went right to bed. Before he found sleep his mind stopped to review the day's events. It played a scene that was beginning to haunt him when he was involved in a death. Essentially the thoughts could be summarized in one question, "*Am I ever going to be through with the need to kill or be killed? I am getting weary of death and destruction.* When he fell asleep, Patsy was waiting for him. Her presence helped him through the trauma of having to be involved in killing again. Sleep acted as a healing balm for his troubled mind and he woke up rested and restored.

There were lots of questions asked and answered during breakfast. It was as if no one wanted to say goodbye. The parting was delayed until it couldn't be ignored anymore. It had turned into a long, long Minnesota farewell before they started down the trail home.

Chapter 41

Fort Abraham Lincoln

I t was a welcome sight when the travelers reached the Missouri River bluff where they could see their tribe's teepees spread out before them on the bank of the mighty river. Several changes were visible that would help with the care and safety of their new herd of cattle. A spacious rope corral enclosed a large plot of prairie grass. This would provide adequate forage for the herd for at least a month. The gate was open like welcoming arms to make it an easy task to drive the herd in. Several water troughs had been built, spotted around the rope perimeter and filled with water. All was well in the cattle's new world.

Someone must have spotted the herd coming down the hill because a crowd had gathered around the corral by the time the herd entered. There was excited talking and pointing as the tribe greeted their future.

Within a month seven of the cows had dropped calves and the herd had grown to 17 head. Bill rode into Sioux City, Iowa and one of the things he bought was a branding iron for the tribe. The brand selected was the **=MMS** (double bar Mdewakanton Minnesota Sioux).

As soon as Bill arrived back in camp, a contest between the young men of the tribe and the calves was arranged. A fire was built to heat the branding iron. In order to win a feather in this contest one had to catch, wrestle the calf to the ground and bind its feet together with a pigging string.

The whole camp turned out to watch the fun. Many laughs and squeals of glee rippled through the crowd as they watched the calves lead the boys on a merry chase around the pasture. The first calf went down and was dragged over to the fire. The branding of the tribes first calf was greeted with a great roar from the watchers. The next six captures came shortly after the first one.

The summer was a continuous heat wave. The young men had their hands full keeping the water troughs full. The rope corral had been moved three times to provide fresh graze for the herd. The good news was that the cattle were doing well. The calves were growing and putting on weight.

One day in the middle of July an army patrol

stopped in. The troopers were dusty, sweaty and thirsty. The people greeted them warmly and provide water to quench their thirst and wash their faces.

The Lieutenant leading the patrol asked, "What's going on here?"

Bill spoke for Fox Feather, Bold Otter and Erect Bear. "This is a band of Mdewakanton Sioux who were exiled from their Minnesota home lands after the Sioux uprising in 1862. "The people here were exonerated by the war tribunal and were deemed to be non-combatants in that war. Regardless of their bystander status they were stripped of their reservation land, the Government money owed the tribe for land they had ceded to White settlers was cancelled and they were exiled here just the same. We are trying to learn to live where Whites are in control. If you look closely at them, you will see they have changed their hair styles and clothes to blend in with the Whites instead of standing out from them. We are making every effort to be allowed to return to our homes in Minnesota. The people are determined to earn their way back to the land of their fathers. Right now, we are working on skills that will help us live in harmony with whites who will control the land."

"And who are you and these gentlemen with you?

Bill gestured toward each as he said, "This is Fox Feather, Chief of this tribe, Bold Otter, chief of police for the tribe and Erect Bear, assistant police chief. I am Bill Cheever, formerly a Sergeant-Major in the Union Army. And you are?"

"Lieutenant Sheely, 7th Cavalry. It is good to meet you Bill, Chief of the tribe and police force."

"What are you and your patrol doing here in the east? I thought the main action was to the west."

"This patrol is searching for a band of Kiowa's who were raiding along the eastern border of Indian territory. They are taking everything they can and killing/burning everything, they can't.

Bill asked, "Where are you and your men stationed?"

The Lieutenant replied. "Were out of a new fort the army built near Bismarck. It is named after Abraham Lincoln. It is now the headquarters for western field operations of the U. S. Army. The commanding General is Winfield Scott Hancock. However, in September General Phil Sheridan, Commander of the Armies in the west, is coming to conduct the court martial proceedings in the trial of General George Armstrong Custer."

"What has Custer done now?"

"I'm not sure what all he's charged with, but I'd bet a dollar against a hole in a donut that it is something he did without proper administration authority. He has always thought his shit doesn't stink but his farts have always given him away. "Well good luck on your efforts to get your land back. I see my men have finished their water, so we best get going. Thank you and your friends for their hospitality. I shall note it in my report."

"Thank you, that would be most appreciated."

The Lieutenant said, "Sergeant, let's get this parade under way.

"Yes Sir. **Patrol prepare to mount, mount. Column of twos, forward ho!**" The soldiers moved out smartly heading south.

Bill said to his friends, "The people did a good job, acting their part as pseudo whites. We have got to give them some praise for it. Is there anything we can do as a reward for their performance?"

Bold Otter said, "We haven't had a dance or village party since the Grand Council this spring. I think a real Indian dance would make them forget any shame they might feel about hiding their Indian self in order to look and act like whites."

That afternoon, Fox Feather had the Tribe Crier announce the summer dance to be held the following evening. He also called a council meeting to see what it thought should be done about the Kiowa threat.

The council decided that a screen of young braves would be deployed around the cattle corral each night backed with a mounted patrol of warriors. The young braves would take their positions at twilight and the warriors sneak out of camp at full dark to take a position outside the screen.

The dance was held and did a lot to bolster the tribe's pride in their Indian heritage.

Life returned to its old routine about a week later when one of the scouts found out the Army had rounded up the Kiowa's and shipped them off to a detention camp.

The tribe had resolved another issue during this time. They found a valley where the cattle could winter protected from the wind. It had abundant grass and a small stream running through it. They would not have to worry about filling water troughs this winter. There was a forest to help shelter the Tepees and provide ample wood for the winter fires. The village moved there, and the rope corrals were set up.

One day near the end of September Sam and Charlie showed up leading a bull. They knew the tribe would need a bull if there was to be calves in the spring. They had used the money they had earned during the summer to purchase this one. They became instant heroes to all the people.

Erect Bear and the hunters had been gone three weeks when they returned with enough Buffalo to provide every lodge food for the starving time.

With everything ready for the harsh conditions

that were approaching Fox Feather and Bill started thinking about the future. When news came that General Sheridan had arrived at Fort Lincoln, they decided to try to see if they could make any progress on the tribe's desire to move back to Minnesota. Bill, Fox Feather, Gray Wolf and Fighting Elk got ready and left camp bound for Fort Lincoln. Their primary objective was to ascertain what the army's position might be regarding such a move. The goal was to see if they could get an audience with General Sheridan to make a plea to be allowed to return to their Minnesota homes.

The little cavalcade headed north by northwest toward Bismarck. They moved quickly but cautiously across the open prairie. Early on the third day they crossed a trail that Gray Wolf estimated to have been made by a party of about 20 riders on unshod ponies. Gray Wolf and Fighting Elk were sent to find out who made the trail. Fox Feather and Bill continued on their way toward the Fort. A couple of hours after they left, the two scouts were back. They had seen the trail makers and ID them as Blackfeet.

The Blackfeet inhabited the area north of the Missouri River around the border with Canada. About the only time they ventured this far south was to raid the tribes that lived here. They were hated enemies of the Sioux Nation.

Since Bill and his friends were moving in the opposite direction, they ignored the raiders and continued moving toward Bismarck. They arrived there two days later. They stopped at the Mandan Village just north of the city to ask for shelter during their stay. They were treated as honored guests. Not only were they provided lodging for their stay but also a welcoming banquet.

The next day Bill rode over to the Fort on sort of a scouting expedition. It was on the west side of the Missouri almost directly across from the settlement of Bismarck. The Fort had no walls for its defense and did not resemble most people's idea of a Fort. It consisted of four prominent buildings arranged around a quadrangle/parade ground. There were several squads of soldiers on the quadrangle going through drills. Their cadence calls were mixed together to make a confusing babble of noise. This scene brought back memories of his early days as a raw recruit. These were not fond memories, but they were reminders of his time in the army.

Three of the buildings were big boxy things three stories high. Bill recognized them as barracks for the troops. They paralleled the south, the east and the north edge of the quadrangle. On the west edge was a long, low building with a porch across its front. Bill took this to be the Fort's business center. The Fort's officer corps would run all things Army out of this building.

Bill thought, *maybe I could arrange an audience with the General. I guess it wouldn't hurt to try.* He found the General's office and entered. The Sergeant at the desk looked familiar but Bill could not remember why. He presented himself at the desk and stood quiet until the occupant looked up.

"What can I do for you?"

"I represent a delegation of Mdewakanton Sioux who would like to present a grievance and ask for restitution of the land of their fathers that was confiscated by the government for actions they did not participate in. Is it possible to obtain an audience with General Sheridan?"

"Who are you?

"My name is Wilber James Cheever, formerly a Sergeant Major in the Union Army. Have you worked for the General for a long time?"

"About 15 years, why do you ask?"

"You look familiar, but I couldn't place where I might have met you. I decided that the only possibility was the General's headquarters in Jackson, Mississippi in 1865 just as the war ended."

"I remember now. You had foiled a train robbery and the General was so impressed with your feat that he gave you a special breakfast to celebrate the event."

"You're right, the only omelet I have ever had. That was mighty fine vittles."

"Your name came up a few weeks ago in a report of a Lieutenant Sheely of the 7th Cavalry. He was most impressed with the hospitality your tribe showed him and his men on that hot summer day."

"We were happy we could help."

"Come back tomorrow and I will have your answer for you."

"Is there a best time to show up?"

"I would say about 14:00 hours might work best."

"Do you think it would be okay to bring a friend with me?"

"I can't see how that would do any harm."

"Thank you! I'll see you tomorrow at 14:00." With that Bill turned and left the office. On his way back to the Mandan Camp he tried to think of how and what they should say to the General when they got to see him if they got to see him.

At 13:45 the next afternoon Bill and Fox Feather were setting in General Sheridan's office waiting room. The Sergeant had informed them that the General would see them as soon as he completed some pressing business.

Bill and Fox Feather rehearsed their story again.

The General called them into his office at 14:22 and greeted them warmly.

Bill introduced Fox Feather as the Mdewakanton Chief.

The General asked him how civilian life was treating him.

Bill's heart sank to the floor as he thought of Patsy's untimely death but then he remembered what they were there for and replied fine right now.

The General then asked them what they needed to see him about.

Bill and Fox Feather repeated the story they had rehearsed.

Sheridan listened intently. When they finished, he said, "I wish I had the authority to right the wrong I believe was perpetrated in this case, but I don't. The best I can do is give you a letter of introduction to General Sherman. The problem is it would have to be delivered to him in Washington D. C. to be effective."

Bill replied, "We will deliver it there if you write it."

By 15:00 hrs. they had their letter and were back at the Mandan Village with happy news of their progress. They thanked their hosts for their hospitality, packed up their gear and with their companions were soon on their way home.

On the way to the fort they had taken their time but now they hardly ate or slept. Three days after leaving the fort they were climbing the ridge protecting the village from the north by northwest and west wind when they ran across sign that a sizable group of Indians had passed this way this morning. The trail led right toward their village. Gray Wolf slid off his pony and studied the tracks. He said, "This trail made by about 20 riders."

They cautiously followed the trail with Gray Wolf riding point and Fighting Elk riding drag. A short distance later Gray Wolf signaled a stop. He dismounted again, walked to the side of the trail and bent down to pick something off the ground. After examining it, he signaled the others to come to him. When they arrived, he said one word, "Blackfeet."

Fox Feather added, "They must be getting ready to attack our village."

Bill said, "I don't hear any shooting, so I assume the fracas hasn't started yet. We must take some bold action to warn the Tribe of the danger surrounding them. I could just ride into the village as if just returning and having no clue to the impending danger."

Fox Feather said, "That is a job for the Chief. I can demand immediate obedience without a long explanation. Besides Bill your rifle will serve us better out here where you will be free to move around to support the defense if any point gets in trouble." The two others nodded in agreement.

Gray Wolf and Fighting Elk said, "We will scout the perimeter to locate our enemies so we will know what we are up against." They tethered their horses and disappeared around the south side of the clearing. Bill and Fox Feather followed leading their mounts. As they neared the south edge of the clearing, Gray Wolf reappeared wiping his bloody knife on his loincloth. Soon Fighting Elk rejoined them. "This side is clear." he said. His knife was bloody also. The three rifle men took positions to cover Fox Feathers ride into the village.

All went as they hoped it would. When Fox Feather was safely in the village the three rifles went looking for targets. On the northwest edge of the clearing they found plenty of them. They were squatting down in a circle with the leader describing his plan of attack. The three Sioux riflemen spread out and Bill took the first shot. The Blackfoot leader went down and did not move. The three marksmen kept shooting and shooting. The Winchesters and the Henry's barrels were too hot to touch by the time their magazines were empty. The ring of Blackfeet was decimated. Their death cries filled the forest. A few were trying their best to disappear into the forest. About this time a backup force of braves from the Village arrived and started the mop up operation.

As the three marksmen made their way back to

their horses, a Blackfoot warrior surprised them with an attack out of the bushes.

Bill's swift draw of his Colt revolver ended that threat with another dead Indian.

The three rode into the Village and were greeted with a hero's welcome and feast.

Chapter 42

Return to Redwood Falls

A rmed with Sheridan's letter, Bill and Fox Feather decided it was time for them to visit General Sherman in Washington. They rode out of the village with the cheers of the tribe ringing in their ears.

Two days later, they were setting on the road looking at Bill's former home. Bill's view brought on a feeling of loss for what might have been. Bill thought, '*Patsy and I were sitting just about here when we saw the house for the first time. That was June of 1865. We certainly came to love the place. The last I was in it was that fateful day in March, 66 when my world came crashing down around me*'

Bill's big surprise was the field after field that had been cultivated. It looked like most of the property was under production. The farmers appeared to be doing a marvelous job.

They broke off their inspection and rode up to the hitchrack in the front of the house. Bill tied Butch to the hitch rack and went to knock on the front door. Emma greeted him with surprise and pleasure emphasized with a big hug and kiss. Bill declined an invitation to come in for coffee and pie. He wasn't ready for that yet. The pang in his heart from just seeing the place was enough to warn him away.

He beckoned Fox Feather to join them on the porch and introduce the two of them. It seems they had just missed Hal. He was on his way to town for supplies. Billy, of course, was in school. Bill was pleased how well things were going for his friends. They said "Farewell" to Emma and rode away toward Redwood Falls.

They didn't stop in Redwood Falls but proceeded directly to the warehouse. Bill knocked on the door and it was answered by Cora (nee McHugh) Mensch. "God are you a sight for sore eyes!" With that she delivered a hug and a kiss on the cheek.

"Good to see you Cora, how are you and Grady getting on?"

"He is a wonderful husband and father. Jamie just adores him and so do I. Come on in. You know that was a great thing for Grady when you showed confidence in him and made him a deputy."

"His war record was a better description of the

man then his condition at the time I met him." Bill waved at Fox Feather to follow as they entered the door.

Cora looked Fox Feather over and said, "Who is this gentleman Bill?"

Bill introduced them to each other.

Cora said, "Please excuse me if I act a little strange around you Chief Fox Feather, we haven't seen an Indian around here since the uprising."

Fox Feather's reply was, "I will excuse you if you will excuse me, mam, if I forget my Whiteman's manners from time to time. I haven't lived close to the whites since the uprising either."

Bill said, "If there are any people in the world who should understand each other's predicament it's you two. Both of you were casualties of the same war."

Peace, or at least a truce was established between the two of them. Cora served them coffee and pie as they sat at the table while Bill satisfied his curiosity about the status of the warehouse residence. Cora's replies were most gratifying to Bill.

As soon as they finish their treats, Bill got up to leave. With his hand on the door handle he said to Cora, "I'm hoping to get together with some old friends for dinner this evening and I hoped Grady could join us. It will be at Milly's at 6:00 o'clock. It would be nice if Jamie could come along with Grady, that is if it's ok with you. Please let Grady know about it. I would really like to see him. Thank you for everything."

As Bill and Fox Feather rode into town Bill said, "I hate putting you through this ordeal Fox Feather. It is hard not knowing how your friends are doing. I suffered many times worrying about where my Sioux brothers were and how you were surviving. Your well-being was unknown to me then." They were now riding down Main Street when Bill spotted Hal coming out of Emmon's with bulging bags in his arms. Bill was elated both with getting to seeing Hal and the opportunity to invite him to this evening's dinner. "Please bring Billy along too if it's ok with Emma."

When they left Hal, they went to Schroder's Livery. They planned to stable their horses there for the duration of their trip to Washington D.C. As they tied up, a voice called out a hearty greeting, **"Hello there!"** It was Michael Schulze coming out of the livery's office. "It is so good to see you again."

"Hello yourself, aren't you playing lawman anymore?"

"No, lots has changed for me this last year. My Uncle Carl had a heart attack and is an invalid who needs the constant care of his wife. He is no longer able to run this livery stable. He asked me to take over. It has given me a solid future, so I married the girl I was sparking the night I saved your ass. I don't have to hide anymore to steal a kiss, in fact we are expecting a baby this spring.

"Wonderful!" Bill said without revealing the momentary flash of jealousy that took over his mind. It was immediately replaced with joy for Michael and his bride. "Can you put up our horses while we make a trip to Washington D.C. I'm not sure how long that will take, will that be a problem?"

"Not at all." replied Michael. He turned and whistled. It was immediately answered by a scrawny young man in oversized, worn bib-overalls, oversized tattered plaid shirt and oversized shoes that looked like they were taped together. "This is my new hostler, Homer. He is one of your forgotten casualties of war from up St. Cloud way. He heard about the warehouse and hoof it down here. Doesn't know much about horses but he's learning. Please don't judge his care by his clothes, we couldn't find any store clothes or shoes to fit him, so my wife is sewing him the needed clothes and another of the flock you started is making him shoes. Homer take these horses and store the gear, they will be with us a while, give them a chance to drink, rub them down and give them a portion of oats. When their ready, bed them down for the night."

"Thanks, Michael. I'm throwing a little party

tonight for my Redwood Falls friends and I'm hoping you will be there." Bill recited to details of his plans for the evening. Michael said he would be there with "Bells on".

With the horses taken care of the travelers moved on to Milly's for a late lunch. When Milly showed up and their hellos had been said, Bill rented the whole restaurant for the evening starting at 5:30. He insisted on paying Milly twice her usual weekday evening take plus the cost of the food and drink.

With the arrangements made and their bellies full they proceeded on their merry way. Bill received some smiles, hellos and glad to see you again from some of the towns people with whom he was acquainted. Surprisingly to him, Fox Feather received some glaring looks and grunts of disgust from a relatively small number of people they met on the street. Until this moment Bill had not thought of the possibility of push back from Minnesotan's if he were successful and the Mdewakanton Sioux returned to their previous reservations.

Their next stop was at Don Williams office. He was in and accepted Bills invitation for the evenings get together. He also treated Fox Feather with respect and dignity. They shook hands and promised to talk more during the evenings get together.

They left Don's office and crossed the street to

the county sheriff's office. Charlie was at his desk working on some papers. He looked up as they entered and said, "Bill, you 'old son-of-a-gun'. How are you?" The usual small talk was exchanged, introductions made and the invitation to the evening festivities delivered. Bill asked if Charlie knew where Zeke or Terry might be.

Charlie said, "I guess you haven't heard; Terry is now Sherriff over at Olivia."

Bill replied, "That's great, that's what he told me he wanted the day he came to work for me."

"I expect Zeke back sometime this afternoon. I'll give him your invitation for this evening's meet and eat as soon as he shows up."

"Thanks Charlie. See you this evening."

"We still need a place to sleep tonight." Bill said to Fox Feather as they turned into the riverboat freight office to pick up their tickets for tomorrow's voyage to St. Paul.

They noticed a small hotel across the street from the freight office as they came back on the street with their tickets. "Let's see if they have a room. this would be very handy tomorrow morning." With that the friends walked across the street and entered the hotel.

"We need a room for tonight." Bill said.

The clerk looked at the two of them and said,

"I've got a room I can rent you but 'Indian Joe' will have to sleep in the stable."

Suddenly the clerk was staring down the barrel of Bill's pistol," I fought in a war so that all Americans are to be treated equal and with respect. **Now,** give me the key to the best room left in the house."

The clerk reached up on the board where the keys were displayed and snatched one labeled Captain's Suite and handed it to Bill.

"One last thing before we go to our room. It has been my experience that some people who have been bullied as I just bullied you try to get back at their bullier with some skullduggery. I just want you to know that you better be sure that nothing disturbs us tonight or happens to our things because I'm coming straight for you if anything does. Whether you did it or not won't matter."

Bill and Fox Feather were at Milly's at 5:30. Bill as host and Fox Feather as special guest formed a reception line. They greeted and shook everyone's hand as they arrived. The rumble of talking grew and grew as the crowd grew. Both Billy and Jamie came but Homer didn't. Michael explained that Homer was too aware of his raggedy clothes to have been comfortable meeting new people. One surprise quest was Mr. Qual. He had begged Grady to be allowed to come along. Bill was delighted to see him and told him so. Mr. Qual was as proud as a peacock when he told Bill he had passed out of third grade and was now in the fourth.

They said grace, devoured lots of food and shared many a toast before the evening ended. The glow of comradeship would warm Bill's heart for months to come.

The next morning, when the two travelers got to the dock Bill was taken aback. The same side wheeler packet that had started Patsy's last trip home was tied up there waiting for them. Bill got tears in his eyes and Fox Feather had to lead him to and up the gangplank. The past was ruthfuly after his sanity.

The trip to Carver took the better part of a day and a half. At Carver they only had time to transfer from the packet to the bigger riverboat to St. Paul. Bill only had time to wave to Dick as the boat pulled away from the dock.

In St. Paul, dad met them at the dock and before they went out to the house, he took them to a near-by men's clothing store. Both Bill and Fox Feather found clothes appropriate for their time in the east and Washington. Fox Feather could have passed for a swarthy white man except for his long, black hair with the Fox tail in it. Each now carried a suitcase with a spare set of clothes in it. Bill still wore his

Stetson and Fox Feather took a shine to a Bowler hat. They were the fashion rage this year.

That evening mom served Shepherd's pie as usual. It didn't have the appeal it had all those years before. Bill kept seeing Patsy sitting across the table from him.

Chapter 43

Washington, D. C.

T he next morning, dad got them to the train on time. The train went through the Wisconsin countryside of farms and small villages until it reached Chicago. They had a twelve-hour layover there. Fox Feather was treated as a curiosity, but they did not encounter any ethnic trouble at the hotel or restaurant. They enjoyed their evening of sightseeing downtown and along the shore of Lake Michigan. Both Bill and Fox Feather were impressed with the horse drawn trolleys. Fox Feather was in awe of the crush of people living that close to each other, packed into tall buildings called tenements.

Fox feather said, "I would not like to live here Bill."

"Nor would I, brother."

The next morning, they boarded the train for New York City. This time it was the farms villages and cities of Indiana and then Ohio that filled them with awe. They stopped in Cleveland for their over-night stop. Cleveland was very much like Chicago with its crush of people and the presence of Lake Erie. Fox Feather was once again treated as a curios-ity, but they suffered no other ethnic discomfort.

In the morning they were off to New York City. This stretch of their journey was dominated by views of the New York and Pennsylvania mountains, the Hudson River the tracks followed and cities like Buffalo, Rochester and the overwhelming spectacle of New York City itself. They didn't have any time to look around the city because the train for Philadelphia was scheduled to leave Grand Central Station a half-hour after they arrived. They had to run with their suitcases banging on their legs, but they were settled in their seats when the Philly train pulled out.

As the train moved down the east coast through New Jersey it seemed that the country became more and more crowded with towns and farms. They reached Philadelphia by mid-afternoon and took a taxi from the railroad station to their hotel. When Bill started to sign the register the clerk said, "Is the Indian staying with you?"

"Is that a problem?"

"Yes, the only non-whites welcomed here are for-eign dignitaries."

"Then we do not have a problem. This gentleman is the Chief of the Mdewakanton Sioux on his way to see General Sherman in Washington with a message from General Sheridan."

All resistance to lodging an Indian collapsed and the clerk apologized for the establishment's policy regarding non-whites. After making themselves comfortable in their room, they spent the afternoon and evening as tourists in this famous City.

Early the next morning they were on the train again, on their way to D.C. All day long the size and strength of the United States was on display again. Fox Feather been quiet and thoughtful on several stretches as the train traveled across the country and down the east coast. Now, as they approached the Washington station he said," Bill, the Chiefs and warrior clans never had a chance, did they? They were like a small rag trying to wipe up a mighty ocean."

"No, they did not. It is too bad the Tribes still on the warpath haven't seen what you have seen nor learned the lesson you have learned on this trip." Bill said in a solemn voice. Continuing in the same voice he said, "They will fight with great courage and skill as your elders and warriors did but in the end the result will be the same. It seems that sometimes the only thing that can bring peace between two different ideas is war."

"Such a waste. The people paid such a high price for an impossible dream." said Fox Feather.

Both men fell silent, wrapped in deep thoughts of their own. The conductor broke into their thoughts as walk through the car shouting, **"Washington D. C.' End of the line."**

They caught a cab to take them and their suitcases to the only hotel in D.C. whose name they knew, Willards. They had no trouble checking into the Hotel. It was the Washington Hotel where most of the foreign dignitaries stayed. So, it wasn't unusual to see a bejeweled Prince from India or a man from China dressed in his traditional clothes. The sight of a man with reddish skin tone, dressed in a tailored suit and wearing a Bowler hat didn't even warrant a second look. Even his raven hair with its foxtail feather didn't get a great deal of attention. They had a snack in the hotel coffee shop and went to bed early.

In the morning after breakfast, they asked for the location of the War Department Offices and since it wasn't far, they decided to walk there. They found the building that housed it where their directions had told them it would be. As they walked in, they were confronted with a big board filled with names and numbers on it. It revealed that General Sherman's office was on the third floor, number 301 to be exact.

The friends walk up the magnificent central stairs to the mezzanine where they were confronted with a reception desk. A Lieutenant behind the desk said. "State your business please." Bill replied, "We are here to request an audience with General Sherman for the purpose of delivering a letter from General Sheridan to him. The Lieutenant at the reception desk ask for the letter and told them to wait on a nearby bench while he found out if the General would receive them.

Bill and Fox Feather sat on the bench wondering, hoping and worrying about General Sherman's willingness to see them. Shortly the Lieutenant reappeared and said," The General will see you now. Follow me." Turning, their guide stated up some back steps to the third floor. Bill and Fox Feather followed a long.

The Lieutenant stopped at an office door with a plaque alongside it which read 'Lieutenant-General William T. Sherman, Commander of the Army.

Their guide rapped on the door and a voice said "Enter." As the door opened, the smell of cigar smoke came out to greet them. The General stood up and offered his hand to each as they entered.

He was a tall man, Bill guested him to be just under 6' and maybe close 200 lbs. His hair was dark brown, but his beard was scruffy in texture and dark rusty in color. His uniform was immaculate as befit his rank and position.

After the greetings and introductions were done the General said, "I have read the letter from General Sheridan and concur with his sentiments completely. We need to find room and stability for the Indian Nations within the structure of our White society. Your proposal is within the current thinking of the Government. However, all I can do is order the Army to give you any help that's in their power when you receive permission to move back to Minnesota. Furthermore, I will give you a letter of introduction to General Grant. He is on the President's cabinet and may have connections that can cut through the red tape and provide you with the permission you seek. Come back tomorrow at 10 bells and the documentation will be waiting for you at the front desk. Bill, after you and your friend made application for an audience, I had my Adjutant look up your service record. It is impressive.

"Thank you, sir."

"That will be all."

The friends left and returned to their hotel room. After dinner they went for a walk around the Capitol grounds looking at the monuments, statues and magnificent buildings.

The next morning, they were back to get the

documentation they had been promised. They inquired at the front desk and received an envelope with their names on it. In the envelope was a note that read, "Bill and Fox Feather. I sent my recommendation and all the documentation to General Grant yesterday afternoon. He will see you in his office at 15:00 today. Your friend W. T. Sherman.

Toting their envelope with its note the two found their way to Grant's office in the Capitol Building. The clock said it was about 11:00 hrs. With that much time to wait they decided to take in more sights and have lunch at Willards.

The maître d' greeted them as old friends and seated them immediately. "Enjoy your meal gentlemen."

"Thanks Hans, what's on the menu today?"

"I recommend the Ruben Sandwich. The corned beef and sauerkraut are especially good today."

"Thank you, Hans. That sounds like a winner."

After lunch they tried sightseeing, but they couldn't get the pending meeting with General Grant out of their minds. After a short time, they gave up and returned to the General's offices. When they reported to the General's reception desk, they were told they would be called at the appointed time. They found some convenient, plush, comfortable chairs to sit in while they waited. The place was bustling with activity as soldiers of every imaginable rank scurried here and there and everywhere. Time dragged by as they waited with their rollercoaster emotions. The highs were high, but the lows were equally low.

Just as Bill looked at his watch for what seemed the umpteenth time and found it was a minute or two before three o'clock a Lieutenant walked up to them and said, "General Grant will see you now. Follow me please." So, they did. They were led past the reception desk and down a long hallway. The name plaques on the doors announced the Captain or Major or whatever that was assigned to it. At the end of the hall the plaque read Secretary of War General Ulysses Simpson Grant.

The Lieutenant rapped on the door and a gruff voice said, "Come in." Once again, the smell of cigar smoke was a physical attack on one's senses. Grant sat behind a gigantic desk with a dead stub of a cigar clamped in his teeth. The giant desk did nothing to enhance his stature if anything it diminished it. His hair had streaks of gray in it and his beard was gray with streaks of black in it. There were ashes on the front of his uniform coat.

"General Grant this is former Sergeant-Major Wilbur James Cheever of the 6th Minnesota and Fox Feather, current Chief of the Mdewakanton Sioux. They were sent to you by General Sherman to consider their plea for being allowed to reoccupy the Sioux Minnesota reservations."

"Welcome, please be seated. I have read all the documentation sent to me by Generals Sherman and Sheridan. I concur with their assessment of the facts. Thus, I spoke to the Secretary of the Interior and after some discussion he came around to seeing the Army's point of view. Therefore, with his help we have come up with the following. The reservation land will be deeded back to the ancestors of the people that owned it. Chief, you, and your people can start moving back immediately. The Army Corps of Engineers will be ordered to provide river boats and barges to transport your people and all their property back to the reservation lands. There is one glitch in this. The reservation land around Mendota has all been sold and settled since the lower reservation was evacuated, therefore the government is substituting a parcel of land in Scott County, located between Shakopee and Prior Lake. The upper reservation will be located on its former land near Morton in Renville County and Redwood Falls in Redwood County. The upper agency land near Granite Falls will also be ceded back to the Sioux.

"Bill, we are asking you to take the job of Indian Agent for this one but split in three parts reservation. What do you say to that offer?

Bill said, "Depending on the details of the job that sounds perfect. And, yes, I will be proud to serve as Indian agent for as long as needed. Thank you, sir!"

"I, as Chief of the Mdewakanton Tribe, I say thank you from all the people. This will go a long way toward closing the gulf that has developed between our people over the last few years."

"Lieutenant take these people to the proper places to obtain the papers they will need and get Bill sworn into his new job. Gentleman it has been a pleasure working with you. Have a good trip home. Dismissed."

It was after 1800 hrs. before all the loose ends were tied up and the two travelers got back to their hotel. They were elated by the success of their mission and what it would mean to the whole Mdewakanton Tribe. They would start home tomorrow but right now all they wanted was a good meal and a night's sleep.

In the morning Bill and Fox Feather came down for breakfast and were met by Harry Pound. Harry was sent by the Interior Secretary to be the new Indian Agent's man of many hats. He was a small, wiry individual who never seemed to tire or sleep. His Bowler hat, rolled up sleeves, bow tie, gaudy vest and horn-rimmed glasses were his uniform of the day, every day. He and Fox Feather were quite a spectacle when they were together with their Bowler hats and all.

His job was to manage the details of Bill's office. This morning he had all the travel arrangements made so all they had to do was get to the train on time. Harry said they had to hurry because the train left in 45 minutes. He also said their luggage was being packed for them and would meet them at the train.

At the depot they were met by Carl Schurtz, Secretary of the Interior. He said, "I wanted to meet you two before you left. One reality of the future is that Native Americans will be living in areas dominated by the Whites. The more they can blend in will be the key to their ability to live peacefully within their surroundings. Your tribe, Fox Feather, is our best present hope of finding out how to intermingle Whites and Indians harmoniously into a community. I wish you luck in your efforts." With that Schurtz shook both of their hands. "God's speed in your travels and good luck in your efforts.

They boarded the train, the whistle blew, and the drive wheels churned and the three of them were off to attempt to homogenize two vastly different cultures.

Chapter 44
Indian Summer

It was January 1868 when Bill, Fox Feather and Harry Pound arrived back in the Mdewakanton Village from which Bill and the Chief had started. The good news for the Tribe was they were getting their Minnesota land back. Announcement of this brought joy and celebration to the Tribe. The messengers were the heroes of the moment.

When the excitement settled down a council meeting was called. A big fire in the fire ring of the Tribe's Council Lodge warmed those seated around it, Chief Fox Feather, the ten members of the tribal council including Fighting Elk, Gray Wolf, Bold Otter and Bill in his new role as Indian Agent and Harry Pound, as Bill's clerk, taking notes so in the future he could create an official record of the meeting.

The topic under discussion was the pending move of the Tribe, "lock, stock and barrel" back to their land in Minnesota. Actually, there wasn't much left to discuss since most of the decisions had been made or were no brainers or were in the hands of the Army.

Most of the Tribe and their belongings would be transported on barges pulled by U. S. Army Corps of Engineers tugs. The Army would handle the loading and distribution of cargo, both human and material. However, the provisioning and grouping of the people would be up to the Indian Chiefs. Thus, for organizational reasons, Bill, as the Tribe's 'Indian Agent', designated Shakopee as the 'Lower Agency', Morton as the 'Middle Agency' and Granite Falls as the Upper Agency. The people had already been given the opportunity to decide which part of the reservation they wanted to live in, upper, middle or lower and were assigned barges accordingly. The people who optioned to live at the lower agency had elected a council to govern them with Charlie, the cowboy, as subchief in charge. The Upper Agency people elected their council also, with Sam, the other cowboy as their subchief in charge. The Middle Agency elected their council with Fighting Elk as their subchief. Fox Feather chose the central location of the middle agency to locate the overall administration of the tribe. The Central Government Council Lodge would be in the center of the middle agency village but the council that would meet there would be elected from the three reservations based on their population split.

Each council's delegations had been informed that the boats with their barges would dock at a convenient spot on the bank of the Missouri River closest to the village to make it as convenient as possible for the people to embark. Each barge would have a banner on it so the people would know its destination and load accordingly. The occupants of each barge would be responsible for providing provisions and water for themselves and their fellow passengers.

The councils of the reservations were reminded it would be a long ordeal until they disembarked on their Minnesota land. Just how long the trip would be was impressed on them by repeating the following, several times: This voyage will take us down the Missouri to St. Louis, then up the Mississippi to St. Paul, then up the Minnesota to Shakopee where the barges designated for their will be left. The rest will continue to Morton/Redwood Falls reservation land where the Middle Agency barges will be left. The Upper Agency barges will continue from there to their destination. The Army will expect the people on the barges to endure until they are put a shore. The Army expects the voyage to take about a week on the boats if everything goes smoothly. The Grand Council recommends that the people prepare for at least a two-week trip.

The cattle herd had increased to over thirty head. The Grand Council decided the herd would be driven overland to their new home. The cattle drive would begin as soon as the spring grass was up. It was expected to take three weeks. Any of the cattle believed to be so weak they would not survive the overland trip would be butchered and their meat distributed to the people taking the boat trip.

Bill was tasked with the responsibility to let the Army know that the Indians could be ready to leave if given a days' notice.

Bill also accepted the responsibility, in his role of Indian Agent, to do the work necessary to prepare for the return of the Sioux to their home ground. He and Harry were starting back to Redwood Falls as soon as the council adjourned. They were taking Fighting Elk and Gray Wolf with them as couriers to keep communications open between the Tribe and reservation. Bill and his team were going early to play the role of advance men, clearing as many obstacles out of the way of resettlement as possible. The Council ended on that note.

Early the next morning the vanguard of the Mdewakanton Sioux Tribe's return to their

Minnesota land left the village in the dust as they hurried northeast toward the reservation land along the Minnesota River.

The four riders pushed their mounts hard all day and didn't stop until about nine o'clock that night when they reached the -DB ranch. The Blocker family was still up but the kids were about ready for bed. Dan sent his two oldest boys out to take care of the horses and build a fire in the bunkhouse stove. The younger ones wanted to stay up and listen to the adult's conversation, but they trundled off to bed when Molly insisted. Molly fed the visitors and while they ate, Bill filled Dan and Molly in on the upcoming return of the Sioux to their old reservations.

Dan said, "I wish I could go with you; I haven't had a good scrap for a good cause in a long time."

Bill asked, "Do you really think there will be resistance to the Indian's return?"

"It seems there will be the natural objections of those who lived through the uprising and those that have heard the stories of the atrocities that took place. It is hard for people to separate the good from the bad when they are evaluating an emotional issue such as the Indian uprising. To many Whites, there are no bad or good Indians, only savages who pillage, torture, rape and murder with unholy glee. The good news is these perceptions can be changed by positive personal experience."

After eating the visitors found their way to the bunkhouse and immediately fell asleep.

About five o'clock, the next morning the ranch house came alive with a light in almost every window. Soon there were lights in the barn also. Not long after that, Dan knocked on the bunkhouse door, **"Breakfast in fifteen"** he shouted.

After the meal, the travelers thanked the Blockers and as they swung into their saddles, Dan brought the wagon up to the house and the kids climb in for their ride to school. The resulting cavalcade left the ranch yard together.

They waved goodbye as the wagon turned east and the rider's northeast. This was going to be another grueling day on the trail for the riders and their mounts. The four riders reached Redwood Falls about 7:15 that evening.

Bill headed directly to the Hotel he and Fox Feather had stayed at on their trip to D. C. As the four walked through the doors into the lobby, Bill saw the same clerk as he had tangled with before was behind the registration desk. When the clerk looked up and spotted Gray Wolf and Fighting Elk, He lifted his hand in a stop gesture and said, "We don't allow Indians in here, get out."

Bill stepped to the front and said, "I thought we agreed that was not a very friendly policy the last I was here."

The clerk cringed a little and said, "Oh, it's you again!"

"Yes, it's me again and I still won't allow this flea-bag to undo all that for which I fought. I will not stand aside while the taint of the South sullies Minnesota. Now reach back and give us the keys for two of your finest rooms. These rooms will be rented to the U. S. Government for an indefinite time. Harry, take care of the details, please.

Harry stepped up to the desk while the other three took the keys and hunted up their rooms. After locating them and settling in, the four travelers took care of their horses as best they could and grabbed a bite to eat at Milly's before turning in for the night.

The next morning Fighting Elk and Gray Wolf put on their White man blend in clothes and joined Bill and Harry at Milly's for breakfast, Bill made arrangements with Milly to meet Ed there for dinner that evening to discuss the possibility of Ed and his crew building a new Agency House on the site of the previous one.

Breakfast over, Bill and Harry went off to spread the word that in the spring the Mdewakanton Tribe would be returning to the Shakopee, Morton/

Redwood Falls and Granite Falls reservations. They contacted all the town and Redwood County officials so Bill could introduce himself as the new Indian Agent for the tribe and to expect the tribe back in the spring.

Fighting Elk and Gray Wolf took the map of the reservation and headed there to inspect it and stake its boundaries. They also plotted where the best graze and water for the heard was located. As part of their exploration they discovered that Chief Little Crow's house had survived undamaged.

At the end of the day. when all four of them were gathered back in the hotel Fighting Elk told Bill of their discovery. Bill was delighted. "Now we can have a home of our own until the Agency House is finished." he exclaimed.

At dinner time they joined Ed at Milly's. Ed was still doing handyman contracts even though he expected the farm to start paying for itself by fall. He was delighted to get this big a contract. It would allow him to retire and enjoy the farm a lot sooner than he had expected. After dinner, they all shook hands before going their separate ways.

The next day, the four homeless front men stopped at Schroder's Livery so Bill could pick up Butch and board their extra horses. Michael was there so he and Bill caught up on recent events. Carl was dead and Michael now owned the livery. Anne's pregnancy was going smoothly, and they still lived in the Schroder's home with Mrs. Schroder. Terry and Ellie were wed and living in nice home provided by the county. It was located just outside Olivia.

Bill said, "I'm so happy for all of you. Please give them my regards when you see them."

"You take care."

"You too. I'll see you again soon."

They four riders left the livery and rode out to Little Crow's house. Their mission was to assess what was needed before it would be comfortable enough for them to move in. When their assessment was completed, Bill and Harry rode over to Bill and Patsy's house of joy and sorrow to enlist Hal's help with collecting and hauling the stuff they need out to the new Agency Headquarters. With Hal and the wagon, the stop at the hotel to check out and load the few belongings the travelers had left there. Next, they shopped the town for the things they had to have to setup housekeeping. Last they stopped at the livery to pick up the tack Bill and Fox Feather had left there on their way to Washington last fall as well as the two horses still stabled there. Harry paid the bill with a U. S. Government Chit.

When Bill, Hal, the wagon load of stuff they had

collected, and Harry arrived back to the Agency's temporary Headquarters they got a big surprise.

Gray Wolf told them the story. About mid-morning four riders rode up to the house and when Gray Wolf went to see who was there, the four guys jumped off their horses and attacked him. I was being sworn at, hit and kicked while trying to protect myself from the blows as best I could. Fighting Elk on hearing the commotion caused by the cursing and yelling came into the fight with his blood curdling war cry. That turned the tables and we started gaining the upper hand. These guys were not in the best of shape. I caught one's arm and dislocated it. I heard one of the arms of the guy Fighting Elk was grappling with snap. I caught another of the attackers with the edge of my hand across the nose. I'm sure I broke it. By this time, they wanted nothing more than to get out of here alive. They shouldn't be hard to identify with a broken arm, a broken nose and a dislocated arm.

The thugs were quickly identified as they sought help for their injuries. The three damaged assailants not only identified the fourth, they identified the instigator of the attack. It didn't surprise Bill that the main culprit was the prejudice hotel clerk. The trouble coming the way of these five guys had just begun. The Federal Attorney for Minnesota indict them for assault of a person or persons on federally protected land. They were being held in Fort Snellings until their trial.

"I'll bet it will be a long time before anybody bothers you again." Bill said. And he was right. In fact, the two Indians became great ambassadors for the Mdewakanton. They made many friends among the people of the area, changing many people's negative feelings about the prospect of the Tribes expected return into an at least a, 'let's wait and see' attitude.

The tugs with their barges reach Shakopee near the first of June and unloaded their cargoes without a hitch. Everything was arranged so their move to the reservation land was accomplished without any problems.

The day after the Shakopee unloading started the middle agency tugs and barges set out for Morton/Redwood Falls. They arrived at their destination about five days later and found out their arrival was also planned and executed perfectly. It took another three days to reach the upper agency.

The same day as the barges arrived at the upper agency, the cattle herd showed up. The Mdewakanton's return to the land of their fathers was complete.

Chapter 45
Wrap-Up

A couple of years past, Bill and Fox Feather were kept busy with the move and resettling of the Tribe back to Minnesota. There were some difficulties between the residence of the surrounding area and the new occupants of the reservation but nothing that wasn't handled by the County sheriff's office and the reservation police. It was somewhat galling for some of the Indians to imitate White people, but the Grand Council and reservation police kept reminding them what blending in with the Whites had gained them this far.

The tribe was well organized and functioning at a high level. All locations were carrying on cattle operations and farming. The herd at each reservation was approaching a hundred, they provided meat for the reservation and a small cash dividend as the herds became large enough to market a few head each fall.

Bill settled into his job as Indian Agent. He and Harry moved into a new house constructed by the government to replace the one burned down during the uprising. Mrs. Betters accepted the job of housekeeper for the two bachelors. She and Louise moved into the downstairs and kept the place in tip-top shape.

Don Williams was still the ever-reliable Town Marshal. He and his wife had to break in a new person to take care of their needs. Luckily, Carla Gray still lived in the warehouse and was eager to find a job, so she jumped at the chance to take over where Cora left off.

At first Bill was approached by many sleaze bag traders with their, 'you scratch my back and I'll scratch yours' schemes. Bill thought, *Nothing seems to have changed. Don't these guys know what fate had befallen their predecessors at the beginning of the great up rising? Maybe they didn't know what had happened in the past, but they will soon find out what happens now days.* When approached with some shady scheme, Bill would immediately send Harry to summon Erect Bear. His instructions to his friend were as follows. "Escort these scoundrels to the boundary of the reservation. Do not cross the line but do boot the bastards in the ass and throw them across it." The traders with shady deals for this Indian Agent dropped drastically as word got around but they were replaced by honest traders who knew they would get a straight deal.

Harry Pound was the maestro of organization. He kept the entire venture together with his energy and skill. He had never been further west then Saratoga, New York but he took to Minnesota like a duck takes to water. By the end of his first year in the west he found a soul mate in Louise Betters. Cohabitation may not make strange bedfellows but it sure speeds up the bedfellow process. She and Harry were married moved into their own home and now as true bedfellows got busy on the process of turning out children of their own. A few days after their first anniversary, Harry Jr. showed up. He was a healthy, happy little tike with an engaging smile, a dimple in his chin and a mop of blond hair. Bill would have been lying if he told you he wasn't jealous.

Hal and Emma lived in the house Bill had essentially given them. They had been together for so long; they decide to make it official and got married. Billy loved Hal so that worked out to everyone's satisfaction. Billy was growing up and filling out. He had become a fine-looking specimen during his early manhood years. He was working at the livery in Redwood Falls and breaking girl's hearts all around the surrounding area.

The three farmers, Cassy, Lee and Chris, were keeping everybody in fresh vegetables and making a nice profit besides. In order to be closer to their work they built a small sleeping quarters behind the barn and slept there now. They took their meals with Billy, Hal and Emma. Bill as Indian Agent hired the three farmers from the warehouse as his Agriculture Consultant. They rotated in that position as suited them. It was working out splendidly.

Cora McHugh and Grady were enjoying life together. Grady had won Jamie over completely. Jamie now called him dad. Jamie like Billy had matured and was becoming a very handsome young man. Grady and his family still lived in the warehouse that Cora managed. Grady was still a deputy for Zeke and Charlie still ran the sheriff's office.

Terry had moved on to Olivia where he was appointed Town Marshall. Before he left, he married that saucy little redhead, Michael's sister Ellie, he had never stopped courting her after he saw her that morning at breakfast.

One day, out of the blue, Bill asked Billy and Jamie if they would have any interest going to West Point together. After thinking it over for a day or two they said it would be an honor. Bill sat down with Harry and they composed a letter asking everybody they knew in the government if there were any

West Point appointments that might not have been filled for this fall? The response was almost immediate. Two appointments were being held open for the boys. They would have to appear at Fort Snelling to take the qualification test on or before August 25. Arrangements were made for them to leave as soon as possible. They bunked with Bill's mother and father while they were in St. Paul.

Bill received a letter from his mother which raved about the two boys Bill had sent them,

Bill had run out of excuses. Everything he should do, and everything could do was now done, accept one thing. The one thing that he should have done long ago. The one thing he had avoided doing day after day, month after month and year after year. He now couldn't think of anything to stop him from going to face Mel and Patricia in Des Moines. He packed his bag and was on the next riverboat to Carver. He had a connection there for a boat to St. Paul. This time he was able to meet with Dick and share the news. When he arrived in St. Paul, he spent a night and a day with his parents before taking the night train to Des Moines.

In Des Moines he planned to stay in the Hawkeye Hotel. He knew he couldn't stand to stay in the Armour's home, the memories of Patsy would drive him crazy in short order.

So, on the morning of his arrival he found himself standing at the desk at the hotel waiting for the clerk to get around to him. Eventually the clerk said, "Your name?"

"Bill Cheever."

"A gentleman is waiting in the lounge for you. He didn't leave his name, but he said you would recognize him when you saw him."

"Where is the lounge?"

"Around the corner and a little way down the hall. It will be on your right. You can't miss it."

"Can you keep my bag for me until I get back?"

"Certainly."

Bill lifted his bag onto the counter and said, "Thanks." He then followed the clerk's directions to the lounge. There setting at a table in the middle of the lounge was Blair.

Blair's face lit up with a big smile when he saw Bill enter the room. Bill returned that smile with one of his own. They advanced on each other and shook hands and then hugged; a man hug of course. "God, it's good to see you!" they both said almost in unison.

"You must be starved." said Blair. Let's have breakfast and catch up on what's going on in each other's lives."

"Good idea, I am hungry."

Blair signaled the Maitre d' who hurried right over.

"Table please. Somewhere we can talk undisturbed."

The Maitre d' led them to a corner table, "Will this do sir?"

"Yes, we will need menus and a waiter; we are going to have breakfast."

"Yes sir, right away sir." he raised his arm and waved a waiter over with his hand. The waiter arrived armed with menus and water.

He said, "Good morning gentlemen, my name is Tony. May I get cocktails for you this morning? Bloody Marys are the specialty of the house. "

Bill said, "I'll take a bottle of Schlitz Beer and a cup of black coffee."

"Make mine the same." said Blair.

Bill had been appraising Blair since they met. His hair was thinning, and he looked overweight and out of shape. However, he had picked up an air of authority and decisiveness about him that Bill thought fit him well. "How are things going for you and your family?"

The waiter returned with their drinks. "Are you ready to order?"

"Give us a minute, will you?" Both picked up a menu and scanned it. Bill immediately spotted omelets as a choice and ordered one with cheese, bacon and onion. Blair said "I've never had one of those. I'll try the same thing."

"Very good choice. Those will be coming up shortly."

Bill said, "Thank you Tony."

Bill repeated his question, "How are things going for you and your family?"

"We will be adding another baby to the brood come spring." Mel and Patricia have been superb and Artie, I think already has his eye on my daughter. He has grown up to be a fine young man. I guess that was a given when his parents are Mel and Patricia. No two finer people ever lived. Mel Jr. is a rugged woodsy who disappears for weeks at a time to go camping and see this or that wonder of the world. Dru is a beauty that has her hands full managing all her beaus. No one's won her heart yet but it's kind of entertaining watching them try. Milly is engaged and planning a spring wedding. That is quick update of the family."

The waiter interrupted them with the dishes of food. Their conversation went on hold as they ate. The only sounds emitted at their table were those of appreciation. As they pushed their empty plates back Tony appeared with a pot to refresh their coffee and a busboy to clear their table.

Blair said, "Thank you Tony. That will be all for now."

As Tony retreated, Bill renewed the conversation by asking, "How is John's family doing?"

"John is now General Manager of 'Armour Packing' and Lisa has opened her own dress shop. Zeke is the meat packing plant manager. He is married and he and his wife are waiting for their first child. Mel and John went together in a joint venture and opened a restaurant and catering business run by John's girls and staffed by some of his boys as waiters and such."

"How about Mel?"

"Mel is doing about as well as can be expected. His stumps are healed, and his general health and mental health are good. When I couldn't find wood to carve him a new leg for him, I made him a peg leg. He doesn't like it much, but he can get around on his own with his foot, a cane and the peg leg. Life seems to be ok for him right now."

"You have certainly been a gift from God to Mel. I hope you appreciate the great job you have done with him."

"Thanks, I look at it like this opportunity has made two lives better, Mel's and mine. I had little to look forward to in civilian life except the grind of daily living. Helping Mel has given my life a purpose and satisfaction I never expected.

"And last, what about Patricia?"

"She was devastated by Patsy's death but there is no person on Earth more resilient than Patricia. She mopped, sobbed and wept for a few days and then returned to the Patricia she has always been. She said it is what it is, and I can't change it by grieving my life away. I lost a daughter and a grandson in one terrible moment, but I still have a loving family to care for while Bill has nothing left. I understand why he didn't show up for the funeral. It was a ceremony to bury he's future. I talked to Mel about it and he agreed with Patricia. Mel was sure when you came to terms with Patsy's death you would come and face them so you could all say a last goodbye together. My wife and I have made room in our house for your stay. Nobody could imagine your being able to stand staying in the house where your love affair blossomed and bloomed."

Blair insisted on paying the tab and leaving the tip. "This meal is on Mel and Patricia, they insisted."

The visit went off without a hitch. Bill spent a couple a day's setting a long side the grave of his wife and son deep in thought.

A week later he was back on the train heading home with all the usual stops on his agenda.

Bill lived until just after his 84th birthday. He never had a serious affair in all those years. He explained it thus, "It was all but impossible to say" I love you to someone with three in the bed. Patsy never really left my side all those years."

Lightning Source UK Ltd.
Milton Keynes UK
UKHW010636280920
370660UK00001B/41